AF541538

Bhakti

KRISHNAJEE AYYAGARI

A Critical Appraisal of Madhusūdan Sarasvatī

(Based on Doctoral thesis approved by BHU Varanasi)

Adventure of Consciousness

9

- Analytical Ayurveda
  Dr. K A Latheef
- Upanisads and Edith Stein: *A Dialogue on Models of The Person*
  Thomas Marottipparayil
- Tīrthaṅkarāsana: *A Work on Jaina Yoga*
  Shantilal D. Parakh
- Aparokṣānubhūti: *The essence of Self Realization*
  Dr. Shrikrishna D. Deshmukh
- A Critical Study in The Schism in Early Buddhist Monastic Tradition: *Dasavatthu and Pancavatthu*
  Lokananda C. Bhikkhu
- Mystical Poems of Jnaneshwar
  Ananda Mundra
- Exclusion of Sudras from Brahmajijnasa
  Jaison Vadakkan
- The Theory of Karma Revisited
  Vibha Chaturvedi
- Bhakti: A Critical Appraisal of Madhusūdan Sarasvatī
  Krishnajee Ayyagri

Bhakti

Krishnajee Ayyagari

A Critical Appraisal of Madhusūdan Sarasvatī

(Based on Doctoral thesis approved by BHU Varanasi)

Bhakti: A Critical Appraisal of Madhusūdan Sarasvaī
by Krishnajee Ayyagri

First Edition : Delhi, 2021

ISBN : 978 81 948 1587 7

Published by

MOTILAL BANARSIDASS PUBLICATIONS
93, Shyam Lal Marg, Darya Ganj, New Delhi - 110002
Email: mlbd@mlbd.com; Website: www.mlbd.com

MLBD CATALOGUING-IN-PUBLICATION DATA
Bhakti: A Critical Appraisal of Madhusūdan
Sarasvatī by Krishnajee Ayyagri
ISBN : 9788194815877
I. Preface II. Acknowledgment III. Foreword
IV. Bibliography

Printed by
Repro Books Ltd.

ACKNOWELEDGEMENTS

I offer my obeisance to Lord Visvanātha and Goddess Annapurna the presiding deities of Varanasi, for their grace in giving me the opportunity to spend nearly four years at this sacred place and blessing me with health and enthusiasm to pursue my study in the evening of my life. Being a research scholar at the century old Banaras Hindu University famous for study of Philosophy is also a great opportunity.

I offer my humble homage to my parents. I lost my mother at an early age. My father is my role model in integrity, honesty and living with the motto "There is no substitute to hard work".

I am fortunate to have Prof. Dr. R .K. Jha, as my supervisor for my doctoral study. I am fortunate to have a professor who has in-depth knowledge in Advaita and very methodical in his approach and he is an ideal guru and he has given loving guidance at every stage. I offer my thanks from the bottom of heart.

I am thankful to Prof Mulkraj Mehta (head of dept.), Prof S.P.Pandey and Prof K.S.Ojha, for their valuable guidance right from my admission. All the professors for their kind word of encouragement and assurance of their readiness for help I needed.

The non-teaching staff and the library staff have always offered their cooperation and I thank and appreciate their friendly attitude.

My respectable pranams to Śrīpāduka, K.Avatara Sarma, who retired as Head of Dept. of Sanskrit at P.R.Goverment College, Kakinada in A P and now living at Varanasi. He holds three doctoral degrees in Sanskrit (Education, Vyākaraṇa and Alaṅkāra Śāstra). He has,as a special favor, explained the entire content of the text BhaktiRasāyana (in Sanskrit) and elaborated to me (an Illiterate in Sanskrit) the poetical technical terms with patience. This helped me to have better understanding of BhaktiRasāyana text. I am deeply indebted to him and have no words to express my gratitude and I offer my humble pranams.

I am thankful to Dr P. Śaṇḍilya of Sanskrit Dept., who has carefully examined the translation of my Bhakti-Rasāyana into English and accuracy of diacritical marks and also explained Sanskrit verses in other texts with patience whenever I approached him.

I consider myself fortunate to have the moral and emotional support of my loving wife - Mrs. Neeeladevi – during all the four years stay at Varanasi, thank you Neela!

I appreciate the loving encouragement given by my entire family, my son, daughter and their spouses who love me (as two sons and two daughters) enquiring about our health and welfare all the way from USA so frequently as if all were in Varanasi and visited Varanasi twice to cheer me in person.

I pay homage to my elder brother Late A.M.Sarma who was my friend philosopher and guide and treated me with fatherly affectionately affection. He is unfortunately no more to share my thoughts and my success. I thank my sister-in-law Dr. Indira Devi who shared the ideas and gave positive feedback.

Last but not least, I do not hide my pride for the cheer and encouragement given by my loving granddaughters - twin sisters Chy Sneha and Raga who are Alumni of Stanford University and Chy. Pooja, a high schooler. Their loving cheers and reassuring messages of 'Tata! You can do it' gave boost to my spirit.

I thank Dr. R,K.Jha for having graciously agreed to write the foreword to this publication which is based on my doctoral thesis which was done under his supervision and guidance.

I thank the Banaras Hindu University authorities for giving their consent permitting me to publish the book based on my thesis for which they have copyright.

My thanks to Pranav Jain, of **M/s Motilal Banarasidass Publications**, New Delhi, for publishing the book in the shortest time in spite of their busy schedule.

My thanks to Mrs. Manju Arya in setting the book.

AYYAGARI KRISHNAJEE

PREFACE

Madhusūdana Sarasvatī (1540-1647), was one of the greatest exponents of Advaitism in the Post-Śaṅkara era. He made valuable contribution to the knowledge of Advaitism with his works like Siddhāntabindu, Advaitasiddhi, and Vedāntakalpalatikā etc. The most famous among them is Advaitasiddhi, in which he has upheld the Advaita and forcefully refuted the criticism by SriVyāsatīrtha in his work ***Nyāmrṛta***. He flourished during the period when the Bhakti movement is gaining widespread popularity throughout the country which influenced scholars as well as laymen. The Interreligious rivalry and wrangles were at peak. He was an ardent devotee of Śrī Kṛṣṇa since his childhood and continued the worship of his Iṣṭa, even after resorting to Sannyāsa. He wrote an exclusive treatise on Bhakti to Śrī Kṛṣṇa called Bhakti-Rasāyana, based on Bhāgavatapurāṇa, in which he asserted that Bhakti is an independent path for liberation. Bhakti is the highest goal of life, and it is not a mere path but an end itself and Kṛṣṇa is none else than Parābrahman.

The Advaitic system has Mokṣa as the highest goal and only through Jñāna one can achieve that goal. Brahman is the only realty. The above assertion of Madhusūdana ,who is an exponent of Advaita is considered as a paradox and intriguing.

A review of the literature we find that there are only few studies on the subject and there is no unanimity. One scholar observed that Madhusūdana in spite being a great non-dualist Vedāntin, he admits his paradox of his personality.

He simply makes a synthesis between Advaita Vedānta philosophy and theology of pure love for Bhāgavan , the supreme being without losing sight of the concept of the non-dual Reality.

Another scholar observed that he has written Bhakti-Rasāyana more from a devotionalist view than as an Advaita Sannyāsi. The commonly accepted view that he was a champion of cause pf Bhakti who, successfully integrated devotion and Advaita cannot be accepted without serious reservations.

A detailed study has been made of the author's devotional works and the sentiment of devotion expressed sporadically found in other works and is presented in this book to make a logical conclusion about the authors concept of Bhakti. The study is presented in a systematic manner by dividing it into six chapters in a logical sequence. The brief contents of each of the chapters are given below.

Outlines of The Chapters

I. ***The first chapter has been divided into the following sections.***

(i) The Review of the available literature and the scope and objective of the study.

(ii) Madhusūdana Sarasavatī's life and his works., his skills his personal traits and attitudes. His social achievements even as a monk and his benevolence as a teacher are noteworthy. It can be presumed that he was greatly influenced by the Kṛṣṇa Bhakti movement of Chaitanya which was widespread in Bengal and spreading in other parts of the country.

II. The second Chapter is titled as 'The concept of Bhakti'.

The Basic concepts of Hindu religion are briefly narrated to have a clear understanding before proceeding with the discussion on the concept of Bhakti. The structure of Hindu society with Varṇa, Āśrama (stages of life) and the respective functions and responsibilities and moral and ethical conduct for harmonious living, as given in the scriptures, besides eligibility for pursuing spiritual disciplines, have been discussed as Varṇa Āśrama dharma. The Indian ethical ideals has certain goals of life or Puruṣārthas are (i) Dharma, (ii) Artha, (iii) Kāma and (iv) Mokṣa is as the highest goal of life or 'Parama Puruṣārtḥa'. By attaining mokṣa one is freed from the cycle of births and deaths and all the sufferings.

The principal means for attaining Mokṣa are (i) Karma (action) (ii) Bhakti (devotion) and (iii) Jñāna (Knowledge). The broad concepts of these means have been discussed in a concise manner. Bhakti in the following literature has been studied and salient points are narrated briefly. (a) Bhagavad-Gītā, (b) Bhāgavatapurāṇa, (c) Bhakti Sūtras of Śaṇḍilya and Nārada and (d) It is considered pertinent to examine the concept of Bhakti in Advaita Vedānta of which, Madhusūdana was a prominent exponent. For study of the concept of Bhakti of Madhusūdana, it is considered essential to devote separate chapters for the major devotional works authored by him,

(a). Bhakti-Rasāyana. (b). Gūḍhārtha-Dīpikā. (c). The other minor works have been discussed in a separate chapter.

III. The third chapter is devoted to study the concept of Bhakti in the important composition on Devotion called "Bhakti-Rasāyana" by Madhusūdana. This is the exclusively devotional treatise on Bhakti ever authored by any Advaita Philosopher. The text consists of three Ullāsas. The first Ullāsa is named as 'Bhakti Sāmānya Nirūpaṇa', for which the author himself has written an elaborate commentary. Anannyā Bhakti and Brahmavidyā have been compared with respect to their different parameters.The phenomenon of the modification of mind and retaining the image or impression of the cause of that modification has been explained. If the cause is due to loving devotion towards the Lord, the mind takes the form of the Lord, or 'Bhagavadākārata', which is its inherent nature. He has articulated the development to resemble the Advaitic theory of Bimba - Pratibimba Vāda. Rasa is a blissful experience. Bhakti rasa has been logically proved to be adequately qualified to be called a rasa and also to be declared as the most superior rasa. The supreme love for God is impossible without higher Non-attachment. Non-attachment cannot exist without knowledge of self and Brahman, and so the two are to be cultivated to obtain steadfastness in devotion. Bhakti is a gradual process and there is no shortcut. The eleven progressive stages of the practice of devotion, beginning with association with great saints up to the culmination of supreme love towards God have been elaborated. The second Ullāsa called "Bhakti viśeṣa nirūpaṇa", presents the rasa concept of Bhakti as per Aesthetics, which has been adopted and explained. The various means that modify the mind (as per aesthetics) and the Ālambana, Vibhāvana and Sthāyī - bhāva (permanent sentiments) which gets established as rasa depending upon the Vibhāvana associated with it, have been mentioned. The various types of rasas have been mentioned with examples. After discussing various combinations of Vibhāvana and Anubhāva, he discarded some as they were antagonistic to bliss and only the few rasas that qualify to be considered as Bhakti Rasa are mentioned. The types of Bhakti based on the Guṇas, motives and types of results are also narrated. The third Ullāsa is called "Bhakti Rasa Nirūpaṇa", which aims about the concept of rasa has been explained in detail and Bhakti is established as rasa with scriptural authority.

IV).The fourth chapter is devoted to analyze the concept of Bhakti in the commentary on Bhagavad-Gītā called Gūḍhārtha-Dīpikā (illuminating the hidden meaning), written by Madhusūdana. It was written with the Shaṅkar's Bhāsyṣa as the basis. The special feature of it is that it has an annotation consisting of forty-six verses which gives an over-view of the commentator's views and objective of writing the commentary. The author has divided the text into three sections as Karma, Bhakti and Jñāna. He has interpreted the three sections in consonance with the Upaniṣadic verse 'Tattvamasi' or 'Thou art That'. The annotation has been discussed in detail. The author considered that Bhakti is essential at all stages to avoid any possible obstacles that may arise. This division of Bhagavad-Gītā is unique. Although Bhagavad-Gītā states that there are only two paths, Karma and Jñāna, yet Bhakti has been stressed in several chapters and in a separate chapter called Bhakti-yoga, which shows that Bhakti is inherently integrated with karma and Jñāna.. Bhakti yoga has-been discussed in a separate section of this chapter. Kṛṣṇa clarifies about devotion to the manifest and un-manifest Brahman and explains that both types of worship can be practiced for spiritual development and can give equal results. A devotee of the manifest form will attain 'kramamukti' and ultimately reach Brahman by God's grace, while a worshiper of the unmanifest form attains immediate realization. Those who adopt Bhakti towards the manifest form will also attain the result of worshipping the Unmanifest Lord by practice of Śravaṇa, Manana and Nididhyāsana and realize the Upaniṣadic Mahāvākya "Tattvamasi". This clarifies the doubt about the type of Bhakti to be practiced. Madhusūdana, has generally agreed with Śaṅkarācārya, although he has shown more enthusiasm by making elaborate commentary on Bhakti by giving examples from Bhāgavatapurāṇa. However in analyzing verse 18.66 he has seriously deferred with Śaṅkara. Madhusūdana treats total surrendering to the Lord as the final purport of the scripture and disagrees with others who interpret otherwise. Madhusūdana Sarasvatī has mentioned that with maturity of spiritual practice, there are three types of surrender to God, and the most intense type of surrender is "I am He indeed". Here the distinction vanishes and only the Lord remains which is nothing but an Advaitic concept.

V).The fifth chapter is devoted to discuss the devotional sentiment as expressed by Madhusūdana Sarasvatī in the minor works like Ānandamandākinī, Īśvarapratipattiprakāśa, which are short, independent works and Mahimnastotra-ṭīkā and Paramahaṁsapriyā, which are commentaries, have been explained in detail. The devotional sentiment scattered in different other works have also been covered in this chapter.

Madhusūdana has in all the works has mentioned about Kṛṣṇa Bhakti. The devotees should be humble and seek God's grace which will be duly rewarded. He advised that people can choose any means as per their ability and attitude. He has advised people not to waste time in futile discussions but utilize some time for devotion for God. He also said that although there are several names and forms of the Gods, all are aspects of the same God.

VI). In the concluding chapter, the distinctive aspects about the Bhakti of Madhusūdana Sarasvatī, apart from the conclusions as discussed in the third, fourth and fifth chapters above have been mentioned.

The concept of Bhakti as depicted in various works of Madhusūdan Sarasvati has been discussed and his aim of writing and his attitude as a realized soul in propagating to the common People who are suffering with the miseries of life with cycle of births and deaths to get rid of such miseries by resorting to devotion to the Lord. He has also brought about that self realisation can be achieved by all by whatever path they choose according to their capacity and attitude and practice of devotion to any God. He has emphasized that there is one God with different forms and names. He has also dispelled the misconception about the Bhakti in Advaita framework by highlighting the importance assigned to Bhakti in the system.

His remaining a devotee to Sri Kṛṣṇa is not in any way paradoxical. He has remained as an uncompromising Advaita Philosopher.

VII). A brief note on Rasa theory and Indian aesthetics has has been appended giving the concepts of Bharat's Rasa theory and contributions of scholars and Bhakti rasa to give some a overview of Rasa theory and its aesthetic value and relation with the philosophical and theistic conceptions.

The learned readers may appreciate the effort in presenting this study and the author whole heartedly welcome any suggestions for further improvement of the content which will be taken care of in future editions.

FOREWORD

The present work is a slightly modified version of the doctoral research thesis of Krishnajee Ayyagari, which was completed under my supervision. As such, I have been an active witness to the entire course of its formulation and it is a matter of immense pleasure and satisfaction to see it being presented before the world in the form of a book, dealing with a subject matter which is of immense significance and value for both the advaitic tradition as well as the bhakti tradition.

Madhusūdana Saraswatī represents the full bloom of the advaitic school and he was unique in his effort to work out a synthesis of the advaitic philosophy and the devotional philosophy. The primary introduction to the nature of Brahman in the Brahma sūtra (I-i-2) clearly refers to the saguṇa aspect of Brahman, which is sufficient to indicate its significance in the advaitic framework. Despite this, it is not so uncommon to come across advaitic scholars who think that the pure ontological nature of Brahman refers to its nirguṇa aspect alone, as the saguṇa aspect involves an epistemic element of ignorance and illusion. This misunderstanding has been vehemently challenged, criticised and rectified by Madhusūdana Saraswatī in his works. His early life had been exclusively devoted to the bhakti tradition and he shifted to the advaitic tradition later on after much reflection and critique. Therefore, he was uniquely qualified to comment on the compatibility of the advaitic thought and the bhakti thought. His outlook on this subject is clearly reflected in his various works, but his Bhakti-rasāyana singularly stands out in this matter as he focuses exclusively on this subject in this work. In the course of his elaborate discussion and critique in this work, he presents his novel ideas on the subject of *rasa* and shows it as the meeting and culminating point for both the advaitic and bhakti frameworks. For Madhusūdana Saraswatī, there is no conflict whatsoever between these two frameworks. On the contrary, he rather maintains the complementarity of these two frameworks.

A systematic presentation of the ideas of Madhusūdana Saraswatī would go a long way in enriching the understanding of contemporary advaitic scholars. So far, such a work was not available. Therefore, the present book would certainly enrich the academic understanding of Advaitism, as also the practical spiritual aspect of Advaitism. The author certainly deserves a hearty congratulation for his patience and perseverance in doing this difficult study.

Dr Rajesh Kumar Jha
Professor
Department of Philosophy and Religion
Banaras Hindu University, Varanasi

IN PRAISE OF

The book under review is about the devotional philosophical attitude of Madhusūdana Sarasvati, who has been a prominent advocate of Advaita Vedanta in the post Śaṅkara era and the author of famous Advaitasiddhi among other compositions enriching the Advaita Literature. He was a devotee of Kṛṣṇa from his childhood and continued even after taking Sannyasa. He believed that Kṛṣṇa is none other than Brahman in human appearance as was revealed in Bhagavad-Gīta.

Bhakti Rasāyana is a unique composition on Bhakti by Madhusūdana Sarasvati besides other minor compositions related to the philosophy of devotion. He has argued profoundly that after being an aspirant and purification of mind one can chose Jñāna Mārga or Bhakti Mārga as per his capability and aptitude. Bhakti and Jñāna both culminates into experiencing bliss untouched by any trace of sorrow even though the means, eligibility and results are different. The Brahmavidyā results in eradication of nescience and realisation of Nirvikalpa Samadhi whereas Bhakti results in Ananya Prapatti and realisation of Savikalpa Samadhi and both are blissful states in its nature. He established that Bhakti is superior in the sense that it is Rasa and for that Rasa, Ānanda and Brahman are synonyms. He has advocated the people to drink the Bhakti Rasa which will act as an elixir for the eradication of the melody of cycle of births and deaths which is in consonance with the Bhagavata Purana (verse1.1.3).

Though the author has based this book on his doctoral dissertation, but he has made in depth study of all the devotional works and sentiments expressed sporadically in the major and minor works of Madhusūdana Sarasvati. The objective and content of this book is evidence that Madhusūdana Sarasvati has composed his all most all devotional works with an enlightened attitude for the sake of people to get themselves free from the miseries of cycle of births and deaths by practicing Bhakti. There is no pre qualifying conditions are required so far as Bhakti is concerned. It is most easy way to achieve the state of liberation, for which everybody is eligible without any discrimination of caste, gender, social status and education like prerequisites. It is a commendable work on the Madhusūdana Sarasvati's philosophy of Bhakti. It can be accredited for dispelling the wrong notion that Advaita philosophy is devoid of Bhakti whereas Bhakti to Saguṇa Swaroopa of Brahman is admissible in the Advaita system.

Dr. Ambika Datta Sharma, Professor of Philosophy,
Dean, School of Humanities and Social Sciences,
Dr. Hari Singh Gour University, Sagar [M.P.]- 470003

I have gone through the book "A Critical Appraisal of Madhusūdana Saraswathi" written by Krishnajee Ayyagari which is a book prepared in a publishable form of his doctoral thesis.

This book mainly deals with the works of Madhusūdana Saraswati in general "Bhaktirasāyana" in particular. It has consisted six chapters and each chapter has its own significance by which it upholds the discussion of chapters. Madhusūdana Saraswathi has several books to his credit. Among them SiddhāntaBindu, AdvaitaSiddhi, Vedanta Kalpalatikā, Bhakti Rasāyana etc., a few are famous in the intellectual world. The first three works are to establish the supremacy of Advaita and the book Bhakti Rasāyana is a Book which deals with Bhakti based on Bhagavata. Madhusūdana Saraswathi was a devotee of Sri Krishna. Though he is a staunch supporter of Advaita he gave equal importance to Bhakti which is an instrument to realise the self or attain liberation. According to Advaita Self-knowledge is the only means to attain Moksha. Bhakti is a means to achieve Self Knowledge. But Madhusūdana Saraswathi who profoundly argued the path of Jnana gave equal importance to Bhakti. Therefore, he says. कृष्णात् परं किमपि तत्त्वमहं न जाने Madhusūdana Saraswathi somehow balanced Bhakti and Jnana as a means to attain Moksha.

In the First chapter the author compiled almost all-important information about Madhusūdana Saraswathi from his childhood days to his Sanyasāsrama, and brief note about his works also given. After getting the recognition in the intellectual world through his scholarly works he has started teaching Advaita and many numbers of students studied under him and he was famous for his teaching skills.

In the Second chapter the concept of Bhakti discussed at length. The Hindu ethical ideals and the four Puruṣārthas and the aim of life have been elaborated. One must attain Moksha to get himself freed from the clutches of birth and death cycle. To attain Moksha there are three means such as karma, Bhakti and Jnana are explained in the Scriptures. As per Bhagavad-Gita, Bhagavata and Bhakti Sutras Bhakti Swaroopa explained. The place of Bhakti in Advaita also discussed elaborately.

The Third Chapter is entirely devoted to the study of Bhakti Rasāyana of Madhusūdana Saraswathi. The author has compared Ananya Bhakti or utmost devotion with Brahmavidyā. During this Ananya Bhakti the state of mind and its modifications explained. Though the author has explained both Bhakti and Jnana as Separate means to attain Moksha it is exceedingly difficult to differentiate Annanya Bhakti and Jnana. In my view Ananya Bhakti is nothing but the realisation of true soul. Here I would like to remind that Shankara says in Vivekacūdamani "स्वस्वरुपानुसन्धानं भक्तिरित्यभिधीयते". In my view Madhusūdana Saraswathi professes the above view of Shankara in his Bhakti Rasāyana. Thus, he balanced Bhakti mārga and Jnana Mārga.

The Fourth chapter is devoted to the study of Bhakti in Gūḍhārtha-Dīpikā the commentary written by Madhusūdana Saraswathi on Bhagavad-Gita Shankara Bhāṣya. Madhusūdana Saraswathi in the beginning has clarified his views which are very much reflected in forty six verses. Krishnajee excelled in this chapter. The place of Bhakti according to Madhusūdana Saraswathi well discussed and concluded that Bhakti is also equally important means to attain Moksha. However, I have my own reservation with the opinion of Krishnaji with regard to the commentary of 66th sloka in 18th chapter. According to the author, Madhusudana Saraswati seriously differed with Sankara. Total surrendering to the Lord (Sharanagati) is the final purport of the scripture and disagrees with others. At the same time the author has said among the three types of surrender the utmost or intense surrender is "I am he Indeed". When distinction between Jīva and Brahman vanishes then total surrender cannot be called as means to Moksha. Because the intense surrender itself took the form of Advaita of this is the chapter where the author has reached the highest peak of his intellectual exercise.

The fifth chapter contains the concept of Bhakti in other works of Madhusudan Sarasvati such as a Ānandamandākinī the Mahiṁna stotra tika, Paramahaṁsapriyā, Īśvarapratipatti prakasha etc. Madhusūdana Saraswathi's devotional sentiments are well expressed in his independent works. He advises the human being should not waste his time in wasteful exercises, instead he should devout maximum time to get rid of himself from this bondage of birth and death cycle. For this he should choose any means according to his eligibility. The author has peeped into the sentiments expressed by Madhusūdana Saraswathi in the above said other works.

In the concluding chapter the author clearly states the view of Madhusūdana Saraswathi towards the means to attain Moksha and his love towards Bhakti. Thus, the author of the book establishes a crystal-clear view of Madhusūdana Saraswathi on Bhakti as a means to attain liberation. Along with it a brief explanation about Rasa theory and Indian aesthetics and Bharata's concept of Rasa theory enhances the weightage of the book.

At the end I would like to state that Krishnaji aayagiri has done a tremendous scholarly research exercise, and I have no doubt that his work definitely will receive the applause of the research students and intellectuals as well. I wholeheartedly congratulate the author for this wonderful and commendable work. We may expect some more such works from him. Shubham Bhuyat.

Prof. M.L. Narasimha Murty
Former Vice-Chancellor
National Sanskrit University
Tirupati, Andhra Pradesh, India

This is a first-rate work on Madhusūdana Saraswathi. The central theme of this book is to examine the compatibility of the prominence of bhakti with the non-dualism of the Advaita Vedanta. The author, through an in-depth study and cogent arguments takes us to the conclusion that there is no contradiction in upholding the primacy of devotion yet holding to the view that reality is nondual absolute. The book initiates the reader to the subtitles of a very complex theme in lucid language and convincing logic.

S.Mishra Ex professor &
Head Department of philosophy
And pro vice chancellor
DDU Gorakhpur University

In addition to Dharma, Artha, Kāma and Moksha, Bhakti gets established firmly as the Puruṣārtha in the work Bhakti-Rasāyana of Madhusūdana Saraswati. The work of Krishnāji, an erudite exposition with a strong logical frame of thinking, presents a lucid analysis of the work of Madhusūdana Saraswati. The work being a systematic study of the place of bhakti in the advaitic philosophy of Madhusūdanam reconciles the diverse views that existed on his philosophy.

Prof Balaganapati Devarakonda,
Head of the Department f Philosophy
Delhi University, Delhi,

*Given the essential traits of Advaita Vedānta and the na*ture of bhakti, it looks quite impossible to an inquisitive mind to comprehend a synthesis of both the thoughts. With such an interesting background, it is Ācārya Madhusūdana Sarasvatī who theoretically, logically explores the fraternity between the two with a unique philosophical approach. More importantly, his own life becomes a practical illustration of the same. It Is his exemplary genius to portrait bhakti as rasa, the aesthetic counterpart of emotions and thus to provide a wholly distinctive but remarkable perspective to bhakti which can be recognized as a middle ground for bhakti and Advaita.

It is a matter of immense pleasure that such a unique and profound topic is dealt with in this book. It is a highly appreciable and challenging task carried out by Sri Ayyagari Krishnajee to provide comprehensive information on bhakti, a concept of enormous importance in Śāstra and tradition.

Prof Rajaram Shukla,
Vice-chancellor,
Sampurnanada Sanskrit university, Varanasi.

Madhusūdana Saraswathi was a devotee of Sri Krishna. Though he is a staunch supporter of Advaita he gave equal importance to Bhakti which is an instrument to realize the self or attain liberation. Madhusūdana Saraswathi who profoundly argued the path of Jnana gave equal importance to Bhakti. Therefore, he says. कृष्णात् परं किमपि तत्त्वमहं न जाने

Madhusūdana Saraswathi somehow balanced Bhakti and Jñāna to attain Moksha.

Ananya Bhakti is nothing but the realisation of true soul. Here I would like to remind that Shankara says in Vivekacūdamani "स्वस्वरुपानुसन्धानं भक्तिरित्यभिधीयते". Madhusūdana Saraswathi professes the above view of Shankara in his Bhakti Rasāyana. Thus, he balanced Bhakti mārga and Jnana Mārga.

the author clearly states the view of Madhusūdana Saraswathi towards the means to attain Moksha and his love towards Bhakti. Thus, the author of the book establishes a crystal-clear view of Madhusūdana Saraswathi on Bhakti as a means to attain liberation. Along with it a brief explanation about Rasa theory and Indian aesthetics and Bharata's concept of Rasa theory enhances the weightage of the book.

I would like to state that Krishnajee Ayyagari has done a tremendous scholarly research exercise, and I have no doubt that his work will receive the applause of the research students and intellectuals as well.

Prof. M.L. Narasimha Murty,
Former Vice-Chancellor,
National Sanskrit University.
Tirupati, Andhra Pradesh, India.

This is a first-rate work on Madhusūdana Saraswathi. The central theme of this book is to examine the compatibility of the prominence of bhakti with the non-dualism of the Advaita Vedanta. The author, through an in-depth study and cogent arguments takes us to the conclusion that there is no contradiction in upholding the primacy of devotion yet holding to the view that reality is nondual absolute. The book initiates the reader to the subtitles of a very complex theme in lucid language and convincing logic.

S.Mishra Ex professor
head Department of philosophy
pro vice chancellor
DDU Gorakhpur University

The book under review is a commendable work on the Madhusūdana Sarasvati's philosophy of Bhakti. who has been a prominent advocate of Advaita Vedanta in the post Śaṅkara era and the author of famous Advaitasiddhi among other compositions enriching the Advaita Literature. He was a devotee of Kṛṣṇa from his childhood and he believed that Kṛṣṇa is none other than Brahman in human appearance as was revealed in Bhagavad-Gīta

Bhakti Rasāyana is a unique composition on Bhakti by Madhusūdana Sarasvati besides other minor compositions related to the philosophy of devotion. He has argued profoundly that after being an aspirant and purification of mind one can chose either Jñāna Mārga or Bhakti Mārga as per his capability and aptitude. Bhakti and Jñāna both culminate in experiencing bliss untouched by any trace of sorrow even though the means, eligibility and results are different. He established that Bhakti is superior rasa and that Rasa, Ānanda and Brahman are synonyms with scriptural authority

The content of this book is evidence that Madhusūdana Sarasvati has composed his all most all devotional works with an enlightened attitude that everybody is eligible for liberation through Bhakti mārga which is the easiest means. He has advocated to the people to drink the Bhakti Rasa which will act as an elixir for the eradication of the melody of cycle of births and deaths which is in consonance with the Bhāgavata Purāṇa .

Dr. Ambika Datta Sharma,
Professor of Philosophy, Dean, School of Humanities and Social Sciences, Dr. Hari Singh Gour University, Sagar [M.P.]- 470003

The Philosophy of Madhusūdana Saraswathi is well presented in view of the author's study of almost all his works and therefore the authenticity of the book. Author's exposition on the popular issues of jñāna, bhakti and karma discussed in the book very nicely differentiates Madhusūdana Saraswathi's view from other Vaishnav Vedāntins on one hand and from Śaṅkara Advaita on the other. Advaita- Bhakti is the most attractive theme attributed to Madhusūdana Saraswathi and is the central theme the author has discussed well in the chapters of the book. I wish the book will be welcomed well by the students and the teachers of Vaishnavism ln particular and of philosophy and Religion in general.

Devendra Nath Tiwari,
professor of philosophy and Religion,
Banaras Hindu University. Varanasi.

CONTENTS

CHAPTER 1.

1. INTRODUCTION:

The Indian philosophical thought has enunciated that the highest goal of life is liberation or Mokṣa (eternally free from sorrows and sufferings due to cycle of births and deaths). The means for attaining the goal have also been prescribed as Karma, Bhakti and Jñāna.

The schools of Vedānta are propounded on the basis of scriptures, Upaniṣads, Brahma Sūtras and Bhagavad-Gītā, called Prasthāna traya (the triad). The earliest of them is Advaita Vedānta which preaches non-duality and it is propagated by Śaṅkarācārya (9th century).

The school of Vīśiṣtādvaita (the qualified non-dualism) is propounded by Rāmānuja (12/13thcentury) and Dvaita school (Duality) by Madhvācārya (13th century). Subsequently Śrī Vallabha (15th CE) taking Bhāgavatapurāṇa as a fourth canon has propounded Śuddhādvaita (pure non-dualism).

Śaṅkarācārya preached the theory of non-duality and declared the attribute- less Brahman (Nirguṇa Brahman) as the absolute reality. The jīva and Brahman are one. He has also advocated that the path of knowledge (Jñāna) only is the ultimate means for liberation.

All other schools of Vedānta have advocated that Śrī Kṛṣṇa is none other than the Para Brahman and Bhakti is the superior means. It is not only a means but an end itself. They have also said that everybody without any discrimination of age, gender, caste, literacy and standing in society are eligible for Bhakti.

The basic scriptures are and the aim also being the same, the approaches have been found to be different on account of their interpretations according to individual attitudes. This gave raise to mutual friction and rivalry among the absolute non-dualists and the other theistic schools. All of them claim superiority for themselves and all of them are united to oppose the Advaita School. In the 14th CE the spread of Bengal Vaiṣṇavism and other Bhakti schools became popular and influenced both scholars and laymen.

Although Advaita Vedānta emphasized knowledge as a sole means of liberation, it did not reject Bhakti. It considered Bhakti as an essential component and a means of attaining knowledge by purifying the mind. It is one of the steps in the ladder to reach the pinnacle of knowledge. The devotion to God gradually removes the idea of 'Ego' and ultimately leads to self-surrender which is the highest form of devotion. This helps the devotee to qualify for the realization of true nature of self. Thus, Bhakti is considered an important means of acquiring true knowledge of Ātman or Brahman. However it is never conceived as the final instrument of liberation.

This has been overlooked and misconstrued and the opponents continued their tirade which is like theological wrangles. Vyāsatīrtha, an eminent scholar belonging to Madhva School has written "***Nyāyāmṛta,***" a devastating critique of Advaita.

Madhusūdana Sarasvatī a 16th CE Advaita philosopher has shown his brilliant logic, erudite scholarship and polemical skills and has effectively and in a systematic manner refuted '***Nyāyāmṛta'*** on all counts and upheld the truth of non-dualism by writing "Advaitasiddhi"**.** The important aspects of Advaita Vedānta are dealt in this work. He has earned a prominent place as an ardent exponent of Advaita and an uncompromising defender among post Śaṅkara Advaita philosophers. He has contributed a lot to the total Advaitic literature by his works; Vedāntakalpalatikā, Siddhāntabindu, Saṁkṣepaśārīrakasārasaṅgraha.etc.

Madhusūdana Sarasvatī has exhibited his vast knowledge in various disciplines (śāstras) and deep knowledge of spiritual scriptures like yoga, Vedas, Upaniṣads. He had reputation as a master logician of his time (navya Nyāyā). He had knowledge of aesthetics (Alaṅkāra śāstra) and Vyākaraṇa. This is evident from his works. Thus he was one of the most brilliant luminaries in the firmament of Advaita Vedānta. He had high esteem towards Śaṅkarācārya.

He has shown his independent thinking, and did not hesitate even to differ with Śaṅkara on some occasions in his works. He is also known to have been a Yogī of high attainment, and he attached high importance to yoga as can be seen in his commentary on Bhagavad-Gītā (Gūḍhārtha Dīpikā).

It is interesting to know that Madhusūdana was also a devotee of Śrī Kṛṣṇa from his childhood. He continued to worship his Iṣṭa devata during his stay at Banaras after taking the sannyāsa dīkṣa. The devotional sentiment has found expression in several of his works and he has the distinction of writing an exclusive treatise on Bhakti called *"Bhakti Rasāyana"* besides other devotional works like Mahimnastotra ṭīkā, Ānandamandākinī,Paramahaṁsapriyā. In Gūḍhārtha Dīpikā (a commentary on Bhagavad-Gītā). He has highlighted and glorified Bhakti. He has asserted that total surrender to Lord Kṛṣṇa is the central message of Bhagavad-Gītā.

He has proclaimed In Bhaktirasāyana that Bhakti is an independent path for salvation and Śrī Kṛṣṇa is none other than Para Brahman. Bhakti is not only a means but an end in-itself. He has also mentioned that experience of ecstasy of Kṛṣṇa consciousness is even superior to mokṣa, based on the Bhāgavatapurāṇa, which closely resembles the path propagated by Gouḍīya Vaiṣṇavism which was prevalent in those days.

Madhusūdana Sarasvatī, being an uncompromising orthodox monistic sannyasin and at the same time an ardent devotee of Kṛṣṇa and advocating Bhakti as an independent spiritual path, is paradoxical and quite intriguing

The concept of Bhakti of Śrī Madhusūdana Sarasvatī therefore deserves a detailed study.

1.1. THE SCOPE AND OBJECTIVE OF THE STUDY AND BRIEF REVIEW OF AVAILABLE LITERATURE.

Madhusūdana Sarasvatī was a genius, well versed in several scriptures and an orthodox Advaita philosopher, ranking second only to Śaṅkarācārya. At the same time, he was devoted to Śrī Kṛṣṇa as his personal God identifying Him as Parā Brahman and advocated Bhakti as an independent spiritual path. In spite of this apparent contradiction he remained an Advaitin and there is no room for anybody to judge otherwise. The intention behind his highlighting and glorifying Bhakti deserves a detailed study.

A review of the available literature indicates that there are only few studies on the philosophy and works of Madhusūdana Sarasvatī It is found that the devotional sentiment and adherence to Kṛṣṇa Bhakti has been pointed out and commented by some authors in a more general way. Only few studies have been found which were made on the Bhakti aspects and are briefly discussed below.

i) P.M. Modi[1] (1929)· He has translated Siddhāntabindu into English. The brief details of the life and works of Madhusūdana Sarasvatī were discussed in the Introduction. Śrī Modi added a detailed note on the Bhakti mārga of Madhusūdana Sarasvatī as an appendix to the translation. It was mentioned, in order to establish that Bhakti is the principal aim of human life; one must decide the nature of this aim. Madhusūdana says "the chief object of a man is no other than Bliss unmixed with misery'.[2.] He has observed that Madhusūdana's devotion was not inconsistent with the Śaṅkara Vedānta school. Modi also mentioned that "just as in the days of Kumarila Bhaṭṭa and Śaṅkara the most important problem was the reconciliation of Karma and Jñāna, so in the days of Madhusūdana and Vallabha the great problem was that of Jñāna and Bhakti".[3] But it was left for Madhusūdana to solve it thoroughly and inculcate a new line of thought in the Śaṅkara Vedānta.

ii) Sanjukta Gupta (1966).[4] In her doctoral thesis on the study of philosophy of Madhusūdana Sarasvatī, she has devoted a chapter on Bhakti. She has observed that Madhusūdana did not break his pledge of allegiance to Advaita, yet could not keep himself away from the influence of Vaiṣṇavism of the time and he tried to forge a reconciliation between the Advaita and Vaiṣṇava points of view of Bhakti. She has further mentioned that Madhusūdana has explored a new path in which the doctrine of monism is reconciled to the theory of devotionalism. It is observed that there was no specific conclusion on the concept of Bhakti as an independent path mentioned in Bhakti Rasāyana by Madhusūdana Sarasvatī and its extent of congruence or otherwise with his Advaitic philosophy.

iii) Pradeep kumara khare (2000).[5] In his doctoral thesis on the philosophy of Madhusūdana Sarasvatī (in Hindi) has not made any specific observation on the concept of Bhakti.

iv) The only exclusive study is by Lance Edward Nelson (1986).[6] The thesis titled "Bhakti in Adv-aita Vedānta: a translation and study of Madhusūdana Sarasvati's Bhaktirasāyana". He has made a detailed analysis of Bhakti Rasāyana and Gūḍhārtha-Dīpikā for the Madhūsudan's devotional concept and also noted the devotional sentiment scattered in several other works. He has translated the first Ullāsa of Bhagavad Bhakti Rasāyana. He observed that "Madhusūdana presented the doctrine of Bhakti as an independent path and Paramapuruṣārtha. He has written more from a devotionalist view than as an Advaita sannyasin".

Dr. Nelson has concluded that "the commonly accepted view that he was a champion of the cause of Bhakti who successfully integrated devotion and Advaita cannot be accepted without serious qualification"[7]

v) Niranjan Saha (2014)[8] in his thesis entitled "Philosophy of Advaita Vedānta according to Madhusūdana Sarasvati's Gūḍhārtha-Dīpikā" has concluded that an inclination to Advaita Vedānta school is compatible with devotion, though it may not be of the same flavor as that of the dualist schools. It was further asserted that the thesis will enable the readers to accept the fact, that path of devotion is an important component of Advaita system of philosophy and was forcefully stated and established by Madhusūdana Sarasvatī.

vi) Suresh, K.V (2009)[9] in his doctoral thesis "Bhakti Rasāyana of Madhusūdana Sarasvatī: A critical study" has dealt mainly on Bhakti and Rasa and its combination as Bhakti rasa. The main topic of Bhakti Rasāyana is Bhakti. The conclusion is "Mad-

> husūdana winds up trying to fit an elevated view of Bhakti in to the confines of a system which is not designed to support it. Probably the most striking, from the view point of classical Advaita, and most unorthodox aspect of Madhusudan's presentation of Bhakti in the Bhakti Rasāyana, is his conception of Bhakti-yoga as a distinct and independent spiritual path, not in need of competition with Vedāntic Gnostic"

Thus, it is seen that there is no unanimity, but each has given different views and no definite conclusions.

It is proposed to make a detailed study of the concept of Bhakti as depicted in all his devotional works and devotional sentiments expressed in other works. The salient features of consistency and divergence, if any, will be brought out to make a comprehensive assessment of the concept of devotion of Madhusūdana Sarasvatī.

1.2 MADHUSŪDANASARASVATĪ'S LIFE AND HIS WORKS

1.2.1 LIFE OF MADHUSŪDANA SARASVATĪ

In the study about any philosopher it is necessary to know his heredity and the environment in which he has flourished, the political, social, and religious atmosphere prevailing at that point, that might have impacted and influenced the religious and philosophical thinking of the philosopher, is also to be ascertained.

The biographical details (Place of birth, date of birth and family background) of Madhusūdana Sarasvatī are not available from any of his works. He has written all his works after becoming a saṅyāsi and as per tradition; the enunciates avoid mentioning their past. In absence of authentic information we have to depend upon the accounts that are in circulation orally or claims of certain pundits who claim to belong to the clan. So it is difficult to arrive at any precise conclusion

There are different claims regarding the origin of Madhusūdana. In Vedāntakalpalatikā there was a mention of the name of a deity as Nīlāchalanāyaka[10] (the Lord of Blue Mountain). Many north Indian scholars have identified that Nīlāchalanāyaka is Lord Jagannāth at Puri and the author was a resident of Puri.

On the same analogy some south Indian scholars[11] felt that it would be appropriate to identify the Lord as Lord Kṛṣṇa of Guruvayur or Kṛṣṇa of Udipī, since Madhusūdana was an ardent devotee of Kṛṣṇa and more so has a fascination for BālaKṛṣṇa (Kṛṣṇa in childhood)[12] which is vividly described in Bhāgavatapurāṇa. Madhusūdana has attached importance to Bhakti to BālaKṛṣṇa, and he has quoted from Bhāgavatapurāṇa extensively in Bhakti Rasāyana. These are the places where the Lord is worshipped in the child form and this is the area where Madhva sāmpradāya flourished. It is told that even now there are some Sārasvata Brahmin families around Kochi in Kerala, believed to have migrated from Gaudadesa.

The following details are available from the article by Jagadīswarānanda Swami[13] and the introduction to commentary of Siddhāntabindu by Divanji P.C.[14] Divanji has collected the details from Sri Chintāharana Chakravartī who himself claimed to belong to the family of Madhusūdana Sarasvatī. The information is recorded in the manuscripts called Vaidikavādaṁīmāṁsā held with a famous Bengali poet named Sri Haridāsa Siddhānta Vāgiśa.

Due to persecutions by Muslim rulers, several Brahmin pundit families had migrated from Kanauj district in central India to Navadvīpa in Bengal. Among those who settled in Bengal was a Brahmin family of Kāśyapa gotra called Rāma Miśra in whose illustrious line our great saint was born, seventh in descent. Śrī Chintāharana Chakravartī is the ninth descent being grandson of Yadavānanda. Śrī Kṛṣṇa Gunārṇava had moved from Navadvīpa to Jessore district. His third son Purandara (also known as Pramoda Purandarācārya) had once again moved to Kotilāparā village in Faridpur district (now in Bangladesh). Purandara had constructed a dedicated temple of the Lord Dakṣiṇāmūrti and Goddess Kālī, with a pond facing it, where he used to worship. Thus it can be confirmed that he hailed from Bengal. It is also mentioned that a memorial reading room and library was founded in the locality in 1920, known as Madhusūdana Sarasvatī mandir.

Based on such details a genealogical tree of the family is drawn and is shown below.

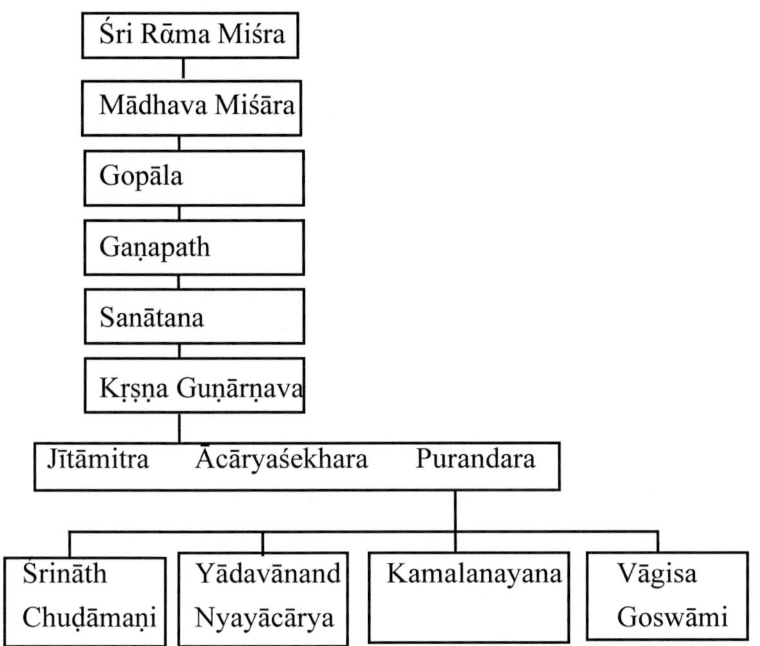

1.2.1.1 EDUCATION

Kamalanayana is the name of Madhusūdana in his Pūrvāśrama. He had shown his sharp intelligence and his prodigy since his childhood. He is reported to be capable of reproducing verbatim only after listening once. His father had identified this trait and arranged for his son's upanayana at an early age of five. Kamalanayana got his early education under the tutelage of his father, who was well versed in several śāstras. The young lad acquired proficiency in Vyākaraṇa, Kāvya, Alaṅkara and other śāstras in a short period of six years. He was able to write poetry by the time he was twelve.

There is a legend that once Śrī Purandara went to visit the king along with his two sons Yadavānanda and Kamalanayana. He apprised the king of the intellectual achievement of his sons, and Kamalanayana had dedicated a poem to the king. However the king who was otherwise preoccupied with his problems did not respond in spite of their wait for few days. Kamalanayana was hurt and told his father that "instead of pleasing men, henceforth I shall endeavor to please God"[15]. His father sent Kamalanayana to Navadvīpa, a premier seat of learning, where he studied Nyāya under Sri Hariram Tarkavāgiśa and further pursued the study of Navya Nyāya under Sri Mathurānātha Tarkavāgiśa, the greatest teacher of Navya Nyāya at that time. He is reported to have acquired proficiency which he had later exhibited in his works.

Kamalanayana since childhood imbibed devotion to Kṛṣṇa. Bhakti movement of Caitanya Mahā Prabhu (1485-1533) was then at its peak and swept the cultural mood all over Bengal and particularly Navadvīpa, the birth place of Caitanya. It was the center of Gouḍīya Viṣṇava movement where young Kamalanayana studied Nyāya. In all probability, the prevailing cultural mood was conducive for further strengthening his Kṛṣṇite devotion. It is told that he accepted the Bhedavāda, (the doctrine of difference). His newly learnt knowledge provided a logical basis to bheda. He then became keen to put the Bhakti cult on a firm metaphysical basis. He then decided to disprove Advaita using the skills he had mastered.

1.2.1.2 HIS JOURNEY FROM DVAITA TO ADVAITA.

It is told that in pursuit of his desire, Kamalanayana proceeded to Banaras from Navadvīpa to make an in-depth study of Advaita in order to categorically disprove Advaita doctrine.

At Banaras he approached Śrī Rāmatīrtha, the renowned Advaitin (who was the author of well-known commentary on Vedāntasāra,) and was duly accepted as a disciple. He has also sought help of Śrī Madhava Sarasvatī to facilitate learning of Mīmāṁsā for a better understanding of basic Advaita texts. Kamalanayana with his inherent intelligence, spirit of dedication and extraordinary concentration soon won the laurels of his teachers. Through his study he was convinced of the superiority and validity of Advaita that made him a staunch Advaitin for the rest of his life.

He approached his teacher Śrī Rāmatīrtha and confessed his original intention of becoming his disciple and sought forgiveness and prāyaścitta. On his Guru's advice he approached Śrī Viśveśvara Sarasvatī to grant him Sannyāsa. Śrī Viśveśvara Sarasvatī has cautioned that it is a great decision and he should firmly makeup his mind before taking a final decision, which should be irrevocable. In order to assess his mental attitude, scriptural knowledge and philosophical insight, Kamalanayana was asked to write a commentary on Bhagavad Gītā as a precondition and he left for a pilgrimage. Kamalanayana sincerely undertook the task and wrote the commentary. On returning from pilgrimage, Śrī Viśveśvara Sarasvatī perused the partially finished Vyākhyā, and having been impressed, initiated him into sannyāsa and from then on Kamalanayana was known as Madhusūdana Sarasvatī.

At Banaras he lived at Gopāla math in Catuḥṣaṣthi yoginī ghāt where he used to worship daily his Iṣṭa deva Śrī Kṛṣṇa. He wrote all his works at this place. He used to give discourse on spirituality and Vedānta and soon gained reputation as a learned scholar and a realized soul. He gathered disciples

1.2.1.3 HIS DISCIPLES

Madhusūdana Sarasvatī accepted everybody who approached him for knowledge without any reservations. It is pertinent to cite the example of Vyāsarāya before we mention his principal disciples. Vyāsarāya was a disciple of Dvaitācārya Vyāstīrtha (the author of ***Nyāyāmṛta,*** a devastating critique of Advaita Vedānta which was refuted by Madhusūdana Sarasvatī through his famous work ***Advaita-siddhi***). At the instigation of his guru Vyāsarāya approached Madhusūdana Sarasvatī to learn the *Advaita**siddhi*** from the author himself to gain in depth knowledge with a clandestine intention of refuting it subsequently. Madhusūdana (even though aware of his intentions) accepted him as a disciple and taught without any bias. After completion of his study Vyāsarāya presented Madhusūdana Sarasvatī, as a token of his gratitude, his work called ***Taranginī,*** in which he has vigorously refuted ***Advaita siddhi.*** Madhusūdana Sarasvatī did not show any resentment but smilingly remarked that he was aware of his disciple's intentions from the beginning, and it would not behoove of him to challenge his own disciple and some other disciple will do so in due course. This was done by his disciple Balabhadra by writing ***Siddhivyākhyā.***

Śrī Vithalesa, son of Śrī Vallabhācārya, who propounded Śuddhādvaita School, is also believed to be a disciple of Madhusūdana Sarasvatī.

The following were his principal disciples.

i) Balabhadra, who is also known as Balabhadra Bhaṭṭācārya, wrote *"Siddhivyākhyā"*, in which he refuted *'Taraṅginī'* of Vyāsarāya. Madhusūdana Sarasvatī had written his *Siddhāntabindu,* a commentary on Daśaśloki of Śaṅkarācārya, at the request of Balabhadra.

ii) Puruṣottama Sarasvatī wrote a commentary on his guru's *Siddhāntabindu* called *Bindusandipana* .

iii) Śeṣa Govinda wrote a commentary on Śrī Śaṅkara's Śarva Siddhānta Saṅgraha. He held his guru in high esteem and is known to have mentioned as follows.

"Sarsvatyavatāram tam vande Śrī Madhusūdanam."

Meaning that Śrī Madhusūdana Sarasvatī is none other than the incarnation of Sarasvatī

1.2.1.4 SOME IMPORTANT EVENTS IN THE LIFE OF MADHUSŪDANA SARASAVTĪ

The following are some of the important incidences that happened in the life of Madhusūdana Sarasvatī, known as per tradition.

a) Madhusūdana Sarasvatī was a contemporary of Saint Tulasī Das (1523-1647), the author of the famous ***Ramacarita Mānasa*** in vernacular, who used to reside at Harișcandra ghāt not far from Gopāla math. Tulasīdās was criticized by orthodox pundits for having written the holy Ramayana in vernacular to which he responded as follows-

Hari Hara yaśa sura nara gira vaarṇahi santa sujana |
Hāṇḍī hāṭaka cāruṭira rāndne swāda samāna ||

Meaning that Food cooked in a golden pot or an earthen pot tastes equally well and so also the glories of God described by devotees in whatever language are equally sweet". When this was brought to the notice of Madhusūdana who was impressed sent a note to Tulasīdās in Sanskrit couplet as follows.[16]

Paramānandapatroyaṃ jaṅgamatulasītaruḥ |
Kavitāmañjarī yasya Rāmabhramaracubitā||

Which means that this moving Tulasi plant (holy basil) has a leaf of supreme bliss, the efflorescence of it is in the form of poetry, kissed by the bee called Rāma.

According to tradition Emperor Akbar (1556-1605) had invited learned scholars and arranged for discussion and honoured them .The scholars gathered in the court of Akbar were so amazed by Madhusūdana's erudition that they paid him the highest tribute as follows[17].

Madhusūdanasarasvatyāḥ pāram veṭṭi Sarasvatī |
pāram veṭṭi Sarasvatyāḥ Madhusūdanasarasvatī ||

Meaning, that Goddess of Learning, Sarasvatī knows the depths of the limits of (knowledge of) Madhusūdana Sarasvatī, and Madhusūdana Sarasvatī attained, the limits of (knowledge of) Goddess Sarasvatī.

b) Madhusūdana Sarasvatī also played a different role in the social life, different from his monistic and religious life. The armed Muslim ascetics in the name of pious duty of their religion used to subject the Hindu sannyāsins to harassment and persecution. Madhusūdana approached Akbar through Bīrbal (a Hindu king). The outcome of the meeting was that Akbar agreed that, the Hindus can also raise a suitable force to protect themselves, who will have same immunity from governmental interference by the sacred character as that applicable to Muslims. The result was that many men with strong physic, Kṣatriya and Vaiśyas and other non-Brahmins were initiated into sannyāsa order by Madhusūdana Sarasvatī.[18] This is rather a radical departure from the orthodox tradition.

c) There is another story that Madhusūdana in his old age had visited Navadvīpa, the place where he had his early training in

Nyāyā and Navya Nyāyā. At that time his guru Mathurānātha Tarkavāgiśa was very old .The flourishing logician Jagadīśa, known from his student days, felt helpless and the upcoming logician Gadādhara Bhaṭṭācārya became insecure on seeing the arrival of Madhusūdana. The following verse is reported to have been circulated.[19]

Navadvīpe samāyāte Madhusūdana vākpaṭau |
cakaṁpe Tarkavāgiśāḥ kātaro abhÊta Gadādharaḥ.||

Meaning, that When Madhusūdana, the master of speech came to Navadvīpa, Mathurānātha Tarkavāgiśa, who was the foremost Nyāyācārya in those times, trembled with fear and Gadādhara another logician, became nervous and insecure.

Madhusūdana Sarasvatī on his return from Navadvīpa went to Hardwar, the holy city on the banks of river Gaṅgā. He spent the last days of his life there. He left the mortal body at a very advanced age of 107 at a preannounced time on the banks of Gaṅgā, sitting in a meditative posture. Hardwar is one of the seven tīrthas,[20] Where mokṣa is granted to all who die there.

a) The renowned south Indian Advaita philosopher Appayadīkṣita (1520-1593) met Madhusūdana when he visited Banaras and he had a high regard for Madhusūdana.
b) Modi, in the introduction to his translation of Siddhāntabindu mentioned that as per Nijavrata (Vallabha literature) that there was a meeting of Madhusūdana and Vallabha. (1478-

1531). Madhusūdana was reported to have recited a Śloka from Gūḍhārtha-Dīpikā with which Vallabha was pleased. Madhusūdana also showed his Bhaktirasāyana and held discussion on the book. However, the episode cannot be true because of the place of their meeting as well as the periods of the two scholars.

1.2.1.5 THE PERIOD

Several scholars after research have arrived at the approximate period in which Madhusūdana Sarasvatī flourished, but the estimate of dates widely varies.

A) Sulochana Nache24 gives it as 1565-1670.AD.

B) P.C. Divanji25 shows it as 1540-1647 AD.

Thus in the absence of any verifiable source, the speculation of the date has been so wide. However correlating some of the incidents mentioned above, the date of Madhusūdana Sarasvatī has been generally accepted between 1540 and 1647AD by the scholars. Still this is open for discussion.

1.2.2 MADHUSŪDANA'S WORKS

There is no authentic record of the works authored by Madhusūdana Sarasvatī. Aufrecht[26] has mentioned that there were six scholars who bore the name of Madhusūdana Sarasvatī and naturally it is difficult to identify our author. However with the works attributed to the scholars, it became easy to identify the author of Siddhāntabindu as

Madhusūdana Sarasvatī, our philosopher.

The following are the works listed under the name of Madhusūdana Sarasvatī by Mr. Aufrecht in catalog rum.[27]

i) Advaita Brahma siddhi[28] .It should be read as Advaitasiddhi.
ii) Advaitaratanarakṣaṇa.
iii) Ātmabhoda-ṭīkā.
iv) Ānandamandākinī.
v) Ṛg Veda- Jaṭādyāṣṭa-vikṛti-vivaraṇa.
vi) Kṛṣṇa Kutūhala Nāṭaka.
vii) Prasthānabheda.
viii) Bhakti sāmānya Nirūpaṇa.
ix) Bhagavad-Gītā Gūḍhārtha- Dīpikā.
x) Bhagavad Bhaktirasāyana.
xi) Bhāgavatapurāṇa prathama śloka-vyākhyā.
xii) Bhāgavatapurāṇādyaślokatraya-vyākhyā.
xiii) Mahimnastotra- ṭīkā.
xiv) Rājñāṁpratibodhah.
xv) Vedastuti- ṭīkā.
xvi) Vedāntakalpalatikā.
xvii) Śāṇḍilyasūtra-ṭīkā.
xviii) Śāstrasiddhāntalesa-ṭīkā.
xix) Saṅkṣepa- Śārīraka-Sārasṅgraha.
xx) Sarvavidyā Siddhānta varṇana.
xxi) Siddhāntatattabindu.
xxii) Harilīlā-Vyākhyā.

Several authors have indicated different number of works. K.L.Potter[29] has mentioned 19 works and Dasgupta, Surendranath[30] has mentioned as 18, and it is difficult to specifically ascribe these works with any accuracy to Madhusūdana Sarasvatī.

The following are not considered as authored by Madhusūdana Sarasvatī for reasons mentioned.

Item3. Ātmabhoda- ṭīkā: It was mentioned by Divanji[31] that is a work of another Saṅnyāsin of the same name of Madhusūdana Sarasvatī.

Item 6. Kṛṣṇa Kutūhala Nāṭaka: and Item 14 Rājñāṁpratibodhah on an examination of manuscript, it was concluded by Divanji[32] that they were written by another namesake who lived in Banaras, whose biographic detail are different.

Item 7. Prasthānabheda[33]: It is found to be not an independent work, but it is a commentary on verse 7 of Mahimnastotra- ṭīkā. (item13)

Item8. Bhakti sāmānya Nirūpaṇa:[34]It is not an independent work but the name given to the first Ullāsa (of item 10 above).

Item12.Bhāgavatapurāṇadyaślokatṛaya-Vyākhyā:[35]When the author has already written a Vyākhyā on the first verse of Bhāgavatapurāṇa once again writing a second commentary on the first three verses of the same work is considered not possible and hence not considered as a different work.

Mahāmahopādhyāya Abhayankara Śāstri has stated that Kṛṣṇa Kutūhala Nāṭaka, Harilīlā -Vyākhyā, Vedaśtuti- Vyākhyā and Ānandamandākinī are written by another Madhusūdana Sarasvatī[36] and not by the author of Siddhāntabindu. We have already noted this point about Kṛṣṇa Kutūhala Nāṭaka.

Item 17. Śāṇḍilyasūtra-ṭīkā and item 18 Śāstrasiddhāntalesa- ṭīkā: are not available and hence not considered.

Aufrecht himself has doubted about item 20 Sarvavidyāsiddhānta-varṇana.

Sanjukta Gupta[37] has opined in her study that only ten works can be considered to have come from the pen of Madhusūdana Sarasvatī based on the internal evidence found in the works and classified and also chronologically although the same is tentative. This can be considered agreeable. The Harilīlā-Vyākhyā which is included in these ten however was not accepted to be the work of Madhusūdana Sarasvatī by many after verification of details of author's biographic details (as mentioned above)

Prof. Modi and P.C. Divanji have strongly pleaded that Īśvarapratipatti-Prakāśa is the work of Madhusūdana Sarasvatī, based on the similarity of the contents with other works like Siddhāntabindu. Mahāmahopādhyāya Gaṇapati Śāstri has also confirmed that it was authored by Madhusūdana Sarasvatī. However but as the style of the work did not show similarity, Sanjukta Gupta remains neutral on the inclusion of this work.

Similarly Ānandamandākinī is also to be considered, as the colophon and the last verse bear the name of Madhusūdana Sarasvatī, a devotee of son of Nanda as it composer. It is also mentioned in Kāvyamālā series, Bombay in the second Guchchha[38].

Thus adding these two to the list of works agreed by Sanjukta Gupta, but by exclusion of Harilīlā-Vyākhyā, we have eleven works, and they are classified as Philosophical works and devotional works as follows. We find that some are independent compositions (prakaraṇa) and some are commentaries (Vyākhyā/ ṭīkā) and are classified as such.

(A) PHILOSOPHICAL WORKS

i) Saṅkṣepa-Śārīrakasāra- Saṅgraha. (Commentary)
ii) Vedāntakalpalatikā. (Prakaraṇa)
iii) Siddhāntabindu. (Commentary)
iv) Advaitasiddhi. (Prakaraṇa)
v) Advaitaratanarakṣaṇa. (Prakaraṇa)

(B) DEVOTIONAL WORKS

i) Ānandamandākinī. (Prakaraṇa)
ii) Mahimnastotra- ṭīkā. (Commentary)
iii) Bhagavad Bhaktirasāyana. (Prakaraṇa)
iv) Bhagavad-Gītā Gūḍhārtha- Dīpikā. (Commentary)
v) Paramahaṁsapriyā. (Commentary on the first verse of Bhāgavatapurāṇa)
vi) Īśvarapratipatti Prakāśa. (Prakaraṇa)

It is now proposed to briefly examine briefly the outlines of thecontent of each of the above works.

Divanji[39] has rightly observed that although the apparently works on Bhakti but in each of them the Advaita doctrine has been anyhow brought in and some one or another new feature thereof is explained in order to clear up doubts. We find that devotional aspects and Philosophical aspects are mixed in many works.

1.2.2.1 ĀNANDAMANDĀKINĪ

The work is an original composition consisting of 102 verses. The main content of the composition is praise of Śrī Kṛṣṇa and his beauty from top to toe (Kesādi Pādānta varṇana).The whole composition is full of eulogizing the beauty and virtues of Śrī Kṛṣṇa in detail. The Bhāgavatapurāṇa described the various aspects of Śrī Kṛṣṇa's childhood deeds, which were brought out in poetical compositions like Śrī Kṛṣṇa Karnāmṛutam, Mukundamāla which delights the devotees. The present work is a crown among such works coming out of the pen of a prominent exponent of Advaita Philosophy. The composition described in detail, the childhood deeds and exploits of Kṛṣṇa with Gopīs and cowherd boys. The episodes of Putanā, Kāliyamardana, lifting of Govardhana giri, the divine dance called Rāsalīlā and killing of Kaṁsa were described. The episode how Kṛṣṇa has humbled Brahma who wanted to test him and similarly Indra, and how he rescued Śiva from Bhaśmāsura were also narrated. The colophon of the composition at the end is noteworthy, that the work is that of a devotee of the son of Nanda. This is perhaps is the first work of the author.

1.2.2.2 VEDĀNTAKALPALATIKĀ

There are two editions of the manuscripts of this work, one in India office and the other at Ānandāśram, Poona. The contents are reported to be almost same. The English translation by Karmarkar, R.D[40] is referred in this study. The author has mentioned Śrī Viśveśvara as his preceptor, and glorified him, which also means the Lord of the universe.

Vedāntakalpalatikā is a well known Sanskrit manual in which important concepts of Advaita Vedānta were discussed. It is a treatise on mokṣa. It is the opinion of the commentator that this and Siddhāntabindu give the views of Madhusūdana on Advaita Vedānta in a nutshell and other works give the exposition of these in detail. The author gave the aim of the book as, bringing out the true nature of mokṣa and means. He refuted the views of Jaimini, Kapila, Patañjali, Kaṇanda and others in accordance with the interpretation given by Vyāsa and Śaṅkara. Madhusūdana was of the opinion like all other Advatins that mokṣa can never be described as a product, as that would show mokṣa as impermanent. He wishes to uphold the invaluable Śrūti passages. He was greatly influenced by devotion and tried to show that while mokṣa require no Kārana for its realization, the vicāra of Śrūti passages, devotion and instruction from a qualified teacher help in preparing the ground for realization of Ātma and removing Ajñāna by ensuring all-round purity of citta, which automatically brings about realization of mokṣa.

1.2.2.3 SIDDHĀNTABINDU (commentary)

This is a commentary on the Daśaśloki of Śrī Śaṅkarācārya. It is told that when Śaṅkara approached Govinda Pāda and sought to be accepted as a disciple, he was asked who he was? Śaṅkara spontaneously answered by these verses which are famous as Daśaśloki.

In the invocation verse Madhusūdana has paid respects to his preceptor Śrī Viśveśvara, whom he considers as the new incarnation of Śaṅkarācārya. In the conclusion of the composition, he has mentioned that the composition is like a desire-yielding Gem, which gives abundant knowledge. He also praised Śaṅkarācārya and Sureśvarācārya for the knowledge of Vedānta given by them. This commentary was composed at the request of his disciple Balabhadra. The Vedāntakalpalatikā was referred in this work and thus confirms that this was written by Madhusūdana. This work like his earlier work gives in-depth knowledge of all important aspects of Advaita Vedānta. His disciple Puruṣottama Sarasvatī has written a commentary on this called Bindusaindipina

There are several translations of Siddhāntabindu by Divanji, P.C[41], Modi, P.M[42], Śāstri, S. N[43] and others.

1.2.2.4 ŚIVA MAHIMNA STOTRA-ṬĪKĀ (Commentary)

The Śiva Mahimnastotra-ṭīkā is considered as foremost of hymns extolling Śiva and is immensely popular among devotees of Śiva all over the country and was considered as the best among the stotras to Śiva. It was composed by a Gandharva called Puṣpadanta prayed to Lord Siva for forgiveness having realized that he has incurred the wrath of the Lord for a fault committed inadvertently. Śiva was pleased with the prayer and restored the powers to Puṣpadanta. Madhusūdana Sarasvatī has written a commentary on the stotra. This was published by Nirṇaya Sāgar press Bombay. It was mentioned that ancient Ācāryas have commented on this but did not mentioned the details. A Hindi translation with original Sanskrit by Pundit Rālarām Śarma published by Chow Kamba Vidyābhavan, Varanasi is referred in analyzing the text.

Madhusūdana while believing the story of Puṣpadanta has commented only on the first 31 verses considering them as relevant and the rest are only routine Phala Sruti. The special feature of this commentary is that Śrī Madhusūdana has commented first as applicable to Śiva (Hara) and then equally applicable to Hari (Viṣṇu) to convey the message that they are not different from each other. The commentary on verse seven is treated as a separate work, by name Prasthānabheda. However, later it was identified as a part of this Mahimnastotra ṭīkā. The conclusion of it is that all prasthānas are meant to establish the non-dual supreme God. The commentator has shown his poetic and linguistic skills. This is mostly a devotional work with some philosophical truths and highlights the need for sincere devotion by which the Lord can be pleased.

1.2.2.5 SAṄŚEPAŚĀRĪRAKA-SĀRASAṄGRAHA (Commentary)

This work is a commentary on the work of Sarvajñātma Muni, called SaṅśepaSārīraka which is a summary in verse of Brahmasūtra Bhāṣya of Śaṅkarācārya. The commentary is an ample proof of Madhusūdana command over the language and Vedānta theory of Śaṅkara. The author has given elaborate and scholarly interpretation. It is found that some of the topics are found to have been discussed in Siddhāntabindu and even more elaborately. This work has not been mentioned in any other work nor has been mentioned in any other work.

Sarvajñātma Muni is one of the favorite philosopher of Madhusūdana and perhaps as he was also sympathetic towards Nirguṇa Bhakti mārga. It will be pertinent to mention that Madhusūdana has also mentioned the possibility of approaching Nirguṇa Brahman through Bhakti Mārga.

1.2.2.6 BHAGAVD BHAKTI RASĀYANA (Prakaraṇa)

This is an independent work exclusively on Bhakti and Madhusūdana can be considered as the only Advaita Philosopher to have written such an exclusive treatise on Bhakti. He propounded a unique devotional theory in tune with Bhāgavatapurāṇa and explicitly recognized Bhakti as a valid, independent path for salvation. He also proclaimed that Lord Kṛṣṇa as none other than Supreme Brahman. The text referred Vedāntakalpalatikā, Siddhāntabindu which confirms that the work is written by the author and all those were written earlier than this.

The text is divided into three Ullāsas. The Ullāsa consisting of 35 verses which is named as Bhakti Sāmānya nirūpaṇa. The second Ullāsa consisting of 80 verses is called Bhakti viśesa nirūpaṇa. Third Ullāsa consisting of 30 verses establishing Bhakti as a Rasa. The author himself has written a detailed commentary on the first Ullāsa.

Madhusūdana has named the text as Bhaktirasāyana which literally means that Bhakti is an elixir for permanent cure for all dreaded ills of Saṁsāra (Cycle of births and deaths).

The Bhakti has been defined and means of Bhakti have been described. He has compared Bhakti with Brahma-Vidyā and the eligibility and fruits of the same have been detailed. Bhakti has been defined as the incessant flow of mind towards the highest God, like Gaṅgā flowing continuously and uninterruptedly towards the ocean, when the mind melts on hearing His names and virtues. He explained that the Lord is himself is the highest form of bliss by his own nature, and who when reflected in the melted state of mind becomes the Sthāyībhava and manifests as rasa. The different divisions of Bhakti and different forms of rasa were explained and established that Bhakti rasa is the only rasa that can be qualified as the supreme rasa which brings immense bliss.

1.2.2.7 PARAMAHAṀSAPRIYA (Vyākhya)

This work is a commentary on the first Śloka of Bhāgavatapurāṇa namely *"Janmādyasyayatah ...Satyam param Dhimahi."*, and is called Paramahaṁsapriyā. The text was published in w.ww. Laitaalitaa.com. The commentary by Madhusūdana is elaborate. The commentary is divided into three parts. The first according to Upaniṣads, the second as Purāṇic and the third as Kevala Bhakti. He has given a Mangalācarana Śloka about Bhakti to Śrī Kṛṣṇa explain the virtues of Kṛṣṇa as per Bhāgavatapurāṇa, evincing interest in hearing and singing them will be beneficial for the devotees. There is a mention of Bhaktirasāyana in this work.

1.2.2.8 ĪŚVARAPRATIPATTI PRAKĀŚA (Prakaraṇa)

This is a small work found on palm leaf in manuscript in Malayalam characters. Although there is name of the author, It is believed to be authored by the famous Madhusūdana Sarasvatī, who wrote Advaitasiddhi and Gūḍhārtha-Dīpikā. Śrī Gaṇapati Śāstri, who wrote the preface of the work, has mentioned these details. This was published in Trivandrum Sanskrit series 1921. The various theories of the conception of God both in heterodox and orthodox schools were described. The commentator of Siddhāntabindu (P.M. Modi) has observed the contents are similar and the theories on God are much bigger account than in Siddhāntabindu and hence concluded that this is a later work of the author.

The author has not given his own conclusion, but it can be construed that the content of the Mangalācarana Śloka which states Śrī Kṛṣṇa son of Nanda as his Īśvara tattva.

1.2.2.9 BHAGAVAD- *GĪTĀ- GŪḌHĀRTHA-DĪPIKĀ (Commentary)*

The commentary on Bhagavad-Gītā called Gūḍhārtha-Dīpikā meaning the illuminator of the hidden meaning thereof was written by Madhusūdana Sarasvatī. It was written after a thorough reading of the commentary of Śaṅkarācārya. Madhusūdana has explained every word including simple words[44].

The special features of Gūḍhārtha- Dīpikā are:

i) An introduction (containing 46 verses) was given by the author which will be helpful for all the readers as a guide.

ii) The test is divided into three sections each covering six chapters. The first dealing in Karma, the last section deals with Jñāna and the middle section deals with Bhakti and also God's grace which enable transition from karma to Jñāna.

iii) The division also explains *"thou art that".* The first clarifies *'Thou'*, the second section 'that' and the last section reveals the essence of the *'thou art that'* that *the* Jīva is identical with Brahman.

iv) Śrī Madhusūdana has given a few verses of his own as the gist of the chapter. He has added some verses, in some chapters at the beginning and at the end of the chapter in some.

v) Bhagavad-Gītā has first time propounded Bhakti as an important component for realization along with karma and Jñāna. Madhusūdana has stated that Bhakti is inherent in all, mixed with karma, Pure and also mixed with Jñāna.

Madhusūdana Sarasvatī, while agreeing mostly with the commentary of Śaṅkara, but has boldly shown his courage to differ in a few instances and gave his own version. The most important difference is while interpreting verse 18.66. He has declared that essence of the teaching of Gītā also other scriptures is self-surrender to the Lord, while Śaṅkarācārya has declared that the essence is renunciation of all actions and steadfastness of knowledge.

The author stated that with maturity of spiritual practice, the following types of surrender to God come about namely *'I belong to Him'*, *'He belongs to me'* and finally *'I am He'* and stated that the same has been described in the Bhakti Rasāyana a treatise written by him.

The devotional sentiment and leaning toward the path of Bhakti are observed to have been shown by him at several places throughout the commentary, however he has given due importance to Jñāna.

1.2.2.10 **ADVAITASIDDHI** (Prakaraṇa)

Advaitasiddhi is considered as the monumental work of Advaita literature. The thorough knowledge and understanding of the test is considered essential for any claim of scholarship in Advaita philosophy. This was written to refute the bitter criticism of Advaita by Vyāsatīrtha, a dualist philosopher belonging to Madhva School in his work called '*Nyāyāmṛta*'. Madhusūdana has shown his brilliant skills as a logician and polemicist and refuted him on all counts and vindicated the truth of Non-dualism.

The work refers to Vedāntakalpalatikā six times and Siddhāntabindu five times. It will not be out of place to mention that this work has been refuted in '***Taraṅginī***' written by Vyāsarāma, (a dvaiti) who became a disciple of Madhusūdana, concealing his identity and intensions. Bal-abhadra- Bhaṭṭācārya, a disciple of Madhusūdana has refuted the same by writing a book called '***Siddhivyākhyā***'.

The colophon at the end of each chapter indicates that it is written by Madhusūdana Sarasvatī, a disciple of Viśveśara, of the illustrious order of Paramahaṁsas.

1.2.2.11 ADVAITARATNARAKṢAṆA (Prakaraṇa)

This work is a original work of Madhusūdana Sarasvatī against the views of dualist Nyayā philosophy and was published by Nirṇayasāgar press, Bombay. This work refers to Siddhāntabindu, Advaitasiddhi and Vedāntakalpalatikā. We find that this was not referred in any of his earlier works, and so it can be inferred that this was his last work. The author has expressed his disgust that the dualist philosophers were making repeated criticism, in spite of his detailed clarifications in Advaitasiddhi.

Notes and Reference

1. Modi.P.M, Translation of 'Siddhāntabindu' being Madhusūdana's commentary on the Daśaśloki of Śrī Śaṅkarācārya, Vohra publishers and distributors, Allahabad.1985.
2. Ibid, Appendix, xii, P156.
3. Ibid, P13.
4. Gupta, Sanjukta, Studies in the philosophy of Madhusūdana Sarasvatī, Pustak Bhandar, Calcutta, 1966.
5. Kare, Pradeepkumar, 'Madhusūdana Sarasvatī ka darśan', Classical Publications, New Delhi.2000.
6. Nelson, Lance Edward, 'Bhakti in Advaita Vedānta, A translation of Madhusūdana Sarasvatī Bhakti Rasāyana, 'McMaster University, Ontario. 1986.
7. Ibid. Piii.
8. Saha, Niranjan, 'Philosophy of Advaita Vedānta according to Madhusūdana Sarasvatī's Gūḍhārtha Dīpikā', Department of the study of religion, SOAS, University of London., 2014.
9. Suresh, K.V, 'Bhakti Rasāyana of Madhusūdana Sarasvatī: A critical study', Śrī Śaṅkarācārya Sanskrit University, Kalady, 2009.
10. Rajagopalan, V, Preceptors of Advaita, Ed By Mahadevan, T.M.P, Samatabooks, Madras, P254, 1984.
11. Ibid P254.
12. Mahimnastotra ṭīkā, Verse 13.
13. Jagadīswarānanda, swamī, 'Śrī Madhusūdana Sarasvatī', Vedānta kesari, Advaita Asram, Kolkata, Dec, P308-14, 1941.
14. Divanji, P.C, Siddhāntabindu (Tr) Gaekwad's Oriental series, Baroda, 1933. --Divanji, P.C has made extensive study of the biographical details of Madhusūdana Sarasvatī and give elaborate details in the introduction of his translation of Siddhāntabindu, (Tr) Gaekwad's Oriental series, Baroda, 1933.
15. Biographies of Indian saints www.Angelfire.com/india/saints/bibo.html.

16. Jagadiśwarānanda Swamī, VK Dec, P313, 1941.
17. Jagadiśwarānanda Swamī, VK Dec, P313, 1941.
18. Farquher, Prof N, *The Organization of Sannyāsa ofAdvaita,* JRAS, July, P483. 1925, also quoted by Modi,P.M,, Siddāntabindu, P9. 1985.
19. Jagadiśvarānandaswamī, VK Dec, P314, 1941.
20. There are seven Mukti tirthas, Places where one will get mokṣa if he dies at this place as per Hindu belief. They are Ayodhya, Avantika, Hardwar, Kanchi, Kasi, Mathura, and Puri.
21. Rajendra Ghose *Introduction to Advaita Siddhi*, Part I, Ed Mm YogendraNāth Tarka saṁkhya Vedānta Tirtha, P115. Quoted by Gupta, Sanjukta, in her book Advaita Vedānta and Vaiṣṇavism, Rutledge, P 5, 2006.
22. Modi, P.M., Siddhāntabindu Tr, Vohara Publishers and Distributors, Allahabad, reprint, Introduction, P1, 1933.
23. Pāndey Ramājña Śarma, Ed *Vedāntakalpalatikā*, with introduction, quoted by Divanji, P.C, in his introduction to Tr of Siddhāntabindu, Gaekwad's oriental series Vol. LXIV, P xix. 1933.
24. Nache, Sulochana, '*The date of Madhusūdana Sarasvatī'*, ABORI, Poona, p326-31. 1945.
25. Divanji, P.C, *The life and works of Madhusūdana Sarasvatī*, ABORI Poona Vol ix P313-23 also mentioned in the authors Tr of Siddhāntabindu, Gaekwad's oriental series Vol LXIV, Pxix. 1933.
26. Note: Aufrecht has mentioned about 15 or16 authors with the name of Madhusūdana and of whom only one has the suffix Sarasvatī, applied to his name. However Mahāmahopādhyāya Abhayankara Śāstri has stated that there are five with suffix Sarasvatī of them. P.C.Divanji has made a detailed discussion on the subject in his Siddhāntabindu Translation published by Gaekwad's oriental series Vol LXIV, pii, 1933.
27. Catalogues Catalororum, Part I-P427.
28. Advaita Brahma Siddhi- It should be read as Advaitasiddhi. (note: Advaita Brahma Siddhi was reported to have been written by Sadānanda Yeti and published in Advaita manjari by Nirnayasagar press, Bombay.

29. Potter, Karl, '*Encyclopedia of Indian Philosophy Part1'*, MotilalBanarsidas, New Delhi, P368-370, 1983.

30. Dasgupta, Surendranath, '*History of the Indian Philosophy'*, Vol2,-Cambridge university press, p225,1932.

31. Divānji, P.C, "*Siddhāntabindu*" (tr) Baroda oriental series Vol L xiv, Introduction Piii, 1933.

32. Divānji, P.C., "*Siddhāntabindu*" (Tr) Baroda Oriental series vol - Lxiv, 1933

33. Ibid. introduction, p iii.

34. Ibid introduction, p iii.

35. Ibid introduction, p iii.

36. Śāstri, Abhayankara, Tr '*Siddhāntabindu*', Government oriental series class A No2 P27.was quoted by Divānji in his work cited 31 above.

37. Gupta, Sanjukta, "*Advaita Vedānta and Vaiṣṇavism-The Philosophy of Madhusūdana Sarasvatī,"* Rutledge, London, 2006. p11.

38. Ānandamandākinī was published in Kavyamala series, Guchha 2, Bombay as the work of Madhusūdana Sarasvatī.

39. Divānji,P.C , *'Siddhāntabindu* ',Gaekwad's Oriental series Vol LXIV,Baroda, 1933, Introduction, p xiii.

40. Karmarkar,R.D, '*Vedāntakalpalatikā*' (tr) in English with original Sanskrit text, Bhandarkar Oriental research institute, Poona, p 1, 1962.

41. Divānji,P.C, '*Siddhāntabindu*', (Tr)in English with original Sanskrit, Gaekwad's Oriental series, Vol LXIV, Baroda, 1933.

42. Modi,P.M, Translation of *'Siddhāntabindu'* being Madhusūdana's commentary on the Daśa śloki of Śrī Śaṅkarācārya,Vohara Publishers and distributors, Allahabad, India,1929.

43. Śāstri, S.N, '*Siddhāntabindu'* (Tr) Ādi Śaṅkara Advaita research center, Chennai, 2006.

44. Gambhīrānanda Swāmī' *Madhusūdana Sarasvatī, Bhagavad- Gītā with the Annotation-* Gūḍh ārtha-Dīpikā', Advaita Ashrama, Kolkata, edition 2013.

*****

CHAPTER 2.

2. CONCEPT OF BHAKTI.

In this chapter the basic concepts of Karma, Bhakti and Jñāna as means of realization, Bhakti in various scriptures, the structure of Hindu society as Varṇa Āśrama dharma, which specifies duties and functions, besides the eligibility for pursuit of spiritual practices, are discussed in a concise manner.

The concept of Bhakti in Bhagavad-Gītā, Bhāgavatapurāṇa, the Bhakti Sūtras of Sage Śāṇḍilya and Nārada are examined and narrated concisely. Madhusūdana Sarasvati whose attitude towards Bhakti is the aim of this study is a prominent Advaita philosopher who has highlighted that Bhakti is also a valid means of self realisation and established with scriptural authority. There is a general misconception that Advaita is antagonistic towards Bhakti and it is therefore proposed to examine the concept of Bhakti in Advaita Vedanta.

2.1. BASIC CONCEPTS OF KARMA, BHAKTI AND JÑĀNA.

Madhusūdana Sarasvatī whose attitude towards Bhakti is the aim of this study is a prominent Advaita philosopher who has highlighted that Bhakti is also a valid means of self realisation and establised with scriptural authority.

All the systems (with the exception of Cārvāka) are in agreement that mokṣa is the ideal, without any tint of sorrow or imperfection. Once that state is reached there is cessation of births and deaths. Mokṣa is thus "the master word in Indian philosophy. It is the supreme ideal"[1] and all cherish the attainment of it, as the highest goal of life. It is an immediate experience, not the result any logical thinking or discursive reason, but by philosophical wisdom obtained through spiritual disciplines. The system combined faith and reason, blending religion and philosophy as inseparable. The philosophical systems hold that there is a permanent spiritual essence, the soul of man. Humans due to ignorance and egotism are blind about their true nature. The removal of egotism and ignorance, as well as moral and ethical living, are the essential pre- requisites for spiritual life.

The Upaniṣads and scriptures lay stress on morality and self control. "One whose mind is restless due to weakness to some mundane pleasure, who is incapable of controlling his mind and who is always craving for fruit of his action can not realize the self through Knowledge."[2]

Bṛahadāraṇyaka Upaniṣad states, "The practice of general rules of morality and special rules pertaining to different professions and different stages of life is a pre condition for spiritual realization."[3]

The word dharma is a broad concept that includes religion, duty, and righteousness. In the context of individuals, it refers to the attitude that prompts a person's action or duty during the present life time, by which he can realize his destiny. All beings have an inherent sense of right and wrong, true and false, good and bad actions, on the basis of which, one is relatively free to choose how to act according to situations in life.

To arrive at a right choice that is beneficial rather than pleasing, is possible only when he realizes the need to take refuge in the Lord or acts as per inner conscience. The Indian ethical ideal, the goals of life of man, are the "Puruṣārthas" or objectives of life namely Dharma, Artha, Kāma and mokṣa. The supreme ideal is mokṣa, while Artha and Kāma are instrumental and secular. In order to gratify the mundane desires, men seek (Artha) wealth for food, clothing, housing and other utilities. Kāma is gratifying to the biological instincts and pleasures.

The Dharma (righteousness) is the guide for righteous living and regulating all acts. One should not be greedy to amass wealth beyond his legitimate needs. This applies to food as well as property and other assets. Men have a general tendency to be greedy and hoard huge wealth.

The gratification of sensory desires has to be morally legitimate, and should avoid indiscriminate indulgence. The man whose desires are so fulfilled legitimately should be content in life and look forward for the higher objectives of life. The greatest enemy of man is lust and sensual pleasures, which blinds their intellect and they do not hesitate to go to any extent. The senses are the chief source of man's pleasure and pain. The immoderate and uncontrolled indulgence in sensual passions, envelopes knowledge and leads to sin and becomes a perpetual foe.

The individual has to win over his internal enemies *Kāma* (sensual desire), *Krodha* (anger), *Moha* (illusion), *Lobha* (greediness), *Mada* (Ego), *Mātsarya* (Jealousy). This is essential not only, not to frustrate the spiritual pursuit but also to avoid miseries in life.

2.1.1. STUCTURE OF HINDU SOCIETY AND STAGES OF LIFE.

The Hindu society has classified the persons in the society into four (Varṇas) based upon the intellect, physical strength and inherent mental guṇas (qualities) and attitudes. It has accordingly assigned them certain functions within society and decided their eligibility for the pursuit of spiritual disciplines. It is import to be noted in this connection that it is not the birth that determines the varṇa but his intellectual and mental qualities (Sattva, Rajas and Tamas).

In a similar manner the Hindu tradition has classified the stages of life and the legitimate and obligatory functions at each stage of life. The stages of life are (i) Brahmacarya–student (ii) Gṛahasta-householder (iii) Vānaprastha-Hermit stage and (iv) Sannyāsa -ascetic stage. In each stage of life the duties to be performed by each category of varṇa have been prescribed to have a harmonious society.

The performance of the functions prescribed in scriptures, as per the varṇa and stage of life is called 'Svadharma'. It is mentioned in Bhagavad-Gītā that 'Better to do, one's own dharma though imperfect, than the dharma of others even well performed.'[4]

No matter how one has spent his life, at a certain point of time, he realizes that his goal is to seek God. Worldly goals immerse men in a temporary delight and joy. He eventually realizes that even after successful accomplishments, one feels restless and continues to search for something which is difficult to identify. Sincere search leads one to seek God.

Now after examining the structure of the society and their duties and functions, the means of realization of the highest ideal of life which is liberation or mokṣa, will be discussed.

The means of realization mainly depend upon the nature of people who seek realization. Their eligibility for pursuit of spiritual disciplines has to be considered. There are people of diverse nature in the world; hence no stereotype or universal method can be prescribed. However it would be better that some means and methods are evolved, as it would be better than having no means at all.

The ancient sages after considering the diverse types of people e mentioned three main means of sādhanā or practices with intent to ensure the highest good of an individual in the shape of liberation.

(i) Disinterested action.(Niṣkāma Karma).
(ii) Devotion (Bhakti).
(iii) Spiritual enlightenment (Jñāna or knowledge).

The observance of certain essential basic moral practices is prescribed for all. They are (i) *Ahiṁsā* (non-violence). (ii)

Satya (truthfulness). (iii) *Asteya* (Non stealing of other's property. (iv) *Brahmacarya* (observance of celibacy). (v) *Aparīgraha* (not accepting gifts).These are to be followed strictly by all people irrespective of varṇas and other classifications. These are not only physical practices but should also be mentally observed with sincerity.

The paths mentioned above, Karma, Bhakti and Jñāna are not mutually exclusive. On the other hand, each blends into the other. Each of the divisions is made in accordance with the type of tendency that prevails in a man; each one may pursue the way that suits his dominant psychological disposition.

The path of Jñāna is for men whose intellect is sharp and who have natural tendency for renunciation. The Karma path is for people with a strong desire for performance of actions, which involves will and physical effort.

Bhakti is for people who have emotions. Man is an integrated whole of mental, physical and emotional aspects and they cannot be separated.

The purification of mind and grace of God are essential pre-requisites of all paths. If any one aspect is purified, it will result in purifying the other aspects as well. Although in the beginning they appear to be different paths, the final goal being same, they integrate into one another later on.

2.1.2. PATH OF KARMA (ACTION).

The doctrine of Karma has been accepted by all philosophical systems of India (except Cārvāka- the materialist system) in one form or other. It is a moral law of cause and effect. Some of the systems like Buddhism and Jainism do not believe in Vedas and the existence of God, but they do give importance to Karma.

The yogīs undertake work through body, mind and intellect without attachment, merely for purification of themselves,All living creatures in the world have essential needs (like hunger, sleep, sex etc) which are there as instincts but human being is superior among them, because they have the ability to think and have a free will to act as a responsible agent and be responsible for its consequences, good or bad as the case may be.

The Upaniṣad says as follows:

"As is a person's desire, so is his will, and as is his will so is his deed (karma), whatever"[5]. It is similar to the age old saying "As you sow, so you will reap". It is similar to the physical law, that every action has it consequence or reaction and every effect has a cause and vice versa, or what goes around comes around.

The word Karma is derived from the root Kṛ (to do) which also generates several words like Karta (doer), Karthavya (duty) and Karma (action) etc.

The totality of a person's karma or actions both physical and mental is the sum total of all actions done by a person during his life time. These actions determine his future existence or destiny. The individual (soul) due to ignorance identifies himself with the body and with ego, exercises his will, and feels that he is the doer and enjoyer.[6] There are some duties to be performed in accordance with Varṇa-Āśrama dharma. One has to discharge such acts diligently without any desire for fruit. Such acts can be called 'Svadharma' and will not attract any liability to the doer. If anybody attempts to perform actions ordained to be done by others, one has to be responsible for its consequences as a doer[7]. One should not give-up the duty to which one is born, even though it is faulty, as all actions are surrounded with evil, as fire is with smoke.[8]

2.1.2.1. NATURE OF KARMA.

The thoughts that are strong and repetitive become our will and desire and they finally become actions. So thoughts manifest our actions. The nature of action is inscrutable. One has to have clear understanding about the action to be done and about the prohibited action. The results of the actions of an individual have to be experienced by him only and cannot be transferred to others.Desire (Kāma) is the cause of action (Karma). Karma (in the form of Saṁskāra) taking form in this world becomes the cause of our birth in this world. Man is a bundle of desires and as one desire is satisfied, another desire crops up and so on. So one should develop contentment and avoid to be entangled in chain of actions.

2.1.2.2. TYPES OF KARMA (ACTIONS).

Karma can be classified into following:

(i) Nitya-karma: Obligatory acts to be performed, egdaily prayers and should not be omitted.

(ii) Naimittika-Karma: Special occasional acts contingent on some occasion such as Bārasāla (on the birth of child) etc.

(iii) Kāmya-karma: Acts performed with the sole aim of fulfillment of certain desires.

(iv) Niṣiddha-karma: The acts prohibited by the scriptures and other religious authorities, besides those which are morally and socially forbidden, like hurting or killing others, to speak lies and falsehood, adultery, stealing etc.

(v) Prāyaścitta- Karma: Karma to atone for some action done inadvertently, and to get rid of the sins.

(vi) Lokasaṅgraha- Karma: There are some acts done with intent of doing good for general public like building choultries at pilgrim centers, providing shelters of homeless, running of orphanages etc. These actions have to be with no desire for fame and social recognition, as that again will become a cause of egoism.

The main features of karma are briefly mentioned below

I). One has to perform action and cannot sit idle and has- to earn his food, clothing and family maintenance and should not became a parasite. All are under compulsion to work by qualities born of nature[9].

ii) One should perform actions and duty that are assigned to him by social as well as religious prescriptions with all diligence, concentration of mind and try to achieve perfection in work which not only gives mental satisfaction and sense of fulfilling his functions, which is a joy.

(iii) The results are bound to come for every action, but expecting results and if not to his expectations (even for reasons beyond his control) results in dissatisfaction and leads to frustrations. If he welcomes and accepts whatever comes (as a gift from God) with contentment it will not upset him. This is an attitude to be developed.

(iv) A person has to develop equanimity (avoid over excitement for success as if it is his own effort, and blaming others or cursing fate if the result is otherwise).

(v) So an aspirant has to perform action with complete non-attachment. Any work done with a desire for enjoyment of fruits here and hereafter will only add to the fetters of life and future bondage.

One has to perform the obligatory duties for which one is competent without attachment, and then the person attains the highest good.[10]

One who keeps his organs of action; speech etc under control, and does work without hankering for results, that one attains the good. [11]

One is advised to perform all works as meant for God without being attached and any action other than this may be cause for bondage. [12]

The action done other than actions done without any sense of doer ship, as a consecration to God, will fructify. The results may be visible (Dṛṣṭa) in this life or mature after a long time in other world or life (Adṛṣṭa) . The fruits of karma accrued are as follows.

(a) Sañcita Karma. (b) Āgāmī Karma. (c) Prārabdha Karma.

(a) The sañcita- karma is result of accumulated past deeds (good as well as bad) for which the results have not started to fructify and may be carried forward to future life. Those have to be experienced or these can be destroyed by Brahma Jñāna.

(b) Prārabdha-Karma: The karma which is to be experienced through the present life. The Prārabdha karma is considered as the cause for the present birth. It is of the nature, that cannot be avoided or changed and has to be exhausted only by actual experience.

c) Āgāmī or Kṛyamāṇa-Karma: The current works performed during the present life that may bring fruit in future.

A man of wisdom can choose the actions to be performed wisely and avoid those that are likely to give negative results. The nature of the karta, his actions will be according to the inherent guṇas (qualities) possessed by the individual.

	Sattva	Rajas	Tamas
Karma	-obligatory actions performed without -attachment or desire for fruit of action -No likes and destitute[13]	-Egoistic actions with desire -for fruits of action[14]	-under delusion -Action done without consideration of consequences.[15]
Karta	-Not egoistic -Free from attachment[16]	-covetous -Desirous of results of action -cruelty nature unclean and subject to joy/ sorrow[18]	Naive deceitful wicked lazy Procrastination[20]
Jñāna	Single, undecaying,Undivided[17].	Different entities, distinctive values[19]	Irrational, not concerned with truth and trivial[21]

All those qualities do inherently exist in every person in different proportions. One is known by the predominance of a particular quality. The aspirant has to strive to reduce gradually, the Tamas and Rajas, and ultimately aim toincrease the proportion of Sattva guṇa,(others may be reduced to insignificant level) and finally aim to achieve Pure Sattva Guṇa.

Those who perform actions with great pains out of greed for petty results will be deprived of the supreme bliss. The yoga of action is imbued with the idea of equanimity, destroying evil actions: therefore it is greatly skillful. If the work associated with the idea of equanimity is performed, one becomes endowed with wisdom through purification of mind and becomes capable of averting evil actions.

Śrī Kṛṣṇa in Bhagavad-Gītā mentioned that "A person has only right to perform action, and never for the results". He advised that "one should not become the agent of the results of action"[22]. One should not hanker for the fruit of action.

One should be equipoise in success and failure. Thus one should perform action skillfully without desires which is called Niṣkāma Karma, by which the mind of the aspirant becomes pure and he can aspire to pursue wisdom[23].

In a nutshell, the message of karma yoga is for us to perform all our karmas without attachment, with a Sāttvika attitude as an offering to the Lord called (Īśvarārpaṇa buddhi) and to receive the results with gratitude (Iśvaraprasāda buddhi),whether they are favorable to us or not. One has to use the experiences to strengthen one's spiritual qualifications, which include purity of mind, one-pointed focus on the final goal and discrimination between the eternal and the ephemeral. The message of Bhagavad-Gītā is, do actions prescribed and others with no desire for results and with a sense of doing for God and be free from bondage. It strongly advocated karma for renunciation and not refraining from work.

2.1.2. PATH OF DEVOTION:

The Word Bhakti is derived from the Sanskrit root 'bhaj' which means to serve.. It has a range of derived meanings like devotion, trust, worship, faith, love religious devotion.[24]

The Bhakti mārga (path) or Bhakti yoga is practiced as a means of spiritual practice in Hindu religion for God realization. The Devotion to the God is practiced in several religions in the world.

Yoga means union with what is valued. The tendency to draw another to oneself is a power of human behavior and this gradually takes a man to Bhakti, to its highest level. We find that love; fondness, attachment and affection are found to be inherent in all living beings including birds, animals and human beings and may arise out of mutual need. The essential requirement for sustained love is faith.

There may be compassion etc, love for those who are less fortunate than oneself (called karuṇa), love between one's equals (friendship) and affection together with reverence to one's superiors.

Although love is seen as a common thread in the above cases, that which involves veneration surrender and self-abnegation and such other traits elevate Bhakti to the higher grade of love: Mātṛubhakti, Pītṛubhakti, and Guru Bhakti. When Bhakti is centered in God it becomes adoring service with a sense of gratitude and blessedness.[25]

All love derived between persons is due to some sort of relationship or association developed but there is also some sort of motive, that gives favorable results of happiness or satisfaction. Love can be for objects like money, cute pets or other things. All these are not everlasting but fade over a course of time and the love is essentially self centered.

Men out of ignorance initially resort to devotion to God for fulfillment of their desires and favourable conditions in this world. They express gratitude to the God if their wishes are fulfilled. This is called lower Bhakti or devotion, but it is very rare that one seeks God for His own sake and shelves aside all other desires.

No Matter how one has spent his life, but at one point he realises that his goal is to seek God, and henceforth lives his life fixed on this goal.

Although there is upāsanā in the Vedas which is same as Bhakti, the word Bhakti is reported to have not been used. The word Bhakti was first mentioned in Śvetāśvatara Upaniṣad. It says that 'one must have great love (Parā Bhakti) for God, for yourself, for your teacher'. This implies that one should also have keenness and determination. Śaṅkarācārya mentioned that in addition one must also be steady or have great faith in them. When one is having love and faith, one will then feel that salvation lies in self knowledge. [26]

Bhakti according to Gītā is the love for God and that love is reinforced by a true knowledge of the glory of God. It is superior to love for all worldly things. This love is constant and centered in God and God alone and unwavering in all circumstances. The supreme ideal Bhakti is a reciprocal love between the Lord and the devotee.

Bhakti presupposes a distinction between the worshipper and the worshipped (God).The doctrine of Bhakti in Hindu system has ultimately grown into a philosophy and religion.

There is a vast devotional literature in India and there are also different sects and deities, principally Śiva, Viṣṇu, and Śaktī. In another dimension, there are different philosophical systems, e.g.; Advaita, Vaiṣṇava, Bengal Vaiṣṇava Śuddha Advaita, Kashmir Śaivism. etc.

Bhagavad-Gītā, Bhāgavatapurāṇa and Viṣṇupurāṇa are prominent texts containing Bhakti to Kṛṣṇa. The Bhakti Sūtras of Śaṇḍilya and Nārada are other principle treatise on Bhakti which are ancient and popular. Nārada Pañcarātra is another work authored by Nārada. In the above cited literature mostly Bhakti to Śrī Kṛṣṇa as the supreme God and his charming childhood deeds and adventurous deeds are propagated.

The name Kṛṣṇa is derived from the Sanskrit root 'kṛṣ', means "to draw or pull in, to draw to one self" Kṛṣṇa, the narrator of Gītā-Śāstra is not just an embodied teacher. He is also the indweller of all beings, calling us all to our self, like a flower whose form and color attracts wandering bees. Kṛṣṇa is the voice of beauty and truth within us drawing us inward to drink from our own beings.[27]

2.1.2.1. ELIGIBILITY FOR BHAKTI

The doctrine of Bhakti is universal and everyone is eligible without any discrimination of caste, gender, culture, birth, wealth or learning. All are eligible for devotion because all are equal before God. The mere desire to achieve spiritual realization with faith is the only requirement.

Bhagavad-Gītā, Bhāvatapurāṇa have categorically stated this. Men born of sin and low birth, even birds, animals also prayed to God and got salvation. God treats all equally and does not show any partiality.

2.1.2.2. DEVOTION NOT FOR NONBELIVERS

The Bhakti is not for the Abhaktas. It is also not for those who hate God and who do not have belief or faith in the divine.

2.1.2.3. QUALITIES OF DEVOTEES

The following are the good characteristics of devotees, commonly prescribed in the purāṇas and Bhagavad-Gītā.

(i) One should be compassionate to all beings (ii) He should be free from ego and pride and the sense of 'I' and 'Mine' (iii) He should be truthful(iv) He should be steady and un-wavering in mind.(v) He should be friendly and bear no ill will against anybody and even to those even hurt him (vi) He should be free from desire and contended with what he has (vii) The devotees should be pure in mind, intellect and body (viii)) The devotee should exhibit equanimity in all circumstances, joy and sorrow, praise or censure, heat or cold, success or failure (ix) He treats a friend and foe equally (x) Respect for other's point of view and avoiding arguments (xi) Strong and unflinching faith in the truth of scriptures and his guru's teachings.

2.1.2.4. AVOIDANCE OF HINDRANCES FOR DEVOTION:

Humans have certain qualities that are potential hindrances for Bhakti and these have to be subdued before any progress can be achieved in the path of Bhakti. They are called internal enemies, namely Kāma (sensual desires), Krodha (Anger), Lobha (greed), Moha (Lust), Mada (Ego) and Mātsarya (Envy).

If these internal enemies are won over, everything can be achieved. These can be subdued only by the individual and no outside help is of any avail. These belong to body, mind and word, like eating too much, craving for taste, egoistic speech, loose talk, thinking of evil etc. and indulging in sensual pleasures.

The association with evil persons, who indulge in talk of women, lust and wealth and envious of other's achievements or gains and atheists are to be strictly avoided.

2.1.2.5. THINGS CONDUCIVE FOR DEVOTION:

(i) Cultivation of association with pious devotees. (ii) Reading of spiritual books and stories of legendry devotees. (iii) Visiting holy places, temples or devotional congregations.

2.1.2.6. TYPES OF DEVOTION:

A) Bhakti has been classified in many ways and some are even overlapping.

i) Sakāma- Bhakti and Niṣkāma- Bhakti (Based on motives and motiveless).

ii) Apara Bhakti (secondary type also called Gauṇī Bhakti) and Parā Bhakti (Higher devotion)

iii) Brahman has two aspects (i) with attributes called Saguṇa swarūpa and (ii) without attributes Nirguṇa Swarūpa.

B) Based on the qualities of devotees like Sattva, Rajas and Tamas which are inherent in all beings in various proportions and dominant cause in mentioned.

i) Sāttvika: Those who are free from attachment and who are not egoistic.

ii) Rājasika: Desire for enjoyment of prosperity and power, a fame.

iii) Tāmasika: which is deluded, unsteady and having wavering thoughts.

C) Based on desires: These can also be co-related with qualities. The devotees who have no motive of devotion can be classified as Sāttvika.

(i) Seekers of wealth, power or property or progeny. They have predominance of Rajas quality.

ii) Men in distress and afflicted by diseases, danger from enmity or protection from miseries. They are people of predominance in Tamas quality.

iii) Seekers of knowledge or wisdom (Predominance of Sattva quality)

iv) Men who have no desires what so ever and have deep love for God (Pure Sāttvika).

2.1.2.7. PRACTICE OF DEVOTION:

The devotional practice is a gradual process.

One has to develop association with great persons and serve them and obtain their grace. Hear the chanting of the names of the Lord and stories of His glory and develop taste for devotion. Once the taste is obtained, chant the holy names and share the sweet stories with others. One can adopt the nine forms of devotion told by Prahlāda in Bhāgavatapurāṇa.

i) Śravaṇa – Hearing the names and glories of the Lord. (ii) *Kīrtana* – Chanting His glories. (iii*) Śmaraṇam* – Remembering the Lord. (iv) *Pāda-sevanam* – Serving the Lord's feet.*(v)Arcana* – Worshiping the Lord. vi*)Vandanā* – Offering obeisance unto the Lord. (vii*) Dāsyam* – Serving the Lord as His servant. *(viii) Sakhyam* – Developing friendship with the Lord. (ix) *Ātma Nivedanam* – Total surrender of oneself to the Lord.

A devotee can practice all or any of these nine forms of Bhakti, whichever best suits his nature. Devotional path is considered as an easy path and there are no prerequisites and qualifications. The devotional path is suitable for all householders and it is described as easier than other means. However, if we see the qualities required for restraining sensual desires and winning over the over the internal enemies and developing the attitude of renunciation and purification of internal organ, it is practically most difficult to achieve. It was pointed by Rūpa Goswāmin that it is difficult, like walking to the high cliff through a narrow mountain path and any mistake on the path is fraught the great risk.

2.1.3. PATH OF KNOWLEDGE OR JÑĀNA YOGA:

The salient features of Jñāna yoga are as follows.

Jñāna yoga also known as Jñāna mārga, is one of the spiritual paths for realisation of the supreme reality and Yoga is used in the derivative sense of that knowledge, through which one gets united with the Para Brahman. It also means self realisation, as Brahman is the indweller of the souls.

Jñāna in Sanskrit language means knowledge.. In Advaita Vedānta it connotes both the primary and secondary meanings that is self awareness in the absolute sense and relative spiritual understanding respectively.

The Bhagavad-Gītā states that "Steadfastness in knowledge concerning the self, contemplation on the purpose of the experience of Realty-This is spoken of as knowledge. Ignorance is that other than this"[28].

The three paths Karma, Jñāna and Bhakti are means of achieving the supreme goal of life. One can practice any one of them as per his ability, aptitude and personal preferences. However, the path of Jñāna involves philosophical reflection which requires study of scriptures and meditation and mostly suitable for intellectually oriented people.

The Upaniṣads have dealt with the Jñāna- yoga which aims at realisation of the oneness of the individual soul (Ātman) with the universal soul, Paramātman or Brahman. The Advaita Vedānta gives primary importance to Jñāna (knowledge of Brahman).

The method for attaining this objective is as follows.

The internal organ should be first purified through the steadfastness in Karma yoga and renunciation[29]. The action is far inferior to the yoga of wisdom[30]. The Karma Yoga also means dedicating the fruits of all actions to God with devotion. The purity of mind and concentration of mind and non attachment to worldly things is possible through devotion and the devotee develops the power of discrimination.

The following is the prerequisite for practice of this Jñāna yoga, called Sādhanā-catuṣṭaya[31].

a) Discrimination between the permanent, eternal and unchanging, from that which is temporary, transitory and changing.
b) Dispassion or *Vairāgya,* indifference to the enjoyment of fruits, here and hereafter.
c) Six perfections (ṣaṭ- sampat).
    i) Śama: self-control, control of internal organ, curbing the mind.
    ii) Dama: voluntary self restraint of sense organs.
    iii) Uparati: withdrawal of mind from sensory objects.
    iv) Titikṣā: Forbearance.

v) Śraddhā: Faith.

vi) Samādhāna : Concentration of mind.

d) Mumukṣutva: Intense yearning for Mokṣa from the state of ignorance.

Thereafter the aspirant has to approach a teacher, who has direct experience of Reality. From the teacher one has to hear the teaching of the Upaniṣadic verses and follow the three step process.

i) Śravaṇa: Hearing and understanding the meaning of the Vedic verses and clear doubts and get answers.

ii) Manana: To contemplate and deliberate on the Vedānta teachings

iii) Nididhyāsana: Profound meditation: unbroken flow of mental modifications in the form of Brahman without any idea of egoism.

One who practices the above with the guidance of a teacher is believed to attain correct knowledge, which will destroy the ignorance (Avidyā) and all psychological and perceptual errors related to Ātman and Brahman.

In Bhagavad-Gītā, Chapter 4 has been exclusively devoted to the exposition of the Jñāna- yoga. Jñāna is considered a sure means of discovery of one's Ātman and given utmost importance and mentioned at several places. The same is specifically mentioned in the following verses.

'That person having discarded pride, egoism, desire anger ... and serene is fit for becoming Brahman."[32]

'One, who has become Brahman becoming same towards all, attains the supreme devotion to Me.' [33]

'Through devotion he knows Me in reality as to what I am and who I am. Then having known Me in truth, he enters (into Me) immediately after that knowledge.'[34] The steadfastness in knowledge is considered as the highest fourth kind of devotion as mentioned earlier[35].

The well ascertained conclusion in the Gītā and all the Upaniṣads is that liberation follows from the knowledge alone.[36] Kṛṣṇa said that 'the man of knowledge is his very self in verse 7.18 and reiterated at several places in Gītā.

Kṛṣṇa has mentioned as his firm Judgment that, "who so ever studies this (sacred conversation between Himself and Arjuna) which is conducive to virtue, and that person shall adore the Lord through the sacrifice in the form of knowledge.[37]"

The Path of knowledge involves an inherent nature of renunciation and high intellectual capability and steadfastness and is therefore suitable for very few people and it is a hard struggle for achievement of the supreme goal. Once the aspirant experiences the unity with Paramātman, he is liberated.

2.2. CONCEPT OF BHAKTI IN BHAGAVAD-GĪTĀ.

Bhagavad-Gītā is considered as the essence of the teachings of the mass of the Indian philosophical and religious thoughts in Upaniṣads. This is a part of the epic Mahābhārata, composed by sage VedaVyāsa. Gītā contains 18 chapters comprising of 700 verses. Bhagavad-Gītā was taught by Śrī Kṛṣṇa to Arjuna. The Epic Mahābhārata is also called the fifth Veda and is very popular and is meant for all, including the common man.

The teachings of Bhagavad-Gītā which is a collection of the quintessence of all the teachings of Vedas are not sectarian and addressed to all human beings irrespective of caste, creed, and gender, high or low birth. Gītā has been translated into many Indian languages and principal foreign languages world over.

The means to acquire knowledge which leads to realization of the ultimate Truth have been taught in Upaniṣads, and there is need for greater detail in simple language for better understanding to all. Gītā is not only the highest teaching of philosophy and religion but also a way of life. Gītā is a comprehensive text that can be used as a guide to lead a righteous path by people in all walks of life. Each of the eighteen chapters is called yoga. Yoga means Union with God and the path leading to it is also known as yoga.

Gītā considers that Pravṛtti mārga (a way of active performance of work) and Nivṛtti mārga (way of renunciation of work), both are needed for functioning of the society.

The dharma characterized by action and enjoined for different categories of men and at different stages of life, even though it is meant to contribute for prosperity and emancipation of the society respectively, when performed without hankering for selfish motives, with an attitude of dedication to God, leads to purification of internal organ and are considered as stages in the spiritual path of an individual[38].

Every one seeks happiness by way of security, pleasure and peace. However happiness is our true inner nature. The core objective of Gītā is to solve the problem of sorrow and delusion, which are caused by cycle of births and deaths, by means of spiritual wisdom[39].

A series of internal disciplines like Japa, Dhyāna, as means of realization are mentioned and the human beings are free to choose.

Gītā states that there are mainly two paths.

(i)Karma -Mārga (Action), (ii). Jñāna- Mārga (Wisdom) and all the other yogas are covered by these.

Bhakti is an integral part of these two. One should perform Karma with steadfastness combined with devotion, and Jñāna with steadfastness of devotion although it is not mentioned as a path. However Bhakti has been given prominence and elaborated in the middle six chapters of Gītā.

It is seen that in the Gītā, the supreme person (taking a human form) has spoken directly to a human being, as a friend and charioteer. The Lord manifested in order to protect the pious and punish the evil and reestablish righteousness in the world[40]. Arjuna is an average man filled with delusion and also egoistic of being born in a royal family and his achievement in archery. His spirits are dampened and he faces a great dilemma and becomes desperate for solutions of the problems faced by him.

Śrī Kṛṣṇa has from the beginning taught that every action has to be performed with a sense of dedication of results to the Lord and with devotion. One has to perform the assigned duties without selfish motives, and dedicate all fruits to God with devotion, and then he will not bind himself and actions will be for his good. It is also called Niṣkāma Karma which involves consecration of all fruits of action to God. He extols karma yoga and says that a man who does not hate and does not crave, should be known as a man of constant renunciation, and one who is free from duality becomes easily free from bondage[41].

Bhagavad-Gītā is one of the earliest scriptures to describe the various aspects of Bhakti. Arjuna had a doubt about how Kṛṣṇa was preaching although he was his contemporary. Kṛṣṇa has indicated at several instances that he is the Lord himself. Kṛṣṇa clarified that foolish people disregard, that He has taken a human form[42]. He continued to state that He is all pervading, and indweller of every living creature. Ultimately, He granted a vision of His cosmic form to Arjuna[43]. For viewing the cosmic form, Kṛṣṇa granted Arjuna supernatural eyes to see. It was mentioned that the cosmic vision is possible only for people with sincere and one pointed devotion to the Lord and others can only have intellectual vision and the devotees have seen in the reality[44].

2.2.1. NIRGUṆA AND SAGUṆA ASPECTS OF BRAHMAN.

There are two aspects of Brahman; one is formless and without attributes called 'Nirguṇa' and the second is a manifestation with form and attributes called 'Saguṇa'. There is stress on worship of the formless (nirguṇa) in several places beginning from chapter two to chapter ten of Gītā.

However at the end of the chapter wherein the cosmic vision is described, Śrī Kṛṣṇa declared God realization is a reward for exclusive single minded devotion to the Saguṇa swarūpa.

Chapter twelve is named as Bhakti yoga which deals exclusively with devotion (Bhakti) and clarifies the relative aspect of devotion to the attributeless and immutable, and also to the manifest form with form and attributes. It was clarified that Saguṇa form is for catering to the devotional and the Nirguṇa is for the intellectual propensity of the seekers. However he eulogized those who choose the Jñāna Mārga[45].

Śrī Kṛṣṇa has elaborated the most pragmatic approach for God realization. He has narrated various alternatives to cater to the needs of diverse kinds of aspirants according to their ability and attitudes[46]. He has given the desirable qualities for a devotee of God. He concluded that devotees who acquire and adopt such qualities are dear to Him.

Nirguṇa or Attributeless Godhead is described as follows.

The object of worship or God is incomprehensible, formless, actionless, and featureless and without any attributes and is an absolute. There is no form. It is eternally silent and immutable. These are the aspects of impersonal God described and emphasized on which one ought to meditate upon.

The features of Saguṇa or personal Godhead are as follows.

He is the Lord of the Universe, Supreme person, (Creator, preserver and destroyer). He is omniscient, omnipresent having a universal form and has great powers of yoga. He is the Master; He is immanent in all things and is the inner controller of living beings.

The Characteristic features of the un-manifest are given in Bhagavad-Gītā[47] are (i) *Anirdeśyam*: The indefinable–being unmanifest, beyond range of words; (ii) *Avyaktam*, It is not comprehensible through any means of knowledge. (iii) *Sarvatragam*: All pervading, perceived like space.(iv) *Acintyam*: Incomprehensible. It is not an object of the mind. (v) *Kūṭastham*: changeless. It is seated in Māyā. (vi) *Acalam*: Immovable.(vii) Dhruvam: it is constant and eternal Thus discussing various Upaniṣadic utterances, it was concluded that the worshipper attains Him alone, the imperishable Brahman. The statement that the man of knowledge is the very self of mine, is the firm conclusion.

The devotees who meditate on the un-manifest, who have the following qualities will attain Brahman.[48]

(i) They have to restrain all senses. They have to withdraw their senses.(ii) Even minded: They have to be equipoised in both favorable and unfavorable situations at all times (iii) They have to be kind and engaged in welfare of all beings. (iv)The devotee is not hateful towards any creature; he is friendly and compassionate and does not have any idea of 'Mine" and is ever content and has self control. The Lord mentioned that a man of knowledge is His very self.[49]

However, He concludes that reaching the unmanifest God is extremely difficult for embodied ones and also that those who seek the unmanifest, and those who seek the manifest, both reach the same goal. When the end result is the same the path that is easy and reaches the Goal earlier is superior to the other[50].

It is easy for the aspirant to seek the Lord in manifested form, they have a tangible idol or image to which they can direct their love, energies and knowledge. The choice whether to adopt the pravṛtti dharma (the path of works) or Nivṛtti dharma (the path of renunciation) is left to the aspirant as per his temperament.

The struggle for the aspirant worshipping the manifest Brahman is also great; similarly for those who meditate on the unmanifest, the trouble the is greater for the reason that they need to give up their self identification with the body. [51]Those who dedicate all the actions to the Lord, who accept the Lord as their supreme God and meditate with one pointed concentration, they will be taken by the Lord across the sea of the world and deliver them from the sea of transmigration.[52]The upāsanā should be with an intention of becoming one with the Lord.

Those who have accepted Vairāgya or renunciation, who are not very much attached to the world, the Path of devotion is most suitable. [53]

After explaining the above details, the devotee has been advised to fix his mind on the Lord, (giving up all thoughts of sense objects) and placing his intellect on the Lord (with discrimination), he will dwell in Him alone.[54]

If these are followed, the individuality ends and one can merge with the infinite. One should obtain the condition of one-pointedness by constant practice, which can be achieved gradually.

Arjuna was given several other options. If one cannot practice rigorously, one can do all actions for the Lord.[55]

The Lord has given one more option, if the above method of performing action for the sake of the Lord is not possible, then one can surrender the fruits of all actions by taking refuge in Him. [56]

The gradation of these in order of importance is as follows:

i) Practice of meditation on the Lord in external images.(ii) Practice of religious activities related to Viṣṇu or Kṛṣṇa. (iii) Dedication of fruits of action[57].

2.2.3. CHATACERISTICS OF A DEVOTEE.

After describing the methods of worship both on the manifest and unmanifest, the characteristics of the God realized/ devotee are given[58] : Some of the twenty four qualities are enumerated below.

(i) Not hateful to any creature. (ii) Friendly and compassionate to all. (iii) Free from ego and attachment to worldly desires. (iv) Even-minded to pleasure and pain (Pairs of opposites). (v) Forgiveness. (vi) Always having contentment.(vii) Steadfastness in meditation, with full devotion to the Lord. (viii) Self-controlled. (ix) Mind and intellect centered on the Lord, Firm conviction. (x) Who has serenity and also cannot be agitated by external unpleasant conditions. He is freed from all that create inner agitations like joy, anger, envy, fear. (xi) He is pure internally and externally. (xii) Observance of silence or only few words, both mentally and physically.

The devotees with the above qualities are dear to the Lord. These qualities indicate the dharmic (righteous) way of life. One should realize the self and live in that wisdom at all levels (physical, mental and intellectual). The yogi who adores the Lord, with his mind fixed on Him, with faith, is considered as the best of the yogīs". [59]

Śrī Kṛṣṇa is satisfied and accepts anything given with love by a devotee, who is pure. It may be a leaf, a flower, a fruit or water (whatever is available within his means) offered with love.[60]He does not value the gift, but values the affection with which it is presented.

Śrī Kṛṣṇa advises that whatever one does, eat and whatever sacrifice or any kind of austerities undertaken, may be offered to the lord[61]. This is the yoga of renunciation. Thus one gets free from bondage and attains the Lord. The result of such dedication makes one free from bondage and he reaches God.[62]

The Lord treats all beings as equal. However those who worship Him with devotion, they surely exist in Him and He is in them.[63]

2.2.4.1 TYPES OF BHAKTAS (BASED ON MOTIVES).

Śrī Kṛṣṇa has stated that there are four classes of people of virtuous deed who adore the Lord out of which three have desires and one is without desire. [64]

(i) Ārtaḥ: One who is afflicted with disease, danger from enemies etc.

(ii) Arthārthī: one who seeks wealth.

(iii) Jijñāsu: One who is a seeker of knowledge.

(iv) Jñānī: The man of knowledge who knows the identity of self with Viṣṇu and who seeks no other God for realisation..

2.2.4. 2.TYPES OF BHAKTAS. (Based on Guṇas).

The Bhaktas are also classified according to inherent nature of soul, Guṇas (qualities) and their attitudes.

(i) Sāttvika: not egoistic, free from attachment.

(ii) Rājasika: desirous of result of fame.

(iii) Tāmasika: unsteady, deluded action, wicked etc

All these are on account of the divine Māyā; it is difficult to cross over except for those who take refuge in God[65].

Even those who are born of sin, animals or birds, who are women, Vaiśyas, Sūdras will reach the highest God by taking shelter under Him.[66]

Even if a person is of very bad conduct but who worships the Lord with one-pointed devotion, he is considered to be good because he resolves to worship the Lord.[67]That person surely gives up his bad conduct and takes to god conduct. For the devotees of Vāsudeva there is never any misfortune[68].

2.2.5. MODES OF WORSHIP

The aspirant has to fix his mind on the Lord, devoted with mind, body and speech, take refuge in Him, bow down to the Lord, accepting Him as the Supreme Goal.

The Supreme Lord assures that He will grant wisdom (through which the aspirant can reach Him) to those who are ever devoted to Him.

He resides in their hearts out of compassion and destroys their ignorance and darkness by bestowing knowledge (like a luminous lamp). [69]

The Lord concludes "One who seeks the unconditioned Brahman as a result of perfection in meditation on the conditioned Brahman, who is distinguished by virtues such as 'Lack of hatred', of equanimity etc; who is a preeminently eligible person, who pursues Śravaṇa, manana, Nididhyāsana, it is possible for him to directly experience the reality which forms the content of the great Upaniṣadic sentence "*Tattvamasi*", 'That thou Art' which logically leads to liberation (one should seek the meaning of this mahavākya. [70]

Chapter twelve on Bhakti in Bhagavad-Gītā has clarified many doubts about, the superior way of Bhakti' and that one may adopt according to his choice either Saguṇa or Nirguṇa and both give the same result of cessation of cycle of births and deaths. The qualities of devotees enumerated are the ways to live in complete practice of virtuous life (according to dharma) in perfect harmony in the world.

The various other means like meditation, spiritual practice, and renunciation of desires will help attain Supreme peace.

Thus, although Gītā mentioned only two paths Karma and Jñāna, but Bhakti is intertwined with both and the middle six chapters have given significance to devotion. The devotion practiced to reach one-pointedness and without wavering and considering Vāsudeva as the only source of refuge will attain the highest good called ananyā Bhakti and is also called Parā Bhakti[71].

The Bhagavad-Gītā thus elaborated that Bhakti is an integral path of Karma and Jñāna Mārga. Karma-yoga is Niṣkāma Karma and dedication of all fruits of action to God with devotion. By dispassion and detachment to worldly things, purifying and developing concentration of the mind, through one-pointed devotion, one should obtain knowledge of the glory and greatness of God. Thus one can get rid of the miseries of the cycle of births and deaths by going to Brahmaloka. By grace of the Lord, one can get the knowledge of the identity of the self with Para Brahman in due course. It is also possible that after realization of the manifest form of the Lord through one-pointed devotion, one can continue through the practice of Śravaṇa, Manana and Nididhyāsana and get the intellectual realization of the of Upaniṣadic verse '*Tattvamasi*' that is identity of the Jīvātman and Paramātman.

The status of devotion in Bhagavad-Gītā has been summarized as follows in the introduction to the commentary of Bhagavad-Gītā by Śaṅkarācārya, translated by A.G.Krishna Warrier as follows.

"Bhagavad-Gītā is a unified work that has arrived at an ultimate monism; that God is a personal-impersonal combining attributes of a monotheistic deity and those of the Upaniṣadic Absolute. Devotion to God of the Bhagavad-Gītā is logically capable of being synthesized with knowledge of Nirguṇa Brahman. Devotion is only a means, may be an indispensable means, to the winning of the saving knowledge. The two, devotion and knowledge, have been intimately blended as means and end in Bhagavad-Gītā."[72] The Jñāni Bhakta is considered as the very self of the Lord.

2.3. CONCEPT OF BHAKTI IN BHĀGAVATA PURĀṆA.

2.3.1. INTRODUCTION.

Śrīmad Bhāgavata-Mahāpurāṇa, also known as Bhāgavata, commands universal appeal to all sections of people. It was composed by sage Veda Vyāsa. The essence of Vedas and Upaniṣads, which are in a language and idiom not intelligible to ordinary human beings, is brought out in epics and purāṇas out of compassion for humanity.

Among the purāṇas authored by Sage Vedavyāsa, Śrimad Bhāgavata outshines the others being the crest jewel of the entire purāṇic literature.

Bhāgavata alone is described time and again, as one without a second and incomparable as an instrument for freeing humans from bonds of samsāra and help attain liberation (Mukti).

Bhāgavatapurāṇa emanated from the essence of Vedas and Upanishads, having separate existence from them but representing their very fruit essence and appears to the very best.[73]

The Purāṇa named 'Bhāgavata' which is on par with Vedas has been authored by sage Vyāsa for stabilizing Bhakti,

Jñāna and Vairāgya[74]. Jñāna -yajñā (sacrifice of knowledge) has been recognized as righteous actions leading to liberation. Jñāna-yajñā has been extolled by Śuka and others.[75]

Five significant words of Bhāgavatam are mentioned in the introduction to Critical study of Bhāgavata published By Tirumala Tirupati Devasthānam, (on web site).[76]

Bhā - for Bhakti (devotion)
Ga - for Jñāna (knowledge)
VA - for Vairāgya (dispassion)
Tha - for Tattva (the real nature of the Supreme)
M - for Mokṣa (liberation or Emancipation from worldly bonds)

The purāṇa consists of 12 Skandhas or cantos with 18000 verses and thus it is the biggest Purāṇa. It has exercised profound influence on the philosophy of life.

The following will show its popularity.

There are nearly 81 commentaries of Bhāgavata in Sanskrit alone. It has been translated into several Indian languages, the first being by Śrī Bammera Pothana in 15th century into Telugu. It has been translated into French, English and Persian languages. The Glorious Bhāgavata is surely considered to be the cream of the Upaniṣads. A man satiated (completely satisfied) with it's nectarine flavor will not find delight anywhere else[77].

Sage Nārada's counseling to Sage VedaVyāsa;

Sage Nārada once visited the hermitage of Sage VedaVyāsa and found him in a despondent mood. After making due enquiries about the cause of the dissatisfaction in spite of his glorious achievements (dividing Vedas, composing epic Mahābhārata to make divine knowledge available to all those who are ineligible to recite Vedas). Nārada thereupon advised that he has not yet sung the glories of Lord Kṛṣṇa and his Lilās.

Nārada revealed how he himself became a Bhakta (devotee) in his former life and his present life.[78]

Vyāsa, after keenly listening to Nārada's counseling was satisfied and purified his mind by the spiritual discipline of Bhakti-Yoga.

Sage Nārada taught Sage Vedavyāsa, the knowledge he got from his father Brahma (creator), who got it directly from the Supreme Lord.

The Supreme Lord Nārāyana having been pleased with the penance of Brahmā, revealed to him his Supreme abode. He then imparted the most esoteric knowledge in the form of four couplets (Catuśloki Bhāgavata-Purāṇa) (i) Brahma Tattva. (ii) Maya Tattva. (iii) Jagat Tattva. (iv) Jijñāsā Tattva and its realization. He also imparted the true knowledge about Him and His greatness, His essential character, also the number of forms He manifests, His virtues and doings. He is the self of all embodied souls; therefore a man should dedicate his love to Him alone, for the body and other things are dear only on His account. One should establish oneself fully in the doctrine of Mine (Brahman), thereby avoiding falling a prey to egotism.[79]

Sage VedaVyāsa felt that he has not until then adequately expounded the Bhāgavata dharma i.e. virtues that enable one to attain the Lord. It is these virtues that are practiced by God realized saints and they alone are dear to Lord Viṣṇu.

This resulted in the composition of "The Glorious Bhāgavata" as a faultless scripture, which stands celebrating as the one Supreme Reality, which is all consciousness, all truth and bliss, free from all impurity (in the form of contact with Māyā) and which is the goal of Paramahaṁsas (ascetics of highest order). In this Purāṇa withdrawal from all mundane activity, developing spiritual enlightenment, dispassion and devotion, has been expounded[80].

The purāṇa begins with and concludes with same words *"satyam param dhimahi"*[81].

The purāṇa is meant to be an exposition of the highest truth,[82] which is explained as Para Brahman, Paramātman and Bhagavān.[83] The way it proposed to elucidate the ultimate truth is clearly given.

The Supreme has been described as:

"He is pure, absolute consciousness uniformly abiding as the inner self of all. He is ever true and perfect; has no beginning or end, and is attributeless, eternal and one without a second".[84]

"The knower of truth declares knowledge alone as the reality, that knowledge which doesn't admit of duality". The Supreme is called by different names such as Brahman (the Absolute), Paramātman (the Supreme Spirit or universal soul) and Bhagavān (the God).[85]

Nārāyaṇa is the Supreme teacher of ascetics of the highest order and the Lord of those who revel in the self and the beloved of his devotees and ascetics of the highest order. Bhāgavata purāṇa could be rightly called the 'Paramahaṁsa- Saṁhita' (i.e.) the hand book of the Paramahaṁsas[86].The colophon at the end of each skandha in the Śrīmad Bhāgavata Mahāpurāṇa "The great and the Glorious Bhāgavata-Purāṇa, otherwise known as Paramahaṁsa -Saṁhita"[87].

In this connection it is pertinent to mention that Śrī Madhusūdana Sarasvatī has named his commentary of the first Śloka of Bhāgavatapurāṇa as "Paramahaṁsa Priya".

Bhāgavata is a practical guide for all. It preaches that God-realisation alone can give salvation for man and shows the way to God realisation. Bhāgavatapurāṇa teaches that God alone really exists and God is everywhere and in every situation of life. God-realization is be-all and end-all of life.[88]

Bhāgavatapurāṇa played a significant role in the Hindu Philosophy and is the most revered book for "Vaiṣṇava" sect of devotees, Caitanya's Kṛṣṇa Bhakti (in Bengal) and Vallabha School of 'Śuddhādvaita'. The Bhāgavata-Purāṇa is an important canon of their philosophy.

Both the Bhāgavatapurāṇa and Bhagavad-Gītā do not rule out knowledge as the means of salvation. Jñāni is described as Nirguṇa Bhakta and Jñāna- yoga itself is spoken of as the best means for the highest bliss.[89]

The Bhāgavata purāṇa also glorifies knowledge as follows:

"The knower of the truth declare that knowledge alone is Reality – "The knowledge which does not admit of duality, in other words, which is indivisible and one without a second and which is called by different names such as Brahman (the Absolute), Paramātman (The Supreme Soul) and Bhagavān (The deity)"[90].

2.3.2. MOKṢA IN BHĀGAVATA PURĀṆA.

"A study of the conception of Mukti or Mokṣa in Bhāgavata literature will reveal the importance laid on *Ekatva* or Sāyujya. Mokṣa means the cessation of all worldly existence and a sense of identification with the Supreme Being. It is also described as "the return of Brahman into His own true nature." It suggests the ultimate union of the emancipated soul with Brahman.[91]The Bhāgavatapurāṇa abounds with verses which proclaim the return of the Individual soul to the Absolute and the fusion into Absolute.

The Bhāgavatapurāṇa describes the release of soul as follows. "It is through nescience the astral and material bodies are superimposed on the self.When the superimposition is removed through knowledge, that very moment takes place the realisation of Brahman" and "The knowers of the truth are aware that when the Lord's sportful Māyā withdraws, the Jīva becomes one with Brahman and gets established in the Glory of the self."[92]

2.3.3. BHAKTI IN BHĀGAVATAPURĀṆA:

Bhakti has great importance in the Bhāgavatapurāṇa which was revealed by the Supreme Lord himself. The highest duty of a man is devotion to Kṛṣṇa, a devotion which is motiveless and uninterrupted as a result of which the soul realizes the all- blissful Lord and thus obtains his objective.[93]

2.3.3.1. BHAKTI IS A MEANS AND AN END IN ITSELF:

In Bhāgavatapurāṇa Bhakti has been treated in two different aspects as follows.

(i) It is an end in itself or identified with Bhagavān. Bhagavān is Himself an embodiment of Bhakti and Bhakti is God.

ii) Bhakti is a means to the attainment of supreme bliss that is Bhagavān. 'The devotees remembering Śrī Hari, the destroyer of their sins, their devotion turning into divine love filled with rapture experience a thrill of joy'[94].

It is proposed to be discussed briefly as follows:

2.3.3.2. Definition of Bhakti.

2.3.3.3. Nature of Bhakti.

2.3.3.4. Characteristic features of a Devotee (Bhakta).

2.3.3.5. Practice of Bhakti.

2.3.3.6. Types of Bhakti.

2.3.3.7. Bhakti can be with different emotions.

2.3.3.8. Teaching of Bhakti in Bhāgavata purāṇas.

2.3.3.2. Definition of Bhakti:

The motiveless devotion to the Lord may be defined as the natural inclination towards the Lord, who is an embodiment of Sattva (goodness),of the senses of a man of undivided mind, which are the only means of perceiving the objects, as well as his organs of action, which are engaged in the activities enjoined by the Vedas.[95]

The distinguishing character of unqualified Bhakti-yoga was mentioned by the Lord as "The uninterrupted flow of mind-stream towards the Lord, dwelling in the hearts of all, like the waters of the Gaṅgā towards the ocean-at the mere mention of My virtues, combined with motiveless and un remitting love to Me, the supreme person."[96]

2.3.3.3. NATURE OF BHAKTI.

Bhakti yoga is open to all irrespective of age, caste, gender, stage of life, education or any mark of distinction. Daityas, Yakṣas and monsters, women folk, Śūdras cowherds and those living by sin, even birds and beasts, all can attain immortality through devotion[97].

There are several examples of all kinds of individuals who attained salvation and the only common characteristic was constant meditation on Kṛṣṇa by any type of emotion. The following are the examples:

a) Prahlāda, Dhruva, and even Nārada were children when they became devotees and became as Mahā Bhāgavatas. (b) Nārada (believed to be son of a maid servant in earlier life), and Vidura, belonging to lower caste, similarly Vālmīkī the composer of epic Ramayana.(c) Draupadī, Kuntī and Gopīkas of Vraja are all women. (d) Śuka renounced the worldly life and took sannyāsa at an early stage of his life. (e) Prahlāda (the son of a demon King Hiraṇyakaśipu), Vibhīṣaṇa (a devotee of Rāma) is also demonic origin, MahaBali, a demon king also got liberation.(f) A person of previous record of vicious life like Ajāmila got salvation by just uttering Nārāyana,(his son's name) at the time of death.(g) Gajendra (the elephant king) who sought help in distress also got liberation[98].

2.3.3.3.1.BHAKTI IS THE HIGHEST GOAL OF LIFE. (PATAMA PURUṢĀRTHA)

Indian philosophy has a doctrine of Puruṣārthas, the goals of life of human existence namely Dharma, Artha, Kāma and Mokṣa. Artha and Kāma are considered of worldly nature. These are not denied but have to be achieved within the principles of Dharma. Thus having contended with the Artha and Kāma, man can strive for the superior goal of Mokṣa or liberation to obtain freedom from the cycle of births and deaths.

The means to achieve this Goal are different for different people according to their physical, mental and intellectual attitudes and the predominance of Guṇas (qualities) of Sattva, Rajas and Tamas. They are Karma, Bhakti and Jñāna or knowledge.

2.3.3.3.2. BHAKTI MĀRGA IS EASIEST AND BEST MEANS

Bhakti is advocated as easiest and safest means and is accessible for all without any discrimination and can be practiced at all times. The adoration of Śrī Hari's feet is the only means for him who seeks his own good in the shape of Dharma (virtuous life), Artha (worldly riches), Kāma (sensuous enjoyment) and final beatitude, Mokṣa[99].

The Bhāgavatapurāṇa declared that propitiating Lord Hari through unalloyed devotion is conducive to the pleasure of the Lord. Exclusive devotion to Govinda is the same as beholding Him in every creature and this alone has been declared to be the highest interest (or Goal) of men in this world[100].

Śrī Kṛṣṇa has advised Uddava as follows:

For those who dedicate themselves to His service, all their objects are accomplished as a matter of course through devotion (Absolving love for the Lord) alone.[101] Thus it can be concluded that devotion is not only the best means to fulfill the puruṣārthas but also Goal of all puruṣārthas of all human endeavor.[102]

It was mentioned "for striving souls there is no blissful road to God realization than devotion directed to the Lord, who is the soul of the universe. The attachment was considered as an unyielding fetter for the soul, it serves as an open door to liberation if it is directed towards the saints"[103].

2.3.3.4. CHARACTERISTICS OF A DEVOTEE.

The ideal devotee must have certain qualities to gain the grace of God. The following are the virtues enumerated in Bhāgavatapurāṇa.

(i) Who does not hate a single being and who regards all beings as himself.

(ii) Who is friendly and compassionate to all (even to those who cause him pain).

(iii) To whom pain and pleasure are equal, who is not attached for pleasure or hates suffering.

The Lord concludes, that those devotees who follow the immortal Dharma with devotion and faith looking upon "Kṛṣṇa" as the Supreme Goal are very dear to Him.[104]The same is mentioned in Bhagavad-Gīta also.

2.3.3.5. PRACTICE OF DEVOTION.

The devotion for attributeless Brahman, as well as the absence of attachment to the world of matter, both are easily developed through intense faith, through discharge of duties consecrated to the Lord. The desire for knowing higher truths, and by firmly abiding in the Yoga of knowledge, by worshipping the Lord, and ever listening to the stories of the Lord leads to practice of devotion. One should develop distaste for the company of those delighting in sensual enjoyments and eschew wealth and sense gratification. One should live a life of an ascetic.

One should get rid of the six internal enemies (i) Desire (Kāma), (ii) Anger (*Krodha*), (iii) Greed (*Lobha*), (iv) Passion (*Moha*), (v) Arrogance (*Mada*), and (vi) Ego (*Mātsarya*).

The Practice of following twelve forms of self-discipline is essential: (i) Non-violence. (ii) Truthfulness. (iii) Non-stealth. (iv)Absence of attachment. (v) Modesty. (vi) Non-accumulation of wealth. (Except for the interest of others). (vii) Faith in God. (viii) Habit of meditation. (ix) Firmness. (x) Forgiveness. (xi) Fearlessness. (xii) Continence[105].

The observance of religious vows is also prescribed.

(i) Internal and external purity. (ii) Muttering divine names. (iii) Austerity. (iv) Offering oblations into sacred fire. (v) Reverence. (vi) Worship of the Lord. (vii) Pilgrimage to holy places. (viii)Endeavour for the good of others.(ix) Contentment and Waiting on the preceptor. (x) Refraining from calumny and abandoning all activity for hoarding worldly goods. (xi)Enduring pairs of opposites (like cold and heat).(xii) Devotion to Śrī Hari and uttering His Praises.

2.3.3.6. TYPES OF BHAKTI.

The discipline of devotion (Bhakti) is manifold according to the ways of approach (attitude of mind) and the natural characteristic qualities of the devotee. The devotees are classified into four different types according to the way in which they worship.

(a) One who is devoted to the Lord with a mind full of violence, hypocrisy and jealousy is called Tāmasika Bhakta. (b) One who worships with a view of gaining objects of senses, fame and power is called a Rājasika Bhakta.(c) A devotee who adores the God with an intention of getting freed from bondage of action is called Sāttvika Bhakta.(d) One who has absolutely no motive in the mind, in devotion to God is called Nirguṇa Bhakta. His mind just enters the all-pervading deity "like that of waters of the Gaṅgā towards the Ocean". He is in constant meditation.[106] The Nirguṇa Bhakta is often described as Jñānī.

The Bhāgavatapurāṇa mentions that enquiry into Truth is the object of the body and soul together. The knower of Truth declares knowledge alone as Reality – that knowledge which does not admit duality (the distinction of subject and object). In other words, which is indivisible and one without a second and which is called by different names such as Brahman (The Absolute), Paramātma (The Supreme Spirit or eternal soul) and Bhagavān (The deity)[107].

The sages who are full of faith perceive that Truth as their own self in their own heart through devotion coupled with knowledge and dispassion, acquired through hearing of Śrīmad Bhāgavatapurāṇa etc[108]. Thus we find the keynote of the Bhāgavatapurāṇa, as an attempt to reconcile that all three yogas Karma, Bhakti and Jñāna, aiming at the realization of Supreme Truth. At the stage of perfection Jñāna and Bhakti are included in each other and are not exclusive.

2.3.3.6.1 CHARACTERISTICS OF NIRGUṆA BHAKTA.

Bhāgavata Purāṇa describes the Nirguṇa Bhakta who has absolutely no motive. [109]

The devotee does not seek, much less, solicit anything. The devotee bestows his love on the Lord alone, because He is dearest of all dear ones. He is the self of all embodied souls.The devotion should be steadfast, and knows no obstructions, *ahetukī* and *aprathihata*[110]. The mind should be firmly established with the Lord and the uninterrupted flow of the mind stream towards the Lord, like the waters of Ganges towards the ocean by mere mention of His virtues, combined with motiveless and unremitting Love to God is another distinguishing character of unqualified Bhakti Yoga[111].

The example of Prahlāda is appropriate to denote such a steadfast devotion, even in most trying circumstances (of even threat to life).[112]

The Nirguṇa Bhakti is exclusive and its only object of love is God. Thisis mentioned at several places in Bhāgavatapurāṇa with examples.

Śuka was a great yogī whose mind was exclusively set upon God.[113] Kuntī used to constantly and exclusively find delight in Kṛṣṇa, like Gaṅgā incessantly pours its water into the ocean[114]. Vidura after ascertaining the truth of the spirit from Maitreya felt his heart welled up with exclusive devotion to Govinda.[115]The Lord mentioned about the devotion of the saints, who practice uninflinching devotion and even forsake their obligatory duties and their relatives[116].

2.2.2.7. BHAKTI CAN BE WITH ALL TYPES OF EMOTIONS.

Narada mentioned that one should, fix one's mind on the Lord either through constant devotion (free from any enmity towards any creature) or with fear or enmity or affection or love. By doing so, he will not perceive anything other than the Lord. Anybody fixing his mind on the Lord through concupiscence, hatred, fear or attachment as through devotion, and getting rid of the sins standing as barrier for His realization may attain him. Nārada has narrated that Lord Kṛṣṇa being the universal spirit, and the one without the second, no violence can influence Him. So by any means whatsoever one should fix his mind on Kṛṣṇa[117]. It is interesting to note that Nārada has also said that a mortal may not attain such absorption into Him by fixing his mind on Him through devotion as through constant hostility.

The example of a caterpillar imprisoned by a wasp was mentioned. The caterpillar out of fear of being killed constantly thinks about the wasp with intense hatred and fear and metamorphoses as wasp. The people who hate and are afraid have by constant contemplation on the Lord get all their sins washed off and attain the Lord.

Nārada has clarified as above to the astonishment of Yudhiṣṭhira, how the sinful characters like Śiśupāla, Dantavaktra, King Vena getting absorbed into Śrī Kṛṣṇa, which could not be obtained by even those exclusively devoted to Him.

The following examples are cited for the different emotions:

(I) Compupiscence (strong sexual desire-Kāma).: Gopīs of Vraja .
(ii) Fear (Bhaya) : Kaṁsa
(iii) Hatred (Dvesa): Śiśupāla.
(iv) Kinship and affection (Sneha): Pāṇḍavas, Uddhava.
(v) Devotion (Bhakti): Nārada and other sages, Prahalāda

Śrī Ramaṇa Maharṣi said "Hate or love, it is all the same, the thought of Him will take you there". He has also said that, if you abuse good people, they may not retaliate; but they are hurt, and because of that the abuser will have to suffer.

If you want to curse at all, curse Bhagavān. He will not hurt you and you are safe in cursing Him. He wants only to be remembered, the mood in which you remember is of less importance."

2.3.2.8. TEACHINGS OF BHAKTI IN BHĀGVATAPURĀṆA.

In Bhāgavata the narration is by Sage Śuka to king Parīkṣita and there are several other devotees of Śrī Kṛṣṇa who are not only the devotees but have also taught doctrine of Bhakti like Prahlāda, Uddhava. Kapila (who is considered as another incarnation of the Lord) taught devotion and means for obtaining liberation to his mother Devahūti, who revealed that his objective of birth is to revive the knowledge for self realisation which has become obscure..

Kṛṣṇa, the main character, about whose glories the Bhāgavata Purāṇa was composed, has directly taught to his friend and follower Uddhava.

The teachings of Bhakti by the following are discussed in a concise manner:

i) Nārada. (ii) Śuka. (iii).Kapila. (iv). Prahlāda. (v) Śrī Kṛṣṇa.

2.3.2.8.1. TEACHINGS OF SAGE NĀRADA.

Nārada is a celestial sage and one of the spiritual sons of Brahmā (the Creator) and needs no introduction. The Bhāgavatapurāṇa is a consequence of his counseling and advice to Śrī Vyāsa to get rid of his despondency. The story of his birth and how he got devotion is a significant teaching for all to practice devotion.

Nārada is the first teacher of Prahlāda (even before his birth). Nārada protected the pregnant wife of Hiraṇyakaśipu from Indra when the latter captured her and wanted to kill the child at birth. Nārada identified that the embryonic baby is a Mahā Bhāgavata and warned Indra of incurring the wrath of the Lord. He gave hospitality to her at his hermitage. Nārada narrated the essence of Dharma and knowledge to her. It was the fortune of Prahlāda to have this knowledge of immediate apprehension of Truth as well as pure cult of devotion to the Lord.

Nārada is also the teacher to Dhruva, the young boy who was hurt mentally by the harsh remarks of his step mother and resolved to seek Nārāyana on the advice of his mother.

2.3.2.8.2. TEACHINGS OF SAGE ŚUKA.

Śuka, the son of Veda Vyāsa, has renounced at a very early age and does not want to indulge in worldly attachment and he was a fully realised soul. He was sixteen years when he met King Parīkṣit, who was awaiting his death due to the curse of a sage and sought Śuka to teach him how to find God.

Śuka proposed to recite Bhāgavata with an intent to convey that by listening, and reposing full faith in it will quickly conceive the disinterested Love for Śrī Kṛṣṇa (the bestower of Liberation)[118]. The chanting of Śrī Harī's name is concluded to be not only the means but also the end for those who seek liberation and also for the realized souls who have attained union with God[119]. He narrated the story of Ajāmila, who in spite of his past deeds has been liberated for uttering the name of Nārāyana, addressing his son (even though not intended to the Lord).

The greatest reward for human birth is to put one's mind on the almighty Śrī Harī even for one moment during the entire life. It may be through knowledge, devotion or through steadfastness to one's sacred duty[120].

One who wants to attain fearless state (mokṣa) should listen to, recite and dwell on the stories of almighty Śrī Hari (the sole of the Universe)[121]. Śuka advised Parīkṣit to shun fear of death, cut the ties of world with a sharp sword of renunciation[122].

Śuka taught the detailed procedure for meditation with concentration upon the Lord, to be absorbed within and get the calmness and transcendental bliss. One should, though living in the world, not be attached, not to seek gratification of senses and understand that these pleasures are not real and should resort to practice renunciation and observe austerities.

In his final teachings to King Parīkṣit, Sage Śuka advised him to distinguish himself from the body (which may perish) and identify himself with the Absolute (the self within) which is undying and unborn, to realize his true nature by identifying "I am Brahman, the Supreme self,"[123]

In his teachings Śuka gave due stress to the Importance of Bhakti but the overall narration has reflected his Advaitic belief.

2.3.2.8.3. TEACHINGS OF KAPILA.

Kapila is said to be another incarnation of the Lord which was foretold by his father Kardama[124]. On his birth the whole world has rejoiced and heavenly flowers rained from heaven and gods and demigods danced with joy. Kapila has informed his father, who wanted to take leave of him to lead the path of recluse as follows: "My present birth in this world is meant to expound the true nature of the categories which will be helpful to those seeking realisation. The path of self- knowledge will be revived which has been in obscure[125] and he promised to impart the spiritual knowledge to his mother."

The mind is responsible for both the bondage and emancipation of the soul. Attachment to objects of senses leads to bondage. Attachment to the Supreme brings liberation to the soul[126]. One needs a mind equipped with true knowledge, dispassion as well as devotion to obtain liberation. The blissful road to God realization is devotion to the Lord[127].

The following good virtues of yogis are mentioned:

They are compassionate and composed, friendly to all beings and inimical to none and follow the injunction of Śāstras. They have unflinching devotion to the Lord with an undivided heart; they forsake their kith and kin. They like to listen to and narrate delightful stories of the Lord.

He advised his mother Devahūti to seek association with such holy men and listen to the Lord's stories through which one will get true and full knowledge of the Glory of the Lord. This will surely develop reverence and fondness and devotion to the Lord. The ignorance will cease leading to realization.[128]

The renunciation of materialistic worldly objects of senses through wisdom supplemented with dispassion, through concentration of mind by yoga and through devotion to the Lord enables men to attain the Lord (who is also the self of all embodied souls) in their very life.

In order to fulfill his mother's desires Kapila has expounded the systems of Sāṅkhya and elaborated devotion and yoga (process of mind control).

Motiveless devotion to the Lord is superior to final beatitude itself. Some devotees of the Lord do not even crave for absorption into His being, but are delighted in service to His feet and in activities for His sake etc. Such devotees will secure themselves in His subtle abode even though they never seek it. For Such devotees, the Lord is not only their object of love, but the very self, son, friend and preceptor. They crave not for anything else including wealth, the place in Satya Loka, any of the eight kinds of supernatural powers that come to them. The Lord takes those who have such exclusive devotion to Him, once for all to the other side of death (ocean of birth and death).For lasting happiness, the yogis betake themselves through the practice of devotion accompanied by spiritual knowledge and dispassion. The intense practice of such devotion is the only means for final beatitude. [129]

The discipline of Bhakti yoga is recognized as manifold according to the attitudes of the men with regard to it. Men have different attitudes depending upon their natural characteristics of Tamas, Rajas and Sattva and again divided as adḥama, madḥyama and Uttama in each according to the intensity of attitudes. They are in the ascending order of commend ability. The attitude of difference between the deity and devotee remains[130].

The motiveless devotion of a Nirguṇa Bhakta has been mentioned as follows.

The devotees are willing to continue the service of the Lord, and do not accept any form of final beatitude even if offered to them.[131]

A man who dedicates all his actions and their consequences, even his very self to the Lord and sees no difference in himself and the Lord, who has no doership and regards all equally .He treats all living beings with great respect with the belief that almighty Lord has entered their body as the inner controller of the soul tenanting it, One should mentally bow down to them.[132]

Kapila has also mentioned the following to his mother:

"The discipline of Jñāna (spiritual knowledge) and discipline of devotion (which is free from the three guṇas) directed to the Lord, lead to the same goal, which is signified by the word 'Bhagavān'.[133]

Through two fold yoga (viz) (i) that which is accompanied by worldly activity and that which is characterized by renunciation, (ii) through the realization of the true nature of the self through dispassion do we attain the same self-effulgent Lord, who is both with attributes and without attributes[134].

2.3.2.8.4. TEACHINGS OF PRAHLĀDA.

The demon king Hiraṇyakaśipu, who is the enemy of Indra and Vāsudeva. has pleased Brahma with his penance and got boon that he could not be destroyed by any being. He became arrogant and declared Himself as God and that everybody should worship him.

He has one son called Prahlāda and he wished that his son follows his ideals. He sent him to school for proper education. Hiraṇyakaśipu once asked Prahlāda to tell something he learnt from the teachers at school.

Prahlāda answered as follows:

"(i) Listening the names and praised stories of Lord Viṣṇu(ii) To Chant them(iii) to remember Him (iv) to wait upon Him (v) to worship Him. (vi) To make Salutations to Him (vii) to dedicate one's actions to Him (viii) to cultivate friendship with Him.(ix) Completely dedicating everything including self to Him. Devotion marked by these nine features is considered as the highest lesson."This can be considered as Prahalāda's first teaching (to his father)[135]. The nine types of

Bhakti is very popular in Hindu religion and is considered as a Gauṇi or preliminary Bhakti by Nārada and Śāṇḍilya.

The king got angry that his son is praising his enemy (Viṣṇu). On enquiry from where he got this teaching, Prahlāda replied.

"The people whose mind indulges in worldly pleasure, not knowing them to be transitory, will fall in the whirlpool of transmigration. Those whose minds are impure continue to hanker on the enjoyment of sensuous pleasures and their minds do not therefore, be inclined towards Lord Viṣṇu and thus bound themselves"[136].

In spite of several severe, cruel and gruesome persecutions Prahlāda remained unscratched due to his mind in rapport with the indefinable Supreme[137].

One day in the absence of teachers, and being requested by fellow students, Prahlāda narrated the significance of human birth and how to utilize the short span of life to get rid of the whirlpool of births and deaths through devotion to Lord Viṣṇu[138].

The daitya's sons wholly accepted his teachings and got interested on the realization of a single purpose (devotion to the Lord)[139].

On getting this information from the teachers, Hiraṇyakaśipu could not tolerate this misdemeanor of Prahlāda, accused him of violation of his command and shivering in a fit of anger announced to put an end to Prahalāda's life. However Prahlāda humbly informed about Viṣṇu to his father as follows:

"He is unquestionably the strongest in the world and all creatures including Brahma (the creator) are under His sway. He is the Supreme Ruler, who creates, protects and dissolves the Universe with his potencies". Prahlāda urged his father to abandon his demonic disposition and keep his mind equipoise. "There is no achievement in conquering the entire external world, unless one curbs his six internal thieves (five sense perceptions and the mind). There can be no enemies in the eyes of pious soul and all embodied beings."[140]

Hiraṇyakaśipu declared that he himself is the Lord of the Universe. He challenged his son, "If He is present everywhere, why is he not seen in the pillar over there. I will severe your head and let Hari, who is the asylum you sought, protect you".

The king forcibly knocked the pillar with his fist and immediately a weird sound was heard by which all are afraid. The Lord assuming a queer form which was neither a beast nor a human, appeared in the pillar. It looked like a man-lion. Hiraṇyakaśipu tried to attack, but the demon king has fallen in the nimbus of Lord Nṛsiṁha, like a moth in the flame. All the Gods in heaven rejoiced.

Prahlāda is the only one who could approach the Lord and praise the Lord at length. The prayer is full of Bhakti and Jñāna integrated as a Lyric in praise of the Lord. The elaborate manner of the eulogy of the Lord by Prahlāda is itself a big treatise on devotion which is being concluded with the following verse.

"A man can develop devotion to you only through whole hearted service consisting of using the six limbs viz. (i) salutations. (ii) Glorification. (iii) worship in the form of one's actions to you.(iv)Waiting on you. (v) Concentrating one's mind on your lotus feet.(vi) Listening to your stories".[141]

The Lord was pleased with his devotee (Prahlāda) and offered to grant him any boon he wished for. The Lord revealed that it is difficult to perceive Him for those who do not propitiate Him. One who beholds Him have no reason for grief.

Prahlāda did not hanker after them, not even as being tempted with alluring boons and exclusively devoted as he was to the Lord[142].

The entire conversation between the father and his son is a teaching for all about the futility of worldly enjoyments. One who is arrogant and proud of his wealth and powers, and filled with hate are doomed to meet with disaster in this world itself. The significance of devotion to God for the ultimate realisation of bliss without being tempted by boons that are so alluring to the world is highlighted.

2.3.2.8.5. TEACHINGS OF ŚRĪ KṚṢṆA.

The teachings of Śrī Kṛṣṇa to Uddhava, his childhood friend and follower are an important part of Chapter eleven of Bhāgavatapurāṇa, which is mostly concerned with Bhakti. The teachings of Kṛṣṇa to Uddhava are spread over sections 7 to 29 of Chapter eleven. It is popularly known as "UDDHA-VA GĪTA".

Śrī Kṛṣṇa explained to Uddhava about several aspects like spirituality, religion, code of conduct for various classes of society and stages of life. The mind is the root cause of all miseries and one needs to control it. He also imparted various means of enlightenment and highlighted the supremacy of devotion.

This is considered the farewell message of Kṛṣṇa and indicating his impending departure from the earth to his celestial abode.

Śrī Kṛṣṇa described the qualities of pious souls. Compassionate to all and cause harm to none, forbearing, Faithfulness, faultless mind, self disciplined, soft by nature, pure, free from passions and to maintain equanimity. One must have conquered the six waves (cold, heat greed, infatuation, hunger and thirst). One has to be capable of imparting right knowledge to others, sincere and altruistic and possessed of the right knowledge[143]. Men of such exclusive devotion are considered by the Lord as foremost of all His devotees.

The devotion to the Lord consists of the following:

i) 'Touching and worshipping His images and people devoted to Him, rendering physical service and bowing down to them and repeatedly contemplating on the Lord.(ii) Celebrating festivities in temples with vocal, instrumental music, dance and worshipping with flowers on important festival days.(iii) Building temples and other infrastructure around the temple, growing garden etc. and keeping the temple tidy and clean etc.(v) Offering whatever is most favoured by the world as well as by the devotees to the Lord. Such offerings are capable of yielding immortality'[144].

On seeing Uddhava developing liking for devotion, Kṛṣṇa once again described the royal road to devotion, in addition to the already mentioned methods, adding the following.

i) Saluting the Lord with all eight limbs.(ii) Plucking of basil leaves and flowers for worship.(iii) Foregoing other pleasures and devoting time for His works etc. All these are stepping stones for devotion. The devotion in all-absolving love towards the Lord is the reward of all endeavors, after which nothing remains to be achieved. One should enjoy the Ātma Ratī (psychological orgasm)[145].

Śrī Kṛṣṇa declared that a devotee is dearer to Him than anybody else including His own consort[146]. Only exalted souls who are devoted to Him in their minds free from all passions and have no wants at all, will be able to know His blissful characteristic[147].

Intense devotion is better than any other means (like Japa, austerity, renunciation etc.) and only devotion can purge the mind of its impurities[148].

Listening to and recounting and singing the stories of His glories help jīva to develop discrimination of the reality. Devotee should avoid from a distance the company of women or men indulging in women. To avoid affliction, one should conquer the mind and go to a solitary place and unweariedly think of the Lord[149].

2.3.8.6 CONCLUSION

The concluding skandha can be considered as a synopsis of the whole text of Bhāgavata and it deals with the ceremonial way of studying it and the significant place of this purāṇa among all purāṇas.

The Bhāgavata portrays the essence of Vedas and the Upaniṣads, of the truth of non-duality characterized by the oneness of Brahman (the absolute) and the individual soul—and has detachment of the spirit from matter as its ultimate objective.[150]One that enjoys the nectarine flavor of this will never have delight for anything else[151].

This faultless Purāṇa occupies the same pride place among the purāṇas just as Gaṅgā is superior among the holy rivers, Viṣṇu among divinities and Lord Siva (the source of all blessings) among the devotees of Viṣṇu. This Purāṇa is unexcelled among purāṇas like Kāśī among the holy places[152].

Bhakti (love for Bhagavān) is claimed to be the main theme of Bhāgavata. However it is a judicious mixture of Jñāna (the knowledge of the Ātman) and Vairāgya (total renunciation and dispassion) with emphasis on Bhakti and through Bhakti the other two.Bhakti is easy to practice. It is universal and all are eligible without any discrimination on account of age, caste, gender, status in life or other factors. Parā Bhakti (motiveless Bhakti) is even superior to Muktī. Bhakti is both a means and an end.

By developing Bhakti or love towards the Lord and as it intensifies, the Love and attraction for other worldly things will drop off, resulting gradually in complete renunciation. As the renunciation gets intensified the devotion towards God simultaneously intensifies. Bhagavān will shine as Jñāna in the devotee. Sri Ramakrishna Paramahaṁsa once expressed about Bhāgavata that it is "Fried in the butter of Jñāna and soaked in the syrup of Bhakti"

The Bhakta (devotee) will become unconscious of everything else. The Bhakta (devotee) will be conscious of Bhagavān and nothing but Bhagavān. The idea of Bhakta that he is conscious of Bhagavān (consciousness) will drop off and Bhakta himself will become conscious of self. The fusion of Bhakti, Jñāna and Vairāgya thus leads to the ultimate self realization.

Śrimad Bhāgavata is the fruit essence of the wish yielding tree of Vedas dropped on earth from the mouth of the parrot-like Śuka and is full of the nectar of supreme bliss. It is an unmixed sweetness (devoid of rind, seed or pulp or superfluous matter). The devotees who have taste of divine joy can go on drinking this divine nectar again and again till there is consciousness left in him[153]

2.4. CONCEPT OF BHAKTI IN BHAKTI SŪTRAS.

2.4.1. INTRODUCTION.

The doctrine of Bhakti which has its origin in Vedas was gradually systematized into a regular philosophy and religion. It has come to be known as Bhāgavata religion. The main sources for this are Bhagavad-Gītā, Bhāgavatapurāṇa, Pañcarātra Āgamas and the Bhakti Sūtras of Śāṇḍilya and Nārada.

In the Upaniṣads the impersonal Nirguṇa Brahman is advocated, however one personal God, known with several names like Kṛṣṇa, Rāma, Īśvara, Vāsudeva, Nārāyana has been popularized. His grace is the supreme factor in realizing Him, which can be obtained by single minded unconditional devotion to Him. God also reciprocates the love for His devotees. He is known as *Bhaktavātsala* and *BhaktaParādhīna*.

The doctrine of Bhakti is dealt in the Bhakti Sūtras, in the ancient Sanskrit literature. The profounder of the doctrines or knowledge have composed in the form of Sūtras or aphoristic statements. They are brief statements containing deep meaning and are difficult to understand the implied meaning. Therefore some others who are well versed usually write Bhāṣya, ṭīkā or commentary which will help the readers to have better understanding of the purport of the Sūtras.

In order to have a comprehensive understanding of the doctrine of Bhakti, a study of the Sūtras of Śāṇḍilya and Nārada is considered very useful to have knowledge about Bhakti and also to sincerely practice. The two great sages although dealt the same doctrine, they have different mode of approach to the subject.

2.4.2. ŚĀṆḌILYA BHAKTI SŪTRAS.

The Śāṇḍilya Sutras is one of the oldest of the Bhakti Sūtra literature. There are two well known Bhāṣya on the Sūtras, One by Svapneśvara (A.D 900) and another by Nārāyana Tīrthas (A.D.1700) called Bhakti- chandrikā. The Bhāṣya of Svapneśvara is considered as a pioneering and important work. The English translation by Swami Harshānanda with a detailed introduction was published in 1969 by Mysore University, which was subsequently reprinted and published by Ramakrishna math, in 2002. There is also a translation by E.B.Cowell published by Asiatic society of Bengal, Calcutta in 1878.

Swami Harṣānanda in his introduction has observed that the approach of Śāṇḍilya is intellectual and has mentioned about Pramānas, Prameyas, reality of the world etc .He propounded that devotion is the only means of liberation and delineates the form of devotion. While dealing this Svapneśvara emphatically denies any place for knowledge as a means of liberation and at best can be subservient to devotion. Some have made observations that it can aptly be called Mīmāṁsā of Bhakti and it does not profess to teach the doctrine of devotion, and it is a compilation and exposition of illustrative authoritative texts on the main points of devotion. The philosophy of Sūtras is proposed to be discussed briefly the following headings. The Bhakti (devotion) and its means of practice will be discussed in detail.

2.4.2.1. THE FOLLOWING CONCEPTS ARE ACCEPTED IN THE SŪTRAS

(a) Īśvara or God. (b) Jīva or the individual soul. (c) Jagat or the created world.

(a) Īśvara or *Bhajanīya* are the words used to denote God. He is the Lord and ever free. He is of the nature of consciousness. He has Śaktī or power called Māyā through which, He creates the world. He and His powers are identical, and so the creation is also is identical. He does not undergo any change and it is only the Prakṛiti that undergoes modifications. God out of pity to the created beings incarnate in the world with a divine body out of his own free will through His powers. The devotion to Him or his incarnations will grant liberation to the soul. Any one mode of devotion out of several modes available, when practiced sincerely and intensely will please Him to grant liberation. The devotees that give up their bodies before reaching the supreme devotional stage, they are born again in this world and continue their devotion and will ultimately attain liberation. He specifically mentions that only devotion and not knowledge as the cause for liberation.

The Individual soul or Jīva is essentially identical with Brahman. The separation of the soul from God is caused by the Individual intellect or Buddhi which consists of three guṇas. This is called Upadhi (limiting adjunct) which is real and not an illusion caused by ignorance and hence cannot be removed by knowledge. Since the soul is eternal, the Upadhi has to be dissolved and then only the soul can realize its original state which can be done only by supreme devotion to God.

The God is one and the souls being identical to Him, however because of the multiplicity of the buddhi there are multiplicity of different Individuals. This is like the same Sun is reflected as separate in several different mirrors. If one soul is liberated others continue in the samsāra, just like the reflection of sun continue in other mirrors when one mirror is removed.

There are only two realities that exist. The soul and Brahman (in twofold form) and the other, is Prakṛiti created by the Māyāśakti of God. This being the power of God is also real. Hence the world and the whole of the creation is also real. This creation is possible only by God and not by any intellect of an ordinary being.The philosophy of the sūtra Kara upholds the sat-kārya-vāda or the doctrine of preexistence of the effect in the cause. The creation and dissolution takes place as in the Sāṅkhya School of philosophy.

It is proposed to briefly discuss the Mukti or liberation thereafter the Ṣādhanā will be discussed in detail.

2.4.2.2. MUKTI OR LIBERATION:

The soul due to its adjuncts of buddhi and body gets separated from its real identity of Brahman and it is the root cause of the bondage of cycle of births and sufferings. The limiting adjuncts are not illusion that can be removed by knowledge and can only be dissolved and liberation can be attained by supreme devotion to God. The soul if it is free from past karma which is the cause of this body, he gets immediate liberation. Otherwise he continues to live as a jīvanmukta (until exhaustion of Prārabdha karma) and is merged in God when the body falls.

The liberation can also take place in a gradual way as follows. The soul that has been purified by practice of means like lower forms of devotion and those who have not yet obtained supreme devotion will either reborn or take the path of light leading to the world of conditioned Brhaman. They continue the devotion till they get supreme devotional state and then obtain liberation. Thus Mukti is assured to all that are devoted, but only when they reach the supreme devotion either in this world or in the higher region (world of conditioned Brahma).

2.4.2.3. DEFINITION OF BHAKTI.

The devotion is defined as the highest love for God.The use of the word highest, indicating that excludes other lower forms of devotion. It also indicates that the devotion with mind, body and soul without any motive.

2.4.2.4. THE SĀDHANAS OR PRACTICES OF DEVOTION:

The practice of Bhakti is classified into two types (i) Supreme devotion or primary devotion. (ii) The secondary devotion or Gauṇī Bhakti.

2.4.2.5. NATURE OF DEVOTION:

(i) The higher devotion is absolute attachment to the Lord[154].The higher devotion indicates that is the supreme form of devotion (also there is a secondary or lower form of devotion).The general import of definition of devotion is that the object of devotion is the Lord worthy of being worshiped.

(ii) The unalloyed devotion to the Godhead makes one immortal[155].

(iii) Jñāna (knowledge) is inferior to devotion[156].

(iv) Bhakti is antagonistic to hatred. As it is nectar, blissful and gets manifested on its own (*ahetukī*).However knowledge has to be acquired by one's own effort[157].

(v) Bhakti is the principal means and others, Jñāna and karma are subordinate to it and depend on it[158].

(vi) Bhakti is essentially affection; because it will bear fruit (Mukti).It is only affection that brings one nearer to the indweller, and thus inferred that one gets affection for the self and not that which is separate and remote[159].

(vii) Devotion (Bhakti) that alone make aspirant to realize the divinity and not prior knowledge. The same is confirmed in BG as 'he knows me by devotion'[160].

(viii) The meditation and attaining of Samādhi are due to secondary type of devotion and are secondary to devotion[161].

2.4.2.6. ELIGIBILITY FOR DEVOTION:

The devotion is open to all without any discrimination of as gender, age etc. Sūdras, who are forbidden to study Vedas but they can obtain the same through epics and purāṇas. All irrespective of gender, age, learning and status in society etc. and even to the despised by birth are entitled to practice of devotion. All have desire for escape from miseries of mundane existence. Even with those, immature in devotion can perfect it in due course[162].

2.4.2.7. THE MEANS OF DEVOTION.

The devotion cannot be produced directly by an effort and so one has to resort to other methods. The author has mentioned (i) internal means and (ii) external means and the other as secondary or lower form of devotion.

The internal means is to ascertain the knowledge of Brahman. This knowledge will help purification of mind of all its impurities. This is obtained by śravaṇa (hearing of Vedic verses) and understanding the meaning, Manana (pondering) over the truths and clarification of any doubts and Nididhyāsana (meditating).One has to follow the supporting practices like obedience to the preceptor, self restraint. The practice should be continued till the purification of mind is fully obtained.[163]

2.4.2.8. TYPES OF DEVOTION:

The author classified the Bhakti into two broad categories.

i) Supreme Bhakti or primary Bhakti:

The supreme Bhakti is onepointed devotion and that only will bring liberation[164]. It is also called Parā Bhakti. All others forms will be useful and enable to produce supreme devotion.

(ii) Gauṇi Bhakti (The secondary form of devotion).

The secondary forms of devotion will be helpful for leading to the primary Bhakti[165] and involve several forms. The devotion depends on the guṇas and motives of the devotees. The primary and secondary forms can be considered as the pair of tongs. The secondary type of devotion will also have some result like eradication of sins and help purification of internal organ and is an integral part and not an extraneous means.[166]The forms of such devotion are many like celebrating the names of the lord, bowing down to Him, offering gifts as per available means like fruit or flowers, some adore through sacrifice of knowledge and some always contemplate on the Lord and some observe vows of fasting on *Ekādasi* days etc.[167]

The offerings made to the lord can be can be taken by the devotee as a prasāda and it is considered as auspicious.[168]

The subsidiary means may be practiced, either all at a time or any one of them as per convenience as efficiently as possible to please the Lord.[169]

The remembering the names of God, singing of hymns and narrating the glories of the Lord are considered as penances for expiation of sins in case of distressed devotee (Ārtha Bhakta)[170].

The supreme devotion which is directed toward Kṛṣṇa can also be done to the other incarnations of the Lord.[171]

The secondary devotion culminates in attaining the supreme devotion and when the supreme devotion is perfected, emancipation comes to all such devotees.[172]

2.4.2.9 THE OBJECT OF DEVOTION.

The Author has in the verses 85 to 92 has described the object of devotion.

The excellence of devotion depends on the excellence of the object of devotion, and by devotion obtains His state.

The śāstras have established that knowledge is existence, knowledge is Brahman. The objects have no separate existence of their own. So the soul, the devotion and the Brahman are one and the same[173]. The Brahman is oneness. The diversity or unity appears due to the Upādhi (adjuncts). The soul feels that he is different due to ignorance and when the ignorance is removed by knowledge the false notion is removed, the individual Soul and the universal soul becomes one.[174]

The souls are not subjected to change, but change is in the senses, due to ego that one feels the sense of 'I'. The complete disappearance of the intellect with onepointed devotion, realisation of self takes place, which is nothing but knowledge of Brahman, the eternal bliss. The ego is absorbed like camphor in fire; the mind is absorbed in Brahman.[175]

The liberation may be delayed and life will last till the un-fructified merits and demerits called Prārabdha karma is exhausted. All others karmas are however destroyed. This state is called the state of Jīvanmukta (living liberation).[176]

The author has stated that there are three types of liberation, Mukti, the Heaven, and Jīvanmukta. The Mukti and qualified Jīvanmukti is the highest, which is obtained due to supreme devotion. He denied that the mistake of rope for snake is not due to absence of knowledge. The cycle of births and deaths and sorrow are due to the Jīva turning away from the Lord. The identification of 'I' and 'Mine' is due to ego (*Ahaṅkāra)*, and not due to lack of knowledge, but absence of devotion towards God thus want to elevate Bhakti to higher level than Jñāna [177].

The author mentions that just as Rudra has three eyes, all beings have three eyes viz. The Vedas, symbols and senses and they are means of attaining knowledge. (To ascertain the nature of objects, the words are descriptive symbols to get inference and get perception through sense respectively.)

The verses 85 to 100 discussed under the objective of

the devotion show that the concept is in consonance of Advaitic unification of jīva and Brahma when the ignorance is removed.(Including the state of Jīvanmukta till the exhaustion of prārabdha karma.)

In the concluding verse, Śāṇḍilya says, that God is the creator, preserver and destroyer of the universe,with Brahma as His creative aspect, Viṣṇu as the preservative aspect and Rudra as the destructive aspect. The final emancipation is through the realisation of oneness with Brahman[178].

The verses are useful to have a clear concept of Bhakti and also the gradual stages by which one can proceed to practice, even by a householder pursuing his normal activities without knowledge of scriptures.

The need of Knowledge which is rejected has been accepted in the final stages is a bit perplexing

2.4.3. NĀRADA BHAKTI SŪTRAS.

2.4.3.1. INTRODUCTION:

Nārada is a yogi, a Jñānī and foremost among the devotees. He is a divine ministerial and a great ascetic. He rose from humble position with self effort and, with divine grace attained highest spiritual glory. He revealed his life story to Sage VedaVyāsa. He is one of the ten spiritual sons of Brahma (the creator).

Nārada is well known as having either initiated, propagated or inculcated devotion towards God and divine knowledge to spiritual personalities like, Sage Vālmīkī (The composer of Rāmāyana, Sage VedaVyāsa (The composer of

Bhāgavatapurāṇa).He inculcated Bhakti to Prahlāda (Son of Hiraṇyakaśipu) and Dhruva (a young prince) and several others. He is considered as friend, philosopher and guide to all. He is a perfect and ideal personality and he always roams about in the three worlds singing glory of Viṣṇu. He declared to the humanity that each individual has inherent Love within and advises to experience of supreme Bliss by love towards the supreme Lord. He emphasized that devotion is every body's birth right. He advises to strive for it, leaving aside the allurements of the world, to obtain God realization which is the most important goal of human birth, and thus get freedom from cycle of births and deaths and accompanying sorrows.

Nārada composed a simple text consisting of eightyfour Verses on Bhakti (devotion to god).It is one of the two in Bhakti Sūtras literature, the other being the Sāṇḍilya Bhakti Sūtras . In fact his treatise on Bhakti can be considered as a spiritual autobiography of Nārada.

Nārada Sūtras are simple; however as the very nature of Sūtra literature itself, need elaboration for better understanding by the readers. There are numerous commentaries on Nārada Sūtras.

Nārada emphasized on devotion (Bhakti) as it is considered the easiest and more efficient and it is universally eligible. He did not discord the Jñāna and Karma mārgas. The Bhakti Sūtras are considered as very important comprehensive guide intended to be followed by sincere aspirants for God realization and not for mere acquiring spiritual knowledge about the subject. The Bhakti Sūtras literally mean the formula that defines what constitute Bhakti (devotion) to God in all its dimensions from the nature, characteristics, and types of devotees and a progressive means of practice. The above aspects are discussed below, briefly but comprehensively.

2.4.3.2 NATURE OF BHAKTI.

(i). Bhakti is of the nature of Parama Prema and intense love towards God[179] and it is the source of eternal freedom from (the cycle of births & deaths) and obtaining immortality.[180] It is clarified that Parama Prema is of the nature of renunciation (of worldly lust).[181]

(ii). The nature of Parama Prema cannot be described and analyzed precisely.[182] It is like the taste of sweet by a dumb man (he will fully enjoy but cannot express).[183]

(iii) A person attaining which, desires nothing else, he does not grieve, nor hate. He does not rejoice[184].

(iv) The person will be fully immersed in the enjoyment of bliss of the Ātman (His true self).[185]

(v). Bhakti is devoid of attributes and free from all characteristic selfish tendencies. It is of the nature of integral subjective experience and manifests itself automatically after certain conditions are fulfilled.[186]

(vi) Bhakti works up to the highest spiritual realization which consists in seeing God in everything, loving or serving Him in all beings[187].

(vii).The renunciation means, consecration of all activities secular as well as sacred to the God. A distinction between love for God and love in worldly object is to be noted when the nature of love is being discussed. If the attachment to worldly love and secular activities is avoided and renounced, the attachment to God is strengthens automatically. The activities cannot be abounded but one has to consecrate all to God, for the purpose of realization[188].

2.4.3.3. ELIGIBILITY FOR BHAKTI:

(i). Bhakti is universal and there are no distinctions based on varna, culture, birth, gender, physical beauty or fitness, wealth, learning and profession.[189]

(ii) All are equal to the God.[190]

(iii) The highest spiritual realization alone is worthy of being acquired by all beings for release from bondage.[191]

2.4.3.4. BHAKTI AS A MEANS OF REALISNATION.

There are three paths for God realization

i) Karma.(ii) Bhakti and (iii) Jñāna.

Although it has been mentioned that different paths culminate into one goal and are mutually dependent, there is still some discussion based on eligibility, ease of practice and quick fructification. Some are of the opinion that Jñāna or Knowledge is instrumental in production of Bhakti,[192] while others say that they are mutually dependent.[193] However Nārada is of the opinion that the spiritual realization is its own fruit[194]. The following are cited as the reasons for it:

i) Bhakti arises by purification of mind by giving up of desires of sense organs and attachment to worldly things and egocentric intellect or renunciation.[195] (ii). By Practice of uninterrupted and continued worship.[196] (iii)By listening to and singing about the glory of the Lord while engaged in activities of ordinary life.[197] (iv) Primary to the grace of great men and a measure of the mercy of divine grace.[198] It is believed that to get the association with great people is very difficult, but it is obtained by God's grace. In fact there is no difference between Him and His devotees.[199]

2.4.3.5 HINDERANCES FOR DEVOTION.

There are usually certain hindrances and obstacles encountered by a devotee and one has to consciously adopt means to avoid them.

(i). Evil company is to be avoided by all means as they are the source of breeding anger, lust, and delusion. They will disturb the sense of discrimination and divert towards evil deeds. They spread like pests in crops and ultimately ruin the aspirant. They start slowly like ripples on the surface and gradually become like an ocean.[200]

(ii) One has to refrain from listening to talk about women, wealth and conduct of atheists as they will be provocative for such tendencies.[201]

(iii) One should give up pride and egotism.[202]

(iv) The aspirant should not indulge in argument about the devotion and God and comparative merits of devotees and one should understand that there is always scope for difference in views and none is final and conclusive[203].

2.4.3.6. THINGS CONDUCIVE FOR DEVOTION.

The following are considered as conducive for devotion.

(i) The aspirant has to diligently study scriptures and develop the devotional practice[204].

(ii) One should not spend even a moment of idle time, to ensure that his practice becomes continuous without stray diversions of mind to other pursuits.[205]

(iii) There is need to cultivate truthfulness, purity, Kindness, compassion, faith in higher spiritual realities and observe moral values of non-violence etc to develop character[206].

2.4.3.7. CLASSIFICATION OF BHAKTI.

Nārada has classified the stages of Bhakti as

i) Apara Bhakti (Initial stage)

ii) Parā Bhakti (mature stage)

The Apara Bhakti is further classified as (i) Gauṇī Bhakti (ii) Mukhya Bhakti.

The Gauṇi Bhakti is further classified into two categories.

i) According to the guṇas (qualities) Sattva, Rajas and Tamas.

ii) According to the distinction of the worshipper.

The above is represented by a diagram which will show at a glance the above mentioned structure.

The Apara Bhakti also called Guṇa Bhakti as they are associated with is of three kinds of guṇas according to the disposition of nature (ie) Sattva, Rajas and Tamas.

One should improve progressively in stages, by reducing Tamas and correspondingly increasing Rajas and finally to achieve prominence of pure Sattva, purifying the mind which will be finally beneficial to his highest good.

The Bhakti can also be classified as Ārtha, Jijñāsu, Arthārdin and Jñānī according to the motives of the Bhakta for resorting to devotion to God. The fourth type of devotee loves God for the sake of love only, having realized the knowledge, that there is none other than Vāsudeva to whom he can look to. Such devotee is very dear to the Lord, as mentioned in Bhagavad-Gīta.[207]The first three categories of devotees have motives of getting their desires fulfilled.

The following means are to ensure the Apara Bhakti for making it possible.

i) Having interest in worshipping God. (ii) Developing interest in listening to the stories about the glories of the Lord. (iii) Engrossed in the thought of self (Ātman). (iv) Consecration of all activities to the lord by completely surrendering to Him, and diligent in remembering Him and feeling anguish even a moment of forgetfulness[208].

The Bhakti is thus easily obtained and is self evident and does not need any Proof, and the aspirant feels peace of mind.[209] The devotee will have onepointed devotion or love towards God for His own sake. The devotee rejoices in himself and with other devotees conversing in chocked voice and eyes filled with tears.[210]

Bhakti (devotion) or divine love, though only one in kind, manifests itself in several forms according to the attitude of the devotee. Nārada has indicated eleven forms in which the devotee can relate to his beloved lover (God)[211].

(1) Guṇa Mahatmya Śakti.

The love of glorious qualities and divine attributes of the God.

Example: The great sages Nārada, Vedavyāsa, Śuka, Sūta, Śauṇaka, Parīkṣit, and Janamejaya are delighted in singing the glories of the Lord.

(ii) Rūpā Śakti: Love for the enchanting form (beauty of Spiritual form) of the Lord.

The Gopīs of Brindāvanam, Riṣis of Dandakāranya etc. are examples.

iii). Pūja Śakti: Love for worship of the Lord.

Example: Ambarīṣa, Bharata and Lakṣmi.

iv) Smaraṇa Śakti: Love of constant remembrance.

Example: Dhruva, Prahlāda and others

v). Dāsya Śakti: Love of Service like a servant to master.

Example: Hanuman, Akrūra, and Vidura.

vi). Sakhya Śakti: Love as a friend.

Example: Arjuna, Sudāma, Uddhava and Guha.

vii). Vātsalya Śakti: Love for Him as a parent.

Example: Kausalya, Dasaratha, Yaśoda, Nanda, Devakī, and Vāsudeva etc.

viii). Kāntā Śakti: Love as a loving wife.

Example: Rukmini and Satyabhāma.

ix). Ātmanivedana Śakti: Loving self surrender and cherishing self-knowledge.

Example: Hanumān, Ambarīṣa, Sibi, and Vibhīṣaṇa.

x). Tanmaya Śakti: Cherishing, absorption or oneness with the beloved.

Example: Sanat kumāras and Sūka.

xi) Parama Viraha Śakti: The pain of separation of the attachment in which one feels. Ex: Uddhava, Gopīs of Vraja, and Arjuna.

The personal love is found in the preliminary stage, gradually the relationship is developed as servant, friend, parent, and the devotee becomes one in spirit like that of a loving wife and complete self surrender and self absorption when the devotee feels the presence of God anywhere and everywhere and the devotee loses his own self in the lord.

The Love culminates in reaching the Parama viraha Śakti, attachment in extreme separation in which the devotee though he is metaphysically permanently united with the Lord, still feels as if he were separated from Him. A stage that cannot be described in words, but can only be experienced[212]. This situation will prevail till the fall of the body. The devotee will has agony outwardly due to separation but experiences delight due to constant immersion in the contemplation about the beloved inside and he loses himself and only the beloved exists in his thoughts.

Nārada mentioned the great teachers of Bhakti who unanimously declared the above (viz) Kumāras, Vyāsa, Suka, Śaṇḍilya and others[213].

The concluding verse mentions:

"Who so ever believes in this auspicious gospel of Nārada and has faith in it become lover of God, attains the highest beatitude and goal of life"[214].

CONCLUSION

The Nārada Bhakti Sūtras are very practical and are very clear that he has narrated his personal experience in the form of a simple treatise for the benefit of the people with a spirit of altruism. He has given equal regard to other means and considered that a synthetic approach with amalgamation of various means is desirable to achieve the final goal of liberation.

2.5. BHAKTI IN ADVAITA VEDĀNTA.

2.5.1. INTRODUCTION.

The three major Vedānta schools of Indian Philosophy were formulated considering the Upaniṣads, The Brahma Sūtras and Śrimad Bhagavad-Gītā as the three cannons called 'Prasthāna Traya'.

(i) Advaita (Non-duality by Śrī Śaṅkarācārya).

(ii) Vīśiṣṭādvaita (qualified non-duality) by Śrī Rāmānujācārya and

(iii) Dvaita (duality) by Śrī Madvācārya.

All though all the schools are based on the same scriptures they have different approaches based on interpretation by the respective philosophers.

Advaita Vedānta was originally propounded by Śrī Goudapāda based on the monistic view (Advaita or non-duality). He wrote a commentary (kārikā) on Māṇdukya Upaniṣad which laid foundation for Advaita. Śrī Gaudapāda was a teacher of Śrī Govinda who was the preceptor of Śrī Śaṅkarācārya.

The same was systemized both metaphysically and philosophically by Śrī Śaṅkarācārya to become a prominent school of thought with missionary zeal of propagation, consequently the Advaita Philosophy is popularly known as Śaṅkara Advaita Vedānta.

Śrī Śaṅkarācārya was born in Kalady, a village in Kerala State of India. His parents were Śrī Śivaguru and Śmt. Āryāmba belonging to a poor Brahmin family. He was brought up by his mother as he lost his father at a very early age.

He was given the traditional Vedic education. He was a child prodigy. He mastered the Vedas, Upaniṣads, Śāstras by the time he was eleven years old. He has shown his strong desire to renounce the world at an early age to become a sannyāsī. He could obtain the consent of his mother after great persuasion, by giving her promise that he will be by her side at the final hour and perform his duties as a son.

He set out towards north and approached Śrī Govindapāda on the bank of river Narmada who accepted Śaṅkara as a disciple having been fully impressed with the spontaneous reciting of verses that are now famously known as Daśaśloki, a short treatise on Advaita Vedānta[215].

The following are the core features of the Advaita Vedānta.

(i) *"Brahma Satyam"* (Brahman is the only Truth and eternal)

(ii) *"Jagat mithyā"* (The Universe is transient)

(iii) "*Jivo Brahmaiva na Paraḥ*" (The individual soul (Jīva) and the universal soul (Brahman) are not different.

iv) Jñāna (knowledge) is the only way to realization.

Śaṅkara composed commentaries on Upaniṣads, Brahma Sūtras and Bhagavad- Gītā, and also several prakaraṇa granthas, Stotra granthas and devotional hymns on several deities

Śaṅkara made extensive tour covering the entire country by foot and played a great role in successfully unifying several fragmented sections of Hindu religious groups.

Advaita teachings are mainly based on Upaniṣads and Vedas which give due importance to 'upāsanā' which is another name for Bhakti, in a broader sense. Therefore no one can imagine any system based on Vedic literature which would decry importance of Bhakti as a means of liberation.

Śaṅkara gave more importance to Jñāna (knowledge), as liberation is possible only through knowledge of one's own true nature for which one has to overcome his ignorance (Avidyā) and get free from false identity of self with the body; however karma and Bhakti were never discarded. Bhakti is considered essential for purification and concentration of mind and then only there will be progress in gaining knowledge. If we consider it as a lower rung of a ladder, it is obvious that the lower rung cannot be ignored even after the top Jñāna stage is reached one should try to achieve steadfastness in devotion or Jñāna-Bhakti.

Many highly erudite Advaitins assert that there is no conflict between Advaita and devotion. Śrī A.P.Misra, in his book based on in his doctoral thesis on 'The development and place of Bhakti in Śāṅkara Vedānta' observed as follows.

"Only a casual and brief perusal of the system brought me to the conclusion that monistic ideal of the Śāṅkara Vedānta is not against Bhakti, but on the contrary, it preaches it in positive and assertive terms.[216]"

Prof. Umesh Mishra observed in his foreword to the above cited book as follows.

"The subject sounded to many, apparently contradictory, but with a little thinking one can explicitly realize that all these-Jñāna, Bhakti and Karma are so related that one cannot be cut off from the other ..... They are the three aspects of one ultimate path to the highest goal." [217]

It is also seen that several Advaita Philosophers viz. Sureśvara, Sarvajñātma Munī, Advaitānanda, Vācaspati and few others have mentioned about the need of Bhakti in their works.

Sureśvara, the great author of Vartika was emphatic in teaching Bhakti. In his Pañchikarana Vartika states as follows. "A self controlled and composed yogī, equipped with Śraddhā and Bhakti should realize the Ātman through concentration." [218]

The same author in the concluding verse of Dakṣiṇāmūrti Vārtika repeats the words of Śvetāśvatara Upaniṣad which states that the essence of the teachings, revealed only "to those persons who are unflinchingly devoted to the deity and the preceptor."[219]

2.5.2. CONCEPT OF BHAKTI IN ADVAITA VEDĀNTA:

Bhakti is the attitude of Supreme love towards the Lord. Everyone has some amount of love towards the lord. However, it is generally found to the extent of fulfillment of certain desires.

Every Jīva has love, as an inherent quality. People may love several worldly things; one loves his children and also pets. The child loves his mother and father, his siblings, relatives, but all the love between them is short lived and will diminish in due course.

In the dialogue between Yājñavalkya and his wife Maitreyī (in Bṛahadāraṇyaka Upaniṣad), Yājñavalkya says that the husband and wife love each other due to one's own self, not due to love on each other. In the same way the sons, cattle, wealth is dear due to one's love for the self because of self fulfillment (hence arose co-operation and dearness).Yājñavalkya says that one has to know the self, especially one should see, hear, think and ponder over the self (Ātma).[220]

It is only one's own self is always the object of Supreme love (Parama Premāspada). It is that ĀtmaikaVastu. This is desirable to all at all times. If the self is known, everything in the world is known.

This love for self is mistakenly placed on the body and mind. It is instead to be recognized as love for the Primal source, from which one has arisen, which is nothing but the Supreme Lord.

It is that Īśvara, who himself is residing in the heart of the Jīva (the individual soul). This kind of love which one has towards oneself has to be placed towards the Lord (Īśvara who is the source of everything). Thus the love towards Īśvara is supreme and no other object is greater than Him.

There should be uncompromising love for God. One should have contentment and also the mind should not be fixed on any other external objects but engaged always thinking about the lord and His nature. This is called 'placing His feet on the mind'.

This type of contemplation is assumed when the devotee and Īśvara are different. However according to scriptures, even during the offering of worship, one should have an attitude of "He is I" Thus one has to develop the attitude of the non- difference from one's innermost self.

This type of attitude is true for both kinds of meditative Pūjā (Worship) on Nirguṇa, Nirākāra Brahman (The Attribute less Absolute Brahman) as well as Saguṇa Īśvara (The Lord with all qualities and form).

In case of Nirguṇa, Nirākāra Brahman, apart from Brahman there is nothing else. Thus the Individual has no separate existence apart from true Lord and there is only oneness.

In case of Saguṇa Brahman, one has to take absolute care of the Lord (as one make sure for himself) with faith (Śraddhā) and due diligence. One should never show an attitude that it is only a mūrtī or picture (and cannot adopt casual attitude as a formality without reverence) and remembering that it is a conscious entity.

One's mind should be bound with Bhakti and memory of the Lord, holding that Ātma-Jñāna is the only fruit worthy to be obtained.

One should realize that, if the devotee is sincere and devoted to the Lord, He Himself takes care of the welfare of His devotee even without being approached seeking help from Him.[221] Similar assurance is found in B.G. "The Lord will arrange to secure what the devotee lacks and preserving what they have".[222]

Śaṅkara in his famous composition 'Vivekacūḍāmaṇi' (meaning the crest jewel of discrimination) has given supreme place to devotion among the things conducive for liberation. Bhakti here is mentioned as seeking after one's real nature (the Ātman or supreme self immanent in beings)[223].

2.5.3. ŚAṄKARA'S RELIGIOUS ACTIVITIES:

2.5.3.1. ESTABLISHING OF MAṬHS (MONASTERIES)

Śrī Śaṅkara established four Maṭhs (monasteries) spread in four different directions of the country for the propagation of Sanātana dharma. They are called Āmnāya pīthams. They are located at the following places.

i) Dakṣināmṇāya Śrīngeri Śāradā Pītham at Śringeri, in Karnataka state in south India.(ii) Pūrvāmaṇāya Govardhan pītham at Puri in Orissa State.(iii) Uttarāmṇāya Jotiṣ pītham at JoŚīmaṭh near Badrināth in Uttarākhand State.(iv) Pascimāmṇāya Kālikā Pītham at Dwārakā in Gujarat State. Each pītham has been assigned principle divinities specific Veda and specific tradition of worship to be adopted and a mahāvākya as detailed below

Maṭh.	Divinities.	Veda.	Mahāvākya.
Śrīngeri	Malahānikareśwara. Śakti--Sārada	Yajurveda	"Aham Brahmāsmi"
Puri	Jagannādha. Śakti-Vimala	Ṛgveda	"PraJñānam Brahma"
Jotiṣ Pītham	Nārāyaṇa. Śakti--Poornagiri.	Atharva Veda	"Ayamātma Brahman"
Dwārkā	Siddheśvara. Śakti --Kāli.	Sāma Veda	"TatTvam Asi"

Note: The information in the table above was obtained and adopted from the book *Perspectives of Śaṅkara,* published by Dept of culture, Ministry of Human resource Development, Govt of India, 1989.appendix. P.423.

2.5.3.2. Pañcāyatana Pūjā and Ṣaṇmata.

It is believed that the system of Pañcāyatana-**Pūjā** system of worship of five deities of Vedic Religion has been established by Śrī Śaṅkara (Others think he only reinforced the system) and is followed by Sṁārthas. There are five deities and the individual can choose any one of them as his chosen God and all of the deities are equal and there are no ranking among them. All the deities are represented by Śālīgrāma" (certain type of stone collected from different Rivers). Śaṅkara added 'Kumāra' to the Pañcāyatana system and named it Ṣaṇmata.Thus the six kinds of faiths prevalent at that time, by means of his Philosophy of 'non-dualism' of reality.

In the life time of Śrī Śaṅkara there are different practices of worship among the Hindu religion. The Worship of (i) Lord Śiva.(ii) Vaiṣṇava : worship of Lord Viṣṇu and his other incarnations (Śrī Rama, Śrī Kṛṣṇa etc.(iii) Śakti: Worship of Goddess. (iv) Gāṇāpatyam; Worship of Gaṇapati (son of Lord Śiva).(v) Kumāram: Worship of Lord (son of Lord Śiva). (vi) Sauram: Worship of Lord Sūrya.

They adopted practices of worship which Śaṅkara found to be deviation from the practices prescribed in scriptures, not only claiming that ,what they have adopted as correct, but also each claiming that, only their deity is superior. It is alleged that some have even adopted Narabali (Sacrifice of human).

Śaṅkara made strenuous efforts and united them by establishing Ṣaṇmata. The Ṣaṇmata involves the worship of all the six deities in the tradition envisaged in Vedas. Thus the Ṣaṇmata has contributed to minimize the earlier controversies besides eradicating the undesirable abnormal practices and reverting to Vedic practices.

2.5.4. WORKS OF ŚAṄKARĀCĀRYA.

Śrī Śaṅkara has composed several works in a short span of his life of 32 years. They are classified into three categories. Only few considered as very important among them were mentioned.

(a) Bhāṣya Granthas (Commentaries). (b) Prakaraṇa Granthas (original compositions). (c) Stotra Granthas (hymns to deities).

(A) Śrī Śaṅkarācārya has written commentaries of (i) Bhagavad-Gītā. (ii) Brahma Sūtras and (iii) Upaniṣads. It is understood that he has also written commentary of Viṣṇu Sahasranāma stotra.

B) The prakaraṇa Grandhās are the compositions, where in the fundamental concepts in the scriptures are explained for easy understanding of the seekers. The following are the most important of such compositions.

i) Aparokṣānubhūti. (ii) Vivekacūdamanī. (iii) Ātma-bodha. (iv) Daśa- Ślokī. (v) Upadeśa-sahasrī.

C) The stotra Granthas are hymns and verses in praise of different deities using poetic language that can be recited by the aspirants in their daily worship and in temples.

The following are some of them

a). Lord Gaṇeśa:	i). Gaṇeśa Pañcaratnam
b). Lord Subrahmanya:	i). Subrahmanya Bhujanga Stotram.
c). Lord Śiva:	i). Śivānandalaharī.
	ii). Dakṣiṇāmūrti Aṣṭakam.
	iii). Kālabairavāṣṭakam.

	iv). Śiva Pañcākṣara stotram.
	v). Śiva Mānasa Pūja.
d). Goddess Śakti:	i). Soundaryalahari.
	ii). Tripura Sundari Aṣṭakam.
	iii). Kanakadhāra stotram.
	i v). Annapūrṇa Aṣṭakam.
e) Lord Hanuman:	i). Hanumān Pancaratnam.
f). Lord Viṣṇu:	i). Laxmi Nṛsiṁha stotra.
	ii). Acyutāṣṭakam.
	iii). Govindāṣṭakam.
	iv). Bhaja Govinda stotra
	v). Prabodha Sudhākara.
g). In Praise of Rivers:	i). Gaṇgāstotram.
	ii). Yamunāṣṭakam.
	iii). Maṇi- Karṇika Aṣṭakam.
h). General:	i). Nirguṇa Mānasa Puja.
	ii). Sāḍhanā pañcakam.

It is now proposed to examine and highlight the devotional aspects (Bhakti) in the following Works.

(i). Śivānandalahari. (ii). Saundarya-laharī. (iii) Bhaja Govindam.(iv). Śiva Mānasa Pūjā. (v). Sādhanā Pañchakam.

2.5.4.1. Bhakti from Commentary of Śaṅkara on Bhagavad-Gītā

In Bhagavad-Gītā, Śrī Kṛṣṇa told "I am the origin of all; everything moves on owing to Me. Realizing thus, the wise ones filled with fervor adore Me."[224] Meaning, I the supreme Brahman, called Vāsudeva, is the source of the world. The wise who knows this supreme reality worship me ardently engaged in contemplation of the Supreme reality."

This is considered as a pre requisite of Bhakti.

The ways of practicing Bhakti has been given. The devotees with their thought on the Lord (with all their senses) , the eyes are absorbed on the Lord. They speak of the Lord as prospect of supreme wisdom, Power, might and other qualities. Thus they are satisfied and they are delighted as if in the company of the beloved"[225].

The fruit of devotion is given as follows by Śrī Kṛṣṇa.

"To those, ever devoted and worships 'Me' with love, I give that devotion of Knowledge by which they come to me"[226]

It may be recalled that Śrī Kṛṣṇa mentioned in Bhagavad-Gīta:

"All the devotees are noble and are dear to Me. There is however one difference, man of wisdom is excessively dear to ME. It is My conviction that such a man is the very self, not different from ME. The wise strides to reach Me, firm in faith and that is Myself is the Lord Vāsudeva and is no other than ME, and seeks ME only, the supreme Brahman as the highest God to be reached"[227]. Śaṅkara has mentioned that "He is realized through Bhakti having that Jñāna as its prerequisite which has Vāsudeva as its object". The Jijñāsu, who has desire for knowledge, after Bhakti has been practiced brings this devote with a desire for the study of Upaniṣads. Thus we see that Bhakti is considered essential in all the three stages (ie). Śravaṇa, manana, and Nididhyāsana in the process of self-realization.

Thus after discarding of all cravings and with sincere pure Bhakti to the Supreme Being is the ideal way of achieving right vision, the samyag darśana. Śaṅkara accepted that such a Jñāna-Bhakti as a means only and not an end. Thus Bhakti is of great significance has been accepted by Śaṅkara.

"The devotee who works for the Lord, and who identified that He is the Supreme goal, he serves Him in all manner of ways with heart and soul. Such a devotee is devoid of all attachments like from wealth, with kith and kin, relatives. He is free from any form of enmity towards all beings (even to those who severely harmed him).Such a devotee of the Lord only attains Him and no other goal."[228] This is given in Bhagavad-Gītā. Śaṅkara called this "Ananyā Bhakti". The devotee perceives only Vāsudeva and nothing else.[229]

The prerequisite of Bhakti was given in verse BG X.8. "The wise men , who are the knower of the supreme reality, filled with fervor of ardent longing for the supreme reality, filled with it, imbued with that adore ME". The next verse gives the various ways of practicing such devotion. In Verses X.10 the result of such devotion is given as, 'That the

Lord will grant the wisdom by which the devotee will realize their own self' The Lord , who is the indweller of the hearts destroys the darkness born of ignorance with the luminous lamp of knowledge.

In the commentary on BG verse Xii-18, the summary of Vedas and Gītā is given as the devotee of Vāsudeva is mentioned as " My devotee, who attributes the fact of being the self of all to Me who am God, Vāsudeva, the omniscient, the supreme teacher, and whose conviction has been saturated with the idea that whatever he sees, hears or touches, all that verily is Lord Vāsudeva. Such a devotee of Mine having realized the afore said true knowledge becomes qualified for My state of being the supreme self: He attains realization". This type of ananyā Bhakti arises out of selfless love and reaches the climax of Ātma-samarpaṇa or self- surrender that enables to reach true knowledge which is the purport of teaching of Bhagavad-Gītā (verse XVIII.66).

COMMENTARY ON VIṢṆU SAHAŚRA NĀMA STOTRA.

The commentary on Viṣṇu Sahasranāma, verse fourteen is a splendid example of Śaṅkara's Bhakti to Lord Kṛṣṇa. It reads as follows 'It is better to fall in the flames of fire rather than live with those who never remember Lord Kṛṣṇa'[230]

2.5.4.2 BHAKTI IN STOTRA GRANTHAS.

The following stotra granthas have been examined and the devotional sentiment expressed therein by the author and the attitude towards Bhakti, is highlighted.

2. 5.4.2.1. ŚIVĀNANDA-LAHARĪ:

The composition consisting of one hundred verses, in glory and worship of Lord Śiva. Śivānandalaharī is acclaimed as the most inspiring among Śaṅkara's monumental contribution to devotional literature, besides the beauty of the poetic composition, the concepts are helpful in providing intellectual nourishment, and abundance of Bhakti which penetrates the hearts of the devotees. Many verses seek the God's grace by planting His lotus feet in the mind of devotee.

A few verses are selected to bring out the devotional sentiment and the importance given by Śrī Śaṅkara.

The Bhakti is defined as an attraction to God as natural and steady by giving illustrations.

i) The seeds of Ankola tree (a forest tree) are attracted back to the tree.
ii) The Iron fillings or Needle are attracted to the magnet.
iii) A virtuous lady is always attracted to her beloved husband, always thinks about him.
iv) All rivers after eventful course ultimately join the Sea from where its water originated as Vapors and as clouds.

All these illustrations are of Philosophical significance about the relationship of the soul to the supreme Soul which compels Bhakti.[231]

The following quotes from the verses illustrate the devotional sentiment expressed in the text.

Bhakta is accepted and protected by God whatever be that person's station of life, or Caste or community if he offers his heart to the Lord.[232]

The devotee just offering the lotus of his heart at the feet of the Lord is considered as the best Pūja and there is no need for various hard means and methods for redemption like yogic practices.[233]

Gītā also says "yogi who adores me with his mind fixed on ME with faith is considered to be the best of the yogīs"[234].

It is hardly matter whether one is born as a celestial or human being or an animal, a bird in forest, or insect and even as a worm so long as ones heart is given to almighty God. The nature of the body is not important for the soul to receive the waves of bliss of the Lord, if one contemplates on His lotus feet.[235]

Vedas and Upaniṣads say that Supreme Being is both immanent and transcendent. Such an entity is also gracious, benevolent and easy of approach of a devotee who has only to cherish Him in heart.[236]

A wise person will use his intense Bhakti, with a one-pointed concentration to obtain the lord. It is like the concentration of an Archer to hit the target aimed.[237]

The mind has to concentrate on the holy feet of the Lord instead of being engaged on rambling thoughts. Bhakti is indispensable for all Mārgas, as the Lord's holy feet, is a fertile field for growth of spiritual realization.[238]

The devotee prays to the lord to plant His the fragrant lotus feet in his mind to purify it of all odors (mind is considered as a box filled with multitudes of desires and attachments and thus polluted and emanate bad odor).[239]

Śaṅkara exhorts that a devotee should not indulge in arguments exercising the oral organs on debates to establish one's own views. Instead devote has to make it a habit to mediate on the lotus feet of the lord. One should make that he himself an instrument of God when doing work instead of doing things with ego centric desires[240].

The only means to obtain the grace of the Lord is sincere Bhakti and no need to be proficient in learning of arts or other fields.[241]

The weakness of a person in body, mind or spirit is due to the past Karmas, but they can be overcome, only by receiving the grace of the Lord through sincere Bhakti and worship.[242]

God is generous and showers unlimited grace. (Even if the recipient is undeserving).[243]

Bhakti generated by contemplation on the Lord's Lotus feet is incomparably beneficial to the soul and nourishes it like the pure rain water from a tank that nourishes the plants. Bhakti used in any other way is useless.[244]

QUALITIES OF THE BHAKTA:

i). The devotee should be truthful, wise and dutiful[245].

ii). One should be humble and worship God expressing his helplessness, (as any valuable and costliest offering to God is nothing compared to what God has).[246]

iii). The devotee addresses the Lord that His feet are tender and he danced on hard surfaces of hills and forests with a forethought that he had to plant his feet on the devotee's hard heart. Thus intense love for the lord is brought out and the Lord is compassionate to even those who are hard hearted.[247]

iv). A few fortunate persons perform arcana at the Lord's feet, some by meditating on form, some by Vandana, some in darśana of forms, some by singing hymns. Thus several people adopt various means of worship. Some keep the Lord in mind and dedicate his mind to Him. Such a person attains Mukti. All these methods are to train the mid to think of God. Śaṅkara reiterates that Bhakti is Mukti.[248]

Śaṅkara affirmed that Bhakti, by its very nature enables one to see God everywhere and in everything including ones own soul and that is Mukti.[249]

It is well known that the mind of a man is wavering, like a monkey, which always wanders and very difficult to control (although the intellect is above it can control, but very often fails). The more one tries to control, the more it slips away. Therefore, the devotee addresses the Lord that his mind is like a monkey always wandering around the forests of bewitching sensual desires. It dances and leaping on the hillocks of the damsel's breasts and jumping as it pleases over the branches of multifarious evils.' The devotee pleads with the Lord to take charge of the monkey (of his mind) tying it with bond of Bhakti. Śaṅkara here addresses Śiva as one with a begging bowl and offers the monkey (of his mind) so that it will of some use to a beggar. Thus appeals not only to control but also to take charge of the mind. Thus indicating that, one has to pray the Lord even to divert the mind towards Bhakti to God[250].

2.5.4.2.2 SAUNDARYA-LAHARĪ.

Saundarya-laharī composed by Śaṅkarācārya, is considered as great devotional stotram in praise of Goddess. It occupies a unique place among the works associated with Tantric system of Philosophy and Śakti Worship.

It consists of one hundred verses. It has been mentioned by Śrī C.P. Rāmaswāmī Ayyar in his foreword that the work occupies in the Tantric system the same position that Bhagavad-Gītā occupies in the orthodox system of Indian Philosophy[251].

The forms of worship intended for people of lower intellectual capacities were described in the first 21 verses. There after about the form of worship to pure Śvarūpa, a contemplation which is attainable by advanced men.

The devotee addresses the Goddess, O! Bhavānī!, be pleased to cast a compassionate glance on me, thy poor servant". The Goddess Bhavānī at once, even before he finishes the sentence, bestows Sāyujya on him[252].

The verse illustrates the peak of Bhakti, the devotees oneness with the deity, a concept which is meaningful only in Advaita.

The essence of the verse is that when a devotee with a pure heart and austere piety begins to pray to Her for blessings, She at once condescend to recognize the piety and sincere devotion of the devote, takes him to the highest spiritual level by granting him Sāyujya. (The state being oneness with Herself and makes him Immortal).

Bhavāni is the consort of Śiva. Brahma (Creator) and Viṣṇu (the protector and Preserver) worship her lotus feet and prostrate at her Lotus feet. The brilliancy of the gems adoring their crowns sheds a luminous luster over Her feet.

The Goddess has several names and the name Bhavānī is very important and the very utterance of it attracts Her attention, and She will at once be pleased. Bhakti leads to four grades of spiritual realization according to the degree of the strength of devotion[253].

Bhavānī has two meanings, when we consider as noun or as verb. As a Noun it means the consort of Bhava (Bhava is name of Śiva), Amba (mother). Goddess as a verb it would mean "may I become you"

The humble devotee addresses Her as a servant, requests her to cast Her glance of grace and compassion to him. She is an ocean of compassion and grace and when the devotee addresses her, even before he completes his sentence grants the sāyujya status. The devotee may be an ordinary person, even may not be aware of the status of Sāyujya and prays for grace (with n attitude of duality but she grants him the oneness (which is of the Advaitic oneness).

2.5.4.2.3. BHAJA GOVINDAM.

The Bhaja Govindam is one of the poetical works of Śrī Śaṅkara and is the smallest in volume, but could be ranked one of the foremost. It is a Bhajana song, but it is considered as a 'Prakaraṇa Grantha'. It is believed that this was composed during his Kāśī yātrā. He was pained to observe an elderly man trying hard to learn Sanskrit grammar. Śaṅkara felt that the man should be calling on God (Govinda) instead of wasting on learning language. In spite of its exotic poetic beauty and perfection, the composition is a sort of hard rebuke to the old man in particular and a general advice to all people entangled in worldly pleasures.

Śrī C.Rājagopalācārī in his commentary on Bhaja Govindam has observed as follows:

'Śrī Ādi Śaṅkara himself, who drank the ocean of knowledge as easily as one sip of water from the palm of one hand, sang hymns to develop devotion. It is enough to show that knowledge and devotion are one and no other testimony is needed. Śrī Śaṅkara has packed into the "Bhaja Govindam" song, the substance of all Vedāntic works that he wrote and has set the truth of Union of devotion and knowledge to melodious music, which is a delight[254].

The concept expressed in some select verses is mentioned in this discussion.

"When the God of death, beckons to you to come to his region you cannot argue with him with the aid of books you have mastered. The only way to escape is to worship Govinda. Book learning without devotion will not avail in the presence of death".[255]

Bhaja Govindam was sung for everybody. Wisdom and devotion are the invaluable birth rights of everybody. It is advised that everyone has to be content with what he earns one has to conquer the lust for money as it is a folly to grieve over what you don't have without feeling contentment with what you have earned by honest labour. Such an attitude of not wanting is a victory over ones cravings.[256]

Śaṅkara advices against lust as follows:

"Woman looks pretty. If you cast covetous glances at a woman, it will breed more lust in you. Your firmness of mind will be lost without your knowing. Do not be overpowered with lust. Craving and lust are seeming pleasures conceding a core of inevitable pain. Such restraint of senses is essential for everybody for welfare and mental peace.[257]

After initial advice against arrogance of, learning, wealth and sensual desires, Śaṅkara speaks of nature of the life.

The life is like a water drop precariously resting on lotus leaf feeling quite safe which is in fact most unstable. Man's mind always skips from one thing to other and is never stable. Afflicted by disease and tossed by attachments, the life is enveloped in grief. The pleasure of attachments to wife and children is not real, in truth they are cares and sorrows.

One has to seek to Nārāyaṇa to rescue from the danger of disease and attachment like the Purāṇic elephant which cried to Him for rescuing from the crocodile.[258]

Śaṅkara further advises that one must perform his duties as a house holder, but a wise man, will act realizing the limitations. Those who act with proper understanding of things can reduce the cause of grief. The family and kinsfolk are attached as long a man earns and body is able, when the body becomes inform and no longer earn, no one will speak even in your own home.The wife who cares for him bestowing all love and affection as long he is alive, but she is scared and afraid of the same body when he dies.

Śaṅkara only warns of undue attachment, but not to abandon wife and family life.

The man is engrossed in play, sex, and wife and wasted on things of transient and deluding pursuits of family cares and related anxieties. He hardly finds time to turn to the quest for wisdom.[259]

It is now proposed to bring out the way Śrī Śaṅkara has highlighted the need and importance of devotion to Govinda.

i) Once a man is free from attachment, he will attain equanimity and divine peace. These will come in succession to attain salvation at the end. One must start with company of devotees at the same time avoid company of non believers, but not to hate, but hope and wish that they too must receive the grace of God.[260]

ii) The dawn of knowledge will abate all sorrows and the delusions will vanish. The state of mind that looks the wealth and fame as mere trivialities, sensual pleasures must be avoided and obtain such a maturity and firmness of mind but not simply becoming a Sannyāsī to show that he is a renunciate.

The company of the good people is the only boat which will take you across the sea of life. One should become pure in heart and mind and meditate on God with love and devotion in whatever form (father/mother/teacher). There cannot be spirit of renunciation without devotion to God. It cannot be attained merely by book learning without devotion. It has been mentioned that man is a bundle of desires and he will cling to them even when he becomes old and goes about leaning on a stick.[261]

It is immaterial in what form and by what name, devotees offer devotion to God. The traditional names are only different ways of calling the same God. Śaṅkara said "you will be liberated if you worship Murāri (i.e.) Govinda, with devotion at least now and then.[262]

Let us beg God for this grace, He will surely protect us and take us across the ocean of births and deaths.[263]Śaṅkara has further mentioned that if one reads a even a bit of Bhagavad

-Gīta,(which is the essence of Vedas).sips few drops of Gaṅgā water(which is the holy water that has dropped from the feet of Nārāyaṇa) on the head of Śiva and then on to the earth and even prays to Murārī will be freed from the fear of cycle of births.

Thus Śaṅkara, who himself reached the height of spiritual knowledge cried out that nothing except His grace can protect us.

In the concluding verse Śaṅkara gave the message "our body and heart is the temple of God. It is our duty to keep and guard them from defilement. Trust yourself wholly to the Lotus feet of the teacher to get freed from the shackles of saṁsāra. "With your senses and mind controlled in this manner, you will see God residing in your heart."

Thus we can see importance of devotion (to Govinda) displayed by Śrī Śaṅkarācārya, the foremost Advaita preceptor.

2.5.4.2.4. PRBHODHA SUDĀKARA.

This is a lesser known work of Śaṅkara consisting of 257 verses in19 sections, which presents the monistic Vedānta. The outstanding fact is that it completely reconciles knowledge (Jñāna) and devotion (Bhakti) as equally valid methods of direct experience of Ultimate reality. The divine Lord is omnipresent, immanent in all beings, pure Awareness and absolute bliss.[264]

The divine grace and its significance was highlighted section 19 of the text. 'The divine grace is the force that can remove the ignorance and make the individual soul realize its true nature as undivided being-consciousness, bliss, non-different from the divine Lord or supreme self.'[265]The Saving grace of the Lord is like a magnet attracting and drawing to itself even dull witted or apathetic persons who seek Him unwittingly.' 'The divine grace does not differentiate between the physical and mental qualifications of different recipients.' 'The selfless devotees for whom nothing other than the love of the divine Lord matters, experience the bliss born out of the divine grace,' 'The selfless devotee who has totally surrendered to the divine is sure to be rewarded by the dawn of the divine consciousness in his heart which makes him blissful and immortal.'[266]

2.5.4.3. BHAKTI IN HYMNS.

The following hymns are examined (i). Śiva Mānasa Pūja. (ii). Sādhanā Pañcakam:

Many of his words are of eight verses, called Aṣṭakam (viz) Viśvanādhā-Aṣṭakam, Bhavānī Aṣṭakam, Bilvāṣṭakam are very popular. Some are five verses only called Pañcakam or Pañcaratnam (viz) Śiva Mānasa Pūja, Gaṇeśa Pañcaratnam, Kāśī Pañcakam, Sādhanā Pañcakam are similarly very popular.

Śaṅkarācārya composed several hymns on different deities. These are called stotras. All are with deep meaning and with great poetic skill. All though these are apparently convey dualism; they are filled with the essence of non dualism inside them.

Śaṅkara is of the firm opinion that in practice of devotion, involvement of mind is of utmost important. Mind is always fluctuating with different thoughts and such a mind is impure and do not focus on the object of worship. Hence mental worship is more appropriate and preferred to physical worship. Most of these compositions are spontaneous.

In many devotional hymns and works there is a shift from dualism to non- dualism which perhaps is possible only for Śaṅkarācārya who had an ocean of knowledge and abundant intellectual power.

2.5.4.3.1. MĀNASA PŪJĀ.

Mānasa Pūja is doing worship on the Lord, mentally without any external material. The entire Pūja is imagined in the mind, including all the materials necessary for worship (which are offered in formal worship).

This kind of worships of the Lord is more powerful which involve concentration of mind and will be more effective than physical action. The devotee imagines the Lord (Śiva Liṅga) which resides in the Lotus of one's inner heart.

The ablutions are done from the river of devotion; the lotus of meditation is the flower offered. The offering of, tasty eatables with ingredients like honey, curd etc are imagined along with the offering of musical entertainment, dance with eight limbs etc.

"O! Lord you are myself, my intellect is Goddess Pārvathī, My vital airs are your attendants, my body is your temple, all enjoyments of sense objects are your worship, my sleep is Samādhi, all movements of my feet are circumblations of you, whatever I speak is your praise and every action of me is your worship".

The devotee appeals to the ocean of compassion of the lord for forgiveness of all wrongs that are committed due to ignorance, advertently or inadvertently. When a devotee totally surrenders himself to God, then what ever he does is as per God's will. The devotee gives up all sense of doer ship and enjoyer. Thus the Advaitic oneness is established.

2.5.4.3.2. SĀDHANĀPAṄCAKAM.

Sādhanā Pañcakam is a means to self realization. It is a small composition of five verses by Śaṅkarācārya. It expresses in an elegant nutshell what we should do imperatively if we are to overcome the great fear and attain peace that passes understanding.[267]

i). Study the word of God and adhere to its practice with devotion, dedicate all your actions to the Supreme. Eschew all kinds of desires and sensual pursuits. Yearn for knowledge of Ātman and renounce forthwith all attachments. Leave at once your own limited identity.

ii). Remain in company of holy saints and cultivate deep devotion to God. Practice virtues like calmness and give-up all works producing bondage. Resort to a self realized Guru and seek him earnestly for the knowledge of Brahman and listen to words of the scriptures.

iii). Reflect over the meaning of the scriptures and stand by them in spirituality. Avoid all vain arguments, and with self realized persons cultivate the awareness that you are Brahman and give-up ego and identity of 'I' with the body.

iv). Do not crave for taste of food and be content with what you got and treat the decease of hunger with medicine of food obtained through alms.Avoid likes and dislikes, hot or cold and be above such and keep equanimity, remain indifferent to social relations, abandon all harshness towards others, and do not lose yourself completely in pity at the suffering or misdeeds of others.

v). Learn to live in solitude and focus the mind on the Ātman, feel the same Ātman existing in all and notice how it eliminates the fleeting existence called the world. Through the power of consciousness dissolve the results of good and bad of your Prārabdha karma, remain unaffected by your later karma and experience your present karma. Thus remain in your awareness of the Supreme self and live in bliss forever.

We see from the Prakaraṇa granthas, Stotra granthas, and in the hymns of Śaṅkarācārya discussed above, the devotional fervour is abundantly exhibited and the aspirants are strongly advised to pursue the path of devotion with a sense of seeking His grace. Thus it is an ample proof to that Devotion (Bhakti) has been recognized and given prominance and advised to be followed by the aspirants irrespective of the philosophy they follow. The Bhakti to a personal God is adoptable in Advaita Vedānta.

Notes and Refrences

1. Rao, Nagarāja.P, Fundamentals of Indian Philosophy, Indian Boo-Company, NewDelhi, P11.
2. Katha Upaniṣad 1.11.24.
3. BU 4.4.23
4. BG 3.35.
5. BU 4.4.5.
6. BG 3.27.
7. BG 3.35.
8. BG 18.48
9. BG 3.5.
10. B.G. 3.19
11. BG. 3.8
12. B.G. 3.9 & BG 3.19
13. B.G. 18.23.
14. Ibid 18.24
15. Ibid 18.25
16. Ibid. 18.26
17. Ibid 18.20
18. Ibid. 18.27
19. Ibid 18.21
20. Ibid 18.28
21. Ibid18.22
22. Ibid2.47.
23. Ibid 2.50.

24. Werner Karel Love divine, studies in Bhakti and devotional Mysticism, Rutledge, P. 168, 1993.
25. Vimalānanda, Swami, VK, Advaita Ashram, Kolkata, Jan, P 17,1978.
26. Lokeswarānanda Swami, (Tr.) S.U. with Śaṅkara's Commentary, RMIC, Kolkata P254. 1994 (edition2016)
27. Rolf Sovik, 'Bhagavad-Gītā on love', yoga international journal, (www. Yoga international. org.) Feb2015.
28. BG 13.11.
29. Ibid 2.53.
30. Ibid 2.49.
31. Ibid 6.37. see also GambhīrānandaSwamī, Madhusūdana Sarasvatī Bhagavad-Gītā with annotation Gūḍhārtha- Dīpikā Advaita Ashram, Kolkata,.P1007,1017,1021.1022, 2013.
32. Ibid 18.53.
33. Ibid 18.54.
34. Ibid 18.55.
35. Ibid 7.16
36. GambhīrānandaSwamī, Bhagavad-Gītā with commentary of Śaṅkarācārya,(Tr) Advaita Ashram, Kolkata, p131,2012.
37. Ibid 18.70.
38. Gambhīrānanda swāmī. Bhagavad-Gītā, with commentary of Śaṅkarācārya, Advaita ashram, Kolkata, 2012,7-
39. Ibid P58.(commentary on Verse2.18)
40. BG verse. 4.6-8.
41. Ibid. verse5.2-3.
42. Ibid.Verse 9.11.
43. Ibid Verse 11.3.
44. Ibid Verse 11.54.
45. Ibid verses 12.3-4.
46. Ibid Verse12.8-12.

47. Ibid.12.3-4.
48. Ibid Verse1.4.
49. Ibid verse 7.17
50. Ibid verse !2.5.
51. Ibidverse 12.7.
52. Ibid.verse 12.6.
53. Bhp verse11.20.7.
54. BG Verse12.8.
55. Ibid verse. 12.10.
56. Ibidverse 12.11.
57. Ibid verse12.8.
58. Ibid verses 12.13-19.
59. Ibid verse 6.47.
60. Ibid verse. 9.26.
61. Ibid Verse 9.27.
62. B.G. verse 9.28.
63. Ibid Verse 9.29.
64. Ibidverse. 7.16.
65. Ibid. Verse 7 14.
66. Ibid.verse 9.32.
67. Ibidverse. 9.30.
68. IbidVerse 9.32.
69. Ibid. verse10.10- 11.
70. Ibid.verse 12. 20.
71. Ibid verse 8.22.
72. Warrier,A.G.Krishna,(TR) ŚrĪmad Bhagavad-Gītā Bhāyṣya of Śrī Saṅkarācārya, Sri Ramakrishna Math, Madras,. Introduction Pxv, 2017
73. Srimad BhāgavataMāhātmya 2.67. Śrimad Bhāgavata Mahāpurāṇa (part-I,- Bhagavad-gītā press, Gorakhpur 2014.

74. Ibid 2.71
75. Ibid 2.60
76. Introduction to Critical study of Bhāgavatam published By Tirumala Tirupati Devasthanam, web site.
77. BhP 12.13.15.
78. Ibid 1.5.23-40 and 1.6.5to.37.
79. Ibid 3.9.30-36
80. Ibid 12.13.18.
81. Ibid 1.1.1 and 12.13.19.
82. Ānand Subhash, The way of love, M M Publishers, New Delhi 1996. P5.
83. Ibid 2.10.7.
84. Ibid 2.6.39.
85. Ibid 1.2.11.
86. Anand Subhash, The way of love, M M Publishers, New Delhi 1996.P14.
87. Srimad Bhāgavata Māhapurāna,Gita press, Gorakhpur 2014.
88. SethumadhavanTN,Bhagavatam a comprehensive blend of Bhakti,-Jñāna and Vairāgya www.Samsktiti.com June 2010.
89. BG 4.33.
90. Bhāgvatapurāna 1.2.11.
91. Quoted By Rukmini TS in her book, A critical study of the Bhāgavatapurāna, Chowkamaba Sanskrit series office, Varanasi1970.P133.
92. BhP 1.3.33-34.
93. Ibid 1.2.6.
94. Ibid 11.3.31.
95. Ibid 3.25.32-23.
96. Ibid 3.29.11-12.
97. Ibid 7.7.54.
98. Ibid 11.12.7.
99. Ibid 4.8.41.

100. Ibid 7.7. 55.
101. Ibid 11.19.24.
102. Ibid 11.29.33.
103. Ibid 3.25.19-20.
104. Ibid 11.11.29-31 see also BG 12.13-14.
105. BhP 4.22.22-25.
106. Ibid 3.29.8-10.
107. Ibid 1.2.11.
108. Ibid 1.2.12.
109. Ibid 3.29.11-12.
110. Ibid 1.2.6.see also3.9.42,Ibid 11.20.35
111. Ibid 3,29.11-12.
112. Ibid 7.9.55.
113. Ibid 1.4.4.
114. Ibid 1.8.42.
115. Ibid 1.13.2
116. Ibid 3.25.22.
117. Ibid 7.1.22-31.
118. Ibid2.1.10.
119. Ibid 2.1.11.
120. Ibid 2.1.6.
121. Ibid 2.1.5.
122. Ibid 2.1.15.
123. Ibid 12.5.2 -5.and 12.5.11-12.
124. Ibid 3.24.2
125. Ibid 3.24.36-37.
126. Ibid 3.25.15.
127. 3.25.17-19.
128. Ibid 3.25.21-27

129. Ibid 3.25.32-44.
130. Ibid 3.29.7-10.
131. Ibid 3.29.13.
132. Ibid 3.29.33-34.
133. Ibid 3.32.32
134. Ibid 3.32.34-36.
135. Ibid 7.5.23-24. These are the most famous important ways of devo tion to the Lord known as navdha bhakti
136. Ibid 7.5.30-32.
137. Ibid 7.5.38-47.
138. Ibid 7.6.1-18.
139. Ibid 7.8.1
140. Ibid 7.8.7-11.
141. Ibid 7.9.50
142. Ibid 7.9.55.
143. Ibid 11.11.29-31.
144. Ibid 11.11.34-41.
145. Ibid 11.19.19-24.
146. Ibid 11.11.15
147. Ibid 11.14.17
148. Ibid 11.11.21-23.
149. Ibid 11.14.29.
150. Ibid 12.13.12.
151. Ibid 12.13.15.
152. Ibid 12.13.16-17.
153. Ibid 1.1.3.
154. S.B Sutra verse 2.
155. Ibid verse 3. See also CU 2.23.2.
156. Ibid verse 5.

157. Ibid verse 6 and 7.
158. Ibid verse 10.
159. Ibid verse 12.
160. Ibid verse 15. See also BG 18.55.
161. Ibid verse 20.
162. Ibid verse 78 and 79.
163. Ibid verse 27and 28.
164. Ibid verses 83 and 84.See also BG 18.68.
165. Ibid Verse 56.
166. Ibid verse 59.
167. Ibid verse 58. See also BG 9.14, 15, 22,25to29.
168. Ibid verse 68.
169. Ibid verse 63.
170. Ibid verse 74.
171. Ibid Verse 46.
172. Ibid verse 84. See also BG 18.66.
173. Ibid Verse 85.
174. Ibid Verse 93.
175. Ibid Verses 95 and 96.
176. Ibid Verse 97.
177. Ibid verse 98.
178. Ibid verse 100.
179. NBS verse 2.
180. Ibid verse 4.
181. Ibid verse 7.
182. Ibid Verse 51
183. Ibid verse 52.
184. Ibid Verse 5.
185. Ibid verse 6.

186. Ibid Verse 54.
187. Ibid Verse 55.
188. Ibid Verses 8-14.
189. Ibid Verse 72.
190. Ibid Verse 73.
191. Ibid Verse 33.
192. Ibid Verse 28.
193. Ibid Verse 29.
194. Ibid verse 30.
195. Ibid verse 35.
196. Ibid Verse 36.
197. Ibid Verse 37.
198. Ibid Verse 38.
199. Ibid Verse 39-41.
200. Ibid Verse43-45.
201. Ibid Verse 63.
202. Ibid verse 64.
203. Ibid Verse 74.and 75.
204. Ibid Verse 76.
205. Ibid Verse 77.
206. Ibid verse 78.
207. BG 7.19
208. Ibid Verse 16-19.
209. Ibid Verses 58-59.
210. Ibid Verses 67-68.
211. Ibid Verse 82.
212. Nandalal Sinha, Bhakti sutras of Nārada, Motilal Manoharlal publishers, NewDelhi.Pxxii, 1998.

213. NBS Vrse 83.

214. Ibid Verse 84.

215. Madhusūdana Sarasvatī has written an elaborate commentary for this known as 'Siddhānta Bindu"

216. Misra A.P, The development and Place of Bhakti I Advaita Vedānta, Allahabad university, Preface pii, 1967.

217. Ibid. Foreword.

218. Ibid. P.158.

219. Ibid.P158.

220. Brahadāranyaka Upaniṣad 2.4.5 and 4.4.6.

221. Śivānada-lahari ,Verse 35.

222. Bhagavad- Gītā , verse 9.22.

223. Vivekacūdāmani , verse 31.

224. Ibid10.8.

225. Ibid .10.9.

226. Ibid. 10.10.

227. Ibid7.18.

228. Ibid11.55.

229. Ibid 8.22.

230. Misra,A.P. cf P124.

231. Bāla Krishnan S, Śaṅkara an Bhakti, Bharatiya Vidyabhvan, Mumbai. P90, 2000.

232. Ibid verse11.

233. Ibid verse 9.

234. BG. 6.47.

235. Śivānada-lahari, verse. 10.

236. Ibid verse 70.

237. Ibid verse 71.

238. Ibid verse 73.

239. Ibid verse 74.

240. Ibid Verse 6and 7.

241. Ibid verse 5.

242. Ibid verse 6.

243. Ibid verse 18

244. Ibid verse 76.

245. Ibid verse 84.

246. Ibid verse 85.

247. Ibid verse 80.

248. Ibid verse 81.

249. Ibid Verse 91. See also BG 18.73.

250. Ibid verse 20.

251. Saundaryalahai of śankarācārya with commentary ,Ganesh and co, Madras 1957

252. Ibid verse 21 commentary by Prof V.Krishnamuty.

253. The four types of liberation are (a.)Sālokya (Reaching the Loka (abode) of the deity worshipped).(b). Sāmipya (Staying in the presence or vicinity of the deity) (c). Sārūpya (Attaining the form or quality of the deity).(d). Sāyujya (Becoming one with the deity)

254. Rajagopalachari Bhajagovindam, Bharatiya Vidya Bhavan, Mumbai, page , 2011.

255. Bhajagovindam, Verse 1.

256. Ibid Verse 2.

257. Ibid verse 3.

258. Ibid verse 4.

259. Ibid Verse 5 to 8.

260. Ibid verse 9.

261. Ibid verse 10-15.

262. Ibid verse 19-20.

263. Ibid verse 21

264. Śrī Śaṅkarācārya, (Tr) saṁvid ,Prabhodasudhākara,Samatabooks, Madras.Section18,P70-80, 2002.

265. Ibid verse 244.

266. Ibid verses 251-257.

267. Gambhīrānanda Swāmī, V.K. Nov. 1920, P 440-447.

CHAPTER - 3

3. BHAKTI IN SRI BHAGVAD BHAKTI RASĀYANA

3.1 INTRODUCTION

Śrī Madhusūdana Sarasvatī is a prominent philosopher belonging to the Śaṅkara school of Advaita..

He is credited with writing an exclusive treatise on Bhakti ever written by an Advaitin entitled "ŚRĪ BHAGVAD BHAKTI RASĀYANA". (Here after mentioned as Bhakti Rasāyana). It is exclusively devoted to the devotion of Śrī Kṛṣṇa.

The following texts are available.

i) "Śrī Bhagavad Bhakti Rasāyana", with the original text and commentary in Sanskrit and a translation and commentary (in Hindi) by Sri Janārdan Śāstrī Pandey, published by Chowkamaba Vidyābhavan, Varanasi (2008).

ii). A translation and commentary (in Telugu) by Śrī Potukuchi Subramanian Śāstrī published by Sāḍhanā Grandha Mandali, Tenali in 1953 (2nd edition 2002).

iii). The book entitled "BhaktiRasāyana" with original verses in Sanskrit and commentary in Hindi; authored by Dr. Jayakumar Jha, published by Hemadri Prakashan, Delhi, 2013.

iv). A book in Sanskrit with the three ullāsas is reported to have been brought out by Śrī Goswāmī Dāmodara Śāstrī in the

Atchyuta Grandhamāla series, Varanasi with commentary of Madhusūdana and his own commentary of the of the other two in1934. However, this is not available for reference.

It is proposed to discuss the content of the text and bring out the devotional and Philosophical aspects in convenient sections. The work consists of three Ullāsas (a term used by aestheticians for chapters).

The first Ullāsa consists of 35 verses. It is significant to mention that the author himself has written a commentary (ṭīkā) in prose on the first Ullāsa only.It is named as Bhakti sāmānya nirūpaṇa meaning general characteristics of Bhakti. The second Ullāsa consists of eighty verses named as Bhakti viśeṣa nirūpaṇa, different varieties of devotion based on rasa theory and establishing Bhakti as a rasa but also as the most superior rasa with valid justification. The third Ullāsa consists of thirty verses named as Bhakti rasa nirūpaṇa..

It is proposed to analyze the content of the text and bring out the devotional and philosophical aspects in the following convenient sections. The text by Sri Janārdan Śāstrī Pandey is mainly followed for the discussion.

i) The analysis of the first Ullāsa.

ii) The analysis of the second Ullāsa.

iii) The analysis of third Ullāsa.

iv) Conclusion.

3.2 ANALYSIS OF THE FIRST ULLĀSA OF BHAKTI RASĀYANA

3.2.1 TITLE OF THE TEXT.

Title of the text Bhaktirasāyana is aptly chosen and can be understood as follows:

3.2.2.BHAKTI AS RASA:

The rasa is established with combination of Vibhāvana, Anubhāva and a catalyst called Sancāri bhāvas. When a stable state is established it will manifest as rasa. In case of Bhakti, God is both Vibhāvana and Anubhāva and the fragrance of Sandal paste and the Tulasi (Basil) leaves etc. items are Uddīpana. The combination produces cittavṛtti and remains stable, then manifest as rasa is Bhakti Rasa which is a blissful inexplicable experience of the devotee.

3.2.3.BHAKTI + RASĀYANA

Rasāyana, in Indian Ayurveda system of medicine is an elixir or tonic for cure of chronic disease. Bhakti acts like an elixir to cure the maladies of the people due to cycle of births and gain spiritual health.

3.2.4. BHAKTI RASA + AYANA

Ayana in Sanskrit means a path or course of progress (like Uttar Ayana of the Sun) and likewise a course of development in spiritual journey. The author has described the eleven progressive stages of development of Bhakti starting from association with and service to great people till the final consummation of love for God.

3.2.2 PRAYER AND INTRODUCTION

The first verse has described that devotion, either as a combination of the nine rasas or as only pure devotion in the form of Parā Bhakti (as a means of Liberation) to Śrī Kṛṣṇa can be aptly called Bhakti yoga. This devotion is an experience of incomparable bliss and is untouched by even a trace of sorrow. The author proposes to describe Bhakti in a systematic manner supported, by scriptural texts, to bring contentment to everyone.

The Mangalācaraṇa Verse (auspicious Verse at the beginning) also relates to devotion to BalaKṛṣṇa being worshipped by Śiva (Rudra) in his eleven forms. (Ten reflections in the toe nails of Kṛṣṇa as images and the eleventh is Rudra in person) who is bowing down at the lotus feet of Kṛṣṇa who is playing in the palace of Nanda, the yudukula chief.

3.2.3 MEANS OF LIBERATION

The author has made elaborate commentary on the first verse as follows:.

There are four yogas (disciplines or paths) called Karma yoga (yoga of performing disinterested actions), Aṣtānga yoga, Bhakti yoga and Jñāna yoga (the yoga of knowledge). The author mentions that the Aṣtānga yoga can be included in the Jñāna yoga.

The means of liberation, the highest goal of life, as told by Kṛṣṇa in Bhāgavata are viz. karma, Bhakti and Jñāna (knowledge) and no other way is found anywhere in the scriptures.

The Path of Jñāna is efficacious to those who have inherent dispassion. The path of action is effectual to those who hanker for the fruits of action and who has attachments for worldly desires.

However for a person who is neither disgusted with the pleasures of the senses nor deeply attached to them, who have by the stroke of good fortune a zeal for hearing and chanting of the Lord's names the path of Devotion brings success in the form of God realization.

The performing of duties enjoined in sāstras and disinterested actions (Karma) is prescribed till the mind is purified by getting rid of attachments to worldly objects, abstaining from doing prohibited acts and development of dispassion. In such a pure mind only, there is possibility for the practice of devotional disciplines and attaining knowledge of reality, or devotion to the Lord (which is considered superior to self-realization). The author declared that the one-pointed devotion (Ananaya Bhakti) to the Lord is the aim of the Jñāna-yoga and it cannot be achieved without Bhakti- yoga.

Mokṣa (liberation), which results in experience of bliss, is designated as the highest goal of life. The other goals of life are Dharma, Artha and Kāma. The author is of the opinion that Artha and Kāma are only means to bliss and they do not bring any bliss by themselves and refutes that Bhakti (devotion), which brings bliss should not be included as a goal of life. He mentioned that, once the mind is purified after performing actions, without attachments and gaining dispassion, there are only two paths to be chosen.

i). Jñāna yoga to those who have dispassion and whose minds are not melted, by the knowledge of reality.

ii). Bhakti yoga to those whose minds are melted and there is devotion, preceded by faith in spiritual disciplines prescribed by the Lord's devotees.

We therefore have to distinguish the mental attitudes of the persons that are capable of following the appropriate path suitable for them.

3.2.4 DEVOTION AS THE HIGHEST GOAL OF LIFE.

(Glories of the Lord and chanting His holy names)

The author categorically declares that devotion (Bhakti) is the highest goal of life (Paramapuruṣārtha). "The yoga of devotion is the highest Good of life beyond which there is nothing greater. Those who know its essence and those who have experienced it declare as such". This fact was also made clear in the first verse. The Ananya Bhakti which is developed with firm belief that there is no other than the Lord as the savior results in experience of Jñāna. The eternal bliss to be experienced by the mind is not possible in absence of Bhakti.

This assertion is in accordance with Bhāgavatapurāṇa will be in consonance with the Vaiṣṇava followers and other Bhakti schools of Vedānta. The Advaitins believe that Bhakti is an important means of Mokṣa which is the highest goal (Paramapuruṣārtha).

The scriptural authority quoted from Bhāgavatapurāṇa indicate that Bhakti is the means to the highest good and with devotion, what is possibly obtained through other means can be obtained more easily and quickly.

The author stresses that "Bliss unmixed with any trace of suffering is the highest goal" and that is devotion. The perfect happiness, bliss and God are synonymous terms and to obtain that devotion is a means. (The dictionary meaning of bliss is perfect happiness.)

Madhusūdana declares that devotion to the beloved Lord is the highest goal of life. "The experience of incomparable bliss without trace of sorrow or suffering" says Verse1. He thus refutes all notions that devotion is not included in the commonly accepted four goals of life.

He puts forth his firm conviction that only bliss is to be the goal of life like the bliss of perfect meditation. So like meditation, bliss of devotion can be included as a goal of life. The author concludes that if it is not included, then devotion can independently qualify as the highest goal of life. The various scriptural verses are mentioned in support of the arguments by way of kāraṇavyutpatti and BhāvaVyutpatti. He has tried to establish that devotion will be instrumental in worshipping God. Kāraṇa means which will be a means. Bhakti is instrument to serve the Lord.

The author states that *"Bhajte,sevyati,bhagavadākaram antahkarna kriyate. Anaya"* Meaning that devotion to God will make the internal organ (mind, intelligence and ego) take the form of the Lord. Śaṅkara has also mentioned in Vivekacūdamanī that Bhakti is the most important ingredient in achieving Mokṣa.

Bhakti means to serve the Lord, to worship and get the internal organ (which has mind, Buddhi, cittam and Ahamkāra (Ego) purified and completely absorbed in God.

In case of devotion to Kṛṣṇa the mind will be fully occupied by Kṛṣṇa. Buddhi will think of Kṛṣṇa only and even ego will be Kṛṣṇa which means that all the functions are done as only intended for Kṛṣṇa. Thus the internal organ will be overwhelmed with Kṛṣṇa consciousness.

The devotee imagining that he himself is Brahman as meant by the following Upaniṣadic verses.

i). 'Tattvamasi' - Sāma Veda 'Thou art that.'

ii). *'Prajñānam Brahma' -Ṛg Veda 'conscious is Brahman'.*

iii). *'Aham Brahmāsmi' – Yajur Veda "I am Brahman."*

iv). *'Ayam* ātmā *Brahmā'- Atharva Veda "Brahman is this self."*

Thus the sādhaka meditating and contemplating that he himself is Brahman is called Brahmavidya.

3.2.5 BHAKTI -YOGA- BHAKTI IS BHAGAVĀNA

The definition of Bhakti as given in Bhāgavata-purāṇa is as follows and was adopted by Madhusūdana.

'The uninterrupted flow of the mind stream towards Me, dwelling in the minds of all,-like the water in the Gaṇgā towards the ocean, at the mention of My virtues, combined with motiveless and unremitting love to Me , the Supreme person, is spoken as the distinguishing character of unqualified Bhakti-yoga'.[1]

Rukmini.T.S has observed as follows:

'MS identifies Bhakti results in is same as Bhagavān. His definition itself conveys the same. Bhakti is a state, due to intense devotion the mind melts and flows towards God, who is reflected in the mind. '*Tanmayattva*' is achieved and the mind which is full of Bhakti becomes now fully enveloped by God. Bhagavān is the same as Bhakti'.[2]

The author has stated that if the mind is directed exclusively with one pointed concentration towards God, the same devotion will gradually be experienced as Knowledge. Anannyā Bhakti is the object of the knowledge and without devotion it is not possible. In such a one pointed devotion, there is no other object except the all-pervading supreme person.[3]

3.2.6 BHAKTI AND BRAHMA VIDYA.

Bhakti is the transformation of mind and it takes the form of the Lord, when the mind has melted and obtains the permanent state. The mind of the devotee, due to constant hearing of the holy names of the Lord, remains absorbed in meditation but the duality of the meditator and the object of meditation remains. The result is unconditional love for the Lord in abundance. This can happen to an aspirant whose mind melts on hearing the sweet glories of the Lord.

The aspirant enjoys the inexplicable bliss.

This can be practiced by anybody without any distinction of caste, gender, age or any other considerations and at all times,, but one must nourish love for the Lord with faith and without any motive.

The aspirant who has chosen knowledge after purification of mind approaches a teacher and by the practice of Śravaṇa, manana and Nididhyāsana and developing Vairāgya, identifies himself with Brahman as mentioned in Upaniṣadic verses. Thus the devotee, dissolves himself and identifying with the non-difference between self and the supreme self attains liberation or Mokṣa.

"AHAM BRAHMASMI", "SOHAM BRAHMASMI".

The knowledge to obtain this type of consciousness is called "Brahmavidyā". In the previous discussion it was made clear that devotion to the Lord is knowledge of Brahman. Thus, Bhakti and Brahmavidya are not identical.

Madhusūdana Sarasvatī considers Bhakti as the other name of Brahmavidyā by stating *"NĀMĀNTAREṆA BRAHMAVIDYEVABHAGAVAD BHAKTI RITI"*

3.2.7 DISTINCTION OF DEVOTION FROM BRAHMA VIDYĀ

The two i.e. Brahmavidyā and devotion are distinct in nature and in their means, ends and qualifications. The same are detailed in the chart shown below:

		Devotion	Brahma Vidyā
1.	Nature	It is a conditioned mental mode, the mind taking the form of blessed Lord in the melted state.	unconditioned mental mode whose objective is the non-dual self
2.	Means	The hearing of glories of the Lord.	Great saying of Upaniṣads like "Thou art that"
3.	End result/ Fruit	Abundance of unconditional love for the Lord.	Cessation of (avidya) Ignorance which is cause of all evil.
4.	Eligibility	All are eligible without discrimination of caste/ gender/ stage of life etc. only love for God without any desires.	i) Renunciation of highest degree and practice of fourfold means (Sādhana-Catustaya) Discrimination of Real & unreal. ii) Absence of desire for enjoyment of fruits of action in this and other world. iii) Śama, dama, uparati, titīkṣā, Samādhāna,Śraddhā iv) Mumūkṣutva.

Brahmavidyā is an unconditioned modification of mind, which is in an inflexible state and comprehends the non-dual reality or Brahman. The state of mind is known as Nirvikalpa- manovṛtti. The Avidyā or nescience is destroyed and thus there is eradication of all the causes of sufferings and the aspirant experiences inexplicable bliss.

Bhakti is a modification of the melted mind, also called Saviklapa manovṛtti, and the mind is filled with the reflection of the image of the Lord. The love for Kṛṣṇa intensifies and reaches the climax stage. The aspirant experiences bliss. There is still duality of devotee and the deity. Bhakti it is bound by the limitation, where as in case of Brahmavidyā it is unbounded. The devotion results in the experience of the bliss of Paramapuruṣārtha which is obtained through Brahmavidya. This has the scriptural support of Bhāgavatapurāṇa.[4]

The commentary on first verse is concluded by equating the Devotion and Brahmavidyā, and stating that both will bring bliss.

3.2.8 THE OBJECTIVE OF THE TEXT

People in general are suffering due to afflictions with severe illness and worldly miseries, due to ignorance indulge in mundane attractions. The cessation of the cycle of births and deaths, alone can give them radical relief from this suffering. The elixir of Bhakti now being told, may be relished and consumed abundantly as it is the most effective medicine for a lasting remedy for the afflictions. The wise are advised to consume this BhaktiRasāyana abundantly to their contentment.[5]

3.2.9. BHAKTI AND CITTAVṚTTI

Brahman is sat, cit, Ānanda. He is Truth, Eternal and ever blissful, an indefinable tattva. The Śṛuti mentioned that Brahman is embodiment of rasa. -*"Raso vai saḥ"*

Only devotion (Bhakti) and none else can make the internal organ to take the form of the blessed Lord. Only by contemplation, devotion can completely melt the internal organ. The melted internal organ by devotion to God, takes the form of the blessed Lord and manifests as rasa. Taking the shape of the container is the inherent quality of liquids.

Similarly the devotion melts the internal organ and in that state the mind takes the form of the Lord. The great realised saints also delight in devotion to the Lord even while living as "Jīvanmukta" for the same reason.

3.2.10 NATURE OF MIND AND MODIFICATION IN MELTING STATE.

The mind is by nature hard like lac. When a heating element comes in contact, Lac. tends to melt, similarly if the mind whole heartedly contemplates God, the mind starts melting[6].

Note: The author adopted the theory of rasa in explaining the process (refer chapter 7)

Similarly other mundane emotions like kāma, krodha, bhaya, harṣa, sneha, sorrow, acting as causes for heating, melts the mind. If these subside the mind comes back to its normal state of hardness[7].

The mind in its melted state, taking the shape of the cause of melting, is seen above and this modification is called Cittavṛtti. Even after the emotion that caused Cittavṛtti, ceases to exist, it remains as a Vāsanā (as a past impression) and its remembrance is revived whenever there is occasion to recall it[8]. In respect of devotion, if the Cittavṛtti gets fixed as a permanent state, it is called Niṣthā or Samādhi.

The devotee in whom this permanent state of emotion is established will be able to visualize God in all things and all things established in Him. He is a supreme devotee[9]. The qualities of such devotees are mentioned in Bhāgavata-purāṇa[10].

The mind takes the shape of the cause of melting and if the modification has become stable, then it is called Sthāyībhāva. This Sthāyībhāva is obtained by combination of the Vibhāva, Anubhāva and Sancāribhāva. The mind will experience rati (pleasure, happiness, fear etc.) and this Sthāyībhāva will manifest as rasa and will be experienced is called Rasa[11].

Bhagavān is an embodiment of unbounded bliss, if he enters the melted mind as a reflection, the aspirants in whose mind the Lord enters and attains a stable state called Sthāyībhāva and which manifests as a most blissful state attain rasa. The Lord is Ālambana and Vibhāvana and His image is the Sthāyībhāva. Thus Bhakti rasa is all blissful[12].

In the mundane Śṛiṅgārarasa the Sthāyībhāva is rati and the lover and her beloved are the Ālambana and Vibhāvana (are the cause and effect). The result is Rati. Thus Ālambana and Vibhāvana are two separate entities[13].

However in case of Bhakti Rasa, the result is experiencing bliss the reflection of Bhagavān in the melted mind and the cause for it is also the same Bhagavān. It is explained that the cause and effect are the same due to Māyā, the potency of the Lord[14]. Brahman is Sat –Cit- Ānanda and is self-effulgent, but the doubt is why he is not cognized like that. This is due to āvaraṇa Śakti (Power of concealment) the power of Māyā śakti. The original Image is called the proto type is *Bimba* and the reflection in the melted mind is *Pratibimba*. The *Bimba* and *Pratibimba* are same. Once the Lord enters the mind it takes the form of the Lord and is called *'Bhagadākārata'.* The mind remaining in that state is said to be its nature. It will not become hard any more.

3.2.11. BHAKTI RASA IS THE SUPREME RASA

The ever blissful, Bhagavān who is sat-cit-Ānanda or pure consciousness when reflected in the mind in the modified melted status, a permanent emotion and sentiment will manifest as Bhakti Rasa which is full of Supreme bliss will be experienced by the aspirant.

Even if the modification of mind by melting due to worldly acts like Śṛiṅgārarasa (erotic love) resulting in the sentiment of bliss (Rasa). But the bliss is a very insignificant fraction of the bliss compared to the abundance of the bliss due to manifestation of the Lord, who is a mass of unlimited bliss and consciousness. Thus the author declared the devotional sentiment as the supreme sentiment. The Sāṅkhya school of philosophy also concludes that gradation of bliss is as per the mixture of various qualities and so same degree of bliss is not expressed in every sentiment[15].

The possibility of the difference in characteristic of Cittavṛtti is also mentioned and pain, joy and delusion manifest in a single person, in accordance with the proportion of the composition of Tāmasa, Rajas and Sāttvika guṇas.[16] The objection of the Nyāyā School is that due to the atomic dimension of mind, the melting and its taking shape of the lord is not tenable. The objection has been refuted stating that the mind is all pervasive, '*Vibhūtvam*'.

The mind is composite and is capable of expanding and taking the shape of the stimulus for melting and taking shape of the object and also retain the vāsanā (Semblance of remembrance). Mind will manifest objects (quoting the verses from Vedānta Paribhāṣa). The impression of the object captured in mind remaining undestroyed is called permanent emotion[17]. By various means it was established that whatever is impressed in the mind is of permanent impression and even if the external object changes or even destroyed, the mind recalls whatever is stored in it

The Lord has four supreme qualities:

i). Vibhūtvam: means all-pervading or omnipresent.
ii). Nitya: means eternal (exists at all times)
iii). Purṇa: He is without second (He is substratum of duality)

He is consciousness and bliss.

Thus Bhagavān is the highest goal of life (Parama Puruṣārtha).If such a glorious lord's image enters in the melted mind of the devotee, all extraneous objects that entered the mind from times immemorial will be destroyed (non-else can remain there) and He alone shines in the mind. He sees himself established in all creatures, as in the lord (him-self and sees all creatures established in his own self as the divine soul). The mind takes the form of the Lord (Bhaga-vadākāratā). Henceforth there is no scope of any extraneous things entering in the mind.

For a devotee who experiences this bliss of Bhakti Rasa, there is nothing else that can be cherished. The contemplation of the oneness with Lord and experiencing that state is the highest objective of the Bhakti-yoga.

In the commentary we find that the Bhakti-yoga as mentioned in the Bhāgavatapurāṇa has been highlighted at several places. [18]

In Bhagavad-Gītā it was told that through Bhakti (devotion) men get Brahma jñāna, "know 'Me' in reality as to what and who I am that after that knowledge, they enter me".[19]

The hard mind cannot grasp anything, a slightly modified mind grasps and retain as image.[20]

In order to melt the mind, certain emotions conducive for the melting are needed which are absent in the above two states. In case of a person who does not grasp these emotions and acquires knowledge, such knowledge is called indifferent knowledge. A man who does not exhibit any emotion like joy, hatred or any other is called emotionless and his mind remains hard. So hardness of mind even in respect of the Lord is condemned as stone hearted and cannot be purified[21]

The following emotions (bhāvas) are illustrated as conductive for stimulating the melting of the mind.

i) Stamba (Motionless)
ii) Sveda (Perspiration)
iii) Romānca (Hair standing on end)
iv) Svarabheda: Vibration of Tone (hoarse voice)
v) Vivarṇa (becoming pale or change of colour of the face)
vi) Asuru (Tears)
vii) Pralaya (Fainting)
viii) Vipatu (shivering)[22].

The wise (practitioner of devotion) should constantly strive, in accordance with scriptural prescriptions, to ensure means of keeping the mind in melted state to words God and hardness towards the worldly objects. The objective of all scriptures is to secure the form of the image of the Lord in the mind of devotee[23].

NATURE OF THE MIND

Just as the coolness of water, and hotness of fire are natural characteristics, the cherished objects might have entered the melted mind and been established there since a long time and this appears to be a natural feature of the mind. This is due to the objects coming in contract with the sense organs. However the mind giving room to be filled with worldly objects is not its inherent nature. This is explained as follows. The mind in dream state assumes the form of objects and produce latent impressions within it. However mind in deep sleep state is devoid of such objects. It is thus concluded that only in the dissolution state the nature of the mind can be known.[24]

The inherent nature of the mind is having the form of the Lord. The eternal Lord is dwelling in every self and is the inner controller. The Lord is all pervading and is the substratum of the incomprehensible Māyā which has several powers including being the subtle cause of the world. The pot being filled with ether is its nature, but when filled with water it is displaced by the water (which is an external cause). Similarly the inherent nature of the mind is to take the form of the all-powerful Lord.

However, the Lord inherent in mind does not prevent other extraneous matters entering it. The scriptures are the vital source to ensure the prevention of the mind taking a form other than the form of Bhagavān.

Through the practice of Sravana, manana and Nididhyāsana, the impurities can be destroyed and the mind gets completely purified. The Bhāgavatapurāṇa confirms this "Just as the Light of the Sun shines to clear eyes, so the Truth of the self is directly revealed to the pure heart of the man who is earnestly devoted to the Lord and intensely desires to obtain His holy feet and the mind free from the impurities both of qualities and actions".[25] Just as gold gets purified and getting its shine when melted in a furnace, the mind gets purified by means of devotion to the Lord. [26]

The mind of a man dwelling on objects of senses gets attached to them. The mind entangled in material qualities makes the man of crude nature. A man contemplating on God gets absorbed in Him alone. So a man should give up the thought of the unreal and worthless objects of the world and concentrate the mind purified by devotion to God, as mentioned in Bhāgavatapurāṇa[27].

It was pointed out that the extraneous objects which imprint their forms are not distinct from the lord as they are superimposed on Him. All things arise out of Lord within in Him and dissolve into Him alone. The conclusion is that which is superimposed is annulled by the knowledge of the substratum.[28] The Love, even diverted towards other objects is in reality fixed on the Lord (As there is nothing different in awareness.)

One could firmly establish through such reasoning, that the blessed Lord is non-dual self, a mass of perfect being, consciousness and bliss, the substratum of all. Thus one could acquire mastering of viewing the experiencing of the worldly objects as insignificant as objects in a dream state. Thus a great sense of non- attachment arises.

Non-attachment is of three kinds (i) Mṛudu (mild.), (ii) Tīvra (intense) and (iii) Tīvratara (Very intense).

3.2.12 NATURE OF KNOWLEDGE

It is only through higher degree of non-attachment (because higher non-attachment cannot exist without knowledge) and knowledge, together with dispassion and concentration of mind duly cultivated for the attainment of supreme Love for the blessed Lord is possible.

The knowledge is briefly stated as follows

i). The only reality that exists is the blessed Lord, everything else is false, all else is pain, sorrow, suffering and transient.

(ii) The blissful Lord is self-luminous, omnipresent and eternal. To know this truth is called Jñāna or knowledge. The Jñānī, the man of knowledge is dear to the Lord as told in Bhagavad-Gītā. Vāsudeva is the only reality as he is Paramātman and everything else is false and is the product of Illusionary Power (Māyā).

3.2.13 NATURE OF DEVOTION

A man of knowledge resorts to complete detachment and dispassion from material world realizing that they are transient and false. Thus having obtained the knowledge of reality and developed highest detachment from transient worldly pleasures, one should know the nature of devotion and practice spiritual disciplines.

The nature of devotion is explained briefly. 'One should fix his mind, free from all impurities and with concentration, contemplating omnipresent Brahman and should retire from all activity. If the aspirant is unable to fix his mind irrevocably on Brahman, do all his allotted duties efficiently in a disinterested spirit for The Lord's sake and listening with reverence His stories'.

The aspirant has to approach a good teacher (who is learned and well versed in the knowledge of scriptures, who is self-realized), by worshiping the teacher as God. One has to learn Bhagavat Dharma, how to obtain contentment of Ātman free from illusion and how God will be pleased. (God who is self of all and gives Himself to His devotee)

Learning the practices followed by the devotees of the Lord and practicing the various disciplines, observing moral principles, learning to sing the glories of the Lord and developing love for the Lord, one can easily cross over the Māyā which is otherwise formidable[29].

The means of devotion and how he was blessed by the Lord with self-knowledge which he has acquired in his previous birth were narrated by Sage Nārada to Sage Vedavyāsa[30].The author has in the same way narrated the eleven stages of bhakti with some modifications as the appropriate means of practice of devotion as specified in the scriptures.

3.2.14 THE ELEVEN STAGES OF DEVOTIONAL PRACTICE

The Eleven stages of devotional practices in accordance with the scriptural prescriptions were explained to enable the aspirant for easy comprehension and practice in the last few verses of the first Ullāsa. All these are described in detail with copious quotations and experiences of the devotees from Bhāgavatapurāṇa. They are concisely discussed below.

The Bhāgavatapurāṇa it was Nārada who told his experience of his earlier life how he acquired devotion to the lord and with the Grace of the Lord he could now became the most favored devotee was narrated to Vedavyāsa and encouraged him to write praising the greatness of the Lord and the result is Bhāgavatapurāṇa

Madhusūdana has but with some modifications described the stages of Bhakti beginning from service to Great men to the pinnacle stage of acquiring the beatitude. These eleven stages can be treated as the core of the Bhakti text. The eleven stages are as follows.

i) **Mahatāṁseva;** (Service to Great men).
ii) **Tatdayapāttrata..**(Acquisition of their grace)
iii) **Śraddhātha teṣam Dhrmeṣu.**(Developing taste for devotional practices.
iv) **HariGuṇa Śtuti.** (Praising Holy name of the Lord**).**
v) **Ratyaṃkurotpati (**Sprouting of deep love towards the Lord)
vi) **Svarūpādhigati (**Realisation of the identity of self as Brahman).
vii) **Premavṛuddhiḥ parānade (**Increase in intensity of devotion)
viii) **Tasyātha Sphuranṇm tataḥ** (Revelation of Bhagavān)
ix) **Bhaagavat Dharma NiṢtah. (**Absorption in the service of Bhagavān
x) **Bhagavadguṇa** sālitā.. **(**Manifesting the majesty of Bhagavān.
xi) **Prema Paramākasṭa. (**Reaching the climax of the Divine Love)

3.2.14.1 SERVICE TO GREAT MEN (Mahatāṁsevā)

This service to God is of two ways.

i). **The service to the devotees of God:** To get the association of the devotees of God.[31] (Who are pious devotees of God) is itself very difficult[32]. One can serve them and keenly observe and learn the practice of devotion and get initiated into devotional practice. The Lord has told that several men who have not studied any scriptures and not meditated have attained Him by fellowship of saints[33].

ii). **Service to God:** By mere love and with intense devotion any one can get attachment to the Lord and attain Him. By renouncing and cessation of all activity and surrendering to the Lord (who is self in all embodied souls) one can attain the Lord[34].

3.2.14.2 ACQUISITION OF THE GRACE OF THE GREAT (TAD DAYĀ PĀTRATĀ)

The devotee, with pure heart and sincere service can attain the grace of the great men. This grace is of two types.

a). **That has to be obtained through self-effort:** The aspirant has to make effort by getting inspiration from revered people and serve the great men and when they are pleased they will grant their grace. The approach of Dhruva to Nārada is a classic example[35].

b). **Granted Voluntarily by Great Men:** The great men when they are pleased with the interest evinced by the men and their behavior grant their grace to the aspirant on their own. The obtaining of grace from great saints by Nārada is a classic example.[36]

3.2.14.3 DEVELOPING TASTE AND DEDICATION TO DEVOTIONAL PRACTICES (ŚRADDHĀTHA TEṢĀṂ DHARMEṢU)

The aspirant by association with great men listens to the stories of the Lord and starts to relish them. The mind gets freed from the worldly attractions and reduces it Tāmasic and Rājasic qualities.He acquires a liking for chanting the holy names of the Lord and singing the glories of the Lord practices the Bhāgavata dharma with dedication.[37]

The aspirant after developing taste for devotional practice has to attempt to cultivate dedication to sing praises of the Lord by his own.

3.2.14.4 PRAISING HARI'S HOLY NAMES AND ALL HIS ATTRIBUTES (HARI GUṆA ŚTUTĪ)

With perfection of the practice of devotion, steadfastness in devotion will be established and the aspirants will become free from desires. The practice of nine-fold devotional discipline given in Bhāgavatapurāṇa [38]as per once ability is advised.

i) Śravaṇa (hearing the names and stories of the Lord)
ii) Kīrtana (Chanting the Lord's names)
iii) Smaraṇa (remembering)
iv) Padasevana (Divine service)
v) Arcana (worshipping)
vi) Vandana (salutations)

vii) Dāsyam (servant ship)
viii) Sakhya (comradeship)
ix) Ātma samarpana (self-dedication)

The quintessence of devotional practice is given in theses verses. A devotee may practice any one or all of them as per his capacity.

3.2.14.5 SPROUTING OF LOVE TOWARDS GOD (RATYAṂKUROTPATTÍ)

With the practice of the four preceding stages of devotion, the seed of such practice starts sprouting in the devotee. This is actually the beginning of true devotion. The aspirant has to practice with full faith from this sprouting stage and nurse the seedlings, grow gradually to become a large tree flowering and fruiting stage with utmost care. The devotee will experience joy at every stage[39].

3.2.14.6 REALISATION OF IDENTITY OF SELF AS BRAHMAN (*SVARŪPADHIGATI)*

This is a very crucial stage. This is direct realization of the essential nature of the inner self (pratyagātman) as distinct from gross and subtle body[40].

The spirit is eternal, free from decay, taintless, non-dual, changeless, all pervading, self-effulgent, un-attached and has no sheath of Māyā. One should, with the help of these transcendent characteristics of the self, give up the false notion of 'I' and 'mine'. This stage is the same as that of acquiring knowledge of Brahman, the realisation of which is the highest goal of Advaita philosophy. The Bhāgavata-purāṇa says that the supreme self and all-pervading Lord, for the good of the world, appears as though he is invested in a body (through His deluding power)[41].

3.2.14.7 INCREASE IN INTENSITY OF DEVOTION (PREMA-VṚDDHI)

By this type of knowledge, the intensity of Bhakti is further intensified by continuing the practice of Bhakti- yoga. The relationship with Bhagavān Śrī Kṛṣṇa through devotion speedily awakens dispassion and immediate knowledge[42]. The devotee will visualize that the whole world is full of Kṛṣṇa. The devotee is overwhelmed with the thought of Viṣṇu. He exhibits peculiar behavior, by sometimes crying, sometimes laughing. He will not be conscious of self[43]. The devotee imagining himself as the Lord, completely merge in Him, imitates His doings[44].

3.2.14.8 DIRECT REVELATION OF BHAGAVAT (BHAGAVAT SPHURAṆAṂ)

The preceding seven stages are considered as practice with effort by the devotee. From this stage onwards devotion considered as spontaneously obtained, without any effort, by virtue of the practice of the earlier stages.

The devotees of the Lord ever delight in the service of the Lord and are engaged in activities only for His sake. They do not even crave for absorption in Him. The hearing of His stories, the knowledge of the glory of the Lord is pleasing to their heart as well as ears[45].

3.2.14.9 ABSORPTION IN STEADFASTNESS IN DEVOTION (*BHAGAVADDHARMA NIṢṬHĀ*)

The devotee who is completely absorbed in service and devotion of God will realize that all the worldly objects and achievements are mere illusion and attains the total *nissangatvam* or dispassion will be experienced. The devotee filled with longing for the lord absorbed himself in devotion to the Lord. He offers his mind, body and word to the service of the Lord.

The royal sage Ambarīṣa is a classic example of this type of devotion. He propitiated Śrī Hari with devotion coupled with asceticism as well as sacred duties and gave up all attachment[46].

3.2.14.10 DEVOTEE MANIFESTING THE MAJESTY OF BHAGAVĀNA (*BHAGAVADGUṆA ŚĀLITĀ*)

The devotee who is totally absorbed in God's service and internally absorbed with His thoughts only, will manifest the majesty of the Lord and his imperishable qualities. The devotee considers the Lord as his friend, teacher and cherished God. 'Beholding Me –the self-effulgent sprit dwelling in the heart of all beings,-in your own heart through intellect, you will be freed from all sorrow and attain the fearless state(-Final beatitude)'.[47]

3.2.14.11 THE SUPREME STATE OF DEVOTION (PREMA PARAMĀKĀṢṬHĀ)

This eleventh stage is the climax of the devotional practice or divine love, attained by practicing the successive stages of devotion to the lord. He will be filled with superabundance of loving devotion. He reaches a stage where he cannot imagine even a momentary separation from the Lord which experience continues as long as he is alive.

The lover constantly and continuously visualizes the beloved and feel blissful. They see the beloved everywhere and in all things to the extent that they lose their identity. The Gopīs felt supreme experience of joy in the presence of Kṛṣṇa and even a single moment of separation hung heavy on them as hundreds of yugas[48]. The Gopīs felt every moment of separation as long as myriad years and felt as miserable as the eyes without the Sun[49].

The similar feeling of the devotee has been mentioned in Nārada Bhakti Sūtras[50]. The devotee feels self-consecrated to the Lord with deep attachment. This culminates in parama-viraha or extreme separation. This is a piquant stage although the devotee is permanently united with the Lord, still feels as if he were separated from Him. This can be called parama or pure prema-rati or supreme love, which results in consummation of devotional practice and is the immediate cause of release.

The author concluded about this stage as the feeling of separation through intense love for the Lord (Vipralambha śṛingāra).

The general observation is that the author has not specifically mentioned whether the devotee is identified with Lord or any sort of distinction still remains between the devotee and the Lord. (Which is the belief of Vaiṣṇava schools). The mention of vipralambha indicates the absence of the beloved, the lover naturally experiences pain in separation, feels the immense sorrow of separation. However, due to continuous and uninterrupted contemplation on the beloved internally feels the bliss. The lover sees the beloved in all and the increased intensity to the extent she forgets herself in him and achieves emotional unity. Thus the devotee although emotionally realizes the identity with the God, actually the duality continues till the end.

Bhagavad-Gītā conveys this phenomenon in Bhakti yoga[51]. The meditation well established in the aspirant, it ceases to be mere meditation. It acquires the character of perception. When the supreme object of meditation becomes the object of perception, hankering is transformed as apprehension immediate and direct, meaning intuitive understanding or perception on a direct and immediate level.

3.3.1 BASIC TERMINOLOGY AND DETAILS OF CONCEPT OF RASA

Before proceeding to analysis of the second Ullāsa the understanding of the following brief points about the rasa theory will facilitate clarity of the contents.

The Sanskrit word 'rasa' fundamentally means, 'taste' or 'flavour 'or 'relish'. In metaphorical sense it refers to "the emotional experience of beauty in poetry and drama". According to Bharata, rasa or 'sentiment' is the mental condition of delectation produced in the spectator of a play or the reader of a poem as an inevitable reaction to the bhāvas or emotions manifested by the characters. He gives a detailed account of eight different rasas or 'sentiments'. They are as follows:

i) Śṛingāra (erotic love)
ii) *Vīra* (Heroic)
iii) *Karuṇa* (compassion)
iv) *Hāsya* (the comic)
v) *Raudra* (Furious)
vi) *Bhayānaka* (Terrible)
vii) *Bibhatsa* (the odious)
viii) *Adbhuta* (Marvelous)

It has been mentioned that no single word or phrase is adequate to convey the total meaning of rasa. It is actually, the impression created on the mind of the sympathetic audience by the expression of bhāvas or 'emotions' and is an experience the individual is subjected to on account of these expressions. Bhāva is the emotion that creates the enjoyment or experience and that enjoyment or experience is rasa.

There are three types of bhāvas ('emotions') namely

a) Sthāyī-bhāvas (pervading emotions). The emotions that are retained in the minds of audience till rasa is created are called Sthāyī-bhāvas.

There are eight such Sthāyībhāvas.They areas follows.

i).Rati(love) (ii). Hasa(laughter), (iii). Krodha(anger) (iv). Bhaya(-fear) (v).Soka(sorrow) (vi).Utsaha (heroism) (vii) Jugupsa (disgust) (viii) Vismaya(Astonishment)

b) Sancāri-bhāvas or also called Vyabhicāri-bhāvas (transitory emotions).The passing emotions that contribute in creation of rasa.

Three are thirty six Sancāribhāva stated by Bharata .

c) Sattvika-bhāvas ('Responsive emotions"). The physical involuntary expressions that manifest themselves as a result of the intensity of emotion in the mental plane. There are eight such Sattvika-bhāvas.

The realisation of rasa results from the union of the three elements- Vibhāva, Anubhāva and Saṅcāri-bhāva. As rasa is manifested out of Sthāyībhāva there will be as many rasas as there are Sthāyībhāvas.

The root cause or the excitement that creates the emotion is called Vibhāva or the 'determinant'. So the Vibhāva is the cause and Anubhāva is the effect or 'consequent'. It is to be noted that although the Vibhāva and Anubhāva incorporate the word Bhāva it may be noted that they are not bhāvas. They are intimately connected. The Bhāvas when expressed must be natural with their roots in the actual happenings in the world.

The Nātyaśāstra explains that rasa (sentiment) is produced by the union of the determinants, Vibhāvana and the consequent Anubhāvana and the transitory emotion (sancāri./vyabhicāri bhāva).They are categorized as two classes. The Vibhāvana and Anubhāvana are fundamental (like the lover and the beloved) and there can be no rasa without them. There are two types of Vibhavas (i)Ālambana. (ii)The second is 'Uddipana' which will contribute to the determinants (such as cool breeze, place like garden, moon light, the fragrance of flowers etc for Śṛingāra rasa.)The purpose is to foster the sentiments that arise.

However the emphasis on the essential element for producing rasa is the sthāyī-bhāva.[52]

(**Kindly refer to the theory of rasa(appended at the end**)

3.3.2 ANALYSIS OF SECOND ULLĀSA

The second Ullāsa consists of 80 verses. The general characteristics of Bhakti were discussed in the First Ullāsa and in the second Ullāsa the special characteristics of Bhakti have been described.

The mind by nature, is hard and it requires some stimulation that will excite heat and causes its melting. The mind takes the form of the cause of its melting and thus mind receives the image of the cause. If the cause of melting of mind relates to divine, the mind takes the form of the Lord. If this form of mind is stabilized, it is called Sthāyī-bhāva. This permanent sentiment is called Bhakti. It is also a mental modification or Cittavṛtti. Nine such causes were mentioned in the first Ullāsa. These causes are mutually different and so the Bhakti from them also will be different.

3.3.3 DIFFERENT CAUSES FOR MELTING OF MIND

The following are the causes that melt the mind. Kāma (Love), Krodha (wrath), Bhaya (Fear), sneha (affection), Harṣa (joy/delight), Śoka (sorrow), dayā (compassion), Vairāgya (dispassion)[53].

i) KĀMA (Erotic love)

The intense desire involving physical contact is called Kāma.It is of two types. One is where the desired object is physically present called Saṁbhoga, and the second is where the object is physically absent called (vipralambha)[54]. They manifest as Saṁbhoga- bhāva rati and Vipralambha bhāva rati.

ii) KRODHA (ANGER OR WRATH)

Anger is an emotion which may be due to jealousy, which may be due to fear or loss of security. The cause may be (a) The destruction of the cause or (b) Love for the object of the cause[55].

iii) BHAYA (FEAR)

Fear and hatred are associated with the rati and they are not pure. The anger on account of love for the object is being hated by others can generate indirect benefit of rati[56].

iv) SNEHA (Affection)

The relation between son and father, wife and Husband (nature of protector), between a servant and his master (friendship with reverence) are its examples. It can be dāsya, ruler/ruled or loving relationship. Sneha can generate Dayā Rasa, Vātsalya rasa or Preyo rasa[57].

v) HARṢA (Joy/ delight)

Everyone feels joy and happiness when the object desired is achieved. There are four varieties of Harṣa. The most superior is "*Paramānanadamaya harṣa*" That gives the immense pleasure of hearing the greatness of the God's glories and obtaining knowledge of His greatness. The mind always remembering the glories of the blissful Lord will melt. The rati manifested there is pure and unmixed with any other emotion and is considered as supreme. This is considered as the fulfillment of all Sāḍhanā (practices) and no other sādhana is required.[58]

The other types of Harṣa are the (i) Hāsa: Example; The naughty behavior, teasing words and mischievous action of Kṛṣṇa towards Gopīs causes a feeling of blushing shyness and joy to the Gopīs.(ii) Vismaya (wonder):The actions of young Kṛṣṇa trying to eat clay from the ground, lifting of mountain effortlessly and other superhuman qualities bring astonishment and joy.(iii) Utsāha(Excitement.)The heroic deeds of Kṛṣṇa like killing Pūtanā and other demons causes astonishment.

vi) ŚOKA (SORROW)

The separation from the loved person/object causes mental agony and is called śoka or sorrow. The melted mind due to this emotion results in śoka rati[59].

vii) DAYĀ (COMPASSION)

A sense of pity drives a person's desire to protect a person in distress and it is called Dayā (compassion).This is of three types-

a) ***Dānotsāha***: Enthusiastically offering charity generously in abundance[60].
b) ***Dayotsāha***: Offering assurance of protection enthusiastically[61].
c) ***Dharmotsāha***: Intention to voluntarily to uphold his Śvadharma (prescribed duty)[62]

viii) VAIRĀGYA

A person showing a sense of disinterestedness to all the objects of mundane enjoyment and also aversion towards them is called Vasikāravairāgya. The mind melts by this mode and the modification in this state is called 'śama'[63].

The mundane rasas do not qualify to be considered as Bhaktirasa as the Ālambana, Vibhāvana aspects of them do not relate to devotion[64]. In a similar manner the hatred on account of fear and envy, although may be related to divine do not qualify to be considered as rasa, since there can be no melting of mind and further essential conditions for establishing rasa[65]. The śuddḥā Raudram and the other categories of Raudram also cannot be considered as rasas as there is no element of devotional aspect, and they are also not only antagonistic for pleasure and love but also they also have hatred and jealousy[66].

The nature of the mind and the causes for its modifications were mentioned in the first Ullāsa and the Vairāgya as an eighth cause is now mentioned. It is clarified that there will be no other mode that can cause melting of the mind. If there is no melting and modification of the mind there will be no occurrence of Stāhyī-bhāva and consequently no rasa. It is to be noted that for Bhaktirasa, a divine related rati is essential for the mind to take the form of the Lord (Bhagavatākarata).

There will be as many numbers of bhāvas as there are causes that can melt and bring about modification of mind and there will be corresponding number of Sthāyī-bhāvas.

The following Bhāvas, Śṛingāra (saṁbhoga and Vipralambha), śoka, preeti, Bhaya, (out of love) Vismaya, Uddotsāha and dānotsāha have rati, having divine aspects only can be causes of Bhaktirasa. Among them some have Ālambana and Vibhāvana as separate aspects and then they may manifest as separate rasas. If they have mixture of Ālambana relating to divine nature they can be considered as Bhaktirasa bhāvas[67]. If in the above there is devotional aspect in addition to their own Vibhāvana and they can homogenously mix (like milk and water) they are called Vyāmiśritā rasas. If they relate to divine aspects then they can be called Bhaktirasas[68].

The three types of rati (viz) Śuddhā rati, Vātsalya rati and Preyorati are manifested as respective rasas. There is no scope of these mixing with any other variety of Bhāvas. Hence they are called āmiśrita or pure ratis. The rasās that are manifested from these ratis also cannot mix with any other rasa and are therefore called of the nature of Nisaraga poorna meaning unmixed pure nature[69].

3.3.4 KINDS OF BHAKTI

Bhakti is classified as four types; they are Rājasi, Tāmasi, pure Sāttvika and mixed varieties as per Sāṁkhya School of Philosophy[70].Although Sāttvika quality is Principal one, arising out of joy, they are known by the predominance of particular guṇa (quality).

i) **Rājasika:** This is due to hatred on account of jealousy (like Sisupala and Rāvana).
ii) **Tāmasika:** This is due to hatred on account of fear (Kaṁasa).
iii) **Sāttvika:** This is pure sattvika and is blissful.
iv) **Miśrita:** This is on account of soka, Kama and other causes.

The commentator has compared the types of Bhaktas and their qualities (guṇas)[71]. Arthāthi (Rājasic), Ārtha (Tāmasik), (Sāttvik) and Jijñāsu.

The Tāmasik and Rājasik qualties are antagonistic to pleasure and hence not conducive for attaining rasa. For the Sāttvik and miśrita type of Bhaktas there is pleasure and hence they there will be melting of mind and manifestation of rasa and hence can be classified as having Bhakti rasa characteristic.

The above four types of Bhakti can be classified into three types of according to the fruits they attain, they are:

i) Adṛṣṭa Phala (result invisible or to accrue in future).
ii) Dṛṣṭaphala (visible, fructifying now).
iii) Dṛṣṭa Adṛṣṭa Phal (Mixed result-some to fructify at present and some in future).

Rājasik and Tāmasik devotees have negative attitudes and desires. They don't experience pleasure of divine aspects, hence they have Adṛṣṭa Phal. Rāvana, Kaṁsa they got beatitude is by Nirodha in their next life. For mixed qualities the fruits are both visible and invisible. Pharlāda, Gopīs (They have vision of the Lord for Sāttvika quality and also beatitude). Dṛṣṭa phala (visible results) is illustrated in Sanat Kumāras and others as they are Jīvanmuktas.

The Dṛṣṭa-Adṛṣṭa result is also given in a different manner. A man who wanted to get relief form hot sun bathes in Gaṅgā will get immediate physical pleasure. He may get the other benefit of bathing in Gaṅgā by getting rid of sins as invisible fruit[72].

These concepts have been further analyzed or explained elaborately and concluded that the rati and experience of bliss will be possible only when there is melting of mind for which predominance of sāttvika quality is essential.

The author has further classified rati into eight categories as follows.

i) **Nisarga:** It is natural and obtained from saṁskāra of previous birth.

ii) **Saṁsarga:** Depending upon the intimacy or association with the Lord. (Gopīs, Arjuna).

iii) **Sadruśya Jñānata:** By viewing the Lord's glories in His mūrti.

iv) **Adhyātma:** By viewing the Lord in one's own Ātman.

v) **Abhiyoga:** By openly expressing one's feelings.

vi) **Saṁprayoga:** Rati is generated only out of saṁbhoga.

vii) **Abhimāna:** To forsake mundane attachment even to the most cherished object or person and turn towards divine matters.

viii) **Saṁarūpa:** Rati is generated in relation with śabda, touch, rūpa, rasa and fragrance (gandha) and a mixture of these five will be a sixth rati.[73]

The Bhakti can be classified in another manner as two types.

i) Śuddhā (Pure)

ii) Vyāmiśrita (Mixed homogeneously)

The same are also known as Nirupādhika and Sopādhika respectively.

Nirupādhika or pure Bhakti dawns spontaneously and does not have any other connection. It is an experience of inexplicable bliss and of its own nature and is unique and (non-dual).

Sopādhika Bhakti or Vyāmiśrita Bhakti is with an Upādhi, meaning having some other cause also associated with it. The other cause mixes homogeneously like milk and water. This is of three kinds. Kāmajanīta, Sambandhajanīta and Bhayajanīta.

Kāmajanīta: This is born out of love or desire. This is mixed in śṛingāra (erotic love).

Sambandhajanīta: It is generated out of Vātsalya Bhakti or sakhya Bhakti.

Bhayajanīta: The melting of the mind is due to fear.

If there is a combination of all the above it is altogether another rasa of entirely new experience (like mellow or a mixture of juices of different fruits).

The Kāmajanita rati is erotic love.The Bhayajanīta rati will reflect reverence, respect, protection and astonishment and humbleness.The sambandhajanīta will reflect friendliness and affection. The śuddhā rati will reflect serenity or calmness (śānta).Rati manifested in the various types of Bhakti as above will be relished by the individuals' in accordance to their mental aptitudes[74].

3.3.5 BHAKTI IS THE TENTH RASA

The Rasa which is distinctly unconnected with any type of Vibhāva, Anubhāva and sanchāribhāva and are of one quality exclusively related to God, will evolve to become a unique and superior rasa called Bhakti rasa. This rasa will be become the tenth rasa.[75]

3.3.6 REFUTATION OF OBJECTIONS

The Alankārikas claimed that Anubhāva, Vibhāva and Sancāri bhāva all exclusively related to divine qualities result in rati which is called Bhakti and that can be considered only as a Bhāva and cannot qualify to be designated as a rasa. Their reasoning is that Bhāva relating to divine nature cannot be agreed to give the same type of experience of pleasure as that relating to Śṛingāra rasa relating to love between lovers.

The author has stoutly refuted this objection. This may be true in respect of devotion relating to inferior Gods but not in respect of ever shining embodiment of bliss of Paramātman. There can be no such fulfillment in respect of Śṛingāra rati relating to sensual pleasures which are most unworthy and inferior type of rati compared to Bhakti Rasa. They are like intermittent glow of a glow worm compared to the bright shining Sun[76].

3.3.7 BHAKTI IS THE MOST SUPERIOR RASA

The rasas relating to mundane causes like Krodha, śoka, Bhayānaka, which are devoid of even an element of pleasure and virtuously antagonistic for experience of pleasure with miniscule of indirect pleasure gradually evolving as veera (brave) karuna (compassion) and Bhayānaka (fearfulness) are considered as rasās. However the aestheticians adamantly deny Bhakti to be treated as rasa.

The Bhakti Rasa which actually bestows inexplicable experience of bliss, is many thousand folds supreme compared to other rasās and denying Bhakti to be a rasa is nothing short of Jalp or Vitandavāda by the orthodox Aestheticians[77].

Madhusūdana Sarasvatī thus vehemently declared that Bhaktirasa is the most superior rasa.

3.4 THE ANALYSIS OF THIRD ULLĀSA

The third Ullāsa consists of thirty verses. After discussing the general characteristics of Bhakti in the first Ullāsa and the special features of Bhakti in the second Ullāsa the author proposed to discuss the concept of Bhakti Rasa and established it as the supreme rasa in the third Ullāsa. He adopted a novel method of enquiry through some questions and by giving the answers to them the same are elaborated.

Madhusūdana Sarasvatī raised the following questions and gave answers to them.[78]

i) What is rasa?
ii) Where does it exist?
iii) What causes its manifestation? And
iv) How it is cognized?

3.4.1 What is rasa?

The union of Vibhāva, Anubhāva and sancāribhāva and sustaining continuously called Sthāyī-bhāva (static state of emotion) and realisation of pleasure in that state is called rasa[79]. Rasa is manifested due to modification of mind called Cittavṛtti. The object is reflected in the mind. The pleasure is experienced by the mind. If the Ālambana is divine the reflection is Bhagavāna only and the rasa is Bhaktirasa.

3.4.2 Where does it exist?

The Śṛuti has mentioned *'rasovaisaḥ'*[80] which means that rasa is Brahman and Brahman is bliss. Ātman is Brahman. The bliss experienced due to the rasa is that of Ātma and it has no adjuncts. It manifests in the internal organ or Antaḥ-karaṇa[81]. The rasa described in literature or drama or dance usually relate to mundane nature. The Vibhāva and Anubhāva related to anger, sorrow or anguish etc are presented by the artists with a creative effort adding emotion which is implied in the script. They create imagery on the stage and bring the experience in the minds of the audience and make them thoroughly enjoyable.

The same experience like pleasure or sorrow etc is experience by the audience initially. However the sympathetic audience enjoying the rasa will have a pleasurable experience in their minds. Thus is mundane rasa will be relished as eternal or super mundane experience although no such rati is experienced by the artist and the absence of sorrow is in the person who experiences (the audience). The Sancāribhāva will aid and contribute to intensify the rati in the mind[82].

The structure, nature and basis of the three elements in establishment of the Sthāyī-bhāva are known as the nature of the Sthāyī-bhāva. If this results in pleasurable experience in an individual it will also be bring similar experience in all, called generalization. Thus it becomes a super mundane experience and so a sattva quality[83].

3.4.3 What causes its Manifestation?

The qualities (guṇas) of words, the poetic ornamentation like suitable similes and the appropriate styles or methods and meaningful words will be able to ensure the manifestation of rati and enjoyment of rasa. Harsh sounding words are antagonistic to rasa; similarly in verses glorifying the God it is ideal not to use such language. The pleasant sounding words that will manifest pleasant modification of mind (Cittavṛtti) are conducive for rasa experience. The manifestation of the rasa through Śabda (word) may be considered a direct knowledge[84] although it is experienced in mind. The famous episode *'Daśamatvamasi'* is cited to establish that 'Śabda' can be direct knowledge.

3.4.4 How is rasa cognized?

Rasa is experienced only in mind and how can it be cognized is a doubt. Rasa is eternal bliss, pure and self-effulgent and is inexplicable joy (*nirvikalpa sukhānubhuti*).

The pleasure is of two kinds.

i) Normal pleasure: the pleasure experienced with Sattva guṇa with an element of sorrow is the normal pleasure.
ii) Special pleasure: It is an eternal bliss. However due to the mystical power of God it is concealed (Āvaraṇa sakti) and so inaccessible for normal persons and they know only the verbal meaning. The wise only will be able and visualize the reality (which is known when the veil is removed.)[85]

3.4.5 RASA IS BRAHMAN

The Upaniṣadic verses *'Raso vai saḥ'* and *'vij*ñānam ānand*aṁ brahma'* meaning, Brahman is rasa. Bliss is Brahman. The eternal bliss is rasa and is pure, and self-effulgent. After various arguments and discussion it was confirmed that the ever blissful Ātman is itself rasa. When the veil of cidātma is removed the Paramātman is revealed and He is rasa. Thus Rasa, Ānanda and Brahman are shown as synonyms.

The knowledge of the combination of Vibhāva and other bhāvas involved in the process will ensure appropriate rasa. This can be recognized by only learned people.

There have been different types of rasas, and after eliminating all of them it was finally concluded that rasa, which is of all blissful nature, is the Ātman. The root of the manifestation of rasa is the Śabda. The meaning of the Śabda is known through three different means *Abhidhā, lakṣana* and *vyañjanā*. Rasa is known through the vyañjanā[86].

The various philosophical schools have some differences regarding treating Śabda as pramāna (authoritative knowledge) for mundane words. The conclusion was arrived that Śabda being adopted independently are in conjunction with other Vibhāva will by vyañjanāvṛtti will establish the ever blissful rasa.

3.5 CONCLUSION

The title of the text is aptly given as Rasāyana which means an (elixir or tonic in Āyurvedic medicinal system which serves as a lifesaving tonic) The Bhaktirasāyana is an effective remedy for the afflictions of the cycle of births and deaths being suffered from time immemorial by peple with ignorance. He advised the wise to consume this elixir to their contentment and get rid of the sufferings. It is very imaginative and appropriate.

After the purification of mind he mentioned two different paths as per the attitude of the individuals. One is the Jñāna mārga and the other is Bhakti mārga. He declared the yoga of devotion as the highest, as described by those who have experienced it.

This assertion is in consonance with the Bhakti schools of Vedānta and of the Vallabha School and Bengal Vaiṣṇavas, who have taken the Bhāgavatapurāṇa as the canon of their systems.

He tried to establish that just as the knowledge is established in accordance with the Upaniṣadic sentences, Bhakti yoga is established with the copious quotations and authority of Bhagavad-Gītā and Bhāgavatapurāṇa.

The eligibility, essential pre-requisites, and learned and disciplined mind with inherent dispassion is required for Jñāna ,yoga, the fruit of Brahmavidyā is eradication of nescience and a non-dual realisation and abundance of bliss. The state of mind is Nirvikalpa manovṛtti in un-melted mind.

In case of Bhakti yoga the only requisite is sincere devotion without any motive and it can be practiced by any body without discrimination and at all times. Bhakti is a mental state of Sāviklapa manovṛtti in a melted mind. The intense Bhakti reaches its climax, however the duality between the devotee and God remains but realizes emotional identity. attains bliss. Although the eligibility etc. are different both means result in bliss.

This is perhaps the first time that such a comparison is made which is perhaps untenable for orthodox philosophical thinkers.

Madhusūdana has mentioned that when the cause of melting as well as the result are divine, the resulting rasa will be called Bhaktirasa. The Aestheticians have not considered the Bhakti rasa as it is only a Bhāva and not a sentiment.

Bhakti as a rasa was reported to have been first considered by Lakṣmīdhara, the author of *'Nāmakaumadī'* who lived in the thirteenth or fourteenth century. He viewed Bhakti as a mental state (bhāva) of the mind spontaneously focused on the Lord. He designated this pleasurable mental state as love or rati, thus setting precedent for identification of the sthāyī-bhāva of Bhakti-rasa as Bhagavad-rati. Rūpa Goswāmin has made detailed analysis in his work *Bhakti-rasāmṛtasinḍhu*[87].

Madhusūdana has adopted the rasa theory but there is a distinction that, the modification of the mind due to melting (cittavṛtti)and the mind taking the form of the Lord and having the image of the Lord imprinted therein is a permanent sentiment.

Madhusūdana has shown his deep knowledge in the Aesthetics and has covincigly applied it in establishing Bhakti-rasa.

Bhakti-rasa is distinctly unconnected with any Vibhāva and Anubhāva etc and has only one quality exclusively of divine nature .Thus it evolves to become a unique and superior rasa and Bhakti should be treated as the tenth rasa. The author refuted the argument that Bhakti is only a bhāva and not a sentiment and does not qualifies to be a rasa. He argued that the restriction may be in respect of inferior Gods but this will not apply to Bhakti to Kṛṣṇa, the supreme person who is an embodiment of bliss. He declared that the rasa due to mundane sentiments like Śṛingāra involving sensual pleasures will only give infinitely small pleasure like the glow of a glow worm compared to the Bhakti-rasa which bestows immense amount of inexplicable bliss (without a trace of sorrow) like the bright shining Sun. The combination of the Vibhāva, Anubhāva and sancārī-bhāva will result in a type of mental modification or Cittavṛtti of a sāttvik nature. The moment such a modification occurs there will be pleasure and such experience, is called rasa as was believed by our author while others have disagreed with this opinion. The mundane sentiments have Vibhāva, Anubhāva which are two separate distinct entities, where as in Bhakti the God is both Vibhāva and Anubhāva due to the Māyā power of the Lord. The Bhaktirasa will manifest as supreme bliss which is like a bright shining Sun, whereas the mundane rasas will although manifest rasa the pleasure out of them is very minute like the intermittent glow of light given by a glow worm, thus Bhakti rasa is adequately qualified to be tenth rasa and also it is *Rasarāja* or supreme rasa.

Madhusūdana has composed the text which is a combination of Aesthetics, Advaitic theory and poetry. He exhibited his scholastic knowledge in Navya Nyāyā of which he had great skill. He has given careful definitions and elaborate classifications and besides convincingly and logically refuting objections. He has written a very detailed commentary of the first Ullāsa, but for which the text would have left many gaps in the minds of the readers, about what he intended to communicate through the text. The readers would have been benefitted had he given the commentary on the other two ullāsas.

The object of the composition is to explain the Bhakti -yoga in a systematic manner with scriptural proofs which he has fully achieved. This is with a view of eradicating, the malady with which all people are suffering since time immemorial due to ignorance with miseries consequent of cycle of births and deaths.. The common people who are overwhelmed with their mundane activities and with little time to look towards the spiritual side of life and who imagine that it is beyond scope of their ability to even dare to make an attempt in that direction. He offered an elixir called Bhaktirasa which is accessible to everyone to be consumed to their contentment. Nārada has also declared in his Bhakti sūtras that Bhakti is everybody's birthright.

Thus the self- realized soul has with an altruistic attitude composed the treatise on Bhakti as a benevolent service to the public like Suka has volunteered to teach Parișit the most important Bhakti in a short time of seven days.

This objective is very laudable, which is also the aim of all the scriptures.

The exposition of Bhakti in Bhāgavatapurāṇa which is blend of Bhakti, Jñāna and Vairāgy, has been the major source of the content besides the Upaniṣads.

Madhusūdana's verse in stating the title and objective of the treatise is in consonance of the following verse of Bhāgavatapurāṇa

"O! Devotees possessing taste of divine joy, Śrīmad Bhāgavata is the fruit (essence) of the wish-yielding tree of Veda, dropped from the mouth of the parrot-like sage Śuka, and full of the nectar of supreme bliss. It is like unmixed sweetness (devoid of rind, seed or other superfluous matter). Go on drinking this divine nectar again and again till there is consciousness left in you"[88].

The Bhakti depicted by Madhusūdana has influenced his junior contemporary philosopher, Nārāyaṇatirtha (1650-1750Ad) the author of *Bhakticandrika*, has a close affinity and has made a liberal use of the verses of Bhaktirasāyana in his composition.[89]

Hariharānanda Sarasvatī, popularly known as 'Karapātrī Swāmī,(1907-1982), an Advaitin has in his composition *'Bhakti Rasārṇava* [90](an ocean of Bhakti) has agreed with Madhusūdana that Śāntarasa will not qualify to be called Bhaktirasa as is it is emotionless and does not have cittavṛitti and similarly Krodha and śoka have no bliss in them. He has liberally quoted from Bhaktirasāyana in pages 71-86 of his composition.

Notes and References

1. BhP 3.29.11-12.See also BR 1.3 and Br1.10
2. Rukmini .T.S, Acritical study of the Bhagava Purana, Chowkhamba Sanskrit series office, Varanasi, 1970.
3. BG 8.22.
4. BhP1-5,17,19, also 6-1-19.
5. BR 1.2.
6. Ibid 1.4.
7. Ibid 1.5.
8. Ibid 1.6.
9. BhP 11.2.45.
10. Ibid 11.2.46-48
11. BR 1.9.
12. Ibid 1.10.
13. Ibid 1.11.
14. Ibid 1.12.
15. Ibid 1.13-14.
16. Ibid1.18
17. Ibid 1.26-27.
18. Bhp 11-20.(31-36)
19. BG 18.55
20. Bhp 2.3.24 and 11.14.23.
21. BR1.29
22. BhP11.14.23-25 see also BhP 2.3.24
23. BR 1.30.
24. BS4.2.8.
25. BhP 11.3.40.
26. Ibid11.14.25.
27. Ibid 11.14.26-28. See also11.27.21-23.

28. CU 3.14.1
29. BhP 11.3.21-33.
30. Ibid 1.5.23-40.
31. BhP 5.5.2-3.
32. Ibid11.2.29.
33. Ibid 11.12.1-6
34. Ibid11.12.7-9.
35. Ibid 4.8.35-38.
36. Ibid 1.5.26.
37. Ibid 1.2.16-17.
38. Ibid 7.5.23-24.
39. Ibid 10.51-54. See also 10.47.67.
40. Ibid3.26.2-3.
41. Ibid 10.14.55.
42. Ibid 1.2.7.
43. Ibid 7.4.32-42.
44. Ibid 7.7.33-37.
45. Ibid 3.25.34-37.
46. Ibid 9.4.15-21.
47. Ibid 3.25.39-44.
48. Ibid 10.19.16.
49. Ibid 1.11.9.
50. NBS verse 82.
51. BG Verse 12.8.
52. The note on the rasa theory has been prepared from the content of the article by Srinivasan Dr. C.S., entitled 'significance of rasa and Abhinaya toechniques in Bharat's Natya sastra, Published in IOSR Journal of humanities and social science (IOSR-JHSS), Vol 10 Issue 5 ver iv, May 2015 pp 25-29
53. 000BR 2.25.

54. BR 2.3-4 see also Bhāgavata Purāṇ Krodha (a 10.29.46 and also 10.30.1-4).
55. Ibid 2.5-7.
56. Ibid 2.8.
57. Ibid 2.9-11.
58. Ibid 2.13 see also BhP5.5.5-6.
59. Ibid 2.17 see also BhP 10.39.29.
60. Ibid 2.22.
61. Ibid 2.21.
62. Ibid 2.23.
63. Ibid 2.24.
64. Ibid 2.27-28.
65. Ibid 2.29
66. Ibid 2.30.
67. Ibid2.31.
68. Ibid 2.32.
69. Ibid 2.34.
70. Ibid 2.41.
71. BG 7.16.
72. BR 2.44-47.
73. Ibid 2.63-64.
74. Ibid 2.71.
75. Ibid 2.74.
76. Ibid 2.75-78.
77. Ibid 2.79-80.
78. BR 3.1.
79. Ibid 3.2.
80. TU 2.7.1.
81. Ibid 3.3.

82. Ibid 3.4-7
83. Ibid 3.10-13.
84. Ibid3.18-20-21.
85. Ibid 3.22.
86. Ibid 3.23-24.
87. Goswāmin Rūpa, The Bhaktirasāmṛtasindhu, Translated by Haberman, David L., Indira Gandhi National Centre for the Arts, New Delhi, Introduction pp xiviii-viix, 2003.
88. BhP verse 1.1.3.
89. Kaviraja's preface to Bhakticandrika, sampoornanada University, Varanasi, preface part 1 p 2, 1924.
90. Sarasvatī, Harshānanda, 'Bhaki Rasārnava'Bhakti-sudha sahitya Parishad, Kolkata, 2015.

*****

CHAPTER 4.

4. BHAKTI IN GŪḌHĀRTHA DĪPIKĀ

4.1 INTRODUCTION

Śrī Madhusūdana Sarasvatī (hereafter MS) who is a Prominent Advaita Philosopher has written the commentary on Śrīmad Bhagavad-Gītā with an annotation called Gūḍhārtha-Dīpikā (hereafter GAD). Gūḍhārtha means hidden meaning and Dīpikā meaning that reveals i.e. the deeper implications of Bhagavad-Gītā (Here after BG). This is one of the important of his many works.

Though there are several commentaries of Bhagavad-Gītā, this commentary stands next only to the Gītā Bhāṣya by Śaṅkarācārya as regards to clarity, depth and originality. It is an epitome of Madhusudan's vast learning and mastering of different schools of Indian Philosophy and religion, and his great spiritual experience.

There are several commentaries and translations of Gūḍhārtha-Dīpīkā in English, Hindi and Bengali.

i) The first translation in English is that of Sisir Kumar Gupta titled 'Madhusūdana Sarasvatī on the Bhagavad-Gītā being an English translation of his commentary Gūḍhārtha-Dīpikā', Motilal Banarasidas, New Delhi, 1977. It includes a short biographical sketch of Śrī Madhusūdana Sarasvatī and includes the original Verse of the text in Sanskrit, with translation of meaning and commentary of Madhusūdana Sarasvatī. It does not contain the additional sentiments expressed by Śrī Madhusūdana Sarasvatī (in the original Sanskrit) at the beginning and end of certain chapters of Bhagavad-Gītā.

i). Śrīmad Bhagavad-Gītā with Gūḍhārtha-Dīpikā of Madhusūdana Sarasvatī Hindi Translation by Swami Sanatānanda, Choukambha Sanskrit Śaṇsthān, Varanasi, 1983.

ii). Śrīmad Bhagavad-Gītā, Śrīmān Madhusūdana Sarasvatī ka Varttika, translated and explained (in Bengali) by Pt. Bhutānada Saptatīrtha (edited) Nilakhanta Brahma, Navabharat Publishers, Calcutta, 1986.

iii) Madhusūdana Sarasvatī Bhagavad-Gītā with the annotation Gūḍhārtha-Dīpikā translated (into English) by Swami Gambhīrānanda, Advaita Ashram, Kolkata, 1998.This contains an Introduction covering the brief life sketch of M.S. and other works. It contains general observations on the Philosophical view of the author. A detailed glossary of terms, Alphabetical index of Ślokas were given, which are very useful to the readers.

This book has been mainly consulted for the present discussion.

A special feature of the commentary is that, he has taken pains to explain every word of Gītā and highlighted the significant implications, of even apparently simple words such as ca, tu, va etc. at many places.

The author also gave his own gist of the verses at the end of few chapters and under some verses. He added some verses of his own praising Kṛṣṇa which are not part of the

Gītā at the end of chapter 9, 10, 14, 15and 18 and in the beginning of chapters 7 and 13.

Madhusūdana has mentioned that he has written the commentary after assiduously deliberating on the meaning of the commentary of the venerable Sri Śaṅkarācārya.

The translator of Gūḍhārtha-Dīpikā has observed that Śaṅkarācārya makes several points in his own introduction or upodghāṭa to the Gītā that are quite interesting. There is a Vaiṣṇava (Nārāyaṇa/Vāsudeva) slant to Śaṅkara's introduction that can be observed in three different places, at the beginning, middle and end. It begins with the words nārāyaṇaḥ paro'vyaktāt, which means that Nārāyaṇa is beyond both the manifest and unmanifest forms of creation. In the middle, when he talks about Nārāyaṇa incarnating as Kṛṣṇa, the words he uses are basically those of Gita 4.6 (ajo'pi san, etc.).

The most remarkable of Śaṅkara's statements comes at the end of the introduction. After explaining that the *nivṛtti-lakṣaṇa-dharma* of sannyāsa is the means and ātma-jñāna-niṣṭha the ultimate goal of the Gita's teachings, and that the *pravṛtti-lakṣaṇa-dharma* about self-purification leading to that goal, Śaṅkara' concludes, *paramārtha-tattvaṁ ca vāsudevākhyaṁ para-brahmābhidheya-bhūtaṁ viśeṣato'bhivyañjayad viśiṣṭa-prayojana-sambandhābhidheyavad gītā-śāstram | yatas tad-artha-vijñānena samasta-puruṣārtha-siddhiḥ* |

"The Gita śāstras, through its special (*viśiṣṭa*) object (*prayojana*), interrelations and stated signification, reveals especially that the supreme truth named Vāsudeva is the Param Brahma and the object of knowledge delineated in it (*abhidheya*). From realized knowledge of this meaning, one achieves success in attaining all goals of human life".

Here the use of *sambandha, abhidheya (= viṣaya*), and *prayojana* are the standard terms that form a part of the *anubandha-catuṣṭaya*, by which a book's purpose, etc., are outlined. (The fourth being *adhikāra*.),

The topics are proposed to be discussed in the following sections.

4.2 Analysis of Invocation and annotation.

4.3 Bhakti in various verses in chapters of Gūḍhārtha- Dīpikā.

4.4 Bhakti yoga (chapter 12.) in the Gūḍhārtha- Dīpikā.

4.5 Concluding chapter of Gūḍhārtha- Dīpikā.

4.6 Devotional verses mentioned by Madhusūdana in various places in Gūḍhārtha-Dīpikā that are not part of Bhagavad-Gītā.

4.7 Conclusion.

4.2 ANALYSIS OF INVOCATION AND ANNOTATION

4.2.1 INVOCATION.

The author commenced the work with offering of Mangalācarana prayer to Śrī Rāmacandra who is the form of consciousness, whose lotus feet are worshipped by enlightened sages of the highest order known as Paramahaṁsa. It is customary for Sanskrit writers to commence with a prayer to the Lord for successful completion of the work. Śaṅkara has offered a prayer to Nārāyaṇa quoting a verse from Smṛti.

4.2.2 EXPOSITION OF THE SUBTLE MEANING OF GĪTĀ.

Madhusūdana in the first verse mentioned the purpose of writing the work. After having assiduously deliberating on the meaning of the commentary on Bhagavad-Gītā written by Śaṅkara Bhagavatpāda, Madhusūdana wrote the elucidation, called Gūḍhārtha-Dīpikā (exposition of subtle meaning) of almost every word of Gītā. It has been observed that he has explained even smell words like ca, tu, va, ct at various places and highlighted the significant implication.

4.2.3 PURPOSE OF GĪTĀ.

It was stated that the purpose of the scripture Gītā is, "absolute liberation, which consists in the complete cessation of transmigration together with its causes".

In his introduction to Bhagavad-Gītā, Śaṅkarācārya has quoted the same words but added that results from dharma (virtuous path) consisting in steady adherence to knowledge of the self, preceded by renunciation of all rites and duties. This is very dharma (virtuous path) to be the purport of the Gītā. The scripture called Gītā is the collection of the quintessence of the teaching of Vedas, *"Samasṭa Veda Sāra Saṅgraha bhutam."*

4.2.4 STRUCTURE OF GĪTĀ AND SIMILARITY WITH VEDAS.

It was stated that supreme state of Viṣṇu which is identical with absolute (Brahman), Existence, Consciousness and Bliss (Sat-Cit-Ānanda) for attainment of which the Vedas have commenced. The Vedas are an ocean and Gītā is its essence.

There is a popular support of this. The Vedas are imagined as cows, Śrī Kṛṣṇa is the milkman and Arjuna is the calf and the milk extracted is the Gītā, the essence of the Vedas for consumption by the wise. The first three parts of Vedas is called Karma-kānda and the last part is (Upaniṣads) is called Jñāna- kānda.

The Karma-kānda is called "yoga Śāstra" and Upaniṣad part is called "Brahmavidyā". These two are called pravṛtti mārga and Nivṛtti mārga respectively. The practice of karma-kānda is to prepare the aspirant towards Jñāna- kānda.

Śrī Kṛṣṇa has taught the following two paths to Arjuna as the means of realization of the goal of life.

i) Karma- yoga for the yogīs.
ii) Jñāna - yoga for men of realization.

However we can see that Bhakti is discussed as an integral part of both and Bhakti has been discussed in an exclusive chapter.

The Bhagavad-Gītā consists of eighteen chapters; all the chapters are called yoga viz. Karma- yoga, Jñāna- yoga, Sāṅkhya- yoga, Bhakti- yoga etc. It is not a scripture of yoga like karma, Jñāna or Bhakti etc. and considers all the yogas are conducive for realization. (Except the first chapter which was the reason for the entire text).

The Bhagavad-Gītā is a treatise on different forms of spiritual disciplines for practice by persons of different temperaments and inclinations, so that they can attain highest and best of human life. Each chapter in Bhagavad-Gītā ends with a colophon.

"Śrīmad Bhagavadgītā Upaniṣastu Brahmavidyāyam yoga Śāstre Śrī Kṛṣṇārjuna samvāde - - - - - yoga nāma - - - - - Adhyāya."

4.2.5 DIVISION OF BHAGAVAD GĪTĀ INTO SECTIONS.

Śrī Madhusūdana considers the division of Vedas namely karma, Upāsanā and Jñāna as means of attaining the life's goal (Mokṣa) and correspondingly divided Gītā into three sections.

The first six chapters (1-6) as karma-niṣṭha (steadfastness in action), the next six chapters (7-12) as Bhagavad Bhakti, devotion to the Lord as Bhakti- niṣṭha (steadfastness in devotion) and the last six Chapters (13-18) as Jñāna-niṣṭhā, that leads to the goal (steadfastness in knowledge).

The middle section which involves grace of God makes the stage by stage transition from karma to Jñāna smoothly. The devotion is inherent in both karma and Jñāna and it removes all possible obstacles at all stages.

Śrī Madhusūdana mentioned that devotion (Bhakti) is of three kinds,

i) Mixed with rites (karma- miśrita Bhakti).
ii) Pure Bhakti (Śuddhā-Bhakti).
iii) Mixed with Jñāna (Jñāna-miśrita Bhakti).

4.2.6 RELATING MAHĀVĀKYA TO TEACHING OF B.G.

In the earlier verses the author compared the similarity in the structure of Bhagavad-Gītā and Vedas. In a similar way the author has attempted to establish the Mahāvākya of Upaniṣad "*TATTVAMASI*", "Thou art that", the unity of the individual soul (Ātma) and Supreme Soul (Paramātman) to the teaching of Bhagavad-Gītā.

The individual soul (Jīva) is denoted by the word 'Thou' is established by the performance of actions with steadfastness and their renunciation (karma-yoga). The word 'that' (the Supreme self Paramātman) is established with steadfastness in devotion (Bhakti-yoga).

The unity of the two 'Thou' and 'that' is 'Art' is established by steadfastness in knowledge. Thus, the mutual non-dualistic relationship between them is established. In a similar manner there is mutual relationship between the three divisions of Bhagavad-Gītā as karma, Bhakti and Jñāna.

The Mahāvākya (Great sentences) mentioned in the Vedas have the same meaning.

i) *'Tattvamasi'* - Sāma Veda 'Thou art that'[1]
ii) *'Prajñānam Brahma'* -Ṛg Veda 'conscious is Brahman'.[2]
iii) *'Aham Brahmāsmi'* – Yajur Veda "I am Brahman"[3]
iv) *'Ayam ātmā Brahmā'*- Atharva Veda "Brahman is this very self."[4]

The above division of Bhagavad-Gītā into three sections is unique.

4.2.7 VARIOUS DISCIPLINES AND STAGES OF REALISATION (Verses12-20)

The various steps in disciplines of devotion are presented in these verses. It was indicated that specialty of each chapter will discussed in the respective chapters.

Each chapter in Gītā is called yoga. Yoga means a path by practice of that, which will enable to move forward to unite the aspirant's finite self with the infinite being.

The following different types of Karma have been mentioned.

i) Kāmya-karma.
ii) Niṣiddha- Karma.
iii) Nitya-Karma.
iv) Naimittika Karma.
v) i) Kāmya-karma: The performances of actions with a desire for result of the actions are considered as the cause of bondage and rebirth (either good or bad results) and

which may accrue in due course or in the next birth. ii) Niṣiddha karma is acts prohibited to be performed and will result in liability for reaping the penalty for violation of the scriptural prescriptions. Therefore, one should desist from doing such karmas. iii)Niṣkāma Karma: Doing actions as a duty without motive and not aspiring for results thereof or selfless work. iv) Naimittika Karma: Actions prescribed by scriptures as per varṇa-Āsrama dharma.

Thus, doing actions without motive and aspiration for results, and as prescribed by scriptures does not incur any bondage and can be performed.

The performance of actions and dedication of all fruits of such actions to the Lord will not attract any doer-ship to the Jīva. It will result in purification of the Inner organ[5]. This will be conducive for highest good.

The mind thus purified will become fit for discrimination. The four-fold method is called *'Sādhana-Chatuṣṭaya'*.[6]

i) Discernment of things eternal and transient (*nityānitya-Vastu viveka*).
ii) Renunciation of desire for fruits of actions here and here after (*phala bhoga vairāgya*).
iii) Six-fold inner virtues of calmness, temperance (*Śamadamādi Sādhana Sampat).*
iv) Intense desire for liberation (*Mumukṣutva* or *Brahma Jij*ñāsa).

The Śama *damādi Sampat'* consist of the following;

i) **Śama:** Self-control (control of internal organ and curbing of the mind).
ii) **Dama:** Restraint, control of external sense organs.
iii) **Uparatī:** not allowing the sense organs to revert to their respective objects.
iv) **Titikṣā:** Endurance, forbearance.
v) **Śraddhā:** Faith in the teachings of one's Guru, and scriptures.
vi) **Mumukṣutva:** Intense desire for liberation. The mind gradually following the above, the renunciation is fully established. Thus hankering for liberation will spring.

The aspirant approaches a learned guru for receiving appropriate guidance. The aspirant gets instruction to follow the procedure.

Śravana: (Hearing and understanding Veda etc.). The Vedānta scriptures will be useful to get clarification of all doubts. The Śravana is not mere hearing but, to investigate into the meaning and get full understanding, the purport of the scriptural teachings.

Manana: reflecting the learning and augmenting the knowledge by internal questioning of possible doubts and contradictions and thus firmly establishing the learning and dispensing all doubts and misgivings about the scriptural content.

Nididhyāsana: (profound meditation)[7]: To internalize the Truth through constant meditation.

The author mentions that the entire yoga scripture (Patañjali- yoga) is fully useful to accomplish this procedure.

The process of learning Vedānta scriptures should not be self-learning but from a competent guru through Śravaṇa, Manana and Nididhyāsana. The role of guru (Ācārya) is very much important and the necessity was stressed by Śaṅkarācārya,[8] who stated that knowledge is generated by scriptures (Śāstras) and a teacher helps to attain knowledge of Brahman.[9]

There after the veil of ignorance or Avidyā of the self is removed on rise of knowledge of true reality (Tattva-Jñāna) of identity of the self and Brahman in consonance of the Mahāvākya, "*Tattvamasi*" is grasped.

The following results are obtained through the power of true knowledge (Tattva- Jñāna).

i) The results of action done in the past lives (Sañcita Karma) not yet commenced bearing fruit will be wholly destroyed.
ii) The result of the action done in the present life (after the dawn of the knowledge) that are yet to materialize in future (Āgāmi) will not accrue.

However, the results of past actions that have started bearing fruits (Prārabdha Karma), Vāsanās (Past impressions) do not get destroyed and are to be experienced. This is the view of all Advaita philosophers.

4.2.8 ELIMINATION OF PRĀRABDHA KARMA (Verse (21-24)

Madhusūdana Sarasvatī mentions that the Prārabdha-karma may not be terminated in one life and one may have to undergo the cycle of births and deaths. One may practice various means of yogic practices to eliminate suffering due to it and keep the latent tendencies under control.

The practice of Saṁyama as per Patañjali-yoga is the strongest of all the disciplines. Dhāraṇā, Dhyāna and Samādhi together constitute Saṁyama[10].

Dhāraṇā is fixation of mind on a specific object, Dhyāna is meditation, and Saṁyama is absorption. The other limbs of the eight-fold yoga are Yama (restraint) consisting of (i) nonviolence, (ii) truthfulness, (iii) non-acceptance of gifts (aparīgraha) and (iv) celibacy.

Niyama consists of cleanliness, contentment, austerities like tapas etc., scriptural study, Repetition of 'OM', special devotion to God (Īśvara- Prānidhāna). Āsana (Postures), Prāṇāyāma (control of breath), and Samādhi (Unifying concentration). The eight-fold yoga propounded by Patañjali will enable the aspirant towards attaining Samādhi[11] (a spiritual absorption of the mind).

The special devotion called 'Īśvara Prā*nidhāna*'[12] to obtain God's grace will enable the aspirant to eliminate the modification of the mind and dissipation of past impressions (Vāsanas). Thus, the aspirant successfully accomplishes his goal.

4.2.9 JĪVANA MUKTĪ. (LIBERATION WHILE ALIVE).

If the various disciplines are practiced simultaneously with *'Tatva-jñāna'* (mentioned earlier) the liberation will be achieved while alive (Jīvanmuktī)

The Vedas mentioned that renunciation of all actions as a result of enlightenment is called Vidvat-Saṅnyāsa. When the mind is held back from all fluctuations by means of Savikalpa-Samādhi,[13] the awareness of the subject (knower), the object (known), and knowledge (experience) persists.

It will lead to Nirvikalpa-Samādhi[14] (in this state, the subject object relationship vanishes). It consists of three steps.

i). The yogi emerges from this state by himself (just like from sleep).

The yogi is called Brahmavidvara (a great knower of Brahma).

ii). The yogi experiences absence of object as in deep sleep and he will not emerge by himself from this state (to be awakened by others). This state is called Padārthebhāvani (A great knower of Brahman).

iii) The yogi gradually reaches the next stage of spiritual absorption, which is total absence of perception of duality. He does not emerge from this state either by himself or even by the effort of others and remains ever self- absorbed in Supreme bliss. The bodily functions are managed by others (with no effort by him). Such a yogi is called Brahmavid-vareṇya[15] (A greatest knower of Brahman and he will obtain the next stage of Turīya. In that stage he is called Brahmavid-variṣṭha, the greatest knower of Brahma. Such a yogi is beyond the three guṇas and of steady wisdom is spoken as *'Sthita-Prajña'* (a man of steady wisdom) and a devotee of Viṣṇu. He transcends the stages of life and all varṇas. He is one who is liberated while still alive (Jīvanamukta) and is self- fulfilled.

4.2.10 THE SIGIFICANCE OF BHAKTI AT ALL STAGES OF QUEST FOR LIBERATION.

Madhusūdana stated the significance of devotion at all stages in quest for final liberation (Videha Mukti) citing the scriptural authority of Upaniṣads, Bhagavad-Gītā and Śrīmad Bhāgavatapurāṇa.

M.S. emphasizes that Bhakti (devotion) is always essential along with knowledge of reality (Tattva-Jñāna). The devotion should be one pointed, wholehearted with mind, body and speech and Bhakti for Bhakti's sake with no motive at all. In this connection he has cited the definition of Bhakti from Upaniṣad.

The word Bhakti in the Hindu religion was first used in Śvetāśvatara Upaniṣad. He who has supreme devotion (Bhakti) towards God, and as towards God so towards the teacher (guru) to him verily, the great soul, all these things will reveal themselves."[16]

It was commented by Śaṅkarā that, in addition to devotion one should have steady and great faith in them. Then one will feel that salvation lies only in self-knowledge, and then truth reveals itself immediately[17].

Madhusūdana Sarasvatī mentioned that devotion will gradually progress in stages and should be a continuous process and practiced avoiding any possible obstacles.

For a living liberated (*Jīvanamukta*) no result of devotion is to be imagined. He is free from anger, hate etc. and loves all equally. M.S. states that adoring Hari is natural to such a Jīvanmukta. In this state also he will continue to practice disinterested devotion to Śrī Hari and glorifying the virtues of Śrī Hari[18] citing the example of Śuka who is a self-realized sage.

JÑĀNI IS ALSO A GREAT BHAKTA

Madhusūdana Sarasvatī cited the Bhagavad-Gītā in which Śrī Kṛṣṇa stated as follows. "Of them, the man of knowledge, endowed with constant steadfastness and one pointed devotion excels. For I am very much dear to the man of knowledge and he too is dear to me".[19]

In the commentary Madhusūdana elaborates, "of them the man of knowledge (Jñāni) excels, since he is endowed with constant steadfastness as a result of knower of reality and he also become endowed with one pointed devotion because he finds no one else than Vāsudeva, whom he can adore. Consequently, that person of one pointed devotion excels". " I am the supreme self who am non-different from the indwelling self, very much super abundantly dear, an object of unqualified love to a man of knowledge, therefore he is superabundantly dear to me."[20] Śrī Madhusūdana holds that the Bhakti is a means of self-realization and is superior to knowledge, as Bhakti gives the liberation more quickly than knowledge and there is no difference in degree of liberation (the result).

4.2.11 PURPOSE OF GĪTĀ AND GŪḌHĀRTHA- DĪPIKĀ .

The Lord has revealed all the process of attaining liberation by the Jīva in the scripture Gītā. MS has mentioned the intent of the commentary is that his mind is intensely eager to explain the subtle meaning of this scripture.

4.2.12 SUMMARY AND OBSERVATIONS ON THE ANNOTATI ON

Madhusūdana discussed the means of obtaining the highest goal Puruṣārtha (i.e.) Mokṣa, the main objective of the scripture Gītā (mentioned in verse 1) and all the causes of possible hindrances in the path and measures to avoid or overcome them.

The performance of Kāmya-karmas, with craving for fruits of enjoyment, doing prohibited actions (Niṣiddha-Karmas), actions with ego and involving dominical sins, results in bondage and sorrow and consequent pain. These are serious hindrances for liberation and therefore should be avoided. Therefore, one should perform only the nītya-karmas and Niṣkāma-karma and dedication of all fruits thereof to the Lord, will be conducive to obtain the highest Goal of life. This is uttered by the Lord in the most esteemed scripture to enlighten the persons who are eager and filled with intense desire for liberation. In the commentary he has shown keen interest in high- lighting Bhakti (devotion),

At the end of the commentary mentioned as follows:

"The supreme secret called Gītā which is made sweet by the honey from the lotus like mouth of the blessed Govinda, was specially made public by the Sage Vyāsa. It was commented up on, word for word, by the God like one, named Śaṅkarācārya. It has been clarified once more by the monk Madhusūdana for the refinement of his own understanding.[21]" This shows Madhusudan's reverence to Śaṅkarācārya. Madhusūdana has agreed in most places, however in some places he choose to openly express his opinion.

The purpose of the Scripture Gītā is absolute liberation, which consists of cessation of transmigration together with its causes. The Gītā has declared that Viṣṇu is identical with absolute existence, knowledge and bliss. The Lord has taken Human form (Avatāra) to protect the pious and to punish the evil doers and reestablish righteousness in the world[22].

The following are the observations based on the commentary under discussion. There are only two Mārgas mentioned by Śrī Kṛṣṇa has specified, the yoga of knowledge for men of realization and the yoga of action for the yogi[23].

However, Madhusūdana has mentioned three paths, karma, Bhakti and jñāna and accordingly divided the scripture into three sections and this division has been followed earlier by some Vedāntins including Rāmanuja.

The three sections are attempted to be related to the Mahāvākya *"TAT TVAM ASI"*. This is a unique feature. In verse 7 of introduction it was mentioned that the devotion is inherent at all stages and its practice is stressed to be continued without which attainment of success and avoidance of numerous obstacles would not be possible.

The steps in practicing the spiritual disciplines are as per the Advatic concept of realization are well explained.

The practices of yoga in accordance of Patañjali- yoga have been given prominence.

Although no result of devotion is to be imagined, but adoring Hari is natural to a Jīvanmukta, like other qualities like being devoid of hate etc. and supported the claim by quoting from Bhāgavatapurāṇa[24].

The man of knowledge excels all as mentioned in BG 7.17 is mentioned, the essential qualification for the Jñāni has been stated by Madhusūdana is on account of steadfastness in one pointed devotion to wards the Lord only.

The performance of (Niṣkāma Karma) is the prime cause for liberation. The hindrances to liberation are, sinful and prohibited actions, and actions with desires which the man is prone to do on account of delusion there by inviting sorrow and pain and continued transmigration.

Śrī Kṛṣṇa narrated the means for eradicating sorrow, delusion etc. to enlighten those who are filled with desire to attain the highest human goal (Puruṣārtha).

The author had intense eager to explain the subtle meaning of the teachings of Śrī Kṛṣṇa in Gītā and that is stated as the object of writing this Gūḍhārtha-Dīpikā.

The Karma and how to get the purification of mind and obtain steadfastness in renunciation were well described. Śaṅkarā has also of the same opinion that Niṣkāma- Karma and renunciation will purify the mind and karma can only be a means to Jñāna and cannot directly lead to liberation.

Karma is performed with a sense of dedication of the fruits of the action to the Lord and not hankering for fruits. Thus steadfastness in action can be attained through karma-Bhakti. There after spring a firm hankering for liberation and obtaining knowledge. Then approaching a guru and through Śravaṇa, manana and Nididhyāsana to obtain the universal vision of (immediate knowledge of identity of Brahman and Self) is described in detail for the benefit of the aspirants.

The utility of the Pātañjali yoga has been stressed and admitted as the means of realization. The author has mentioned that devotion will be required even in the higher stages to avoid hindrances that may crop up.

Jñāna or knowledge is to meditate on the knowledge to intuitionally seek the identity of the self with the Lord which leads to liberation. Simply identifying the self with the Lord is not enough and unity is a state to be experienced then only liberation occurs.

Thus, the annotation gives a broad idea of, the author adopted in the composition of the commentary and the emphasis he has given to the disciplines. The commentary is a great addition to the several commentaries on Gītā.

4.3 DEVOTIONAL ASPECTS IN VARIOUS VERSES

The devotional sentiments expressed by the author are examined and it is found that Madhusūdana articulated that Bhakti as the principal factor for to attain the grace of the Lord.

Śrī Kṛṣṇa has mentioned that there are four classes of people of virtuous deeds adore Him[25]. They are (i) **Ārtaḥ** (who is afflicted). (ii)**Jijñāsu:** A seeker of knowledge. (iii**)** **Arthārthī** seeker of wealth (iv) **Jñāni**: A man of knowledge. Madhusūdana has given a detailed explanation giving the examples of devotees in each class quoting characters from Bhāgavatapurāṇa.

i). **Ārtaḥ:** who is fallen in the clutches of affliction, of dangers from enemies, deceases etc to get rid of them.

   a). People of Vraja when Indra caused down Pour of rain as wrath on them.

   b). Multiple princes abducted and confined in prison by Jarāsanḍha.

   c). Draupadi, when she is subjected to shame by trying to undress her by Kauravas.

   d. The elephant king when caught by crocodile.

ii). **Jijñāsu:** Seeker of knowledge with aspiration for liberation (viz)Janaka, the king of Mithila, Mucakunda, and Uddhava.

iii). **Arthārthī:** seeker of wealth, one who is covetous of enjoyment here and hereafter viz. Sugrīva, Vibhīṣaṇa.

iv). **Jñānī:** All the three types of devotees mentioned above have devotion with desires but the fourth one, Jñāni has no desires. He is in possession of knowledge for direct realization of the true nature of the Lord and who consider that there is nobody else but Vāsudeva to whom he can be devoted. viz. Nārada, Prahlāda , Śuka and such others.

The author quoted other type of devotees like Gopīs, Akrūra etc. who are selfless devotees with pure love.

He also tried to have distinction (among the four classes devotees mentioned by Kṛṣṇa, who all are, of virtuous deeds) still a Jñāni because of the predominance of Love consequent on the selflessness generated by abundance of good deeds. Kṛṣṇa has mentioned that He is very much dear to the man of knowledge; therefore, he too is dear to Me[26]. Jñāni is a man of knowledge of reality, who is free from all desires, excels all.

Jñāni is superior to all since he is endowed with steadfastness and no cause for distraction as his mind is absorbed in the Lord (who is not different from the indwelling self). He has devotion and love, only for God because he has no other object of attachment. 'I am supreme self, who am no different from in dwelling self, very much super abundantly dear (an object of unqualified love), he too is superabundantly superior to ME".

In another verse Kṛṣṇa has further clarified that "All these are indeed excellent, but the man of knowledge is very to the self of mine. This is my firm conclusion. He has with steadfast mind accepted Me alone as the supreme goal".

Quoting Upaniṣad verse (Ch.u 1.1.10) Madhusūdana mentioned that 'A devotee who is man of knowledge is very much devoted to me' it certainly follows that even one who is a devotee but lacks knowledge is also dear" for this is to be for the word '*atyartham*' of the Upaniṣad Verse.[27]

M.S. in continuation of his commentary on the earlier verse stated that, at the end of many births which are sources of acquiring virtue little by little, in the final birth in which all virtues will ripen and he constantly adore the Lord.The object of unqualified love becomes 'Jñānavān' imbued with knowledge that Vāsudeva is all, with a vision, "everything and I are Vāsudeva for all love culminates in ME. Therefore he, who is endued with knowledge is full of devotion to ME; is a high souled one, he is very rare, a Jīvanmukta as a result of having extremely pure mind". Thus, Madhusūdana articulates that the Jñāni is distinct only on account of being full of devotion.

The three classes of devotees, other than Jñāni are mentioned as indeed are excellent. All though the effort, the possession and the seeing difference be common, My devotees attains through stages the highest result called liberation as compared with the devotees of other Gods.

Śrī Kṛṣṇa has mentioned that who so ever with unswerving mind and imbued with devotion and concentration etc. will reach that resplendent supreme person[28]. Both Śaṅkara and Madhusūdana have commented that the aspirant to have wisdom, imbued with devotion, deep love and concentration.

Kṛṣṇa mentioned "O! Pārtha, which Supreme person, in whom is in all the created things and by whom all this is pervaded is reached through one pointed devotion."[29]

Śaṅkara has in his commentary mentioned "is reached through '*ananny*ā' (Non other) one pointed devotion, characterized as "knowledge" which is one- pointed which relates to the self, but Madhusūdana commented the same as characterized as 'Love' not in any other way. Thus, he has given his own opinion.

M.S. preferred to make a detailed comment on verse 9.14 the various vows extensively from Patañjali-yoga Sūtras and also mentioned " ĪŚvara *Prānidhāna*) from which direct realization of inner most consciousness and also eradication of impediments as a result of offering salutations etc., remaining always with devotion with supreme love towards the Lord, the supreme guru. "The noble-minded worship Me, they constantly think of Me and after full growth of spiritual disciples, the knowledge 'I am Brahman' citing also the Upaniṣad verse (ŚU 6.23).

Śrī Kṛṣṇa mentioned that he will accept offerings from devotees. "Who so ever offers me with devotion a leaf, a flower, a fruit or water, I accept that (Gift) of the pure hearted man which has been devotionally presented[30].

M.S. has made an elaborate commentary wherein he mentioned that with devotion and belief that there is nothing higher than 'Vāsudeva'. The commentary indicates the following as observed by the Lord.

'All that the devotee is offering me is already mine even though they are insignificant, the Lord accepts. I become satisfied by lovingly accepting like food'. The Śṛuti says that Gods do not drink or eat. They are contended by seeing this very nectar" (Ch.U 3.6.1) but Madhusūdana, adopted the literal meaning of the word *asnami*- "I eat." devotionally presented is classified as presented with love. Thus, he states that exclusive specification of devotion as Love. He further adds that accepting the Gift, there is no distinction of the Varṇa of the devotee (quoting the incident of Kṛṣṇa eating beaten rice from Sudāma his childhood friend and also like a child who do not think of eating whatever is given by its mother, the Lord eats the fruit or the flower etc. offered by devotee.

While mentioning that devotion alone is the cause of the Lord's satisfaction, the author mentions not like "other gods anything else like offering of a valuable, offering present etc. which need expenditure of great amount of money and exertion, Hence avoiding other deities, one should worship the Lord with love alone as the purport of the verse.

Kṛṣṇa has clarified that He is treats all devotees equally and do not favour anybody. "I am equally present in all living beings; to me there is none detestable, or none dear, but those who worship me with devotion, they surely exist in me (and) I too surely exists in them"[31].

Śaṅkara has stated the meaning and given the example of fire warding of cold from objects near to it and not which are far away, that although the Lord exists in all beings equally and there is no partiality whatsoever. However, the devotees exist in the Lord by their devotion to the Him with pure mind as their very nature (not by the love of the Lord), others will not be present in him.

M.S. gave the example of Sun as follows. The devotees will be able to purify their minds, become of predominant in Sattva guṇa, devoid of Rajas and Tamas. The Lord will exist in their mind by way of being reflected in the pure mental modification. The others whose mind is impure will be like an opaque object and will not be able to receive the reflection and hence God cannot manifest in their minds. The author adds that this is the greatness of devotion of Kṛṣṇa that creates the difference even among equals.

Kṛṣṇa in order to clarify the doubts of Arjuna that He is the all-pervading supreme person has revealed His cosmic form to him. The Lord said that the cosmic form can be known and seen and entered into only by those having single-minded devotion. The form cannot be seen even by Gods. Similarly, not through the Vedas, not by austerity, not by gifts, not even by sacrifice this can be seen.[32]

Kṛṣṇa clarified that "By single minded devotion am I, in this form-able to be known and seen, and be entered into, O! Destroyer of foes".[33]

Madhusūdana has made a commentary in which he mentioned, the reality is seen by one pointed devotion, but can be intellectually realized only on the perfection of Śravaṇa, manana and Nididhyāsana on the Upaniṣadic utterances. Then, nescience and its products having been eliminated as a result of realizing the true nature, I am also, able to be to be entered, to be attained in My true nature. O! Destroyer of foes, meaning thereby he, being subduer of enemy, nescience, is eligible for entry." Thus Madhusūdana has adopted the advaitic concept of realisation.

It is stated that "one who has become Brahman and has become pure minded does not grieve or crave. Becoming the same towards all beings, he attains Supreme devotion to me"[34]

The person who, having discarded egoism, pride, desire, anger and superfluous possessions free from the idea of 'me' and mine' and so even with his body is fit for becoming Brahman. Śaṅkara commented that person who become Brahman and attained the blissfulness of self does not grieve for the things lost nor crave for things for what he has not. The devotee becomes the same to all beings, judges' happiness or sorrow in all beings by the same standard as he would apply to himself[35] . The one who has this kind of steadfast devotion knows Me, the Supreme Lord. He attains devotion described as knowledge (described as the last of the four classes of People adore Me. (see BG 7.16.).

Madhusūdana has also referred the devotee mentioned here as Advaita Jñāni and the nature of devotion is *'Jñānā lakṣaṇā Bhakti'*

In a similar manner the devotion is accepted as knowledge both by Śaṅkara and Madhusūdana in respect of Verses 13.10 and 18.54.

The verse 14.26 Kṛṣṇa has mentioned 'any one, a monk or a man of action, who always meditate on 'Me' Nārāyaṇa (residing in the hearts of all beings) through unwavering yoga of devotion (supreme love) having transcended the three guṇas becomes fit to become Brahman for liberation'.

In verse BG 14.27 Kṛṣṇa has stated 'I am the abode of Brahman-the indestructible and immutable, the eternal, the dharma and absolute bliss'.

Śaṅkara made the commentary as follows.

'I am, who is the innermost self is the abode of Brahman which is the supreme self.

- The kind of Brahman is,
- That is indestructible,
- That which is immutable,
- That which is eternal,
- That which is realizable through yoga of Jñāna which is called Dharma (virtue),
- That which is absolute, unfailing bliss by nature.

Since the innermost self is the abode of the supreme self, which is immortal, therefore with perfect knowledge, it is realizable with certainty to be the supreme self. This has been stated in 'he qualifies for becoming Brahman'.

The purport is 'indeed the power of God through which Brahman sets out, comes forth, for the purpose of favoring the devotees etc.'. 'I am that power which is Brahman. A power and the possessor of power are non-different. The Brahman means conditioned Brahman. I myself am the un-conditioned Brahman-and none else- am the abode.'

Madhusūdana generally accepting the above has made further commentary quoting the episode of Brahma (the creator) who has extolling Kṛṣṇa when he was humbled when he wanted to test Kṛṣṇa by hiding the cows and cow herd boys. (BhP10.14.23). He has also mentioned the verse narrated by Śuka to Parīksit ' Know that Kṛṣṇa to be the self of all living beings, the God of the world (alone), even though He appears through his Māyā (deluding power) like one invested with a body'(BhP 10.14.55).

4.4 BHAKTI YOGA SECTION OF GŪḌHĀRTHA-ḌĪPIKĀ

The scripture Gītā has from chapter two till end of chapter ten, the meditation on the supreme self, Brahman, the immutable devoid of any qualifications was mentioned. After The revelation of the cosmic form of the Lord, comprising of the whole universe the manifestation with attributes has been shown for the purpose of single-minded devotion. This has created a doubt in the mind of Arjuna as to which one, those who meditate on the immutable, the unmanifest or the God in cosmic form will best experience of the yoga?

The two different forms of devotion of manifest personal God and the unmanifest and impersonal God are given as follows.

The Unmanifest the Godhead is incomprehensible, form-less, attribute less, and is transcendental absolute Reality. He is not involved in any actions, silent and immutable.

The personal God is the Lord of the universe, the creator, preserver and destroyer. Omnipresent, Omniscient, with universal form and all powerful. He is in all things and the inner controller of beings, immanent in all things.

The Lord has clarified as follows.

"Those who meditate on Me by fixing their minds with steadfast devotion with supreme faith, they are considered as the most perfect yogīs according Me."[36]

The Lord has specified three conditions.

i). Fixing the Mind on the Lord.

ii). Ever steadfast and worship.

iii). Supreme faith.

4.4.1 WORSHIP OF AND FEATURES OF UNMANIFEST

The devotion on the Unmanifest is stated as follows.

"Those, however, who meditate on the imperishable, the indefinable, the Unmanifest, which is all-pervading, in-comprehensible seated in Māyā, un-moving and constant,- by fully controlling all the organs and being even-minded everywhere, they, engaged in welfare of all beings attain Me alone".[37]The adjectives indicating, the characteristics of the immutable Brahman are as follows.

i) ***Anirdeśyam:*** *The* indefinable–being unmanifest, beyond range of words.
ii) ***Avyaktam*:** It is not comprehensible through any means of knowledge.
iii) ***Sarvatragam*:** All pervading, perceived like space.
iv) ***Acintyam*:** Incomprehensible. It is not an object of the mind.
v) ***Kutastham:*** changeless. Seated in Māyā, that which, being unreal, appears as real.
vi) ***Acalam*:** Immovable.
vii) **Dhruvam:** constant, eternal. Thus discussing various Upaniṣadic utterances, it was concluded that the worshipper attains Me alone, the imperishable Brahman after removing through Śravana, Manana, and Nididhyāsana regarding the object of the Knowledge. The statement that the man of knowledge is the very self of mine, tis my firm conclusion stated earlier was mentioned once again.

The Lord has introduced a rider that that for those whose minds attached to the unmanifest the trouble is greater[38].

4.4.2 MEDITATIONS OF QUALIFIED ASPECT OF THE LORD

The devotion to Manifested has been described.

M.S. has made the comment that devotion to manifest is easy, where, as devotion to unmanifest God, involving hardship is with pain for embodied souls. The result obtained being same that which is obtained by easy means is superior in comparison to the other.

The devotee who meditates on manifest form of the Lord obtains Brahmalok. He gets the glory of Hiraṇayagarbha and gets supreme emancipation along with Hiraṇayagarbha.

Madhusūdana has commented that while enjoying the glory, he directly experiences the result of meditation on unqualified Brahman, with self the help of self-emerging valid proof of Vedanta. The self and the supreme self, which is non-different from the inmost self and is non- dual, which dwells in the body, which is penetrated into one's heart, which is different from and superior to 'Hiraṇayagarbha', as a result, he becomes liberated. It may be recalled that Kṛṣṇa has mentioned earlier, 'My devotees will attain through stages the highest result called liberation.'[39]

Thus, the commentary concluded by stating that result of the meditation on unconditioned Brahman is achieved through god's grace by the meditations on qualified Brahman.

MS has made elaborate commentary on meditating on Vāsudeva, maintain uninterrupted current of mental modifications of the same kind of the Lord to be contemplated in the *Dhyāyataḥ* etc and eulogized meditation on the qualified Brahman with a single-minded concentration. It is further stated that the Lord grants the worshipper of the qualified Brahman, gives the support of knowledge, becomes without delay quickly indeed in that very life, holding them up in pure Brahman, which is beyond all obstacles, above the sea of the world. The world itself is fraught with death which is false nescience and its effect. "Fix the mind on Me alone and rest the intellect. There is no doubt thereafter you will dwell in Me alone."[40] The Lord has promised that by constantly thinking of Him alone, eschewing all other objects, further clarifying the doubt, that attaining knowledge hereafter, after fall of the body you will dwell, in identity with Me, In Me alone, in pure Brahman itself.

4.4.3. MEANS OF GOD REALISATION AS PER ABILITY

The Lord has by disparaging meditation on imperishable as being very difficult for many who lack the necessary competence has enjoined the meditation on the qualified Brahman. For those whose who cannot perform even this the Lord is compassionate has enjoined other disciplines giving gradation based on their ability

The Lord has given three more alternatives to Arjuna, if he is not capable of fixing the mind steadily on the Lord. They are (i) Practice of meditation of the Lord in external images. In case of being unable to do so, (ii) Practice of religious activities related to Viṣṇu, or Kṛṣṇa. In case of being unable to do so, (iii) renounce the results of all works.

The Lord has given the relative gradation of the above. "Knowledge is superior to practice, meditation surpasses knowledge. The renunciation of the results excels meditation. From renunciation, peace follows immediately"."[41]

The order of importance of the other means is given as:

i) Renunciation of the fruits of action.

ii) Meditation

iii) Knowledge and
iv) Practice.

M S has made a detailed commentary, in which it is explained as follows.

The renunciation of the fruits of action while practicing self- control and seeking refuge in the Lord destroys all desires in the seeker which is the cause of unrest in the mind. The person attains peace and tranquility which helps to cessation of ignorance without delay. In this way the Lord Vāsudeva, by disparaging meditation on the imperishable as being very difficult for those whose competence is average, He enjoined meditation on qualified Brahman, which is easy of performance. There after that the Lord has enjoined other disciplines also mentioning degrees of inability. Those inferior persons who are incompetent to realize directly the unqualified Brahman, they are being shown compassion through presentation of the qualified Brahman, which is free from imaginations of limiting adjuncts, becomes directly revealed in these person's minds which have become controlled through meditation on the qualified Brahman. MS also mentions Patañjali-sūtrās and the special form of devotion. MS mentions that disparagement of the meditation on the imperishable is meant to eulogizing meditation on the qualified Brahman, but not because of its inferiority.

The Lord concluded that those who meditate on the imperishable alone are, in the highest sense, the best knower of yoga. He has recalled the verses BG 7.17 and 7.18 as being most praiseworthy which were mentioned in Gītā at several places.[42]

4.4.4 ATTRIBUTES OF GOD-REALISED DEVOTEE

The Lord has advised to follow the wisdom and the virtuous qualities and behavior of the devotee who have realized non-duality and are self-fulfilled. These devotees are very dear to the Lord. The same were given in the penultimate seven verses of the chapter entitled Bhakti yoga. A few of these attributes are mentioned below.

i) Who is not hateful to any creature (even to cause hurt to him) and identifies everything to himself.
ii) He is friendly and compassionate to all.
iii) He is always with contentment.
iv) Self-controlled
v) He has equanimity in all circumstances. Pairs of oppo sites like honour and dishonour, Heat and cold etc.
vi) Forgiving nature.
vii) Freedom from attachment and egoism.
viii) Firm in conviction and don't waver.
ix) Steadfastness in devotion.
x) Who has mind and intellect dedicated to God.
xi) Who is free from joy, anger, envy, fear and anxiety.
xii) He is not agitated nor cause agitation to the world around him.
xiii) Who is man of few words and is silent mentally and physically.
xiv) He has no sense of possession and belonging.[43]

Thus, the various moral, ethical and spiritual qualities of a perfect devotee are given. Śrī Madhusūdana has given details of all the above qualities. He has mentioned about devotion repeatedly for emphasizing the idea that devotion, verily, is enough means for liberation. All these qualities, described for a jñāni, are natural to him because of his awareness of Brahman. All these, such as compassion, equanimity, absence of wants etc., are not traits which are consciously practiced by him but they accrue to him as a natural consequence of the knowledge of Brahman. He has gone beyond his limited self and identified with the Supreme consciousness.

The concluding verse of Bhakti yoga mentioned "But devotees who accept Me as the supreme goal, who becomes filled with faith, practice with full diligence this ambrosial virtue as stated before, they are very dear to Me"[44]. It was explained that the devotees who accept Vāsudeva alone as identified with the imperishable and unsurpassable supreme Goal to be attained, it is not enough if one gets the mere knowledge of the law of life. It requires that one is filled with full diligence, practice the ambrosial virtues viz. not hateful etc. stated before and become perfect in life. Such devotees are very dear to the Lord. The devotee of Knowledge is dear to Me is once again stated. Madhusūdana has added, For one who becomes seeker of the unconditioned Brahman as a result of perfection in meditating on the conditioned Brahman, who is distinguished by his having virtues such as 'absence of hatred' etc, who is preeminently eligible person, who pursues Śravaṇa, manana,

Nididhyāsana, it is possible to directly experience the reality which forms the content of the great Upaniṣadic utterance. Since liberation follows logically from this, one should seek for that meaning of *'tattvamasi'*.

In the final verse, Krishna calls this devotion as dharmyāmṛtam – the nectar which abides in dharma. It is supposed to be the dearest to god.

This chapter has given in a broad sense the need for living in harmony with everything in the world basing on basic human values. The practices of Bhakti, Jñāna and Karma and renouncing of fruits of actions are mentioned. Beside the devotion on unmanifest and manifest forms of the Lord, various alternates for aspirants of liberation as per their abilities have been given so that every person can attain the supreme goal of life either directly or in stages has been stated by the Lord.

4.5. CONCLUDING CHAPTER OF BHAGAVAD-GĪTĀ

The concluding chapter of Gīta is summing up of the whole scripture and the Lord's final teaching.

"To you have been impacted by Me this knowledge which is more secret than any secret. Pondering over this do as you like."[45]

Śaṅkara has given the meaning only which is clear. MS has given a very elaborate commentary as follows. The performance of duties as per Varṇa-Āsrama dharma by without the expectation of their result, with an attitude of dedication to God- for dissipating the sins which are bar for fitness to knowledge, the means of liberation- is meant for purification of the internal organ, then renunciation of all actions. Then approaching a teacher is indispensable for knowledge and practicing in a secluded place etc. is only for a Brahmin. For a Kṣatriya and others who are ineligible for saṅnyāsa, but an aspirant of liberation, even after purification of mind should somehow perform duties for the sake of obeying the lord's behest , even while engaged in works Knowledge of Reality dawns here itself as a result of his taking refuse in God or the result of the maturity of monasticism etc., he has resorted in his previous birth or through the grace of the Lord alone as in the case of Hiraṇyagarbha or on being born as a Brahmin in the next birth, he attains liberation as a result of rise of knowledge of reality after his monasticism. (This commentary is rather to be considered as the imagination of the commentator as no such alternatives or discrimination of caste etc. is sounded in the verse.)

The Lord mentioned in the next verse- "Listen again to My highest utterance which is profoundest of all. Since you are ever dear to Me, therefore I shall speak what is beneficial to you."[46] "The knowledge is more secret than, Karma-yoga, which has been spoken before. Now however listen again to My utterance: which is the highest, all surpassing (which is *Sarva-guhyatamam*) the profoundest, extremely secret, as compared to everything and even though stated here and there and is spoken again for favouring you. I am telling because you are dear to me, I shall speak, as it is beneficial, supremely good for you."

In continuation of the above verse The Lord said "Have your mind fixed on Me, be My devotee, be My worshipper, and bow down to Me. (thus) you will come to Me alone. (This) truth I promise to you. (for) you are dear to Me."[47]

Śaṅkarācārya has mentioned that the Lord is true in His promise and knowing for certain that liberation is the unfailing result of devotion to the Lord; one should have dedication to God as his only supreme goal. Madhusūdana has explained the devotion, bow down to Me, offer homage (to Me) by becoming a devotee (to Me) in body, speech and mind. This is suggestive of other acts of piety directed towards Bhagavān such as worship, salutations etc. as also the nine characteristics of devotion as mentioned in Bhāgavata.

The conclusion of explanation for this verse MS mentions, 'The Lord resides in the region of the heart of all creatures' and 'take refuge in Him alone with your whole being' as stated earlier.[48]

In the Verse 18.66 which is considered as the most important and the essence of the Scripture Bhagavad-Gītā there we find a very distinct difference in the interpretation of Śaṅkara and Madhusūdana. The verse reads as follows.

"Abandoning all forms of rites and duties, take refuse in ME alone. I shall free you from all sins. Therefore, do not grieve."[49]

Śrī Śaṅkara has made a very elaborate commentary has mentioned that "abandoning all duties and rites, intended as total renunciation of all actions, take refuse in Me alone, the self of all and existing in all, know that there is nothing besides Me. By revealing My real nature, I shall free you who have this certitude of understanding, from all sins, from all bondages. It has also been stated 'I am residing in their hearts, destroy the darkness born of ignorance with the lamp of knowledge. Therefore, do not grieve." In this scripture of Gītā, the knowledge has been established as the supreme means of liberation.

Madhusūdana has commented that, since the supreme secret of all the scriptures is self-surrender to God, Therefore the Lord has concluded the scripture (Gītā) at that itself. For without that surrender even monasticism does not lead the yielding of its own fruit. The teaching of saṅnyāsa to Arjuna, (who is not eligible being a Kṣatriya is illogical. He has refuted the interpretation of Śaṅkara by quoting verses BG 18.46 and 18.55.

Having found the differences are irreconcilable has made the following observation 'Who are we insignificant people to explain the intention of the venerable one?"

This surrender can be explained in the following way. (i) To whom are we to surrender? It is to Īśvara, the indweller of in everyone. It is the immanent Absolute in our core. Surrender to Me. This Me is the Lord who is the transcendent Absolute. This surrender of Immanent and transcendent absolute is the testifying the identity between them as '*tattvamasi*'.

The surrender is with the firm conviction that the Lord will protect me under all circumstances. It is the abandonment of dependence on any other thing other than the Lord.

Madhusūdana mentioned with the maturity of spiritual practice three types of surrender to God come about- 'I belong to Him indeed', 'He belongs to me indeed', and 'I am He indeed'. They have been classified the three as mild, medium and intense respectively.

These can be explained as follows.

'I belong to Him': The wave belongs to the ocean and not the other way. This is a mild type of surrender.

'He belongs to me': The Gopīka, whom the Lord simply warded off by his hand, says, 'you may have forcibly warded me off by your hand: but 'I will consider your prowess as great only if you can move away from my heart.' This is a medium type of surrender.

'I am He indeed': Lord Yama the deity of death said to his messenger of execution "those who, with regard to the infinite one who entered the heart, have the firm conviction 'All this and myself are Vāsudeva: the supreme person, the supreme Lord, is one'- go away from them leaving them at distance.' This is an intense type of surrender. This is in consonance with Advaitic oneness.

Śri Śaṅkarācārya has stated that this intense type of surrender is what meant by *"mām-ekam śaraṇam vraja."* If we are to realize our destinies, we must stand naked and guileless before the supreme. That is what *'Sarva dharmapari-*

tyāgya'. Means. Without surrender even monasticism does not lead to yielding of its fruit.

In Gītā scripture three kinds of steadfastness, related to each other as goal and means, viz steadfastness in action which culminates in renunciation, steadfastness in knowledge, however the steadfastness in devotion to God is the means to both the above and also fruit of both, therefore it has been summed up last in the text.

Kṛṣṇa has mentioned as follows:

"And he who will study this sacred conversation between us two, which is conducive to virtue, by him I shall be adored through the sacrifice in the form of knowledge. This is my Judgment".[50]

The purport of this verse is that who adores the Lord with sacrifice of knowledge, which has been spoken of in the earlier chapters is superior to sacrifice requiring material. This is my judgment. As compared to with various sacrifices, viz rituals, loud prayer, or prayers in low voice, the sacrifice in the form of knowledge is the best.

Madhusūdana has concluded by paying respect to his teachers and offered at their lotus feet.This easily comprehensible explanation has been rendered by me after receiving the favour of my teachers- Śrī Rāma, Viśveśvara and Mādhava and it has been offered at their lotus feet.

4.6 OTHER DEVOTIONAL VERSES MENTIONED BY THE AUTHOR

Madhusūdana has mentioned several devotional verses in praise of Kṛṣṇa in Gūḍhārtha-Dīpikā at the beginning and some at the end of the chapters which are not part of the Gītā text. This shows his deep engrossment in devotion to Kṛṣṇa for which he was attached from his childhood as his chosen God. This devotional sentiment can be considered has become his very nature and he can be considered as an Ideal devote, like the celestial sage Nārada. These are quoted below.

i). At the commencement of the 7th Chapter of GAD.

"I salute that blessed son of Nanda who is supreme bliss through and through, without devotion to whom there can be no liberation, and who is the object of worship of all yogis"[51]

ii). At the end of 9th chapter of GAD.

"Those whose minds have become purified by Tested the honey of the lotus feet of Blessed Govinda, they quickly cross over the sea of the world and visualize the effulgence in its fullness"[52]

Through the Upaniṣads they understand what the highest Good is; they give up delusion, realize that duality is like a dream, and experience pure blissfulness"[53]. This is to confirm the steadfastness of Madhusudan's advatic realization.

iii). At the end of 10th chapter of GAD.

"There are some able persons who by fixing their own minds on the infinite, certainly bring about the cessation of (hankering) for other objects. (But) My mind. O! Slayer of Madhu (Madhusūdana), gets exhilarated again and again by tasting a drop of honey dripping from your lotus-feet"[54].

iv) At the beginning of 13th chapter of GAD.

(a) "If the yogis, with their minds which have been brought under control through the practice of meditation, see some such transcendental light that is without qualities and action, let them see"[55].

(b) But for filling our eyes with astonishment, let there be forever that indescribable blue light alone which runs about hither and thither on the sands of Kālindī (Yamuna)"[56].

v). At the end of 14th Chapter of GAD.

"I adore the great light, the son of Nanda, who removes the bondage of those who salute him, who is Supreme Brahman in the form of human being, and who is all that is the essence of beauty"[57].

vi). At the end of 15thChapter of GAD.

(a) "I do not know any reality other than Kṛṣṇa whose hands are adorned with a flute whose luster is like that of a new rain cloud, who wears a yellow cloth, whose lips are reddish like the Bimba-Fruit, whose face is beautiful like the full moon and whose eyes are like lotuses".[58]

(b) "The mind is ever merged in the state of constant bliss removes (all) mentation and by eradicating the sorrows consequent of repeated births and deaths it at once attains at once the reality transcending cause and effect"[59].

(c) 'I am that Supreme Auspicious one in whom get identified all the followers of Śiva, of the Sun, of Gaṇeṣa, of Viṣṇu and worshipers of Śakti'[60].

(d) "Those fools go to hell who cannot tolerate the wonderful glory of Kṛṣṇa which is ascertained through valid means of knowledge as well"[61].

vii). At the end of verse 15.8 of GAD.

(a) "The Glory of Nārāyaṇa, the Supreme Puruṣa, whose body is made up of only existence knowledge and bliss, who out of compassion, like a human being taught to Arjuna the Supreme realities and His own God-head, indeed baffles comparison."[62]

(b) "Some persons having pure mind and intellect strive by controlling the organs giving up engagement and practicing yoga. but I have become liberated by tasting the glory of Nārāyaṇa, which is the essence of nectar and is shore less"[63].

viii). At the end of verse 15.19 of GAD.

"O" you who are conversant with good works, worship again and again the light which is by nature consciousness and bliss which has the colour of the rain-cloud, which is the quintessence of Vedic utterances which is the necklace of woman of Vraja, which is other shore of the sea of the world to the wise and which repeatedly incarnate for removing the burden of the earth."[64]

ix). At the end of 18th chapter of GAD.

(a) "I do not know any reality other than Kṛṣṇa whose hands are adorned with a flute whose luster is like that of a new vain cloud, who wears a yellow cloth, whose lips are reddish like the Bimba-Fruit whose face is beautiful like the full moon and whose eyes are like lotuses The following has also been mentioned."[65]

This verse was once again has been mentioned at the end of chapter15 and also in Advaitasiddhi'

(b). "Salutation to that God by whom was composed the scripture, called Gītā, in three sections-consisting of the six chapters in the beginning, middle and end"[66].

(c). 'He, the ancient one, the embodiment of Supreme Bliss, who is here (in the world) enchanting the mind, It is He alone who takes care of our merits and demerits because a man by himself is like a blade of grass'[67].

The mention of Kṛṣṇa as the Brahman in human form shows his firm belief as was revealed by Kṛṣṇa at several occasions to Arjuna and ultimately granting His cosmic form. This aspect has been explained in the next chapter - Bhakti in other works and verses in various other works.

4.7. CONCLUSION

Gūḍhārtha-Dīpikā Madhusūdana Sarasvatī has has made effort to explain every detail that enables even common man as well as pundits to understand the purport of Gītā and it is a great service to the public, although he said that he is writing this for his own understanding. Although Madhusūdana has shown enthusiasm in highlighting Bhakti at various place elugizing devotion to Kṛṣṇa whom he identified as none other than Living Brahman he held to the orthodox advaitic concept of advaitic oneness.

Notes and References

1. C.U. 6.8.7
2. AU 3.3
3. BU 1.4.10
4. Ma U.2
5. The inner organ (Antaḥkarana) consists of citta (mind), Buddhi (intellect), Manas and aḥamkāra(ego).
6. A group of four disciplines necessary for a seeker of liberation.
7. M.S. Has mentioned that śravana, manana, and Nididhyāsana is meaningful in Vedāntakalpalatikā, Karmarkar, P12.
8. Victor p. George, life and teachings of Ādi śankarācārya.Dkprintworld, NewDelhi, 2002 P133.
9. BU bhāṣya, (2.1.20) and (2.5.15)
10. Dhārana (concentration), dhyāna (contemplation) and Samādhi(absorption) together constitute samyama. Also see BG 4.26-8.
11. Spiritual absorption of mind. In Patañjali-yoga it means one wontedness(ekāgratā)
12. Iśvara-pranidāna is self surrender to, remembrance of special devotion to God. from which comes direct realization of innermost consciousness, and eradication of impediments .see also BG9.14 and commentary P585 of GAD.
13. Saṁnyāsa is renunciation, monasticism. Meaning renunciation of all actions so as to be able to devote one's time for practice of Vedānta. There are several (see also BG18.4).Karma- saṁnyāsa means, renunciation after having lived the earlier stages of ashrams successfully. Vidvat-Sannyāsa means, the natural, spontaneous falling off of all actions as a result of one's actions having become enlightened (see also BG 18. 12, 17.)
14. The stage in which the awareness of the distinction among subject (knower), object (known) and knowledge (experience) is obliterated. It is also called a saṁsakti (non-relationship).

15. See GAD P233.
16. Śvetāsvatara Upaniṣad 6.23.
17. Lokeśvarānanda Swamy, śaṅkara commentary on śvetāsvatara Upaniṣad, RK mission institute of culture, Kolkata2016. P254.
18. Bhāgavatapurāṇa 1.7.10.
19. B.G. 7.17.
20. Ibid 7.17.
21. GAD P1000.
22. B.G. 4.8.
23. Ibid.3.3
24. BhP 1.7.10
25. B.G.7.16
26. Ibid 7.17.
27. Ibid 7.18.
28. Ibid 8.10.
29. Ibid .8.22
30. Ibid 9.26.
31. Ibid.9.29.
32. Ibid 11.52 and 53.
33. bid 11.54.
34. Ibid 18.54
35. Ibid 6.32
36. Ibid 12.2.
37. Ibid 12.3.
38. Ibid 12.4.
39. Ibid7.19(commentary of Madhusūdana)
40. Ibid 12.8-11.
41. Ibid 12.10.
42. Ibid12.12.

43. Ibid verses 12.13-19.
44. Ibid. 12.20.
45. Ibid 18.63.
46. Ibid 18.64.
47. Ibid 18.65.
48. BG 18.65
49 . Ibid 18.66.
50. Ibid 18.54.
51. Gambhirānanda Swami, *Madhusūdana Sarasvatī Bhagavad-Gītā with annotation Guḍhārtha Dīpikā.* Advaita Ashram,Kolkata2003, P
52. Ibid P608.
53. Ibid P608.
54. Ibid P640.
55. Ibid P706.
56. Ibid P706.
57. Ibid P775.
58. Ibid P802.
59. Ibid P 802.
60. Ibid P802.
61. Ibid P802.
62. Ibid P800.
63. Ibid P800.
64. Ibid P800.
65. Ibid P1000.
66. Ibid P1000.
67. Ibid P1000.

*****

CHAPTER 5.

5. BHAKTI IN OTHER WORKS OF MADHUSŪDANA SARASVATĪ

5.1 INTRODUCTION

In addition to the two major works on Bhakti namely Bhakti-Rasāyana and Gūḍhārtha-Dīpikā which were examined in the preceding chapters, Sri Madhusūdana has been credited with compositions of the following minor works on devotion. The deep devotional sentiments expressed were also found scattered in some other works. It is now proposed to be discussed in this chapter.

i) Ānandamandākinī.

ii) Mahimnastotra. (Ṭīkā).

iii) Paramahaṁsapriyā (Ṭīkā).

iv) Īśvarapratipatti-Prakāśa.

v) The devotional sentiments were also found expressed sporadically in the following works are also quoted with the meaning.

   a) Saṅśepa-sārīraka ṭīkā.

   b) Advaitasiddhi.

   c) In this connection The sentiment of bhakti as found expressed in verses in Gudhartha -dipika detailed in pages 278 to282 may also be referred

A comprehensive view of the Bhakti of Madhusūdana Sarasvatī can be drawn based on these and will be discussed in the concluding chapter.

5.2 ĀNANDAMANDĀKINĪ

5.2.1 INTRODUCTION

Ānandamandākinī is a stotra work consisting of 102 verses composed by Śrī Madhusūdana Sarasvatī. The work has been printed in Kāvyamāla series in second guchha and was found on internet. There is no other printed publication in Sanskrit or Hindi. I could find a Telugu version of the text and commentary by Śrī Kidambi Narasimhācārulu and published by the author at Hyderabad in 2013.

The theme of the work is praising the glory and eulogizing the beauty from head to toe of the enchanting beauty of GopālaKṛṣṇa, his childhood exploits and deeds based on the stories in Bhāgavatapurāṇa. In a poetic and figurative language, the content shows the fervent devotion and the author's visualization of the blissful experience towards Śrī Kṛṣṇa. It reminds the thrill of excessive joy and flood of ecstasy of Sage Nārada had on having the vision of Śrī Kṛṣṇa described in Bhāgavatapurāṇa.[1]

There are several devotional poets like- (i) Śrī Kulaśekhara Ālwār (Mukundamāla), (ii) Śrī Bilwamangala Swāmī (Śrī Kṛṣṇa Karnāmṛutam), (iii) Vedānta Deśīkan (GopālaVimsati) who have written stotras eulogizing Kṛṣṇa's deeds and this Ānandamandākinī qualifies to occupy a prominent place in that category

The title of the work "ĀNANDA MANDĀKINĪ" signifies that it serves its readers and listeners to the best of its ability by narrating the glory and greatness of the manifest and unmanifest Paramātman (Śrī Kṛṣṇa).

The word 'Nanda' means abundance (no shortage) of happiness. If 'Ā' is suffixed it becomes ĀNANDA.

vi) The holy river Mandākinī which has its origin in Himālayas is said to have emanated from the lotus feet of Madhusūdana (Lord Viṣṇu) and believed to be very sacred and quenches the sorrows of people like Ādhyātmika, Ādibhoutika, Ādidaivika arising out of worldly causes and by will of God. Thus, Ānandamandākinī quenches all sorrows.

The composition mainly consists of the descriptions of the enchanting beauty of Śrī Kṛṣṇa in every visible aspect. The various childhood pranks and heroic deeds of Śrī Kṛṣṇa and devotional praise were described.

5.2.2 ELABORATION OF CONTENT OF SELECTED VERSES

Some select verses were examined to elaborate the meaning and content and their devotional aspects. The work begins with verses which eulogize the greatness of Lord Kṛṣṇa in several ways.

The Goddess of learning, Sarasvatī, Brahma (the creator), Śiva and Ādiśeṣa (with thousand heads) feel short of words and unable to describe the glory of Śrī Kṛṣṇa, implying he has immense glories. As such the author being an ordinary mortal feels unable to praise the Lord.[2]

Brahma, Śiva and a host of Gods offer various delicious dishes. However, the Lord gladly accepted and felt contended with a hand full of beaten rice offered with love by his childhood friend, Śrī Sudāma. In a similar way the author with all humbleness and love do not hesitate to praise the Lord with best of his ability. The author concludes that the Lord gladly accepts the offering with sincere love from the devotees and do not consider the status of the person or the value of the offerings.[3]

The author continues to submit that Brahma, Sarasvatī, Śiva and great poets offer their praises in melodious voice and poetic compositions and hopes that his humble parrot like utterances of devotional verses will also be liked and appreciated by the God.[4]

It is usual for the devotees and poets to describe the beauty of the lord and offer praises beginning from the lotus feet and go up to the crown. Śrī Madhusūdana Sarasvatī starts from the peacock feather and hair on the top down to the lotus feet (*kesādipādānta varṇana*). The author described the beauty of every feature of the Lord starting from head far down to the toes, with appropriate comparisons and choicest poetic language.[5]

Madhusūdana prays for the grace of Śrī Kṛṣṇa which he considers as most cherished and more precious than Mokṣa. The experience is more blissful than cool Gaṅgā, pleasant and delightful than moon light.[6]

The author continues to describe the various exploits and marvelous deeds of Śrī Kṛṣṇa as a child, like humbling the venomous great serpent Kālīya, the lifting of the Govardhan Mountain, killing of the demon Pūtana, who came in disguise of a beautiful lady and offered to breast feed

Him. His mischievous deeds with Gopīs and his play with the cowherd boys based on the stories described in Bhāgavatapurāṇa.

The author mentions that Paramātman is an embodiment of Rasa *'rasovaisaḥ.'*and literature is also full of rasa. Sarasvatī, the Goddess of fine arts and learning got enrichment by adoring the face of Brahma. Listening to music and poetry always brings pleasure to the listeners since these have their origin and emanate from the throat of Paramātman[7].

The author after having described the beauty of the Lord advises the devotees, that they should know and get attracted towards the Lord by his eminent qualities and powers of the Lord and not merely by His external beauty.[8]

5.2.2.1. SIGNIFICANCE OF MELODY OF FLUTE OF KṚṢṆA

The melody of the music of the flute of Śrī Kṛṣṇa has captivating effect on the listeners. The emotional feelings and excitement which kindles love in the hearts of the woman folk of Vraja and more particularly on the Gopīs, how they forgot themselves and enticed towards Kṛṣṇa, are well known and described in Bhāgavatapurāṇa.[9] Even the cows enjoy the music of the flute and consider it as their food and feel excited.

The melody of the flute inspires desire in the minds of Jñānīs, to know about Paramātman. This prompts the devotees to forget and renounce their ego and pride caused by education, caste and status etc. and consider all these as worthless and transient. Thus, reinforces the striving for knowing the self and knowledge of Brahman. This weans away the mundane attractions and an attachment which is the root cause of all miseries and sufferings.[10]

5.2.2.2. GOD IS BENOVOLENT

The devotees whoever they might be of high or low by birth, who are loving and kind hearted or otherwise, who seek the Lord's feet, were all treated alike without any discrimination, just like the hard and soft symbols in the feet of the Lord. The sole of the Lord's feet is decorated with several items (a tender lotus, a disc, a conch, a small barley seed, a thunderbolt, a fish etc.) which are of diverse nature and size. All these are considered auspicious. The following devotes are mentioned as example. Vibhīṣana (brother of Rāvaṇa), Śabarī, Guḥa (the boatman), were all treated by Śrī Rāmā. Sudāmā (childhood friend), and Akrūra by Śrī Kṛṣṇa. A Spider, a serpent and an elephant and Tinnadu (a tribal hunter) were all treated alike by Śiva.[11]

Vedas describe God as having both Nirguṇa and Saguṇa manifestations. Nirguṇa does not mean that He has no qualities but having innumerable vitreous qualities. God is having a great quality of treating all as equal as stated above called '*souseelyam*'. Great sages only could have darśana of the supreme God (Śrī Kṛṣṇa) because of their piousness', but Kṛṣṇa mixed with and played with cowherd boys and Gopīs. He ate food along with them. Śrī Rāma has mentioned "*Ātmānam manuṣam mannye*". Meaning I am a man at heart. He considered himself as an ordinary human being, so mixed with Guḥa (the boat man), ate the fruits offered by Sabarī (after prior tasting by her). Such is the great virtue of God.[12]

5.2.2.3. AUSPICIOUSNESS OF LORD

The Goddess Lakṣmi always remains at the feet of the Lord Viṣṇu, which makes her universally adored. However, the River Gaṅgā has dropped down from the holy feet of the Lord. Gaṅgā is considered as holy and bestows mokṣa to people on earth (even though it has left the feet of the Lord, and this is astonishing). The conclusion is that, one who adores the Lord's feet once (whether remain there or away from Him) gets equally auspicious.[13]

Then the author mentions how Lord Śiva has got auspiciousness despite so many visible inauspicious things in the environment he lives, and apparently with poor looking attire and possessions. Śiva lives and roams in cremation grounds which is inauspicious, he swallowed the deadly poison (emerged out of the milky ocean when it was churned by semi gods and demons) but He is immortal. He is utterly poor with elephant skin as attire and human skull as a begging bowl. However, He obtained 'ĪŚĀNA' hood with unbounded prosperity. All this is possible and occurred as Śiva bears Gaṅgā on his head, which is called Viṣṇupādatīrtḥa.[14]

5.2.2.4. OFFERINGS TO THE LORD

Śiva, Brahma and Indra out of reverence to Śrī Kṛṣṇa were seeking his blessings. Kṛṣṇa brought curd meal and after eating, thrown the leaf and left to play with his mates. Then they want to eat the remnants of Śrī Kṛṣṇa, due to fear of being recognized by others, They went in the disguise of crows and craved to eat from the left over with eagerness.

The author mentioned that the Lord is the provider of all things, and the devotees should offer everything to the Lord first and eat the remnants as the sacred Prasād.[15]

5.2.2.5. BLESSED DEVOTEES

Great sages like Agastya, Dūrvāsa, and Pulahudu are immersed in meditation and there are several other such sages, but Nārada who is a devotee was always delighted with the various deeds of Kṛṣṇa and his punishing the wicked demons and sings His glory. Nārad's eyes were filled with flood of tears of joy when he saw the demon Kesi was killed.

By Kṛṣṇa. Nārada is the most blessed devotee.[16]

Akrūra, who was in the court of Kaṁsa, was ordered by Kaṁsa to immediately bring Kṛṣṇa and produce before him, with an intention of killing him. But Akrūra mentally felt delighted as he would have the opportunity to meet Kṛṣṇa and proceeded to Vraja. On arrival at Vraja by dusk, happen to see the footprints of Kṛṣṇa, which he immediately recognized by the sacred marks on the footprints. He got down the chariot and rolled over the footprints and filled with ecstatic mood. Such is the devotion of Akrūra, who is a foremost Parma Bhakta.[17]

Śrī Kṛṣṇa declared that he would appear on earth from time to time to (i) Protect the pious people, (ii) Punish the wicked and curb their evil deeds and reestablish righteousness.

5.2.2.6. DEEDS OF KṚṢṆA---EPISODES FROM BHĀGAVATA.

Several episodes of punishing the wicked that became a threat to the pious people are narrated in Bhāgavatapurāṇa.

Śrī Kṛṣṇa as a child did some superhuman deeds. He crushed the pride of Indra as an adolescent. He restrained and rescued Brahmā and Śiva in critical situations. He assumed the form of an enchanting beautiful lady (with his illusionary power). These are described in the verses the text, based on Bhāgavatapurāṇa. Śrī Kṛṣṇa's deeds as a child, as an adolescent, and in the disguise of a feminine character are praiseworthy.[18]

Madhusūdana has also felt that the foster parents of Śrī Kṛṣṇa especially his mother Yaśoda[19], his boyhood friends and Gopīs and his admirers as most fortunate, who had the opportunity to take part in his life and shared his memorable childhood.

The stotra 'ĀNANDA MANDĀKINĪ' has an epilogue as follows.

"Whoever desires poetic excellence, progeny, landed property, Life's goals (Dharma, Artha, kāma, mokṣa),[20] Aṇimādi superhuman powers[21], who desires relief from the agony of mundane sufferings will be benefited by reading this Ānandamandākinī stotra.[22]

The colophon is quite interesting and reads as follows.

"The composition 'Ānandamandākinī' is by Śrī Madhusūdana Sarasvatī (who is) like a 'Cakora' bird, blessed with a mind, filled with the glow emanating from the moon-like toenails of the son of Nanda"

5.2.3 CONCLUSION

Śrī Madhusūdana Sarasvatī is a prominent Advaita philosopher. He is known to be an ardent devotee of Śrī Kṛṣṇa from childhood. He is a scholar and a prolific writer. The subject matter being about his chosen deity, he has exhibited his skills in composing the work. He has used very figurative language and poetic skills and choicest adjectives in describing the charming beauty of Śrī Kṛṣṇa. He started describing from the head down to the toes, every feature of Śrī Kṛṣṇa, which is not the usual practice in praise of God head. It is very clear from the composition, his wholehearted immersion in ecstasy appreciating the beauty of Śrī Kṛṣṇa. The Lord's great virtue of forgiveness was highlighted. Śrī Kṛṣṇa is portrayed as Paramātman and the devotion to Him is a sure way of achieving life's highest goal mokṣa. The significance of the title Ānandamandākinī mentioned in the Introduction that it serves its readers and listeners to the best of its ability by narrating the glory and greatness, the manifest and unmanifest Paramātma (Śrī Kṛṣṇa) to obtain unbounded bliss is very significant.

This will be a valuable addition to the literature of devotional praises of Śrī Kṛṣṇa.

5.3 MAHIMNASTOTRA-ṬĪKĀ

5.3.1 INTRODUCTION

The Śiva Mahimnastotra is a famous hymn to the Lord Śiva and is very popular among the devotees of Śiva all over the country. The hymns were composed by Puṣpadanta, a Gandharva minstrel in the court of Indra.

The Legend leading to the composition of the stotra is briefly as follows:

A king named Chitaratha, who is a devotee of Lord Śiva, has grown a beautiful flower garden with a variety of flowering plants, to have ample flowers for the worship of Śiva every morning.

A heavenly singer named Puṣpadanta, also a devotee of Śiva, has seen the flowers and very much fascinated by them. He started plucking the flowers before daybreak for the worship of the Lord; consequently there were no flowers in the morning to be offered to the Lord by the king. It has become a regular feature and the king's men have no clue about the thief of the flowers, since Gandharva has the power to be invisible to the humans. The king thought of a novel idea to catch the thief. He got the Nirmālya (the Bilwa leaves offered to Śiva on the previous day) which is very sacred, spread on the pathways of the garden, It is believed that trampling on them will invite the wrath of the Lord.

Puṣpadanta unaware of this trap, trampled on the sacred Nirmālya and instantly lost his power of invisibility. He immediately realized that it is surely a curse of the Lord for an unpardonable mistake. Puṣpadanta immediately started praying Śiva for forgiveness for the inadvertent mistake. The Lord was pleased with the prayer and restored the divine power of invisibility to Puṣpadanta.

The Śiva Mahimnastotra consists of Forty verses and was translated into many Indian languages is very famous among the devotes of Lord Śiva.

It is reported that the original verses have been found engraved in the inner walls of Amaralingeswara temple in Omkareswara Kṣetram on the banks of river Narmada near Indore in Madhya Pradesh some time in Vikrama saka 985 (ie) 1063 CE.

Madhusūdana Sarasvatī has written a masterly commentary (Ṭīkā) for the first thirty-one verses only and left others as the rest are only deemed as usual phala Śṛuti. (Benefits of reciting the verses). The thirty eighth verse confirms the author of the stotra as Puṣpadanta.

The most distinctive feature of the ṭīkā is that, the commentary is in a dual way in favor of Śiva (as per the original text) and equally applicable in favour of Lord Viṣṇu or his incarnations. The aim is conveying the doctrine of non-difference of Hara and Hari as One God with different names.

It is pertinent to mention that Advaitins do not consider any hierarchy among the Gods, while it is not the attitude of Vaiṣṇava followers.

The following published books are available of the composition.

The original text with the commentary in Sanskrit, with a translation in Hindi by Pundit Rālā Rāmaśarma, published by Chow Kamba Vidyābhavan, Varanasi (2001).

I came across a Telugu translation of the commentary by (Tr) Śrī Kāsi kṣetra vāsi Śrī Jñānandatīrthaswāmī published by M/s. Vavilla Rāmaswāmī Śāstrulu and sons, Chennapuri (Madras) in 1939. The commentaryin favor of Viṣṇu is not there.

It is proposed to discuss a few of the verses to bring out not only the significance of the verse addressed to Lord Śiva but also to bring out the skill and masterly way Madhusūdana described the Verse in favour of Lord Viṣṇu in a novel way.

5.3.2 ANALYSIS OF SOME SELECT VERSES HUMBLENESS OF A DEVOTEE.

1. The introductory verse is addressed to Hara as "*stotrahara*" meaning, one who destroys all sorts of sorrows. One can praise only when the glories of the Lord are known but the Lord's glories are so enormous that even eternal gods like

Brahma (creator), Sarasvatī the Goddess of learning cannot fully describe, then how can the ordinary mortal can praise your greatness? Thus, Puṣpadanta expressed his humbleness.

Madhusūdana mentions that '*Stotrahara*' can be considered as (Stotra+ahara), ahara means protector, also means the destroyer of misfortune or poverty. Śiva is destroys of all sorrows and Viṣṇu is protector of joy (in other words destroyer of misfortune or poverty) as his consort is Lakṣmi (The Goddess of Wealth).[23]

2. The second verse also glorifies the Lord. The Lord is both with attributes (Saguṇa) and, also without any attributes (Nirguṇa) and is beyond the capability of being praised.

In the Saguṇa with attributes the qualities are infinite and beyond description and as Nirguṇa (attributeless) are indescribable. However, the mind or word of a devotee can describe your form and get your grace.[24]

3. Puṣpadanta addressed the Lord as follows "You are the teacher of Brahma (the creator), even goddess of learning Sarasvatī cannot impress you with her praises. As such I feel incapable of even attempting to praise you".

"I am entangled in the mundane world and my mind has become impure and my attempt in praising you is to get purified. My mind is inspired by you and enthused by such inspiration, I am attempting to offer my prayers, and otherwise I don't have such ability. I believe that everything happens by God's will. It is only by Lord's blessings, i venture to try, and hope that you will not find fault for my mistakes in my prayers."[25]Thus Puṣpadanta humbly appealed to the Lord to accept his prayers. (The same prayer applies in favour Viṣṇu)

ONENESS OF GOD- ALL PATHS LEAD TO SAME DESTINATION.

The whole world and the fourteen lokas were all created. There must be someone who has created them. He cannot be any mortal on earth. The process of creation, sustenance and destruction of the world is being done with Sattva, Rajas and Tamas qualities donning different bodies like Brahma, Viṣṇu and Maheśwra in a meticulous precession. Some people of dull intellect who cannot understand the glory of such a Lord are misguiding the unfortunate innocent people. However, their falsehood would not succeed.

The Upaniṣads have categorically stated that the creation of all the movable and immovable, the inert and living, sustaining them and ultimately destroying all this is due to the Brahman and none else can accomplish this. (In favoring Viṣṇu the same holds good)

4. The human beings are too clever. They were born on earth due to their past deeds. They desire to be liberated from the bondage. There are several Gods and sacred mantras, all having different means for liberation, having acceptance by scriptures (Vedas). They are Sāṅkhya, yoga, Pāsupata, Vaiṣṇava etc. and in turn each have different divisions within them.

The men are having different attitudes. They chose any one of them that suits their attitude. Some methods are having direct approach, and some have zigzag routes. Just as, several rivers having straight route and some having zigzag routes. Rivers like Gaṅgā and Godavari having straight flow reaches the ocean soon and others like Yamuna, Sarayu take zigzag routes, joining Gaṅgā and ultimately join the ocean after considerable lapse of time.

Similarly, the Nirguna Brahma Upāsakas, as prescribed in Vedas will attain self-realization quickly. Others who may follow other means even deviating from Vedas will somehow finally reach Brahman. "The entire world is your manifestation and will ultimately merge with you. Your majesty is too vast and is known only to your devotees and others cannot even imagine." "You are an ocean of mercy and you are the refuge for all". Thus, the Lord's infinite glory is described. The author proceeds to describe the Lord's new manifestation (Saguṇa Brahman) which the Lord has graciously taken in order to bless his devotees.[26].

The commentary of Madhusūdana on verse seven is very elaborate. The commentator has quoted from several Upaniṣads, Yoga sutras of Pātañjali and Bhagavad-Gītā and the author has exhibited his knowledge of various Śāstras. Even though there are several Gods and several ways to reach Him in vogue, there is only One God with different names and the aim of all means is to reach the same goal. Thus, a great philosophical truth has been highlighted. Madhusūdana has taken contents of Śiva-purāṇa and Viṣṇu-purāṇa in explaining the terms of the verses.

(The commentary is considered as a separate text called Prasthānabheda for some time)

DEVOTEE SHOULD HAVE TRUE KNOWLEDGE OF THE LORD – NOT MERE EXTERNAL APPEARANCE.

5. Puṣpadanta has addressed Śiva and described the Saguṇa Swarūpa of the Lord Īśvara as follows:

"Your vehicle is an old bull, the Khaṭwānga', Paraśu, and an axe adore your arms, your attire is Tiger skin, the ashes are smeared all over your body, serpents are your ornaments, the human skull is your begging bowl. These are your belongings. The entire universe is your family. The Gods, who are your devotees, are flourishing with great riches with your blessing. In order to make a person wealthy the giver should be much richer than who is being benefited. You are endowed with such glorious qualities. However, your external appearance with antique belongings gives the impression that you are the poorest of the poor". How can an ordinary human incline to pray to such a manifestation? "You are the eternal bliss, a Mahāyogī (Great saint), disinterested in exhibiting pompous paraphernalia and you are satisfied even with this uncaring outer look". To such a great yogi, I offer my prayers". People who have knowledge of the Vibhūtis and devoted with body, mind and soul will be blessed. Only an intellectually impoverished person considers you as the poorest from your outer appearance.

As applicable to Viṣṇu: The big wheel is the Sudarśan Cakra. The blessed Lord made the soft and white Śeṣanāga as his bed, floating on kṣīra Sāgara (milky ocean). The hood of the Śeṣanāga is His umbrella. The Kamal (Lotus) and Saṅkha (Conch) adore his arms. Kaustubha is the most valuable Jewal is His ornament. These are Vibhūtīs of Viṣṇu. (The axe used was as an arm in Paraśurāma incarnation).[27]

EVERYTHING IS POSSIBLE ONLY WITH GRACE OF GOD

6. Puṣpadanta now praises the greatness of Śiva. "You are glorious and bright like a burning fire. Once Brahma and Viṣṇu attempted to find your origin and end of your great liṅga Swarūpa. Brahma took the form of a swan and flew high to see the head and Viṣṇu took the form of a Boar and dug downwards. They made a futile effort and got exhausted, then they realized that it is their egoism that prompted to gauge your personality. When they regretted for their action, Viṣṇu confessed the truth, but Brahma made a false claim and making "Ketakī" Flower as a witness. You have Punished Brahma by removing one of his five heads and made Ketakī flower unfit for worship. When they prayed whole heartedly with their mind, body and spirit, you are pleased and gave them your cosmic vision and endowed them with sacred duties of Creation to Brahma and preservation and protection of the universe to Viṣṇu".

The moral is that for those who shed their egoism and sincerely and whole heartedly with mind, body are devoted, God will show his grace. It is only with devotion that a man can aspire for the grace of the Lord and without His grace nothing is possible.[28]

7. Continuing his prayers Puṣpadanta addressed the Lord as follows: O! Tripuraharā! Rāvaṇa is able to conquer the three lokās effortlessly and got himself free from enemies. Rāvaṇa got the strength to win over his enemies only with the blessing of the Lord who is pleased with his ardent devotion.

In favour of Viṣṇu: Bhagavān Viṣṇu gives his vision to the devotees. That vision will destroy the three stages (waking, dreaming and deep sleep) and they are called three cities (Tripura).

King Bāli prostrated with devotion with his head at the feet of the Lord. Having pleased with his devotion Hari entered (in Vāmana incarnation) the place where has performed yaga and accepted the offerings made.[29]

8. Another instance of kindness of the Lord is narrated: The demon king Bānāsura was a great devotee of Śiva and he got all wishes fulfilled with blessings of Śiva and he was able to make people in the three worlds as his obedient servants and did not care for and refused the prosperity and wealth of Indra. All this glory to Bānāsura is due to his devotion to Śiva.

In favour of Viṣṇu: Indra earned all the riches in the world and able to win over all the demons who are his enemies with one arrow. Indra got such a capacity only due to his devotion to Viṣṇu.[30]

9. Puṣpadanta mentioned, How the Lord Śiva takes care the welfare of all as follows: When the milky ocean was being churned, several spectacular items came out of the ocean which were shared among the demigods and demons. Suddenly a great poison has came out of the ocean and all were frightened. At the request of all, including Viṣṇu, Śiva swallowed the poison, and held it in His throat. Thus, all were saved. But a permanent blue mark was left on the throat of Śiva. The devotees adore it as an auspicious sign.

In favour of Viṣṇu: At the time of the great deluge the entire world was inundated with water. The demigods and demons approached Viṣṇu for rescue. He generously accepted and in the incarnation of Varāha (the great Boar) and dried all the water. As he came out of the slush, a bluish Black layer remained on his body permanently. The praise of this beauty of the Lord by the devotees fills their throats with auspiciousness.[31]

MAGNIFICENCE OF THE LORD.

10. Puṣpadanta is glorifying the immensity of the form of Śiva. Once, Sage Agastya has swallowed all the waters of the oceans, so they all dried-up even without a drop of water remaining.

Śrī Bhagirathi after great penance for Nārāyaṇa could get His consent to send the mighty Ākaṣa Gaṅgā to earth. The great thrust of the turbulence of the falling of the river cannot be borne by the earth, considering the gravity of the situation, Śiva has benevolently agreed to let the river fall on his head and then to smoothly drop on the earth. The mighty river called Gaṅgā, which filled all the seven oceans, looked like a small drop on the divine head of Śiva. This shows that the magnificence of the form of the Lord, which is beyond anybody's comprehension.

This proved that Brahman is immense and that the whole of Universe is contained within Him.

In favour of Viṣṇu: Viṣṇu who took incarnation as Vāmana got assurance from King Bāli to give three feet of land as offering. Then He has laid his one foot on earth, the other on the sky and they were occupied and then the king Bali requested the Lord to place the foot on his head to fulfill his assurance. Thus, the immense stature of lord Viṣṇu is beyond imagination of anybody[32].

11. Puṣpadanta described the mighty authority and sport of the Lord. Śiva destroyed the three sons of Tārakāsura namely Vidyunmālī, Tārakāsura, Kamalālakā. They have three cities and chariots made of Gold, Silver and Iron which can move on land, water and air. They got boon from Brahma (the creator) not to have natural death. They meet once in one thousand years. They die only when all of them are killed by a single arrow. Thus, it would appear almost impossible for anybody to kill them. All demigods are afraid that their existence is threatened if the demons flourish. They all approached Lord Śiva for protection.

Śiva agreed to protect them if all of them co-operate with him by providing a chariot and other armaments. The demigods made the following arrangement.

The earth is made the Chariot, the Sun and Moon as the wheels of the chariot, Brahma to be the charioteer, 'Sumeru' to be the bow, Viṣṇu as the arrow, all the demigods to be horses. On one occasion of the meeting of the three brothers on the bank of river Narmada, they were killed by Śiva in one stroke with one arrow.

Puṣpadanta states, that the Lord could have done by mere a decision and wondered why such paraphernalia has been mobilized. It is only a sport of the Lord and to exhibit his mighty authority over the demigods.

In favour of Viṣṇu:Śrī Viṣṇu in his Incarnation as Rāma has done a similar act.

Rāvaṇa, who was a great devotee of Śiva, got several boons. He won several human and celestial kingdoms. He got a most beautiful palace built by Viśwakarma and his capital city is on a mountain called 'Trikūṭa' and was envy to even Gods. (It is an Island city)

Rāvaṇa kidnapped Sītā (Consort of Śrī Rāma) and kept captive in his capital. Śrī Rāma with great difficulty could get information about her location with the help of Sugrīva (the monkey king of Kiṣkinda). After consulting Sugrīva, Hanumān and others decided to go for war against Rāvaṇa. He has built a bridge across the sea with the help of monkeys (monkeys are by nature fickle minded). Rāma mobilized an army of thousands of monkeys, a warrior force consisting of Lakṣmana, Sugrīva, Hanumān, Vibhiṣana (brother of Rāvaṇa who sought refuge of Rāma) and equipped with a chariot, armaments etc and waged a war against Rāvaṇa and finally killed Rāvaṇa.

Rāma as God's incarnation could have done it without any effort but did all this only to show that he is human in existence (although a God) It is his sport.[33]

12. The Lord's grace and love for the devotees is described in another verse. Śrī Viṣṇu is a devotee of Lord Śiva and every day worships Śiva with thousand lotus flowers. In order to test, one day Śiva has hidden one lotus. Viṣṇu found that one flower is missing, then he plucked his own eye (which is like a lotus) and completed the worship.

Śiva was pleased and gave him the most formidable disc called "Sudarśana cakra" and granted power to Viṣṇu to rule and protect all the three worlds. This shows the lord's love and grace on his devotees.

In favour of Viṣṇu: Indra is a demigod and is known to have thousand eyes all over his body which appear as Lotus flowers. Indra is a great devotee of Viṣṇu.The Lord was pleased with his devotion and gave him the ruler ship of the heaven which flourishes with all riches and the all-powerful white elephant called "Irāvatam", bliss giving tree "Kalpataru", the Nectar that gives immortality "Amrita," bliss giving cow called "Kāmaḍhenu" and the magical horse called "Uccaiśravā". Viṣṇu is always benevolent to his devotees and showers his blessings on them generously even beyond their expectations.[34]

13. Puṣpadanta has continued his praise to Lord Śiva. Parameśvarā! The good results of yagña (fire sacrifice) will not be granted without your grace. The devotees perform the sacrifice after procuring all the material and in accordence with the scriptural prescription only on the firm belief that as a benevolent boon giver, you will bless them with your grace.

Parameśvara bestows His blessings, but some of the results are adṛṣṭa (invisible) and may accrue in this life after lapse of time, or the next life.

In such a case where is the certainty of existence of God?

Similarly, if God, who is 'Ānanda' himself, how is it possible for Him that he gives sorrow by punishing those who does evil deeds?

The whole cosmos is in equilibrium and works with precision only on account of the will of Parameśvara. Similarly, there are several Gods and semi-Gods who bestow boons on devotees, but they only deputize to the ultimate Parameśvara and act as per His will.

NEED FOR VARTUOUS LIFE—EVIL WILL BE PUNISHED

God wills that the human beings to abide by dharma, and He will be prompting those with pure mind to perform good deeds and will enjoy the fruits in due course. However, those who do adhārmic deeds and behave with Dominic thoughts and involve themselves in evil deeds are given opportunity through reformist disciplines so that they may realize their mistakes, atone themselves and follow the dhārmic path again. Otherwise they have to reap the consequences. All should perform actions with steadfast devotion and faith and reverence to the Lord, and any contravention and with hatred will have to undergo the consequence.

Dakṣa Prajāpati, decided to perform an yagña, (Fire sacrifice).He was assisted by eminent Ṛṣis like Bhṛgu and others. He has invited all devatas and Indra. He has due to arrogance and hatred against Śiva intentionally did not invite Śiva who is the principal deity, who has to be propitiated in a yagña. He humiliated his own daughter (Pārvatī) the consort of Śiva. So Dakṣa had to face the wrath of Śiva and the yagña was disrupted. The moral is that where there no Shraddha (dedication) in performing yagña, it would not be fruitful.

In favour of Viṣṇu: Emperor Bali is a pious, follower of Dharma and keeps up his word of promise. However, when he performed a yagña, he has neglected to invite Indra and other devotees of Viṣṇu and, so Viṣṇu could not tolerate the insult to His devotees. He came in the incarnation of 'Vāmana,' (a dwarf Brahmacāri) and destroyed the yagña.[35]

Puṣpadanta in the first 23 verses has offered devotion to Lord Śiva, for the fulfillment of some desires and in the next seven verses has offered motiveless devotion which is of higher order.

14. The Magnificence of the Lord cannot be estimated by mere outer appearance is mentioned by the author as follows: The men in this world cannot estimate the glory and magnificence of the Lord because Śiva is always found to be moving and his sporting venue is burial ground, the ghosts are his associates, He is found smeared with ashes from the funeral pyres and a garland of human skulls adore his neck and all these are considered as inauspicious.

However, whoever chants His name in devotion is blessed with most auspicious things. Śiva has narrated the hidden reason for his activities to his consort Pārvatī as follows.

"I have the ghosts and other cruel and evil forces under my control. If I wander all over, these forces will follow me and make the people frightened and put them to troubles. So I prefer to be in the solitude of the burial ground and confine the evil forces to that place.

The burial ground is a suitable a place for people aspiring for mokṣa and I will be helping them to reach their goal. The ashes, the snakes and bones are the features of my nature. My body is a burning mass. I move about in that type of fearful places looking fearful and so appear inauspicious".

"However, whoever believes me to be auspicious and devoted to me, chant my name, they are granted with all auspicious things and much more than they desired. Thus Puṣpadanta has offered prayers to Nirguṇa Brahman.

In favor of Viṣṇu: Viṣṇu bestows auspiciousness even for people of inauspicious characters. Śrī Kṛṣṇa assured as follows in Bhagavad-Gītā.

"Even if a man of very bad conduct worships me, with one pointed devotion, he is considered verily good, for he has resolved rightly."[36]

The nature of those evil minded is described as follows: "The family in a household, who are always immersed in weeping and other inauspicious environment, will rejoice even for a small happy occurrence. These people are compared to the inauspicious inhabitants of the burial ground. (ii) The people who are responsible for exhausting and while away to make the knowledge gained from the scriptures are like the evil minded ghosts. (They are wife and children). They are the companions who live with the man. (iii)The man who does not realize the auspicious significance of the insignia of the Lord on the face, such a decoration is as good as smearing of the ashes on the body.[37]

15. PURITY OF MIND AND ONEPOINTED DEVOTION

"The yogī's taking off their minds from all senses, controlling breath by practicing eight-fold yoga, with purified mind and with concentration, contemplate on you and visualize your divine form. Thus they are overjoyed. Their eyes filled with tears of joy, their hairs standing on end and they appear to be immersed in an ocean of nectar, is easily visible to any onlooker. They have had the fortune of vision of the unparalleled and blissful Supreme.[38]

16. THE LORD IS OMNIPRESENT

Puṣpadanta believes that God is omnipresent and addresses the Lord that, "Some people who did not acquire enough knowledge about your glory describe you as the Bhūmī (mother earth), the Ākaṣa (Vast Sky),Sūrya (Sun),Chandra (Moon), the performer of sacrifice (yagña), Agni (fire)and Vāyu (Air) and such finite names.

However, we are not aware of any object which is not containing you, and which is not yourself", meaning that the Lord is all pervading Omnipresent.

In favour of Viṣṇu: The work area is related to the solar path, Nārāyana is supposed to be present in sun, Moon and fire and Space. So the Nārāyana is also omnipresent.[39]

17. SIGNIFICANCE OF PRAṆAVA "OM"

The sacred name 'OM' is called praṇava. It consists of three alphabets Aa+Vu+Ma, representing the trinity (Brahma, Viṣṇu and Rudra), three Vedas (Ṛg Veda, Yajur Veda, Sāma Veda) and the three worlds (Heaven, earth and Pāthāla). The three stages (awakening, dream, suṣupata) respectively. The composite world "OM" represent attributeless Brahman the Turīyā state.

The three states is the experience of all people, but the fourth state, Turiya is experienced only by yogīs, Paramahaṁsas and Brahman realized .Those who are devoted to the Lord and repetedly utter Brahma praṇava in their meditation are adequately blessed. The same explanation can be adopted in favour of Viṣṇu.[40]

18. DIFFERENT NAMES OF THE LORD

Puṣpadanta addresses the Lord as follows in eight different names "You are called by Vedās with eight different names as Bhava, Śarva, Rudra, Paśupathī, Ugra, Mahān, Bhīma and Īśāna.

All names described individually are very great. The Śmṛti and Purāṇas describe your praṇava and these eight names as equally powerful. In Ṛg Veda they are called as equal to Agni and there is no contradiction even if we address the Lord as Agni.

When even devatās are eager to utter your auspicious names, what to speak of ordinary laymen like me. By mere hearing or uttering your name all the goals of life are fulfilled. For such a self shinning and glorious Lord I am unable to offer any other type of spiritual service and offer whole heartedly my humble Namaskār.

In favour of Viṣṇu: A similar description is valid and the same names are equally applicable to Śrī Hari, if the Word "Deva" is suffixed to all names, Bhava-dev, Sarva-dev etc. The hidden meaning infers that Viṣṇu is the Lord to Rudra (to be worshipped by Him).[41] The Viṣṇu Sahaśra nāmas also described these names as applicable to Hara.

19. PUṢPADANTA'S SALUTATIONS TO THE OMNIPOTANT LORD

a). O Lord Īśvarā!

i). Salutations to the Lord! Who is very close to (devotees) and also far away (from those who are not devoted to you)?
ii). Salutations to Sṁarahara! The lord who, destroyed Manmadha, who is micro and who is also macro.
iii). Salutations to Tṛinetra! Who existed even before the beginning and also ever youthful?
iv). Salutations to the Lord! Who is existing in everything and who is immutable?

With such most conflicting descriptions, (described in Śmṛti also) I am confused to find the truth and the implications thereof.

I therefore offer my Namaskāras to the Saguṇa and also Nirguṇa forms of the Lord. The Lord is the Cause of the visible world and also the origin of the Māyā (Illusionary Power). I bow down and offer my Namaskāras.

The same explanation can be equally applied in respect of Viṣṇu. However, the following salutary words are made applicable:

I) Priyadava: The destroyer of mundane pleasures by dispassion.

II) Sṁarahara: Who eradicates the attractions for objects with Bhakti to the Lord?

III) Trinayana: The Lord who acts as eye to the three worlds and illuminate them and make them visible.[42]

20. BRAHMAN IS TRIGUṆĀTMĪKA AND NIRGUṆA

The world consists of the three qualities viz. Sattva, Rajas and Tamas. I salute the Lord who adopts the quality of Rajas for the purpose of creation of the world (as, Brahma the Creator) and adopt the quality of Tamas for dissolution of the world (as Rudra, the destroyer), Sattva quality for preserving and protection of the world (as Viṣṇu)

However, Parā Brahman is devoid of any Guṇas or qualities and He Himself assumes the three roles (Brahma, Rudra and Viṣṇu) for creation, Preservation and destruction of the world. He is one without the second and self glowing and is represented by the composite word[43]. The same can be equally applicable in respect of Viṣṇu.

21. PUṢPADANTA HUMBLY ADDRESSES THE LORD AS FOLLOWS

"You have the unending, abundant auspicious qualities and far exceeding than your supreme powers. I am an insignificant mortal with inferior mundane qualities and polluted mental state. The relative stature is incomparable and I dared to address my prayers to you. I am too afraid of this inappropriate action. However the devotion towards you has driven off my fear and prompted to resort to praise you through these verses. I am therefore offering to your lotus feet, the flowers of my vocal praise with utmost devotion and beg your benevolent pardon for all my mistakes".[44]

22. Puṣpadanta has once again mentioned that the glory of the Lord is so magnificent that it is beyond the capability of even Goddess Sarasvatī (The Goddess of learning) as follows.

"If an ocean is made the inkpot, the branch of the celestial sacred tree Pārījāta as a pen, the Earth is made the sheet on which to write and Goddess Sarasvatī herself embark to write uninterruptedly, it will still be incomplete."[45]

5.3.4 CONCLUSION

The composition aims at describing

1) The immense auspicious qualities of the Lord.

2) The nature devotion:

One should have humility, dedication, seeking forgiveness for mistakes committed even inadvertently and deficiencies in seeking grace of the Lord. This is the typical attitude a true devotee has to adopt towards the Lord. The devotional prayer of Puṣpadanta has pleased Lord Śiva, who restored heavenly powers to Puṣpadanta is ample evidence of Puṣpadanta's sincerity in devotion. It is a classic example tshowing how he Lord can be approached by a true devotee with faith and steadfast devotion to get the Grace of Lord, and also benevolence with which God showers His blessings on sincere devotees.

The commentary of Madhusūdana is very interesting. The interpretation as applicable to Śiva was done with much effort by modifying the Sanskrit words grammatically, to obtain a close identity of meaning as equally applicable to Viṣṇu was done which shows his literary skill. There are philosophical truths of the Magnificience of the all-pervading Lord. The devotee can worship the God in any manner that suits his temperament and ability. A person who sheds ego and is devoted with faith and dedication without aspiring for fruits of action will be surely be blessed.There is only One God with different names and descriptions and the goal is same.

The objective of commentary by Madhusūdana Sarasvatī is concluded as follows:

"I, with effort, commented on Śiva Mahiṁna Stotra Verses in dual meaning mode (as applicable to Hari and Hara) so that the understanding of non-difference between Hari (Viṣṇu) and Hara (Śaṅkara) may rise even in those with a low intellect. Let the noble ones accept this as admissible"

The objective mentioned above is very significant and laudable, perhaps need to be widely propagated in the Hindu Society, where different groups with narrow sectarian attitudes, proclaiming "THE ONE GOD" differently and portraying one as superior over the other. They create a void among the people and spread intolerance among them, even more aggressively than other alien Religions.

5.4 PARAMAHAṀSAPRIYĀ.
(Bhāgavataprathamaśloka-vyākhyā)
5.4.1 INTRODUCTION

This is a commentary on the first śloka of Bhāgavata-purāṇa composed by Sage Vedavyāsā. The text is published by www.Laitaa Lalitaa.com (2011). It was mentioned by P.C. Divanji[46] that the text was published along with 10 other commentaries, nine in Sanskrit and one in Hindi by Nityas-warūpa Brahmacāri of Vrindāvan in 1955 of the first volume of his Bhāgavata Mahāpurāṇa. As I could not get a copy of the same, the first mentioned commentary was followed in analizing in this study.

The Bhāgavata-Mahāpurāṇa is also known by two other names as "Paramahaṁsa- Saṁhita", and "Sāṭṭvata Saṁhi-ta". The supreme goal of life is mokṣa or liberation in all spiritual scriptures. The knowledge of the experience of the identity of individual soul (Ātma), and the universal soul (Paramātman) is known as mokṣa. The person who obtains this knowledge is known as Paramahaṁsa. The knowledge is known as "paramahaṁsiyam". The Śāstra that propounds this knowledge is called mokṣa Śāstra. Śrīmad Bhāgavata-purāṇa is topmost jewel among all literature which depicts this knowledge.

Śrī Madhusūdana has written a commentary on the first Śloka and named it as Parāmahaṁsapriya". The subject matter has been elaborated with several headings, and in a way, it can be considered as a synopsis of the Purāṇa. The key sentence is *'Satyam param Dhīmahi'.*

Though the commentary is written in an Advaita point of view, the author has at the very beginning has brought about the aspect, mainly Śrī Kṛṣṇa Bhakti and the cause is Śrī Kṛṣṇa Para-tattva. This is evident in the Mangalācarana stotra as follows.

"Śrī ***Kṛṣṇam Par***āmā***m tattvam natvā tasya pras***ā***datah***
Śrī ***Bhāgava Padhyanam kachittbhavaha prak***āś***yateh"***

The meaning of this is as follows:

"The people are engaged daily in unproductive discussion on mundane and worthless subjects (far-away from the knowledge of Ātmā), and are consequently suffering with so many miseries and wasting their life. However, spending even few minutes evincing interest in hearing nectar like stories about Śrī Viṣṇu will be most beneficial. I am making this effort of writing this in an elaborate manner to explain the Brahman. I feel my attempt as fruitful if anybody thinks and experience the fruit of this even for a moment"[47]

Śrī Madhusūdana Sarasvatī is a prominent Advaita philosopher, and it is found that he has chosen Śrī Kṛṣṇa as the Paramātma and immersed in Bhakti to his chosen God and enjoys blissful experience and seems to be always engrossed in this nature. Usually every work aims to preach something in public interest (Bhahujana hitāya), or else for the author's own contentment. Both the purposes are served in this "Paramahaṁsapriyā". This has been given expression in the objective of writing this commentary.

5.4.2 THE COMMENTARY ON THE VERSE

The contents and the devotional aspects contained therein are discussed briefly.

The meaning of the first Śloka of Bhāgavata-Mahāpurāṇa is as follows:

"We meditate on that transcendent reality (God) from whom this universe springs up in whom it abides and to whom it returns because, He is invariably present in all existing things and is distinct from all non-entities. He is himself consciousness and self-effulgent, who revealed to Brahma, (the very first seer) by His mere will, the Vedas that caused bewilderment even to the greatest sages, In which the three-fold creation (consisting of Sattva, Rajas and Tamas), though unreal appear as real, because of the reality of the substratum. Even the Sun's rays (basically made of element of fire) appear as water (In a mirage) - even water as earth and earth as water, earth as silver (Mica appears as silver) and who ever exclude the Māyā, by His own self effulgent glory."[48]

Śrī Madhusūdana has divided the commentary in three parts as follows:

i). Aupaniṣad Bhakti or Jñāna- Bhakti.
ii). Sāṭṭvata or purāṇik Bhakti and
iii). Kevala Bhakti.

i). Aupaniṣad Bhakti or Jñāna Bhakti: Brahman is the eternal truth (satyam), He can be known as the root cause of the evolution and can be known and experienced as per the

Upaniṣad saying *"tat tvam asi"*. The supreme Ātman is to be first seen in the heart, to be heard in the heart, (Śravaṇa), repeatedly reflecting mentally (Manana), and finally realized by constant mental contemplation (Nididhyāsana). The term *'TAT'* is Parā Brahman (Universal soul), the term *'TVAM'* as an individual soul or Ātman and ultimately identifying the oneness of both. The Vedāntic doctrine was thus established as the Mahāvākya *"Tat tvam asi"*. The commentator concluded that the aspirant thus experiences 'Paramahaṁsa-saṁhita tatva'. The Vedānta philosophy has Brahman as the goal, while advaitins superimpose Ātman on Brahman (identifying Ātman and Brahman). Though Brahman has no form, in the initial stages the sādhakā (aspirant) assumes Brahman in a form suitable for his service. This kind of worship is known as Bhakti.

ii). Sāttvata or Paurāṇika Bhakti: In the sāttvata or Paurāṇic Bhakti, Śrī Kṛṣṇa is worshipped in four forms (viz) Vāsudeva, Saṅkarṣaṇa, Aniruddha and Pradyumna. All the four are one, but the names are different due to the Upadhi or adjuncts. The Vāsudeva tattva meaning all pervading. This Bhagavat swrūpa is praised as Śrī Kṛṣṇa. The Bhāgavata praises Kṛṣṇa as *"Kṛṣṇa swayam Bhagavān swarūpa"*. The others are considered as vyuhāvatarās or partial forms. The Vāsudeva-tattva is related to the eternal love which intoxicates all the three worlds (cows, Brāhmaṇas and all the creatures are thrilled with joy and bliss)

iii). Kevala Bhakti: The third interpretation is kevala Bhakti, the theory of the sentiment of love. The first sentence of the first Śloka reading as *Janmādyaśya* has been grammatically divided as *janma+ ādyaśya*. The Sanskrit word ā*dyaśya* means of the first. This means the permanent mood of love called prema. According to Alaṅkāra śāstra requirement of a permanent mood (sthāyibhava) are Ālambana (the enissuant or the result), Vibhāvana (the cause or kāraṇa) and also saṅcāri-bhāva or Uddīpana (excitant or that acts as enhancing the effect). An interaction of the above results in a permanent mood called sthāyibhāva. The love between a lover and the beloved are classified into two. When both are physically present before each other the love is called saṁyoga (association) and if they are separated apart then it is called vipralamba (separation). Madhusūdana has mentioned the incident from Bhāgavata- Mahāpurāṇa to illustrate the same[49]. All Gopīs and gopas are all directly associated with Kṛṣṇa as friends and lovers. When Kṛṣṇa goes for grazing the cows to forest there is separation from Gopīs. The experience of separation is intolerable for them. They spend every moment of separation as waiting hundreds of Yugas, every minute they feel like long time, (abdakoti pratīkṣana) equal to a period of one crore years. This is (vipralamba)[50] un-abating constant contemplation on the beloved.

The Vāsudeva-tattva has significance that, He is Sarvagya (knower of everything) and Śaktimān (all powerful). This is has been shown by the following incidents.

Once Brahma (the creator) in order to know and test the Vāsudeva- tattva) took away all the cows and the Gopālās (friends of Śrī Kṛṣṇa). Kṛṣṇa could know the mischief and he assumed the form of the cows and Gopālās and they all returned to their respective houses as usual. After the passage of one year period Brahma came and surprised that everything is normal. He realized the *Sarvagyattva* of Śrī Kṛṣṇa and offered his apology. Śrī Kṛṣṇa was kind enough to forgive the misdeed and pardoned Brahma. The forgiveness is another significant aspect of Vāsudeva-tattva.[51]

5.4.3 CONCLUSION

The entire commentary Śrī Madhusūdana Sarasvatī states that Śrī Kṛṣṇa is the center point of the whole work of Bhāgavata- Saṁhita. The commentary has made clear in the objective itself that spending even few moments evincing interest in hearing or singing the nectar like glories and stories of Viṣṇu will be most beneficial to mankind. As mentioned in both the Mangalācarana Śloka and in the objective the significance and need of devotion to Śrī Kṛṣṇa has been highlighted.

5.5 ĪŚVARA PRATIPATTI PRAHĀŚA

5.5.1 INTRODUCTION

This is a small work authored by Śrī Madhusūdana Sarasvatī containing ten pages only. This was published in Trivandrum Sanskrit series in 1921 with a preface by MM T. Gaṇapathy Śāstrī who has confirmed that this work is of venerable Madhusūdana Sarasvatī, the author of Advaita-siddhi and Gūḍhārtha-Dīpikā. The text was secured from palm leaf manuscript in Malayalam characters belonging to Brahma Śrī Subramanian Raja of Edapalli.

The work analyses the concept of ĪŚvara (God) in various orthodox (who accept the authority of Vedas) and heterodox (who does not accept Vedas) schools of Indian thought by way of arguments and composed the work 'Īśvarapratipattiprakāśa'. The author has not mentioned any of his own concept.

5.5.2 CONCEPT OF ĪŚVARA IN VARIOUS SCHOOLS

After examining the concept, he discarded the heterodox schools and the Sāṅkhya system among the Orthodox schools as they do not believe in existence of God. The concept of God in orthodox schools has been discussed briefly as follows.

ORTHODOX SCHOOLS

i) PATAÑJALI YOGA DARŚAN

This darśan has identified God as follows. The Lord is a special self (Puruṣa) untouched by defilement (kleśa)[52], and the results of the actions (karma-vipāka) and a store of mental deposits (āśraya)

A man due to ignorance or Avidyā identifies himself as body and with ego exercises his free will. He indulges in fulfilling of desires and gratifying sensual desires and must reap the consequences and suffering due to cycle of births and deaths. The ignorance can be removed only by acquiring knowledge and realize the self and reflect radiance of godliness. All knowing embodiment of consciousness is Īśvara. In Him the seed of omniscience is unsurpassed[53].

The knowledge can be obtained by Īśvarapraṇidhāna, which is usually translated as supreme devotion to God. The ways for attaining this state are either absorption (Samādhi) or dispassion (Vairāgya).

ii) NYĀYA-VAIŚEŚIKA

The Nyāya-Vaiśeṣika and Sāṅkhya schools are similar in their outlook. The two schools although composed by different philosophers have certain similarities and they gradually came to be discussed jointly in all discussions of philosophical schools.

A literally work should have some author. Similarly, the visible universe is a massive activity, and if this is creation, there must certainly be a creator. Hence the vaiśeṣikās believe that a creator cannot be an ordinary mortal embodied soul. He must be someone, endowed with extraordinary super powers. Such a creator with immense potential may be imagined as Iśvara.

The Nyāya school has agreed with this conclusion and added that such an Īśvara can be only be the recourse, who is all knowing, omniscient.

However, both the schools state the liberation called Apavarga is still an individual effort and Iśvara has no role to play in achievement of the highest goal of life, liberation and it comes about only by correct knowledge of things and Iśvara is one among them.

iii) PĀSUPATAS (Veera Shaiva's)

The followers of the Pāsupatha recognize and believe that Parameśvara is the creator of the universe and he is The Lord of the universe Pasupatī.

iv) PANCARĀTRĀS

The followers of this school take Āgamas as the authority. They believe that the divine who is called by a combination of five names (viz) Vyuha, Vāsudeva, Pradyumna, Aniruḍḍha, Śaṅkarṣaṇa etc. who is compositely known as Viṣṇu is the creator of the universe.

v) HIRANYAGARBHIKAS

A sub school, believe that the Brahma, Viṣṇu and Rudra perform the creation, protection, and the dissolution activities respectively of the universe, consider the Hiranyagarbha as the creator.

vi) BRAHMAVĀDAINS, MĪMĀṂSAKĀS

The followers of Uttara Mīmāṃsa are considered as Brahma Vādins consider and accept Brahman is the material and objective cause (the Upādāna and Nimitta Kāraṇa). He is existence, sustenance and dissolver and omnipresent, Omniscience, and omnipotent. He is attribute less and is eternal, ever blissful. He is considered as the Paramātma or Īśvara.

vii) SĀṄKHYAS

The Sāṅkhya School has rejected all the other schools and only the Most magnificent (Mahattava) is acceptable. The minutest of the minute atom is called magnificent power and similarly mightiest of the mighty and all-pervading is also the mighty, Vibhu (like the sky).

5.5.3 CONCLUSION

The author has concluded the composition of this Īśvara pratipattiprakāśa without any mention of his own conception of the Īśvara.

It is construed that the substance of the mangalācaraṇa Śloka at the commencement of the composition which states Śrī Kṛṣṇa the son of Nanda as the author's concept of Īśvara- tattva.

The meaning of the Mangalācarana verse is as follows:

"The young boy who is blissfully playing in the abode of Nanda (implying Śrī Kṛṣṇa,) who is the inner controller of all beings (Antaryāmin) is beyond the scope of being determined by arguments and counter arguments".

This does not mean that He has no existence, but He is all pervading and also all powerful (omniscience and omnipotent) and is the protector of the universe. His Magnificence is beyond description by word of mouth or imagination of mind and He is none other than the eternal Īśvara. This aspect of the ever blissful Kṛṣṇa is His firm conviction and to that supreme personality Kṛṣṇa, to whom Madhusūdana Sarasvatī, has offered his salutations.

5.6 BHAKTI SENTIMENT FOUND IN OTHER WORKS

The sentiments of Kṛṣṇa Bhakti of Madhusūdana Sarasvatī found sporadically in other works are mentioned below.

5.6.1 SAṄŚKSEPA SĀRĪRAKA ṬĪKĀ

Śrī Sarvajñātma Muni has a written a summary in prose of Śaṅkara Brahmasūtra Bhāsyṣa. Śrī Madhusūdana has written a commentary on this summary. It is purely a philosophical work[54]. He has written a verse praising Lord Kṛṣṇa. The meaning of the verse is given below.

"I offer my humble homage to the cute little boy, son of Nanda, wondering in Brindavanam, playing on his flute with a gleaming face like full moon and beautiful Lotus like eyes and who is flourishing with indescribable bliss which is ultimately visualized by:.

The sages who strived hard with steadfast devotion and service to the gurus, to grasp the truth of that Brahman who is Satya (eternal), Jñāna (embodiment of wisdom), and Anantam (infinite).

And by,

........The yogis who seek liberation by intense steadfastness and one pointed concentration of mind (Samādhi)[55].

5.6.2 ADVAITASIDDHI

Advaitasiddhi is a philosophical work written by Śrī Madhusūdana to refute the views of the Philosopher belonging to theistic School of thought Śrī Vyāsarāya.

There are three verses on devotion are found in this work. The meaning/ substance of the verses are as follows.

i). "The embodiment of Truth (satyam), absolute knowledge (Jñānam), and eternal (Anantam) who can be realized with intelligence as envisaged in Upaniṣads, (the essence of Vedas), who dispels all worldly miseries and gives the bliss of Mokṣa but has taken incarnation in the transient and illusionary dualist world. The joy of directly visualizing Him as Viṣṇu (by virtue of the vṛtti called Vikalpa vṛtti) is brightly radiating.[56]

ii). In the chapter where the effort is made to refute the Vaiṣṇava position and establishing that Brahman is devoid of any form (Ākara) and is pure knowledge and bliss (Jñānattvā, Ānandatatva) a purely devotional verse is written. The meaning is as follows.

"I do not know any higher reality other than Kṛṣṇa, whose hands are adorned with a flute, whose luster is like a dark raincloud, who wears yellow silk, whose lips are reddish like a Bimba fruit, whose face, is like the full moon and whose eyes are like lotus flowers".[57] This indicates that author remembers his chosen deity at all times. The same verse was mentioned twice in Gūḍhārtha-Dīpikā.

i). At the end of the text we find the following devotional verse glorifying Viṣṇu "I offer my salutations to Lord Viṣṇu,

..... Whom the Goddess of wealth (Lakṣmī) has chosen as Her consort, overlooking the other divine gods,

..... The benevolent Lord who is ever ready to protect His devotees for mere remembering His holy name,

........Who saved Gajendra (elephant king) from the jaws of the crocodile by slaying with His disc 'Sudarśan Cakra'.

Who not only granted liberation, but also a stay in His realm to even those that always mentally contemplated (Him with fear or hatred or enmity.)"[58]

5.7 CONCLUSION

The above-mentioned devotional verses depicting ardent devotional sentiment and fervor of eulogizing the Glory of Śrī Kṛṣṇa with episodes from Bhāgavatapurāṇa. The works also have great philosophical truths. The works also show the poetic and literary skills of the author.

In all the works the need and significance of devotion to Kṛṣṇa whom he strongly believed as Brahman has been highlighted.

Madhusūdana as a realized soul was not content with his own achievement and has shown his social concern. He has with compassion towards the general public who are ignorant and struggling in the web of worldly attachments and suffering with miseries, has advised them to divert their minds from mundane attachments towards God. He has also mentioned they can choose any path as per their ability and attitude as all paths lead to the same goal. He can also chose the deity of his liking as all are aspects of one and the same with only difference in name and form. This is considered as a benevolent act with an altruistic attitude.

The author believed that Kṛṣṇa is Brahman in human form.

Nārāyaṇa is none other than the transcendental Brahman. Nārāyaṇa the prime mover took birth as Kṛṣṇa on earth by means of His Māyā power. He is unborn and un-decaying as mentioned in BG 4.6. He appeared as if born with a body for the sake of His devotees for bestowing His grace and protecting the righteous and punishing the evil. In BG 14.26-27 Kṛṣṇa declared that He is abode of Brahman.

Śaṅkara has explained the Tattva of Bhagavān:

By devotion one knows Me with Upādhi-created expansive form (Visvarūpa). In reality 'Iam' free of all Upādhis. I am the supreme puruṣa, Brahman, just like ether, Advaitam (without any kind of second), pure consciousness, eternal and all pervading. In order to know Me in truth the Tattva Jñāna is a must. Tattva means the source of being that cannot be seen with eye. What is apparent is not the truth as it is. What is known as Kṛṣṇa who converses with a mind-body complex is only Sporadic of Brahman. The liberating knowledge is nirupādika. Only an Advaitin can know the Tattva and others cannot grasp this Nirguṇa tattva.

The popular etymology of Kṛṣṇa is as follows:

'Kṛṣiḥ' connotes existence, sat and 'na' is bliss. The combination of these two is supreme Brahman known by the name 'Kṛṣṇa'

In Bhagavad-Gītā the Lord said that 'One who sees me everywhere and all things in Me – I do not become an object of indirect experience to him, and he too does not become an object of indirect experience to Me'[59].

Only knower of reality (realized soul) can visualize Brahman. Madhusūdana being a realized soul and so he visualizes Kṛṣna and constantly remembers Him which he has described in several verses in Gūḍhārtha-Dīpikā and several other works described above. He also mentioned he is delighted to see Kṛṣna (Brahman in human form) which has been visualized by yogīs after steadfast devotion and service to Gurus, to grasp the truth about Brahman as of 'satyam', 'Jñāna' and 'Ananta'.

Notes and References

1. *Bhāvatapurāṇa* 1.6.18.
2. Ānandamandākinī Verse 1
3. Ibid verse 2.
4. Ibid Verse 4.
5. Ibid verses 5-12.
6. Ibid verse 13.
7. Ibid verse 21.
8. Ibid Verse 26.
9. Ibid Verse 68 see also Bhp 10-21.59.
10. Ibid Verse 28.
11. Ibid verse 59.
12. Ibid Verse 44.
13. Ibid Verse 61.
14. Ibid Verse 62.
15. Ibid verses 93 and 80.
16. BhP 10.37.15.
17. Ibid 10.39.26 and Ānandamandākinī Verse 97.
18. Ānandamandākinīi Verse 71.
19.Ibid verse 99.
20. Dharma, Artha, Kama, Mokṣa.
21. Note: Anima, Garima, Laghuma, Prāpti, Prakāmya, Īśhatva, Vasistvam and Astaiśvaryam are siddhis.
22. Ānandamandākinī Verse102.
23. *Mahimnastotra ṭīkā* Verse 1.
24. Ibid Verse 2.
25. Ibid Verse 3.

26. Ibid verse 7.
27. Ibid Verse 8. Note: Ādiśeṣa is described to be Dhavala Varṇa similar to the ash on the body of Śiva.
28. Ibid verse 10. Note: The prayer with mind is mental contemplation (manasa Bhakti), Body (verbal praise, puja (stuti) and soul, means the knowledge of the glory of the Lord.
29. Ibid Verse 11. Note: Rāvaṇa offered nine of his ten heads to the Lord and with remaining head bowed down to the Lord .The Lord was pleased with his devotion and gave blessings.
30. Ibid Verse 13.
31. Ibid verse 14.
32. Ibid Verse 17.
33. Ibid Verse 18.
34. Ibid verse 19.
35. Ibid Verse 21.
36. BG Verse 9, 30.
37. *Mahimnastotra- ṭīkā* Verse 24.
38. Ibid Verse 25.
39. Ibid Verse 26.
40. Ibid Verse 27.
41. Ibid Verse 28.
42. Ibid verse 29.
43. Ibid Verse 30.
44. Ibid Verse 31.
45 . Ibid Verse 32.
46. P.C., Divanji, *'Commentary on Siddhāntabindu'*, Gaekwad's oriental series. Baroda, introduction P vii, 1929.
47. The *Mangalācharana* of the work.
48. BhP Verse 1.1.1.
49. Ibid Verses 1.11.9

50. Ibid Verse 10.31.15
51. Ibid Verses 10.13.61-64
52. Note: There are pañchaklesas. Avidya (ignorance), Asmita (pride), Raga (attachment), Dvesha (aversion), Abhiniveshana (desire for living against fear of death).
53. *Yogasūtras* Verse 1.25.
54. Modi P.M. Translation of *'Siddhāntabindu'*, Vohra publishers and distributors, Allahabad, Introduction P39, 1985. He has mentioned that the author of the Kārika was sympathetic towards the Nirguṇa Bhakti mārga, which Madhusūdana followed.
55. *Saṅkśepa* Śārīraka *ṭīkā*, by Madhusūdana Sarasvatī.
56. Madhusūdana Sarsavatī, *Advaitasiddhi* (in the beginning).
57. *Advaitasiddhi* Ibid P750
58. Ibid at the end of *Advaita Siddhi* by Madhusūdana Sarasvatī.
59 . BG verse 6.30.

*****

CHAPTER 6.

6. CONCLUSION

The concept of Bhakti as depicted in various works of Madhusūdan Sarasvati has been discussed, It is found that as a realized soul With his altruistic attitude and compassionate outlook has felt that all are eligible for liberation and not mere elite few. His aim of writing is propagating to the common ignorant People who are suffering with worldly miseries of life with cycle of births and deaths to get rid of such miseries by resorting to devotion to the Lord. He has also mentioned that people are confused and misguided by certain people with numerous Gods and several means of realisation. He advised that an aspirant can choose any path according to their capacity and attitude. He has emphasized that Bhakti is easy and can be always practiced by all to any deity of their choice without any prerequisites. He also emphasized that there is only one God with different forms and names, and all are aspects of the same God. He has also dispelled the misconception about the Bhakti to Saguṇa Swarup in the framework of Advaita. He also highlighted the importance assigned to Bhakti in the system. Thus, his remaining a devotee to Sri Kṛṣṇa is not in any way paradoxical. He has remained as an uncompromising Advaita Philosopher.

The observations about the distinctive features which give a comprehensive idea of the Bhakti of Madhusūdana are enumerated below:

6.1 CAPABILITY OF SYSTEMATICALLY EXPOUNDING THE DOCTRINE OF DEVOTION

Madhusūdana was a champion of both Advaitism and theism and composed both prakaraṇa Grandhās and commentaries on other works depicting Bhakti. He had vast knowledge of Śāstras and scriptures.

His writing skills, cogent reasoning and ability of adequately substantiating his arguments are well known. He felt that just as the Advaita doctrine could be established with scriptural authority, the doctrine of Bhakti can also be expounded in a systematic manner with the support of authoritative scriptures like Bhāgavatapurāṇa, Bhagavad-Gītā and Viṣṇu Purāṇa etc. The composition of Bhaktirasāyana is a classic example of this attempt.

6.2 BHAKTI IS AN INDEPENDENT PATH FOR REALISATION

Bhakti is mentioned as an independent path after performing desirable actions and obtaining purification of mind. Just like lac gets melted due to contact with heating substance, the minds of devotees who have faith in the Lord, on hearing the holy names of the Lord gets modified and melted. They get delight on hearing the stories of the glory of the Lord. Such a person is neither disgusted with pleasures of sense nor deeply attached to them.

Madhusūdana has given two derivatives, Kāraṇa Vyutpathi and Bhāva Vyutpathi for Bhakti. The Kāraṇa Vyutpathi is a preliminary stage as means of devotion or instruments of devotion. They are Śravaṇa, Kīrtana, arcana, Japa and serving the Lord.Bhāva Vyutpathi states that, constant contemplation on God will result in melting of the mind and obtaining the form of the Lord. This was established as follows. The internal organ consists of citta, Buddḥi, Ahaṁkāra and intellect and it is compositely called mind. One must only think of Kṛṣṇa, remember only Kṛṣṇa, and imagine only Kṛṣṇa by the intellect. Thus, the mind is completely filled with Kṛṣṇa consciousness and the devotee feels that whatever he does is being done as Kṛṣṇa. With such a Bhāva the devotee gets Tanmayattva.

Obtaining the form of the Lord by the mind of the aspirant is considered as Bhakti by Madhusūdana. This is perhaps a unique concept and different from the Bhakti concept adopted by the other theistic schools.

This state is considered as like understanding the essence of Mahāvākya of Upaniṣads like '*TATTVAMASI*'.

6.3 COMPARISON OF BHAKTI AND BRAHMA-VIDYĀ

Madhusūdana says that Brahmavidyā is another name of Bhakti-yoga.

He compared Bhakti and Brahmavidyā and has clearly mentioned the distinctive difference in the nature, eligibility, means and end results. However, both lead to the experience of bliss by the aspirant.

Bhakti results in firmament of Bhakti-yoga and the Bhakta realizes Savikalpa Samādhi, and Brahmavidyā leads to cessation of nescience and the aspirant realizes Nirvikalpa Samādhi.

6.4.BHAKTI IS SAME AS BHAGAVĀNA AND THE PHENOMENON OF BIMBA AND PRATIBIMBA.

Bhakti is defined as the state of mind that melts due to mere mention of God's virtues and flows towards the Lord continuously and uninterruptedly like the waters of Gaṅgā towards the ocean. In that state the mind takes the form of the Lord.

The Image of the Bhagavān is reflected in the mind and the mind is fully enveloped by God. The devotee experiences Bliss. Therefore, Madhusūdana says that Bhakti is same as Bhagavān.

Madhusūdana has adopted the rasa theory but he has given two distinctive aspects about the modification of mind due to melting.The cause of cittavṛtti being Bhakti, the mind the takes the form of the God. The second aspect is that the mind grasps the image of the Lord as a reflection. The prototype is the original image of the Lord and the reflection is Pratibimba and it remains as such permanently. This is an Advatic concept.

6.5.MODIFICATION OF MIND AND MANIFESTATION OF RASA.

The natural state of mind is stated to be hard like Lac. The lac melts due to application of an excitant like heat or emotions that stimulate it to melt it. It returns to its natural state of hardness as soon as the source of melting is removed. However, the impression of the cause of melting remains as a past impression (Vāsanā) and is recalled subsequently.

The Author has adopted the basic features of rasa theory which are as follows. The realisation of rasa results from the union of three elements. The root cause or determinant that creates the emotion is Vibhāva, the consequent or effect is Anubhāva. There is the third element which acts as a catalyst that enhances the effect is called Saṅcāri or Vyabhicārī Bhāva. There is another constituent of Vibhāvana called 'Uddīpana' which contribute for enhancement of to the determinants. The first two are important, without them there is no possibility of rasa and are called Ālambana.

For example, In the case of Śṛingāra(erotic love):The lover is Vibhāvana, The beloved is Anubāvana and the cool breeze, fragrance of flowers in a garden or decorated by the lover, the moon light are Saṅcāri or Vyabhicāri. The Vibhāvana and Anubāvana are necessarily two distinctly separate entities. If the mind continues to stay in the modified condition, it is called Sthāyībhāva or stable state of emotion. This state will manifest as rasa depending on the type of emotion. In Śṛingāra rasa (erotic love) will result in experience of bliss called Rati.

Śrī Madhusūdana has explained Bhakti rasa with Bhagavān as both Vibhāvana and as Ālambana, the fragrance of Basil leaves and the sandal paste as Uddīpana and the rasa established is called Bhakti Rasa, which is experienced as absolutelty blissful. The other feature is the mind taking the form of the Bhagavān and it is called Bhagavadākāratā. When God enters the mind, it will not become hard any longer. Being filled with Bhagavān is its natural state. The mind, due to ignorance, indulges in mundane pleasures and gets clogged with extraneous matter. When Bhagavān enters it, all extraneous matters get flushed out. Even if they enter at a subsequent time, they will only be superimposed on Him. Since everything in this world is Brahman, they will not have any impact on the mind.

6.6 BHAKTI RASA LEGITIMATELY ELIGIBLE TO BE THE TENTH RASA AND ALSO THE SUPREME RASA

The Aestheticians had recognized only eight rasas and subsequently agreed to add Śānta rasa, thus making nine rasas. However Madhusūdana has not agreed to consider Śānta as Bhakti Rasa as was in vogue, as it has only tranquility or emotionlessness (nirveda).

Madhusūdana has examined all the emotions and the corresponding rasas. He analyzed all rasas and argued that if the mundane emotions like lust, hatred, horrifying and intimidating aspects could be qualified as rasas; then the supremely blissful rasa of the divine should also be legitimately classified as tenth rasa without further arguments.

Vallabha also mentioned that Bhakti Rasa should be tenth rasa irrespective of whether the Ālaṅkārikās agreed or not and did not put forth any further reason.

Madhusūdana has conceded that there is a minute amount of pleasure in other rasas but claimed that Bhakti Rasa is the most superior rasa as the bliss experienced through it is abundant. He compared the bliss of other rasas which have mundane emotions with the light emanated by a glow worm and the abundance of bliss from Bhakti Rasa (connected with Supreme person) with the light of the bright Sun. Thus, he declared that Bhakti Rasa is the supreme rasa or Rasa Rāja.

6.7 RASA, BRAHMAN AND ĀNANDA ARE SYNONYMS

Madhusūdana has explained the characteristics of rasa, where and how it can be established and how it can be cognized in a simple way, and how rasa is established in the mind when it has undergone modification.

The important aspect is where it exists?

The Śṛuti has mentioned *'Rasovai saḥ'* which means that rasa is Brahman. Brahman is well known as a mass of bliss. The rasa manifests in the internal organ or *'Antaḥkaraṇa'*. Rasa is like Ātma which has no adjuncts. Rasa is eternal bliss, self-effulgent and its experience is inexplicable (*'Nirvikalpa sukhānubhuti'*).

The pleasure due to Guṇas, which has an element of sorrow, is a normal pleasure but the special type of pleasure cannot be known by ordinary people, because it is hidden behind a veil due to *'Āvaraṇa śakti'*. They can understand not only the verbal meaning and not the real meaning which can be understood only by men of wisdom.

The meaning of Upaniṣad verses *'Raso vai saḥ'*and *'Vijñānam Ānandāṁ Brahman'* is that Brahman is rasa and Bliss is Brahman. The eternal bliss is rasa and self-effulgent. With logic and arguments, it was concluded that the ever blissful Ātman is itself rasa. The same is revealed only when the veil is removed. The Cidātman reveals itself as Paramātman and can be experienced by only the people of wisdom.

6.8 STAGES OF BHAKTI AND POSSIBILITY OF ATTAINING IDENTITY

While describing devotion in Bhaktirasāyana Madhusūdana has given the scripturally approved eleven stages as per Bhāgavatapurāṇa and improvised some stages, starting from service to great people and attaining to reaching the climax of Bhakti. The first four stages are Sādhana Bhakti, and in the sixth stage Bhakti sprouts in the devotee and the intensity of Bhakti increases, the next stage is crucial where the knowledge of identity of self and supreme self is obtained. The further stages are spontaneous and called Sādhya Bhakti. In fact, they are contiguous and not separate. The culmination stage is mentioned as Prema parākaṣṭḥā, where the devotee cannot tolerate even a minute of separation from the Lord. This is the highest stage of Bhaktiyoga.He did not elaborate and left it to the imagination of the reader.

The Vipralamba state, where the lover and beloved are separated, is a very painful state. However the lover constantly concentrating on the object of desire enjoys bliss inside and sees the beloved in all things and at all times and imagines only the beloved to the extent of losing the identity of self, which is a sort of emotional oneness and this state continues till the fall of the body. This realisation, although possible, is not a generalized phenomenon and can be possible only with exceptional intensity of Bhakti. The Vipralamba srigara the lover I separation is considered the sweetest experience which is described in Raslila of Bhāgavata purāṇa.

6.9 THE NATURE OF BHAKTI IS DIFFERENT FROM OTHER THEISTIC SCHOOLS

BhaktiRasāyana states that the devotee will first attain the knowledge of identity of self and Brahman, and thereafter develop intense dispassion and then get purity of mind for concentrating on attaining the supreme love for the God. Thus, Bhakti is a blend of knowledge and Vairāgya and can be called Jñāna-Bhakti, which is different from the Bhakti propagated by the other devotional schools.

6.10 BHAKTI TO KṚṢṆA AS A LIVING BRAHMAN JUSTIFIED

Madhusūdana has shown intense devotion to Śrī Kṛṣṇa and identified Him as Brahman in human form. He has mentioned *'kṛṣṇāt paraṃ kimapi tattvamahaṃ na jāne'* meaning that I do not know any greater truth than Kṛṣṇa.

A study of Bhagavad-Gīta we find that Śrī Kṛṣṇa had revealed several times that He is appearing as if born due to Māyā power and He He is the abode of Brahman.

The second apprehension of the people about Madhusūdana is about devotion to Saguṇa-Swarūpa being an Advaitin. This is due to sheer misconception about Advaita which prominently propagate Knowledge as the means of Mokṣa. Advaitism has recognized the Saguṇa as another aspect of the Nirguṇa and identified them as one and the same. Devotion to Kṛṣṇa is thus justified even in the non-dualistic framework. The bhakti in Advaita Vedanta was elaborated in chapter 2 section 2.5.

In Bhagavad-Gītā, Kṛṣṇa has repeatedly used the word 'devotee' while referring to the jñāni (the realized person). The fact of jñāni being a devotee may appear like a paradox as we understand that a realized person is one who identifies his self as Brahman. In Bhakti tradition, the devotees look at God as something different from them and worship the God in a duality mode. Though it is true that devotion is usually in a duality mode, we see Jñānī who is great devotees, not with a notion of duality but with full awareness that the Lord is not different from oneself. Madhusūdana has thus being a fully realized soul continued his devotion to Kṛṣṇa.

6.11 BHAKTI IN ADVAITA SYSTEM HIGHLIGHTED

In the 16th century when Madhusūdana flourished, Bhakti movement was at its peak and attracted attention of both scholars as well as laymen towards theistic schools. The intense inter-religious rivalry was also high. The Advaita Philosophy was considered only for the elite people as it involved intense discipline and intellectual propensity. Thus, it could be opted only by few who had the inherent attitude of renunciation.

Madhusūdana upheld the superiority of the Advaita philosophy, from the onslaught from the rival dualistic schools, felt the need to highlight the importance given to Bhakti in the Advaitic system and remove the misconceptions of people.

6.12 SOCIAL CONCERN AND ALTRUISTIC ATTITUDE OF MADHUSŪDANA.

Madhusūdana had shown his social concern and advised people not to waste their time in futile arguments and exhorted them to divert their minds towards God even for a few moments in a day and get rid of the miseries of life. He has also written a commentary on Mahiṁnastotra to highlight the significance of devotion to obtain God's grace but also advised that they can choose any path as per their ability. He also mentioned about the non-difference of deities, even though they are known with different names and forms.

In this connection it is pertinent mentioning that Bhāgavatapurāṇa was narrated by Suka. The King Parikshit has incurred the curse of death within a week for humiliating a Saint. Parikshit called all the learned sages seeking solution to attain God in the short time left for him. The assemblage of saints from all over the kingdom were intrigued to find a solution.

Suka (a realized soul at a young age) who is the son of Vedavyāsa has arrived and volunteered to narrate Bhāgavatapurāṇa which he has learnt from his father. Suka has assured the king that listening the sacred Bhāgavatapurāṇa is a perfect solution for attaining God for everyone in all circumstances within a short time. Suka started narration of Bhāgavatapurāṇa which was listened by the king and by all the assemblage with rapt attention

Parīksit by simply hearing about the glories of the Supreme person has achieved the Zenith of spiritual success. Thus it was demonstrated that how perfection in Bhakti can be achieved by any one with sincere desire without any stringent qualifications required by other spiritual practices.

Madhusūdana as a realized soul and as an ideal devotee felt that everybody is eligible for the grace of the Lord which requires only sincere desire for devotion and faith, the benevolent God will shower his grace on his devotees without any discrimination. The ordinary people, who are struggling with their preoccupations with the means of survival, do not ever think of the spiritual aspects. Madhusūdana has therefore thought that Bhakti is the only easy means which can always be practiced by all people. Madhusūdana has brought out compositions like Paramahaṁsapriyā, Mahiṁnastotra-ṭīkā, and BhaktiRasāyana for the benefit of the general public. He appealed to the people, suffering from the miseries of cycle of births and deaths, due to ignorance to avail Bhakti which will serve as a Rasāyana (Elixar) for the radical cure of that disease. He encouraged them to consume this Bhakti Rasāyana in abundance to their contentment.

The object of composing Bhaktirasāyana by Madhusūdana Sarasvatī replicates closely the core concept of Bhāgavatapurāṇa, stated in verse 1.1.3 as follows.

"O devotees possessing a taste for divine joy, Śrīmad Bhāgavatapurāṇa is the fruit essence the wish-yielding tree of Veda, dropped on earth from the mouth of the parrot-like sage Śuka, and is full of the nectar of supreme bliss. It is unmixed sweetness (devoid of rind, seed or other superfluous matter). Go on drinking this divine nectar again and again till there is consciousness left in you".

*****

CHAPTER 7.

RASA THEORY AND INDIAN AESTHETICS

7.1 INTRODUCTION:

Rasa is a Sanskrit word derived from *'Rasah'*. Literally means essence, taste or flavor, sap or juice. The meanings are important constituents of its specialized poetic meaning, a relishable 'sentiment' or 'mood' awakened in the spectator through the combination of elements in a given drama or art work.It connotes a concept in the Indian aesthetics a flavor of any visual, literary or musical work that evokes an emotion or feeling in the audience or reader which can be only suggested but cannot be described. Rasa has been found in ancient treatise as chemistry, medicine and alchemy. In day to day life rasa in reference to flavor essence and taste in cousin which is obtained by a combination of different spices, condiments etc. The resulting substance has a unique flavor not identical with any one of the single elements comprising it.

"Rasa in Indian concept of aesthetic flavor ,an essential component of any visual, literary or performing arts that can only be suggested and cannot be described. It is a contemplative of abstraction in which the inwardness of human beings suffuses the surrounding world of embodied forms" (Encyclopedia Britannica).

7.2 RASA IN SCRIPTURES:

It would be pertinent to examine the mention of rasa in Indian scriptures before we proceed to examine the rasa theory.

The mention of rasa was found in Vedic verses and Upaniṣads and scriptures.

In Rigveda rasa is mentioned as a sap or juice from a plant by way extension the way in which sap or juice conduces taste. The Taittriya Upaniṣad explained metaphysically and identified with the Supreme Brahman. *"Raso vai sah"* rasa is indeed HE the Brahman. The rasa is available only in one's own Ātma, who experiences the Ānanda, which is identical with Brahman. It is further stated

"Rasam hy evayam labdhvānanibhavat
Ko hy evanyat kah pranyat
yad esa akasa anando na syat
esa hy evananandayat" (TU 2,7)

Ānanda is the beginning and end of the world, the cause as well the effect, the root as well as the shoot of the universe.(Aitareya Aranyaka 11.8.1).

In Bhagavad- Gīta we find that rasa is mentioned five instances in Bhagavad-Gīta (ch2.59,7.8,15.13 and 17.10). In 7.8 Kṛṣṇa identifies himself as a taste of water. HE states that HE is the essence of everything in the world. Kṛṣṇa is the embodiment of all rasas.

Bhāgavatapurāṇa displays rasa presenting Bhakti to Śrī Kṛṣṇa in aesthetic terms.

It is found in other Purāṇic literature (viz) Agnipurāṇa. In Viṣṇudharmottara purāṇa experiences mentions *'Rasāsvāda"* experiencing the relish of rasa as the highest goal of art and performing arts.

It is interesting to mention that Clive bell, in his work (Art' Chatto and Windus, London, 1914 P36) has mentioned "Art transports us to a world of aesthetics exaltation, For a moment we are shut off from the human interests, one's anticipations and memories are arrested, we are filled above the stream of life". He has further stated the concept of art also leads him to realize its ethical value." A work of art" is ethical because it is a means to good state of mind. Art is above morals or rather all art is moral because... works of art are immediate means of good...A work of art are immence ethical value because it provokes aesthetic ecstasy" (ibid p82-83).

7.3 RASA SŪTRA

Bharata muni is the composer of Nātya Śāstra, which is a treatise and hand book of dance or drama which include music, poetics, movement of organs and expression through gestures and facial expressions. Rasa is considered as a very significant and as the soul of the poetry .The Rasa has been stated in an aphorisms called *"rasasutra"* as follows

'Vibhāvanubhāva vyabhicāribhāva samyogad rasa nispattiah" (NS6.33)

The interaction of the Vibhāva-s Anubhāva and Vyabhicāribhāva or Sanchāribhāva when stabilized becomes Sthāyībhāva (stable emotion) will culminate into Rasa. The rasa accomplished becomes the source of Ānanda (bliss). It is stated "*Rasayati anena iti rasah*" meaning that which is relished is rasa. (NS 6.28)

7.4.1 BHAVA

The word Bhava is derived from the root 'bhu' meaning 'to be' 'to cause' and create or pervade. The bhava-s are inborn in human heart , permanent in the human psychic as latent impressions and will emerge into consciousness with stimulation.

These feelings are manifested by three elements.

Kāraṇa (cause) various emotions we encounter.

Kārya (effect) the effect will result in the form of gestures, facial expressions and voice.

There will always be some supporting circumstances accompanying the effect.

7.4.2 VIBHĀVA

It is called determinant which the cause or Kāraṇa. There are two types. The main cause stimulating cause is called Ālambana Vibhāva and the Uddipana Vibhāwhich act as an exciting agent to the cause.

7.4.3 ANUBHĀVA

Bhratha mentions *"Anubhāva yete anena vāksangat-vaabhinaya iti Anubhāvata"* which means, Anubhāva consists of speech, physical expressions and gestures of face etc. pure heart or having supreme qualities. It is the reaction following the impact of vibhāva.

7.4.4. VYABHICĀRI or SANCANCĀRI BHĀVA

These are fleeting or transitory feelings that which are moving and changing. They do not stay for long in a person. Bharata has mentioned thirty three such bhavas.

7.4.5 STHĀYIBHĀVA

These are durable psychological states and they are inborn and intimate emotions that cannot be acquired through education or training and are evoked from any emotions or feelings. These are also called dominant feelings. Bharatamini has stated that there are eight such bhāvas

(i) rati (love) (ii).has(laughter) (iii). Soka (sorrow) (iv). Krodha (anger) (v).Utsāha (heroism)(vi).Bhaya (fear). (vii). Juguptsa (disgust) (viii) .vismaya (wonder).

7.4.6 SĀTVVIKA BHĀVA

The involuntary state of mind of a person .They is inbuilt response to situations which are intense bhāvas. There are eight such bhavas identified.

(i).Stamba (Paralysis) (ii). Asru (tears) (iii). Sveda (perspiration) (iv).Romanca (horripilation) (v). Svarabheda (change of voice.) vi). Vivarṇa (change of color, pale) (vii) Pralaya (fainting or loose sense). (viii) Thus there are forty nine bhāvas in total.

7.4.7 TYPES OF RASAS:

The rasa is manifested from Sthāyībhāva and so there will be as many as there are Sthāyībhāva- s. Bharata has mentioned the following eight rasas.

i) Śṛingāra (love). (ii) Hāsya (humor). (iii) Karuṇa(compassion).(iv)Raudra (anger). (v) Veera (Heroism). (vi)Bhayānaka (fear). (vii) Bibhatsa (disgust). (viii) Adbhuta (wonder)

Abhinavagupta a prominent philosopher of Kashmir Saivism has relentlessly advocated for the inclusion of the ninth rasa. A ninth rasa called Śānta (peace/tranquility) was subsequently added making a total of nine Rasas, they are popularly known as Nava rasas. He has mentioned that all rasa are dominated by pleasure *"Sukhapradhāna"*

Rasa is completely different from Sthāyībhāva. The Rasa belongs to the art and Sthāyībhāva belongs to the real life. Rasa is universalized Sthāyībhāva whereas Sthāyībhāva belongs to individual person which may be painful or pleasurable. Rasa is known only through vyañjana, and Sthāyībhāva is known with abhida and laksaṇa.

The aesthetic quality contained in the art may be said as '*Rasavant*". The spectator or who is a connoisseur, who experiences the relish of the rasa is called '*rasika*'. The act of experiencing Ānanda is called *"Rasāsvādana."*

The creator of the art imagines and uses his ability to identify the character, the scenario and utilizes appropriate verses in the poetics, music and other actions etc., to communicated to others and not for his sake

The actor or artist who is performing has to fully understand his role, use his acting skills with gestures, facial expressions and display his proficiency in successfully communicating to the spectator or audience the imaginations intended by the creator of the play.

The spectator who is educated and who has qualified who is absorbed fully by keenly listening to and viewing what is being communicated by the artist in the play forgets everything pertaining to his normal life. Then there manifest in him the flavor of the inborn pleasure from which the yogis draw their satisfaction. Such a spectator is is called as 'Sahṛudaya' such a perceiver is most important for the whole of the aesthetic practice.

In the process of manifestation of rasa we find that the rasa is obtained through the combination of bhavas and there should be a combination of the object and the subject (the spectator) should interact. If the spectator is preoccupied with personal affairs and there by not being able to slip into the aesthetic attitude, will not be able to appreciate and enjoy the otherwise excellent performance. Rasa which accompanies necessarily a detached state of mind would elude such a spectator. This the reason that the spectator with a shṛudaya is very much needed for the performance to succeed in its objective.

The spectator's distance from the real life helps to filter the emotion from all its adverse reactions, the pain, suffering, etc. even pleasurable emotions like love.. The spectator not only distanced physically as well as temporally but also mentally, by reminding himself that what he is viewing is not real. Abhinavagupta has pointed out, that it is nothing but the transformation of ordinary emotion to generalization. It does not imply simply expulsion of disturbing effect of sorrow etc. but primarily purification which leads to exaltation and ecstasy.(AB v134,locana 1.4-5. Also kāvyaprakāsa 4.28 quoted from Sneh pandit P37).

The observation of Lee Siegel is as follows.

"Rasa is at once an inner and outer quality as the object of taste, the taste of the object, the capacity of the taster to taste and enjoy it, the enjoyment, the tasting of the taste. The psychophysiological experience of tasting provided a basis of a systemization of a religious experience.(Sacred and profane dimensions of love in Indian traditions, P43).

In Indian thought there is no distinction between art and aesthetic, aesthetic and Metaphysics. This thought affirms that beauty is capable of being known to man intrinsically and Positioning in the innermost essence of his being. Knowledge and enjoyment are not contradictory terms but synonymous in the highest act of transcendence which secure absolute freedom (mokṣa) from phenomenal ends.

According to the Upaniṣads cosmic creation derives from Ananda, has its being, life and sustenance in Works of art.

The nature of aesthetic emotion, a unique and extra ordinary (alaukika) delight afforded by works of art, and through the experience of which a transmutation takes place, is summed up by Bharata in this concept of rasa. Rasa theory is based on the important concept of Indian philosophy. The aesthetic pleasure 'Ānanda' which is pure delight from Metaphysical concept. According the Upaniṣads, cosmic creation derives from ānanda, has its being, life and sustenance in it. The aesthetic perception is an inward apprehension.

The supreme truth is rasa. The Jīva becomes blissful on attaining this rasa.in Aitareya Aranyaka (11.1.8.1) it is stated "Ānanda is the beginning and end of the world, the cause as well as effect, the root and shoot of the universe" (Manduka ii.2.10), (Translation of Dr. S. RadhaKrishnan. (Quoted from Sneh pandit P4).

In the mirror of gestures, a translation of the Abhinaya darpan by Nandikesavara(1877-1947)Ananda coomaraswamy observed as follows.

" The arts are not for our instruction, but for our delight, and this delight is something more than pleasure, it is the Godlike ecstasy of liberation from the restless activity of the mind and senses, which are the evils of all reality, transparent only when we are at peace within ourselves"(The mirror of gestures ,9.)

7.4.8 COMMETARIES AND CONTRIBUTION OF SCHOLARS.

Rasa theory is fairly complex and long debates have continued about its subtle nuances.

Abhinavagupta is a prominent philosopher, anesthetist and exponent of Kashmir Saivism. He has made an exhaustive commentary on every aspect of Nātya Śāstra called 'Abbhinavabharati 'and on 'Dhvanyaloka' of Ānandavardhana called 'Dhvanyāloka Locana'. In these works he has taken the views of earlier Ācārya like Bhaṭṭa lollta, Samkuka, Bhaṭṭa Nāyaka, and his guru Bhaṭṭa Tauta and taken steps to bring about a unified thesis of all earlier thinkers and systemized the concepts. Thus he has brought before the present generation the wisdom of the earlier scholars. Mammata, Visvanādha and Rajasekhara are some of the writers. The Indian aesthetics has given preference to poetics. The rasa is not in words but it is embedded in poetry.

'Rasāritam gunālankāravṛtti sahitam kāvyam'. Kāvyam is that which is based on rasa embellished with sounds and emotions and also metrical foot. Its soul is the suggested dhvani.

The following are the compositions of various writers who have contributed to the concept of rasa and its manifestation

(i) Bhāmaha (7th CE)--Kāvyalankāra Śāstra poetics. (ii) Dandin (8th CE) -- Kāvayadarse (Guṇa,riti). (iii) Udbhata (8-9CE) -- Kāvyalankāra Saṅgraha. (iv) Vāmana (8-9thCE) – Riti-style. (vi) Anandavardhana (9thCE) – Dhvanyāloka--poetic language, Rasadhvani. (vii)

Mammata - (10thCE) – Kāvyaprakāṣa -- Dvani. (ix) Kuntaka (10Th CE) – Vakṛokti. (xii) Ksemendra(10thCE) Auchityachandrika. (xiii) Visvanādha (14th CE) -- Sahityadarpana-handbook of poetics. (xiv) Nandikesvara(3rd CE) -- Abhinayadarpana detailed commentary on dance. (xv) Rajasekhara (14th CE) -- Kāvyamīmāṃsa about poetics.

Bharata has mentioned that "No composition can proceed without rasa" Abhinavagupta has similar view observed that "There is no poetry without rasa"(dl 2.3). Again he mentioned "The meaning of poetry is rasa"(ab7.1)., Visvanādha (4th CE) in his Sāhityadarpana mentioned that "A composition touched with rasa is poetry" (Sd1.3). Similar expression was made by Visvanādha and others *'Vākyam rasātmakam kāvyam'*(SD1.23).meaning the soul of kāvya is rasa.

The views of Bharata mentioned in NS 6.3 were supported by Abhinavagupta "Rasa is realisation of one's own consciousness as colored by emotion' and rasa cannot be expressed directly through words ,their essence being immediate experience; so they can only be suggested by words(DL 1.4). Similarly Visvanādha mentioned "Rasa is identical with the taste of one's own blissful self "and may be said as the twin of this relish of Brahman".(Sd3.35.

Abhinavagupta has called that the *'Kāvya ras*ā-svādana' is the same as *'Brahmāsvādna'*, Rasa is akin to realisation of Brahman (Locana 85).

Rasa is said to be 'Like the relish of the ultimate reality, (*Parābrahmāsvadasachiva*) (DI 2.4). Similar view was expressed by Visvanātha. Abhinavagupta has mentioned that rasa is exclusively an aesthetic relish and it is not of the nature of an object and not any means of valid cognition nor any means of production. Its existence can be proved only in one's heart and cannot be described in words. Like the taste of a sweet dish by a dumb person. That is why it is called alaukika (super mundane).

Mammata in his Kāvyaprakāṣa observed "Brahman is same as ātma in highest self". In yoga this is relished in its purest form as an indeterminate sprit with no object confronting on it, as it transcends all subject, object duality. In poetic contemplation the self is a subject and aware of the emotions and their determinants and the self is aware through these objects. This mode of self realisation is accompanied by an extraordinary kind of delight called "*Sadya paranivṛitti*" as an immediate higher pleasure. This was described by Abhinavagupta as alaukika camatkara, extraordinary charm.(DL3.33).

Abhinavagupta states that Vibhāva in poetics is '*udbhodaka*' that removes the obstacles to a total manifestation of spirit. He says that the poetical meaning is different from the conventional meaning. It shines out and towers above the beauty of the well-known outer parts....(DAI7.3)

The theory of Dhvani was proposed by Ānandavardhana and is considered as an important aspect of poetics.

The poetry conveys meaning in rasa by means of suggestion (dhvani). There are three types, *'Abhida'*(denotation), *'Lakṣna'*(secondary meaning) and *'Vyañjana'* also called dhvani. In addition to the above, others have suggested that poetics should be suitably ornamented, there should be a style or riti, there should not be harsh words and such defects(guṇa doṣa), it should adopt appropriate words. etc .

Jagannādha pandita who belongs to 17th CE is the last prominent philosopher who stressed the importance of rasa in poetry and stressed significance of rasa-dhvani.

'The aesthetic relish was compared to the metaphysics as it raising one's conscious and therefore of one's essential beatitude"(Ganoli -p87note3).

Abhinavagupta has observed that the rasa and aesthetic attitude underlines the men's fulfillment of Puruṣārthas or goals of life.

The above discussion we find that the aesthetics is closely related to the philosophy.

7.5 BHAKTIRASA:

The medieval devotional movements of Bhakti have found that Bhakti rasa is an intense emotional boost of personal devotion to God.The aesthetic emotion was expressed through Bhakti by a devotee (Bhakta) in the form of divine bliss.

Devotion by nature is grounded in some variety of emotional experience. It can provoke a sense of transformed identity in which one's ordinary state drops away and a universal devotional flavor emerges.(J Mcdaniel " Offering flowers , feeding skulls –popular Goddess in west Bengal Oxford university press New york 2004,P145).

A bhava is also an emotional attitude, which a devotee may adopt towards the God. Dāsya, Sakhya, vātsalya, Santa, Kānta and madhurya.(TMP Mahadevan, in "outlines of Hindu" Chetana Ltd,Bombay,1971,P 251).

J. Mohanty," *in historical overview classical Indian Philosophy*" clarified that in this theory a level of cultivation of sensibility is necessary for this actualization of enjoyment to take place, which will forge similarity with cultivation through practice of Bhakti engender devotion to God. The enjoyment of rasa is said to unfold through various stages, other objects disappear from consciousness until rasa only is left and the particular feeling is universalized(sādhāranikaraṇa) into a essence and finally a state of restfulness(viśrānta)(Rauman& little ,Oxford,200).

The divinity's assertion "I am rasa" in the Bhagavad-Gītā imbues the term with greater theological significance and, again, anticipates later developments of the self, in relation to Kṛṣṇạ who is eventually seen as the embodiment of all rasa.

From "sap" or "juice," the meaning of the Sanskrit word has shifted to the essence of anything, eventually to the theological application in Upaniṣads and now applied to existence itself. Moreover, the state of blissfulness attained from having known or grasped this essence or rasa of existence has important soteriological implications. The Bhakti theologians and theorists of rasa, to engage the word theologically. The ninth rasa,' śānta', "peacefulness," that played the most central role in solidifying the connection between rasa theory and theology in India.

Bhakti was considered as an intense emotional .outburst of devotion to personal God. The aesthetic emotion of rasa experienced through Bhakti by the devotee (Bhakta) in the form of bliss.

This devotional turn of the rasa theory finds it most thorough and influential expression in the writings of Rūpa Gosvāmī (16th cen.), the preeminent theorist on rasa in the bhakti tradition. He was a close associate of Chaitanya the founding father of Gouḍīya Vaiṣṇavism a purely devotional school who consider Kṛṣṇa as the as the reality. In contrast to the theory of Abhinavagupta where the experience of alaukika rasa require the abstraction of all personal details and the transcendence is abstract and nondescript, Rūpa Goswāmi consider the personal details and Kṛṣṇa and his associates are transcendence and beyond temporal world. Thus Kṛṣṇa and his associates of his play called Līla are themselves alaukika and experience the bliss directly.. Thus they are alaukika or extraordinary and rasa finds its original source in Kṛṣṇa and his associates within the transcendent Lilas and celebrated as supreme love. However he recognized the rasa theory and the evoking rasa in the audience.

The very first words of Rūpa Gosvāmī's seminal work on bhakti Rasa, titled 'Bhaktirasāmṛtasindhu', he understands the ultimate and most intimate form of the godhead, identified as the divinity of Kṛṣṇạ , as "the very embodiment of the essence of all rasas" (BhRaAm. 1.1.1

The Vaiṣṇava followers claimed that singing and dancing while uttering the auspicious names of the Lord could reach communion with Kṛṣṇa, a communion patterned after erotic human emotion between man and woman. This erotic love is Śṛingāra rasa expressed in stories of Kṛṣṇa and his intimate companion Rādha.

Mammata in his Kāvyaprakāṣa emphatically denied that love (romantic or erotic) for Godhead cannot attain the status of rasa, and such emotions can only be a bhāva (KP kārika 35c-36a Jha 1967)

Rūpa Gosvāmī ignored and insisted Bhakti should be given a status of Bhakti rasa and presented the bhakti as defining character of rasa.

Rūpa Gosvami's fundamental reinterpretation of rasa theory, is where rasa is simply the fullest manifestation of Bhakti. He has added three more rasas namely Dāsya rasa, Vātsalya rasa and Mādhurya rasa. In the Nāṭyaśāstra, rati is the Sthāyībhāva for śṛṅgārarasa (romance or passion).However, in Rūpa Gosvāmī's theory, various modes of rati are the Sthāyībhāva for each rasa.

The Vaiṣṇava School has classified rasas in to two, one as primary and the second group as secondary. They made a hierarchy. Each rasa, beginning with śānta rasa and proceeding to śṛṅgārarasa, represents a higher intensity of love and progressively greater level of intimacy. Yet each rasa, in and of itself, is also recognized as a perfection of love for the divine. Even so, the rasa of passionate love as śṛingāra or Mādhurya is regarded as the ultimate perfection among all perfect rasas...

The above discussion is based on the article: "*Evoking Rasa through Stotra: Rūpa Gosvāmin's Līlāmṛta, A List of Kṛṣṇa's Names*". David Buchta, International Journal of Hindu Studies DOI 10.1007/s11407-016-9195-4).

BIBLIOGRAPHY

A. PRIMARY SOURCES

1. Ānandamandākinī 'Original text in Sanskrit published by Kāvya- mālaseries. http://ia700702.us.archive.org/0/items/Kavya_Mala_Series_Of_Nirnaya_Sagar_Press.
2. Brahmacāri, Gyan Caitanya, Paramahaṁsapriyā (original text in Sanskrit) published in http://www.lalitaalaalitah.com.
3. C.Rajagopālācāri, "Bhaja Govindam", original Sanskrit text and commentary in English, Bharatiya Vidya Bhavan, Mumbai, 2011.
4. Gambhirānanda, swami, Madhusūdana Sarasvati, "Bhagavad-Gītā with annotation Gūḍhārtha–Dīpikā" (tr) in English with original verses in Sanskrit, Advaita Ashram, Kolkata, 2013.
5. Gambhirānanda, Swāmi, "Bhagavad-Gītā" with commentary of Śaṅkarācārya (Tr) in English with original Sanskrit verses, Advaita Ashram, Kolkata, 2012.
6. Goswāmi, C.L, "Śrimad Bhāgavata- Mahāpurāṇa" (with Sanskrit textand English translation), (Parts 1 and 2). Gita press, Gorakhpur, .2014.
7. Harṣananda, Swāmi, "Śaṇḍilya Bhakti Sūtras with svapneś-varaBhāyṣya" (Tr) In English with original verses in Sanskrit, Ramakrishna math,Bangalore, 2002.
8. Kidambi, Narasimhācārulu, "Ānandamandākinī," with text and commentary in Telugu, published by Author, Hyderabad, 2013.
9. Madhusūdana Sarasvatī. "Īśvarapratipatti Prakāśa", Text in Sanskrit, published in Trivandrum Sanskrit series in 1921 with

a preface by MM T. Ganapathi Śāstrī in English

10. Pandeya, Janārdana Śāstri, "Śrī Madhusūdana Sarasvatī virachita, Śrī Bhagavad Bhaktirasāyana", with original text and translation in Hindi, Choukambha Vidya Bhavan, Varanasi, 2008.
11. Śrī Śaṅkarācārya, "Soundalyalahari", with original text in Sanskrit and commentary in English by Śāstri, Ananatakṛṣṇa, and Karra Ramamurthy, Ganesh and co, Madras, 2016
11. Śrī Śaṅkarācārya, "Prabodha Sudhākara". The nectar –ocean of enlightenment, with Original verses in Sanskrit with translation and notes, by Saṁvid, Samata Books, Chennai, 2002.
12. Sarma, Rala Rama, "Śrī Puṣpadanta pranita Mahimnastotra" with original text and commentary, by Śrī Madhusūdana Sarasvatī" (Tr) in Hindi, Choukambha Vidya Bhavan, Varanasi, 2001
13. Sinha, Nandalal, "Bhakti Sūtras of Nārada" with original Sanskrit verses and commentary in English, Munshi ram Manoharlal, New Delhi,1998.
14. Warrier, A.G. Krishna, "Śrīmad Bhagavad-Gītā Bhāsyṣa of Śaṅkarācārya", with text and English translation, Sri Ramakrishna Math, Madras, 1983 Reprint 2017.

B. SECONDARY SOURCES

1. Abhedānanda Swāmi, "Path of Realisation", Ramakrishna Vedanta Math, Kolkata, 2010.
2. Adiswarānanda Swāmi, "The Four yogas" A guide to the spiritual Paths of actions, Devotion, Meditation and Knowledge, Sri Ramakrishna Math Chennai, 2008.
3. Balakrishan, S, "Śaṅkara on Bhakti", Bharatiya Vidya Bhavan, Mumbai, 2000.

4. Balasubramanian, R, and Bhattacharya, Sibajiban, (Ed) "Perspectives of Śaṅkara", (Rastriya Śaṅkara Jayanti Mahotsav commemoration Volume) Department of culture, Ministry of Human Resource Development, Government of India, New Delhi, 1989.
5. Bhaṭṭācārya, Siddheśvara, "The Philosophy of the Śrīmad-Bhāgavata" (Vol. II Religion), Viśva Bhāratī, Śantiniketan, 1962.
6. Bulusu, Udaya Bhaskaram, "Nārada Bhakti Sūtramulu" (Tr) in Telugu Language, Gītā Press, Gorakhpur, 2012.
7. Dasgupta, Dr. S.N. (Abridged by Agrawal, R.R& Jain, S.N.), "History of Indian Philosophy", Kitab mahal, Allahabad, 1969.
8. Deutch, Eliot, Advaita Vedānta: 'A philosophical reconstruction', University press, Honolulu, Hawaii, USA, 1973.
9. George, Vinus, A, "Paths to divine-Ancient and Indian; Indian Philosophical studies XII", The council for research in values and Philosophy, Washington DC, 2008.
10. Goel, Mukul, "Devotional Hinduism: Creating impression of God" Universe, Bloomington, USA, 2008.
11. Gupta, Sanjukta, "Studies in the philosophy of Madhusūdana Sarasvatī", Sanskrit Pustaka Bandar, Calcutta, 1966.
12. Gupta, Sanjukta, "Advaita Vedānta and Vaiṣṇavism", the Philosophy of Madhusūdana Sarasvatī, Rutledge, New York USA, 2006.
13. Gupta Sisir Kumar, "Madhusūdana Sarasvatī on the Bhagavad- Gītā being an English translation of his commentary Gūḍārtha-Dīpikā", Motilal Banarsidas, Delhi, 1977.
14. Harshānanda Swāmi, "Śaṇḍilya Bhakti Sūtras": A study, SriRamakrishna Math, Bangalore, 1955.
15. Hedge, M.A, Siddapur, "Sri Madhusūdana Sarasvatigalu" (Kannada), Vedānta Bhārati, Krisharajanagara Karnataka, 2012.

16. Karnik, and Visalia, Sunil, "Concept of Mokṣa" Bharatiya Kala Prakashan, Delhi, 2012.
17. Kala and others, "Bhakti Pathway to God", Somalia Publications Printing Mumbai, 2003.
18. Khare, Pradeep Kumar, "Madhusūdana Sarasvatī ka darśan"(Hindi).Classical publishing company, New Delhi 2001.
19. Kidambi, Narasimhācārulu, "Ānandamandākinī- Madhusūdana Sarasvatī" {Text and commentary in Telugu), Published by author, Hyderabad, 2013.
20. Lala, Chagan, "Bhakti in Religious of the World", BR Publicity Corporation, Delhi, 1989.
21. Lamba, B.S. "God realisation", Sterling Publishers (Pvt) Ltd, Bangalore, 1981.
22. Lokeswaranada Swami, "Religion- theory and Practice", R K missionInstitute, Kolkata, 2013.
23. Mahadevan, T.M.P., (Ed) "Preceptors of Advaita", Samata Books, Chennai.
24. Mahadevan, T.M.P, "The Hymns of Śaṅkara", Motilal Banaras DasPublishers (p) Ltd, 1997.
25. Mahadevan, T.M.P, "Śaṅkarācārya", National Book Trust, New Delhi, 2014.
26. Mahāraj Jagadguru Kripalu, "Prem Ras Siddhānta" (The true philosophy of divine love), Jagadguru Kripalu Parishad, Sree Barsanadham, Austin, Tx USA, 2004.
27. Maharāja Swāmi Bhakti Vallabha Tirth, "Śuddha Bhakti"- The Path of Pure devotion, Mandala Publishing Group, New York, 2000.
28. Maharaja Śrīmad Bhakti Vedānta Nārāyana, "Śrī Upadesāmṛita", the ambrosial advice of Śrī Rūpa Goswāmi (Tr), Gauḍiya Vedānta Publication, Vrindāvan, U.P. 2003.

29. Mishra, Adya Prasad, "The Development and Place of Bhakti in Śaṅkara Vedanta", University of Allahabad, Allahabad, 1967.
30. Mishra, Umesh, "The Bhagavad-Gītā"- A Critical Study, Tirabhukti Publication, Allahabad 1967.
31. Misra, G, "Advaita Bhakti-Theoretical dimension and practical possibilities", Bhakti, Utkal University, Bhubaneswar, 2006.
32. Modi, P.M, "Siddhāntabindu" (Tr) of being Madhusūdana Sarasvati's Commentary of Dasa Śloki of Śrī Śaṅkarācārya, Vohra Publishers & distributors, Allahabad, 1985.
33. Nachane, S.A, "A Survey of Post Śaṅkara Advaita Vedānta" Ed by Panda, R.K, Eastern Book linkers, Delhi, 2000.
34. Nelson, Lance E, "Kṛṣṇa in Advaita Vedānta: The Supreme Brahman in Human form" in Krishna, A source Book Ed Edwin F Bryant pp 309-328, 2007.
35. Paniker, V. Sisupala, "Vedāntakalpalatikā-A study", Sat guru Publication Delhi, 1995.
36. Paramānanda Swami, "Path of devotion" Śrī Ramakrishna Math,Chennai, 2012.
37. Prabhavānanda Swāmi, "Nārada's Way of Divine Love: Nārada BhaktiSūtras", Śrī Ramakrishna Math, Chennai, 2005
38. Potukuchi, Śrī SubramanyaSāstrī, "Bhakti Rasāyana of Sri Madhusūdana Sarasvatī", Text and Commentary (in Telugu), Sadhana Grandhamandali, Tenali, AP, 2002.
39. Prabhavānanda Swāmi, "Śiva-Mahimnastotra" (Translation and notes), Advaita Ashrama, Kolkata, 2013.
40. Prakash, Prem "Three Paths of devotion": Goddess, God, Guru, Yes International Publishers, South Parl, Minnesota, USA, 2002.
41. Prakash, Prem, "The Yoga of Spiritual devotion" A modern Translationof Nārada Bhakti Sūtras, Transformational Book

Club, Studio City USA, 2005.

42. Puligandla, Ramakrishna, "Jñāna Yoga The way of knowledge" D.K. Print World (P) Ltd., New Delhi, 1997.
43. Puri, Vishnu, "Bhakti Ratnavali or A necklace of Devotional Gems with original verses" (Tr.) By Swāmi Tapasyānda, Sri Rama Krishna Math, Chennai, 2009.
44. Radhanath Swāmi, "The Journey within" Exploring the path of Bhakti,An Imprint of Harper Collins Publishers, Noida, UP, 2017.
45. S, Radhākrishnan, "Indian Philosophy", George Allen and Unwin.
46. Raghavacār S.S, "The Philosophy of Bhakti and the Significance of Hindu Image worship", The Ramakrishna Mission, Institute of Culture, Kolkata, 2007.
47. Raina, B.L, "VEDANTA: What can It Teach?", B.R. Publishing Corporation, Delhi, 1994.
48. Rao, P. Nagaraja, "Essays in Indian Philosophy and Religion", Lalvani Publishing House, Bombay 1971.
49. Rao, P. Nagaraja, "Fundamentals of Indian Philosophy" Indian Book Company, New Delhi.
50. Rao, Ramakrishna, K.B, "Advaita Vedānta: problems and perspectives" University of Mysore, Mysore, 1980.
51. Rukmini Dr. T.S, "A Typical study of The Bhāgavatapurāṇa" (with special reference to Bhakti), The Choukambha Sanskrit Series office, Varanasi, 1970.
52. Śāstri Bhagvat Kumar Gośwami, "The Bhakti Cult in Ancient India", The Choukambha Sanskrit Series Office, Varanasi, 1965.
53. Śāstri S. Kuppuswāmi, "History of compromises in Advaitic thought", Kuppuswāmi Śāstri Research Institute, Madras, 1946.

54. Singh R.Raj, "Bhakti and Philosophy", Lexington books, Lanhsam MD, USA, 2006.
55. Sharma, Mahesh, "Bhakti (Devotion)", Authors House, Bloomington IN,USA, 2007.
56. Sheridan Daniel P, "The Advaitic Theism of the Bhāgavatapurāṇa",Motilal Banarsidas, Delhi, 1986.
57. Sinha, Jadunath, "Problems of post Śaṅkara Advaita Vedānta", Sinha Publishing (Pvt) Ltd, Calcutta, 1976.
58. Sinha, Nandalal, "Śaṇḍilya Sūtram" with commentary of Śvapneśvara, (Commentary in English), Munshi ram Manoharlal (Pvt) Ltd, New Delhi.
59. Sinha, Nandalal, "Bhakti sūtra of Nārada" (Commentary in English), Munshi ram Manoharlal (Pvt) Ltd., New Delhi, 1998.
60. Śivānanda, Swāmī, "Practice of Bhakti Yoga", The Divine Life Society, Sivanandanagar, Uttarakhand, 2013.
61. Śivānanda, Swāmi, "NāradaBhaktiSūtras, Commentary", The Divine Life Society, Sivanandanagar, Uttarakhand,
62. Śivānanda Swāmī, "Bhakti and Saṅkīrtana" The Divine Life Society, Sivanandanagar, Uttarakhand, 2014.
63. Śivānanda Swāmi, "Essence of Bhakti yoga", The Divine Life Society, Sivanandanagar, Uttarakhand. 2014.
64. Sribhashyam, T.K. and Seshadri Alamlu, "Blissful Experience Bhakti" Quintessence of Indian Philosophy, DK Print World (Pvt) Ltd, New Delhi, 2012.
65. Sribhashyam, TK and Seshadri Alamelu, "Form devotion to Total surrender, Sarangati-yoga" in the light of Indian Philosophy. Print world (Pvt) Ltd, New Delhi, 2012.
66. Sribhashyam T.K, and Seshadri Alamelu "Way to liberation-Mokṣa Mārga, An itinerary in India Philosophy", D.K. Print world (Pvt) Ltd, New Delhi, 2011.

67. Subramanyam, K.N, "Siddhāntabindu", Rishi publication, Varanasi,1989.
68. Śrī Harshānanda Sarasvatī (Karapatri) Bhakti-Rasārṇava" Bhakti Sudha Sahitya parishad, Calcutta, 2015.
69. Taoshobuddha, "The Secrets of Bhakti", (As narrated by Sage Nārada) Aphorisms of Love", Sterling publishers (P) Ltd, New Delhi, 2009.
70. Tapasyānda Swāmi, "Bhakti Schools of Vedānta" Sri Rama Krishna Math, Chennai, India, 2010.
71. Tapayānanda Swāmi, "The four yogas of Swāmi Vivekananda" Condensed and retold, Advaita Ashrama, Kolkata, 2000.
72. Tīrtha, Swāmi Bhoomānanda, "Essential Concepts in Bhagavad-Gītā,"vol4. Based on chapter 7-12 of Bhagavad-Gītā. Narāyanāsram, Tapovanam, Trissur, Kerala, 2010.
73. Tridindi Bhakti Prajnan Yeti, "Sri Śaṇḍilya Bhakti sūtras" (Tr) in English, Gaodiya Math, Madras, 1991.
74. Tripathi, Dinanath, "Madhusūdana Sarasvatī" (Hindi), (Bharatiya Sahitya Ke Nirmata), Sahitya Academy New Delhi, 1997.
75. Tripurari Swāmi, B.V, "Joy of Self", Call Publishing, Oregon USA,1996.
76. Tyāgīsānanda Swāmi, "Aphorisms on The Gospel of Devine Love or Nārada Bhakti Sūtras", Sri Ramakrishna Math, Chennai, 2009.
77. Upadhyaya, S.S, "A Study of Nāradiya Purāṇa," Jñānanidhi Prakashan, Muzaffarnagar, Bihar, 1983.
78. Victor P. George, "Life and Teachings of Adi Śaṅkarācārya", D.K. Print world (Pvt) Ltd, New Delhi 2002.
79. Vivekananda Swami, "Religion of Love", Advaita Ashrama, Kolkata,2012.

80. Vivekananda Swāmi, "Bhakti or Devotion", Advaita Ashrama, Kolkata,2002.
81. Vivekananda Swāmi, "The science and Philosophy of Religion", Advaita Ashrama, Kolkata, 2005.
82. Werner, Karel, "Love Divine-Studies in Bhakti and devotional, Mysticism", Rutledge, Taylor and Francis group, London, 2016.